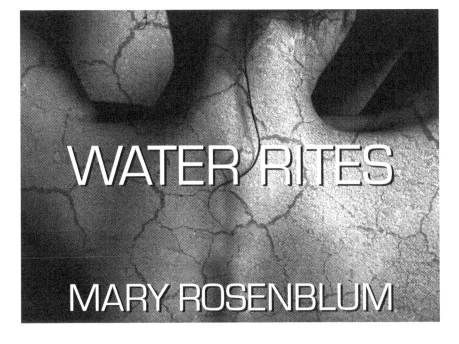

WATER RITES

MARY ROSENBLUM

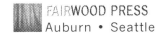

FAIRWOOD PRESS
Auburn • Seattle

WATER RITES

A Fairwood Press Book
February 2007
Copyright © 2007 by Mary Rosenblum

Fairwood Press
5203 Quincy Ave SE
Auburn, WA 98092
www.fairwoodpress.com

Cover & Book Design by Patrick Swenson

ISBN: 0-9789078-1-7
First Fairwood Press Edition: February 2007
Printed in the United States of America

To Nate and Jake,
who were there from the beginning

ACKNOWLEDGEMENTS

"Water Bringer," "Celilo," and "The Bee Man" appeared previously in *Asimov's Science Fiction* Magazine.

The Drylands 1st appeared from Del Rey Books, 1994

CONTENTS

Foreword   10

Water Bringer   12

Celilo   36

The Bee Man   56

The Drylands   73

WATER RITES

FOREWORD

Nearly 14 years ago, back in 1992, I began to read about global warming, and its ultimate effect on our planet. A science fiction writer with a strong interest in "if this goes on" fiction, I decided to set a story or two in a global warming future. So I began to research what the climatologists knew.

And it shocked me.

As I read the vast amount of public information about the major US aquifers, their drawdown rates, and predictions for their depletion, when I looked at the climate models being created by the top climatologists in the field, when I read the numbers on carbon emissions . . . this was back before China came online as a growing consumer of automobiles and coal-fired electricity, remember . . . I was, as I said, shocked.

Why wasn't anyone talking about this? It was scary! I had created a really nasty future in the US with very little water and all that meant in terms of a collapsed US economy. Over the top, I thought, but if I could simply keep one toe in reality . . .

My really nasty future fell within the parameters of predicted climate change.

The Drylands stories appeared in *Asimov's*. The novel *The Drylands* came out in 1994, and won the Compton Crook award for best first novel. We had some wet years. Climate change was not an issue. I wrote more books and more stories. Time passed.

Global warming is now, finally, on everyone's lips. So it was time to revisit Drylands. I picked up the book again, looked over my research.

This time . . . it *frightened* me.

The predictions being made, back in 1992, about melting glaciers, drying forests susceptible to insect damage that would burn in huge wildfires, to be replaced by a different ecosystem as the climate zones shifted northward, the increase in the intensity of storms and droughts, the rise in ocean temperatures . . .

. . . it's all coming true. *Now.* The predictions . . . back in 1992 . . . were, as I recall, for something like forty years out. Forty. Not fourteen.

It is not a comfortable feeling playing Cassandra, when you stare the coming disaster in the face. And you know what? I may see some of those worst case scenarios begin to come to pass before I die. And I'm not that young. Are you listening, Phoenix? Los Angeles? Imperial Valley? The current level of carbon dioxide in the Earth's atmosphere is nearing 400 ppm. That is higher than it has been for the last 650,000 years. It could rise above 500 ppm before the middle of this century. If we don't slow it down.

Do you want that? Do you *really* want to find out if the world that my characters in my Drylands stories inhabit is your future? Do you? It might well come to pass. Think of that next time you vote, or purchase a car. Will you? Pay attention, okay? It won't be a nice world to live in.

Mary Rosenblum 2006

WATER BRINGER

Sitting with his back against the sun-scorched rimrock, Jeremy made the dragonfly appear in the air in front of him. It hovered on the hot breeze, wings shimmering with bluegreen glints. Pretty. He looked automatically over his shoulder. But Dad was down in the dusty fields. With everyone else.

It was safe.

Jeremy hunched farther into his sliver of shade, frowning at his making. It was a little too blue — that was it — and the eyes were too small. He frowned, trying to remember the picture in the insect book. The dragonfly's bright body darkened as its eye swelled.

Got it. Jeremy smiled and sat up straight. The dragonfly hovered above a withered bush, wings glittering in the sunlight. He sent it darting out over the canyon, leaned over the ledge to watch it.

Far below, a man led a packhorse up the main road from the old riverbed. A stranger. Jeremy let the dragonfly vanish as he squinted against the glare. Man and horse walked with their heads down, like they were both tired. Their feet raised brown puffs of dust that hung in the windless air down there like smoke.

Jeremy held his breath as the stranger stopped at their road. "Come on," Jeremy breathed. "There's nowhere else for ten miles."

As if they'd heard him, the pair turned up the rutted track. The man didn't pull on the horse's lead rope. They moved together, like they'd both decided to stop at the farm.

Jeremy scrambled up over the rimrock and lurched into a run. You didn't see strangers out here very often. Mostly, they stopped at La Grande. The convoys stuck to the interstate, and nobody else went anywhere. Dead grass stems left from the brief spring crackled and snapped under Jeremy's feet, and the hard ground jolted him, stabbing his twisted knees with bright slivers of pain.

At the top of the steep trail that led down to the farm, Jeremy had to slow up. He limped down the slope, licking dust from his lips, breathing quick and hard. They'd hear it all first — all the news — before he even got there. The sparse needles on the dying pines held the heat close to the ground. Dry branches clawed at him, trying to slow him down even more. They wouldn't wait for him. They never did. Suddenly furious, Jeremy swung at the branches with his thickened hands, but they only slapped back at him, scratching his face and arms.

Sure enough, by the time he reached the barnyard, the brown-and-white horse was tethered in the dim heat of the sagging barn, unsaddled and drowsing. Everyone would be in the kitchen with the stranger. Jeremy licked his lips again. At least there'd be a pitcher of water out. Even though it wasn't dinner time. He crossed the sunburned yard and limped up the warped porch steps.

". . . desertification has finally reached its limit, so the government is putting all its resources into reclamation."

Desertification? Jeremy paused at the door. The word didn't have a clear meaning in his head, but it felt dusty and dry as the fields. He peeked inside. The stranger sat in Dad's place at the big table, surrounded by everyone. He wore a stained tan shirt with a picture of a castle tower embroidered on the pocket. He had dark, curly hair and a long face with a jutting nose. Jeremy pushed the screen door slowly open. The stranger's face reminded him of the canyon wall, all crags and peaks and sharp shadows.

The door slipped through his fingers and banged closed behind him.

"Jeremy?" His mother threw a quick glance at Dad as she turned around. "Where have you been? I was worried."

"He snuck up to the rimrock again," Rupert muttered, just loud enough.

Jeremy flinched, but Dad wasn't looking at him at all. He'd heard, though. His jaw had gotten tight, but he didn't even turn his head. Jeremy felt his face getting hot, and edged toward the door.

"Hi." The stranger's smile pinned him in place. It crinkled the sun-browned skin around his eyes. "I'm Dan Greely," he said.

"From the Army Corps of Engineers," ten-year-old David announced.

"To bring *water*," Paulie interrupted his twin.

"You're not supposed to go up there, Jeremy." Mother gave Dad an uneasy, sideways glance. "You could fall."

"So, just how does the Corps of Engineers plan to irrigate the valley when the river's as dry as a bone?" Jeremy's father spoke as if no one else had said a word. "God knows, you can't find water when it ain't there to be found."

"Don't be so hard on him, Everett." Mother turned back to Dad.

"I ain't even heard any solid reasons for why the damn country's dried up," Dad growled. "Desertification." He snorted. "Fancy word for no damn rain. Tell me why, surveyor."

"At least someone's trying to do something about it." Mother was using her soothing voice.

They weren't paying any attention to him any more, not even tattletale Rupert. Jeremy slipped into his favorite place, the crevice between the wood-box and the cold kitchen cookstove.

"We'll be glad to put you up while you're about your business," Mother went on. "It would be like a dream come true for us, if you folks can give us water again. We've all wondered sometimes if we did right to stay here and try to hang on."

"What else could we do?" Dad pushed his chair back a mere inch. "Quit and go work in the bush fields in the Willamette Valley? Go be camp labor?"

"I can't promise you water," the stranger said gravely. "I'm just the surveyor. I hear that some of these deep-aquifer projects have been pretty successful, though."

"It's enough to know that there's hope." Mother's voice had gone rough, like she wanted to cry.

Jeremy started to peek around the stove, because Mother never cried. He froze as Dad's hand smacked the tabletop.

"He ain't dug any wells yet. You kids get back to work. Those beans gotta be weeded by supper, 'cause we're not wasting water on weeds. Jonathan, I know you and Rupert ain't finished your pumping yet."

"Awe, come on," Rupert whined. "We want to hear about the cities. Are people really eating each other there?"

"You heard your father," Mother said sharply. "The wash-bucket's too dirty for supper washup. Rupert, you take it out to the squash — the last two hills in the end row — and bring me a fresh bucket."

"Aww, Mom!" Rupert shoved his chair back.

Jeremy scrunched down, listening to the scuffle of his brothers' bare feet as they filed out of the kitchen.

"We don't have much in the way of hay for your pony." Dad sounded angry. "How long are you planning on staying, anyway?"

"Not long. I can give you a voucher for food and shelter. When they set up the construction camp, you just take it to the comptroller for payment."

"Lot of good money'll do me. There wasn't enough rain to make hay worth crap anywhere in the county this year. Where'm I gonna buy hay?"

The screen door banged. Jeremy frowned and wiggled into a more comfortable position. Why was Dad angry? The stranger talked about water. Everybody needed water.

"Never mind him." From the clatter, Mother was dishing up bean-and-squash stew left over from lunch. "You have to understand, it's hard for him to hope after all these years." A plate clunked on the table. "You keep pumping water, trying to grow enough to live on, praying the well holds out another year and watching your kids go to bed hungry. You don't have a lot left for hope. When you're done, I'll show you your room. The twins can sleep with Jeremy and Rupert."

She sounded like she was going to cry again. Jeremy looked down at his loosely curled fists. The thick joints made his fingers look like knobby tree roots. The stranger said something, but Jeremy didn't catch it. He'd only heard Mother cry once before — when the doctor over in La Grande had told her that there wasn't anything he could do about Jeremy's hands or his knees.

This stranger made Dad angry and Mother sad. Jeremy thought about that while he waited, but he couldn't make any sense of it at all. As soon as the stranger and Mother left the kitchen, Jeremy slipped out of his hiding place. Sure enough, the big plastic pitcher stood on the table, surrounded by empty glasses. You didn't ask for water between meals. Jeremy listened to the quiet. He lifted the pitcher, clutching it tightly in his thick, awkward grip.

The water was almost as warm as the air by now, but it tasted sweet on his dusty throat. Jeremy swirled the pitcher, watching the last bit of water climb the sides in a miniature whirlpool.

Absently, he made it fill clear to the brim. What would it be like to live in the old days, when it rained all the time and the riverbed was full of water and fish? He imagined a fish, made it appear in the water. He'd seen it in another book, all speckled green with a soft shading of pink on its belly. He made the fish leap out of the pitcher and dive back in, splashing tiny droplets of water that vanished as they fell. Jeremy tilted his head, pleased with himself. Trout. He remembered the fish's name, now.

"Jeremy!"

Jeremy started at his mother's cry and dropped the pitcher. Water and fish vanished as the plastic clattered on the linoleum. Throat tight, he stared at the small puddle of real water. The stranger stood behind Mother in the doorway.

"Go see if the hens have laid any eggs." His mother's voice quivered. "Do it right now."

Jeremy limped out the door without looking at either of them.

"Don't mind him," he heard his mother say. "He's clumsy, is all."

She was afraid that the stranger had seen the fish. Jeremy hurried across the oven glare of the barnyard. What if he had? What if he said something to Dad? His skin twitched with the memory of the last beating, when he'd gotten to daydreaming and made the dragonfly appear in the church. He shivered.

The stranger's horse snorted at him, pulling back against its halter with a muffled thudding of hooves. "Easy, boy, easy." Jeremy stumbled to a halt, stretched out his hand. The pinto shook its thick mane and stretched his neck to sniff. Jeremy smiled as the velvety lips brushed his palm. "You're pretty," he said, but it wasn't true. It wasn't even a horse, really — just a scruffy pony with a thick neck and feet big as dinner plates.

Jeremy sat down stiffly, leaning his back against the old, smooth boards of the barn. "Hey." He wiggled his toes as the pony sniffed at his bare feet. "It's not your fault you're ugly." He stroked the pony's nose. "I bet you can run like the wind."

The pony's rasping breathing sounded friendly, comforting. Eyes half closed, Jeremy imagined himself galloping over the sunburned meadows. His knees wouldn't matter at all. He drifted into a dream of wind and galloping hooves.

"Jeremy? It's supper time. You don't want to eat, it's not my loss."

Rupert's voice. Jeremy blinked awake, swallowing a yawn. It was almost dark. Straw tickled his cheek, and he remembered.

The stranger had seen him make something.

"I know you're in here." Rupert's voice sounded close.

By now, Dad probably knew about the trout. Jeremy rolled onto his stomach and wriggled under the main beam beneath the wall. He could just fit. Something with tiny feet scuttled across his cheek.

"I hear you, brat." Rupert's silhouette loomed against the gray rectangle of the doorway. "You think I want to play hide and seek after I work all day? If I get in trouble, I'll fix you later."

The pony laid back its ears and whinnied shrilly.

"Jesus!" Rupert jumped back. "I hope you get your head kicked off," he yelled.

Jeremy listened to Rupert stomp out of the barn. "Thanks, pony," he whispered as he scrambled out of his hiding place. He shook powdery dust out of his clothes, listening for the slam of the screen door.

Better to face Rupert later than Dad right now. He'd said never again, after that Sunday. The pony nudged him, and Jeremy scratched absently at its ear. A bat twittered in the darkness over his head. Jeremy looked up, barely able to make out the flittering shadows coming and going through the gray arch of the doorway. His stomach growled as he curled up against the wall of the barn. The pony snuffled softly and moved closer, as if it was glad he was there.

The barn was full of dry creaks and whispers. Something rustled loudly in the loft above Jeremy's head and he started. Funny how darkness changed the friendly barn, stretched it out so big. Too big and too dark. "What to see a firefly?" Jeremy asked the pony. The darkness seemed to swallow his words. It pressed in around him, as if he had made it angry by talking.

He hadn't been able to find a picture . . . The firefly appeared, bright as a candle flame in the darkness. It looked sort of like a glowing moth. That didn't seem quite right, but its warm glow drove back the darkness. Jeremy examined it thoughtfully. Maybe he should make the wings bigger.

"So I wasn't seeing things," a voice said.

The pony whinnied and Jeremy snuffed out the firefly. Before he could hide, a dazzling beam of light flashed in his eyes. He raised a hand against the hurting glare.

"Sorry." The light dipped, illuminating a circular patch of dust and Jeremy's dirty legs. "So this is where you've been. Your brother said he couldn't find you." The beam hesitated on Jeremy's lumpy knees.

The surveyor patted the pony and bent to prop the solar flashlight on the floor. Its powerful beam splashed back from the wall, streaking the straw with shadows. "Can you do it again?" he asked. "Make that insect appear, I mean?"

Jeremy licked his dry lips. "I'm not supposed to . . . make things."

"I sort of got that impression." The man gave him a slow, thoughtful smile. "I pretended I didn't notice. I didn't want to get you in trouble."

Jeremy blinked. A grownup worried about getting him in trouble? The bright, comforting light and the surveyor's amazing claim shut the two of them into a kind of private, magical circle. The firefly glowed to life in the air between them. "What does a real firefly look like?"

"I don't know." The surveyor reached out to touch the making, snatched his hand away as his finger passed through the delicate wings.

"It isn't real. It doesn't look right." Disappointed, Jeremy let it fade and vanish.

"Wow." The surveyor whistled softly. "I've never seen anything like that."

He made it sound like Jeremy was doing something wonderful. "Don't tell I showed you, okay?" He picked at a thread in his cut-off jeans.

"I won't." The man answered him seriously, as if he was talking to another grownup. "How old are you?"

"Twelve. I'm small for my age." Jeremy watched him pick up his marvelous light and swing its bright beam over the pony.

"You look pretty settled, Ezra. I'll get you some more water in the morning." The surveyor slapped the pony on the neck. "Come on." He offered Jeremy a hand. "Let's go in. I think your mom left a plate out for you." He gave Jeremy a sideways look. "Your dad went to bed."

"Oh." Jeremy scrambled to his feet, wondering how the stranger knew to say that. "Are you going to bring us water?" he asked.

"No," the man said slowly. "I just make maps. I don't dig wells or lay pipe."

"I bet you're good," Jeremy said. He wanted to say something nice to this man, and that was all he could think of.

"Thanks," the surveyor said, but he sounded more sad than pleased. "I'm pretty good at what I do."

No, he didn't act like a grownup. He didn't act like anyone Jeremy had ever met. Thoughtfully, he followed the bright beam of the surveyor's flashlight into the house.

Next morning was church-Sunday, but the family got up at dawn as usual, because it was such a long walk into town. Jeremy put on his good pair of shorts and went down to take on Mother in the kitchen.

"You can't go." She shoved a full water-jug into the lunch pack. "It's too far."

She was thinking of the dragonfly. "I won't forget. I'll be good," he said. "Please?"

"Forget it." Rupert glared at him from the doorway. "The freak'll forget and do something again."

"That's enough." Mother closed the pack with a jerk. "I'll bring you a new book." She wouldn't meet Jeremy's eyes. "What do you want?"

"I don't know." Jeremy set his jaw. He didn't usually care, didn't like church-Sundays, with all the careful eyes that sneaked like Rupert when they looked at his hands and knees, or flat out pitied him. "I want to come," he said.

"Mom, no . . ."

"I said that's enough." Mother looked past Rupert. "Did you get enough breakfast, Mr. Greely?" she asked too cheerfully.

"More than enough, thanks." The surveyor walked into the kitchen and the conversation ended.

When Jeremy started down the gravel road with them, Mother's lips got tight and Rupert threw him a look that promised trouble, but Dad acted like he wasn't even there, and no one else dared say anything. Jeremy limped along as fast as he could, trying not to fall behind. He had won. He wasn't sure why, but he had.

It was a long, hot walk to town.

Rupert and Jonathan stuck to the surveyor like burrs, asking about the iceberg tugs, Portland, and Seattle and if LA had really drowned in the rising ocean. The surveyor answered their questions gravely and politely. He wore a fresh tan shirt tucked into his faded jeans. It was clean, and the tower on the pocket made it look like it meant something special.

It meant water.

Everyone was there by the time they reached the church — except the Menendez family who lived way down the dry creekbed and sometimes didn't come in anyway. The Pearson kids were screaming as they took turns jumping off the porch, and Bev Lamont was watching for Jonathan, like she always did.

As soon as they got close enough for people to count the extra person, everyone abandoned their picnic spreads and made for the porch.

'This is Mr. Greely, a surveyor with the Army Corps of Engineers," Mother announced as they climbed the wide steps.

"Pleased to meet you." The surveyor's warm smile swept the sun-dried faces. "I've been sent to make a preliminary survey for a federal irrigation project." He perched on the porch railing, like he'd done it a hundred times before. "The new Singhe solar cells are going to power a deepwell pumping operation. We think we've identified a major, deep aquifer in this region."

"How come we ain't heard of this before?" It was bearded Ted Brewster, who ran the Exxon station when he could get ethanol, speaking up from the back of the crowd.

"Come on, Ted." Fists on her bony hips, gray-haired Sally Brandt raised her voice. "You don't hear nothin' on the Spokane radio news."

"No. That's a good question." The surveyor looked around at the dusty faces. "You don't have internet out here?"

"No power, out here." Sally shook her head. "Bonneville Power didn't put the lines back up after a big storm took 'em out . . . oh, must be eight and a half years ago. Said it wasn't cost effective."

The surveyor nodded and reached inside his shirt. "I have a letter from the regional supervisor." He pulled out a white rectangle. "I'm supposed to deliver it to the mayor, city supervisor, or whoever's in charge." He raised his eyebrows expectantly.

A gust of wind whispered across the crowded porch, and no one spoke.

"Most people just left." Jeremy's father finally stepped forward, fists in the pockets of his patched jeans. "This was wheat and alfalfa land, from the time the Oregon Territory became a state. You can't farm wheat without water." His voice sounded loud in the silence. "The National Guard come around and told us to go get work on the Columbia River Pipeline project. They said they had camps for workers. Camps." He turned his face as if he wanted to spit, but didn't. "That's all the help the government was gonna give us. If we stayed, they said, we was on our own." He paused. "We don't have a mayor anymore, and the Rev, he died in a dust storm a couple years back. There's just us."

The surveyor looked at the dusty faces, one by one. "Like I told Mr. Barlow last night," he said quietly. "I can't promise that we'll find water, or that you'll grow wheat again. I'm only the surveyor."

For a long moment, Jeremy's father stared at the envelope. Then, with a jerky, awkward gesture, he reached out and took it. He pried up the white flap with a blunt thumb and squinted at the print, his forehead wrinkling.

Without a word, he handed the paper to Ted Brewster. Jeremy watched the white paper pass from hand to hand. People held it like it as precious — like it was water. He listened to the dry rustle of the paper. When it came around to Dad again, he stuck it into the glass case beside the door of the church. "I hope to God you find water," he said softly.

"Amen," someone said.

"Amen." The ragged mutter ran through the crowd.

After than, everyone went back to their picnics. After the Reverend had died, they'd moved the pews outside. Families spread clothes on the long, rickety tables inside. There weren't any more sermons, but people still came to eat together on the church-Sundays. The surveyor wandered from group to group in the colored shadows of the church, eating the food people pressed on him, sharing news from Portland and the rest of the world. They crowded him, talking, brushing up against him, as if his touch would bring them good luck, bring water to the wells and the dead fields.

Jeremy hung back, under the blue-and-green diamonds of the stained-glass window. Finally he went down the narrow stairs to the sparse shelves of the basement library. He found a little paperback book on insects, but it didn't have a picture of a firefly. He tossed back onto the shelf. When it fell onto the dusty concrete floor, he kicked it, feeling both guilty and pleased when it skittered out of sight under a bottom shelf. Upstairs, the surveyor was giving everyone the same warm grin that he'd given to Jeremy in the barn last night. That made his stomach hurt.

He wandered outside and found little Rita Menendez poking at ants on the front walk. Mrs. Menendez was yelling at the older kids as she started to unpack the lunch, so Jeremy carried Rita off into the dappled shade under the scraggly shrubs. She was too little to know about his makings or mind his hands. Belly still tight, Jeremy made a bright green frog appear on Rita's knee.

Her gurgly laugh eased some of that tightness. She liked his makings. And she couldn't tell anyone about 'em. He turned the frog into the dragonfly and she grabbed at it. This time, Jeremy heard the surveyor coming. By the time the man pushed the brittle branches aside, the dragonfly was gone.

"Do you always hide?" He reached down to tickle Rita's plump chin.

"I'm not hiding." Jeremy peered up through his sun-bleached hair.

"I need someone to help me." The surveyor squatted, so that Jeremy had to meet his eyes. "I talked to your father and he said that I could hire you. If you agree. The Corps' only paying in scrip, and it's crisis-minimum wage," he said apologetically.

Jeremy pushed Rita gently off his lap. This man wanted to hire him? When he couldn't even pull weeds? Hiring was something from the old days, like the flashlight and this man's clean, creased shirt.

Jeremy wiped his hands on his pants, pressing hard, as if by doing that he could straighten his bent fingers. "I'd like that, Mr. Greely," he said breathlessly.

"Good." The man smiled like he meant it. "We'll get started first thing tomorrow." He stood, giving Rita a final pat that made her chuckle. "Call me Dan," he said. "Okay?"

Jeremy didn't see much of Dan Greely before the next morning. It seemed like everyone had to talk to Dan about watertables, aquifers, deep wells, and the Army Corps of Engineers. They said the words like the Reverend used to say prayers. *Army Corps of Engineers.*

Dan, Dad, and Jonathan stayed in town. Mother shepherded the rest of them home. The twins were tired, but Rupert was pissed because he couldn't stay, too. He shoved Jeremy whenever Mother wasn't looking.

"I hope you work hard for Mr. Greely," Mother said when she came up to say goodnight. The twins were already snoring in the hot darkness of the attic room.

"Waste of time to hire him," Rupert growled from his bed. "The pony's more use."

"That's enough." Mother's voice sounded sharp as a new nail. "We can't spare either you or Jonathan from the pumping, so don't get yourself worked up. You don't have to go with him." She bent over Jeremy's mattress. Her hand trembled just a little as she brushed the hair back from his forehead.

"I'll be okay." He wondered if she was worried that he wouldn't do a good job. He almost told her that Dan knew about the makings and wouldn't tell Dad, but Rupert was listening. "I'll do good," he said, and wished he believed it.

It took Jeremy a long time to fall asleep, but when he did, it seemed as if only moments had passed before he woke up again. At first, he thought Mother was calling him to breakfast. It was still dark, but the east window showed faint gray.

There it was again. Mother's voice. Too wide awake to fall back to sleep, Jeremy slipped out of bed and tiptoed to the top of the steep stairs, just this side of their bedroom door.

"Stop worrying," Dad's low growl drifted through the half-closed door. "What do you think he's gonna do?"

"I don't know. He said he needed a helper, but what . . ."

"What can Jeremy do? He can't do shit, but Greely's going to pay wages, and we can use anything we can get. Do you understand me?" Dad's voice sounded like the dry, scouring winds. "How do you think I felt when I had to go crawling to the Brewsters and the Pearsons for food last winter?"

"It wasn't Jeremy's fault, Everett, the north well giving out."

"No one else has an extra mouth to feed. And I had to go begging."

"I lost three babies after Rupert." Mother's voice sounded high and tight.

"Whatever he wants from the boy, he's paying for it."

Jeremy tiptoed down the stairs, his teeth clenched so hard they felt as if they were going to break.

A light glowed in the barn's darkness. "Hi." Dan pulled a strap tight on the pony's packsaddle. "I was going to come wake you. Ezra and I are used to starting as soon as it gets light. It gets too hot to work before noon." He tugged on the pack, nodded to himself. "Did you get something to eat?"

"Yeah."

Dan gave him a searching look, then shrugged. "Okay, let's go."

It was just light enough to see as they started down the track. The pony stepped over the thin white pipe that carried water from the well to the field. The old bicycle frame of the pump looked like a skeleton sticking up out of the gray dirt. In an hour, Jonathan would be pedaling hard to get his gallons pumped. Then Rupert would take over. The twins would be hauling the buckets, dipping out water to each plant in the bean rows.

"Did your dad build that?" Dan nodded at the metal frame.

"Uh huh." Jeremy walked a little faster, trying not to limp.

He had had a thousand questions about the outside world to ask, but the sharp whispers in the upstairs bedroom had dried them up like the wind dried up a puddle. He watched Ezra's big feet kick up the brown dust, feeling dry and empty inside.

"We'll start here." The surveyor pulled Ezra to a halt. They were looking down on the dry riverbed and the narrow, rusty bridge. The road went across the riverbed now. It was safer.

The pony waited patiently, head drooping, while Dan unloaded it. "This machine measures distance by bouncing a beam of laser light off a mirror." Dan set the cracked plastic case down on the ground. "It sits on this tripod and the reflector goes on the other one." He unloaded a water jug, lunch, an axe, a steel tape measure, and other odds and ends. "Now, we get to work," he said when he was done.

Sweat stuck Jeremy's hair to his face as he struggled across the sunbaked clay after Dan. They set up the machine and reflector, took them down, and set them up somewhere else. Sometimes Dan hacked a path through the dry underbrush. It was hard going. In spite of all he could do, Jeremy was limping badly by mid-morning.

"I'm sorry." Dan stopped abruptly. "You keep up so well, it's easy to forget that you hurt."

His tone was matter of fact, without a trace of pity. A knot clogged the back of Jeremy's throat as Dan boosted him onto Ezra's back. He sat up straight on the hard packsaddle, arms tight around the precious machine. It felt heavy, dense with the magic that would call water out of the ground. Jeremy tried to imagine the gullied dun hills all green, with blue water tumbling down the old riverbed.

Plenty of water meant it wouldn't matter so much that he couldn't pump or carry buckets.

Jeremy thought about water while he held what Dan gave him to hold, and, once or twice, pushed buttons on the distance machine. He could manage that much. It hummed under his touch and bright red numbers winked in a tiny window. He had to remember them, because his fingers were too clumsy to work the tiny keys on Dan's electronic notepad.

Dan didn't really need any help with the measuring. Jeremy stood beside the magic machine, watching a single hawk circle in the hard blue sky. Mother had been right. Dan wanted something else from him.

Well, that was okay. Jeremy shrugged as the hawk drifted off southward. No one else thought he had anything to offer.

The sun stood high overhead when they stopped for lunch. It poured searing light down on the land, sucking up their sweat. "We'll wait until the sun starts to go down," Dan said. They huddled in a narrow strip of shade beneath the canyon wall. Ezra stood next to them, head down, whisking flies.

They shared warm, plastic-tasting water with the pony, and Dan produced dried apple slices from the lunch pack. He had stripped off his shirt, and sweat gleamed like oil on his brown shoulders. His eyes were gray, Jeremy noticed. They looked bright in his dark face.

"Why do you have to do all the stuff?" Awkwardly, Jeremy scooped up a leathery disc of dried apple. The tart sweetness filled his mouth with a rush of saliva. The old tree behind the house didn't give very many apples, most years.

"I'm making a map of the ground." Dan shaded his eyes, squinting in the shimmering heat-haze. "If they're going to drill a well field, they'll have to lay pipes, make roads, build buildings. They need to know what the ground looks like."

"I was trying to imagine lots of water." Jremy reached for another apple slice. "It's hard."

"Yeah," Dan said harshly. "Don't start counting the days yet." He shook himself and his expression softened. "Tell me about your fireflies and your fish that jump out of pitchers."

"Not much to tell." Jeremy looked away from Dan's intent, gray eyes. Was that what he wanted? "If I think of something hard enough, you can see it. It's not real." Jeremy drew a zig-zag pattern in the dust with his fingers. "Don't talk about it, okay? It's wrong. It's . . . an abomination. The Devil's mark. That's why the rain went away. It was God punishing us . . . for living with abominations. We . . . don't let . . . abominations . . . live. Like the Pearson's baby. Like Sally Brandt's baby, born just this spring."

"Who said all that?" Dan asked in a hard, quiet voice.

"The Reverend." Jeremy fixed his eyes on the little troughs in the dust.

Their old nanny goat had a kid with an extra leg last spring. About the time Sally Brandt had her baby. Dad had taken the biggest knife from the kitchen and cut its throat by a bean hill, so that the blood would water the seedlings. The apple slice in Jeremy's mouth tasted like dust. Feeling stony hard inside, he made the dragonfly appear, sent it darting through the air to land on Dan's knee with a glitter of wings.

"Holy shit." Dan flinched, scattering apple slices. "I can almost believe that I feel it."

He didn't sound angry. Jeremy sighed and vanished it.

"I heard your Reverend died," Dan said softly.

Jeremy nodded.

"You got to know that he was wrong. He was just a narrow, scared man, who had to blame this crazy drought on something, because none of us really understand why we didn't stop it from happening, why we can't fix it now."

Jeremy tensed as Dan laid a hand on his shoulder. "In the cities you'd be so hot. What you do is fantastic. It's wonderful, Jeremy, not something wrong. People would pay you money to see what you could create for them." He sighed. "Your Dad's scared of them, isn't he?"

Scared? Jeremy shook his head. Rupert was scared of the brown lizards that lived under the rocks out behind the outhouse. He killed them all the time. But Dad wasn't scared of his makings.

Dad hated them.

"Look at this." Dan yanked a grubby red bandana out of his pocket and shook it. "Watch me make it disappear. Watch carefully now." He stuffed it into his closed fist. "Are you watching?" He waved his fist around, then snapped open his hand.

Jeremy stared at his empty palm.

"Your handkerchief, sir." He reached behind Jeremy's ear, snapped the bandana into view.

"Wow." Jeremy touched the bandana cautiously. "How did you do that?"

"It's pretty easy." Dan looked sad as he stuffed the bandana back into his pocket. "Card tricks, juggling, oh, you can entertain folks, but they all know it's fake. What you can do is . . . real." His pale eyes burned. "I think we'd all give a lot to believe in something real. Like what you do. You should come with me, Jeremy."

Dan acted like the making was a wonderful thing. But Dad had had to ask the Brewsters for food. And the Reverend knew more than anyone in town. Suddenly unsure, Jeremy bent to scoop up the apples that Dan had dropped. "You don't want to waste these."

"I wasn't going to. They're good apples. I'd give a lot for your talent. It's real, Jeremy. And it's wasted here."

Talent? Jeremy dumped the withered rings of apple into the pack. "You're a surveyor," he said. "You don't need to do tricks."

"I guess I am." Dan's laugh sounded bitter. "So I guess we'd better get back to surveying, huh?"

As they worked through the lengthening shadows of the fading day, strange feelings fluttered in Jeremy's chest. Could Dan be right? Would people really look at him like Dan had looked at him? All excited?

He could find out. If he went with Dan.

Jeremy thought about that for the rest of the day, while he steadied the machine and pushed buttons. He didn't say anything to Dan. He might not want Jeremy along.

It seemed like everyone within walking distance was waiting at the house when they plodded back to the farm in the first faint cool of evening. Covered dishes and water jugs cluttered the kitchen table, and Dan was swept into the crowd.

Dan didn't belong to him here, in the dusty house. Here, he belonged to the grown-ups and the Army Corps of Engineers. Jeremy led Ezra off to the barn to struggle with the pack straps and give the pony some water. If he left with Dan, if Dan would take him, Dad wouldn't have to ask the Brewsters for food. He pulled at the pony's tangled mane until the coarse horsehair cut his fingers.

After the first three days, the crowd didn't show up at the farm any more. They'd heard what news Dan had to tell. They'd sold him the food and supplies that he'd asked for, taking his pale-green voucher slips as payment. Now they were waiting for the construction crews to arrive. Even Dad was waiting. He whistled while he carried water to the potato plants, and he smiled at Dan.

Dan was the water bringer. Everyone smiled at Dan.

It made Jeremy jealous when they were at home and Rupert, Jonathan, and the twins hung around him all the time, pretending they were grownups, too. But they weren't home very often. He and Dan trudged all over the scorched hills along the river. Dan talked about cities. He talked about the heart of the drylands, with its ghosts and the bones of dead towns and about the oceans eating the shore. He taught Jeremy how to describe the land in numbers. He asked Jeremy to make things every day, and he laughed when Jeremy made a frog appear on Ezra's head.

Dan never asked outright, but he talked as if Jeremy was going to come with him when he left. To the cities. And the sea.

"Where did you come from?" Jeremy asked on Saturday, just a week after Dan had arrived. They were eating lunch under the same overhang where they'd stopped the first day out.

"The Corps' regional office in Bonneville."

"No, I don't mean that." Jeremy swallowed cold beans. "I mean before that. Before the surveying. Where were you born?"

"South." Dan looked out toward the dead river. His gray eyes looked vague, like he was looking past something far away or deep inside his head. "We came up from LA, running from the water wars and the gangs." His eyelids flickered. "I was pretty little. But the people in the valleys weren't sharing their water, so we moved on. You leave everything behind you when you're dying of thirst, one piece at a time. Everything."

He was silent for a moment. The wind blew grit across the rocks with a soft hiss and Jeremy didn't make a sound.

"I ended up with the Corps," Dan said abruptly.

The transition from *we* to *I* cut off Jeremy's questions like a knife. He watched Dan toss a pebble down the slope. It bounced off an old cow skull half-buried in drifted dust.

"I won't kid you about things." Dan tossed another pebble at the bleached skull. "I'm leaving soon . . . maybe tomorrow. And if you come with me, you're going to find out that things aren't always what they should be. When you're on the road, you don't have any options. You do what it takes to stay alive. Sometimes you don't like it much, but you do it."

The hard thread of bitterness in Dan's voice scared Jeremy a little, but it didn't matter. *If you come with me . . .*

"Can you make a face?" Dan asked suddenly.

"I don't know." Jeremy looked into Dan's bleak, hungry eyes, stifling a pang of fear. He wanted to say no. Get up and go back to surveying. "I . . . can try." Dan's eyes pulled the words out of him.

"She was about sixteen, with brown eyes and black hair. It was straight, like rain falling." His eyes focused on that invisible something again. "She looked a little like me, but prettier," he said. "Her nose was thin — I used to kid her about it — an she smiled a lot."

He could feel it, almost. Dan's memory. Scared, now, Jeremy shaped a face in his mind, watched it take shape in the air. Dan shook his head.

"Stupid of me to play that kind of game." Dan laid his hand on Jeremy's shoulder. "Thanks for trying."

And just that quickly, he felt the awful shiver that seemed to run through his flesh and the air and the dusty ground.

She smiled, her face brining with warmth and sadness, standing there, looking down at them. Jeremy stared at her, sweat stinging his eyes. She was right — the way the land had been right that day he had looked at it and it had turned green and lush and he had seen water running through the creekbed at the far edge of the field.

"Amy." Dan's voice broke.

The sound of Dan's voice pierced him. The making shivered, dissolved, and vanished. "I'm sorry," Jeremy whispered, his skin tight with fear. "Dan, I'm sorry.

Dan buried his face in his hands. Hesitantly, Jeremy reached out and touched him.

"It's all right." Dan raised his head, drew in a long breath. "You did what I asked." He shook his head slowly, his face full of wonder. "That was *her*. Not some image. It was like you called her back for a second. I . . . thought for a minute she was going to say something to me. She was so *real*."

Like the green fields full of alfalfa. Jeremy looked away because he could see fear in Dan's face, too. Not just wonder.

That was why his dad hated them . . . the makings. Because of the green fields.

And hated him.

"Let's get back." Dan stood up, looking down the dead valley. "I'm through here."

"You mean like you're leaving?" Jeremy scrambled to his feet, forcing the words through the tightness in his throat. "Because of . . . what I did?"

"No." Dan looked down at him, forced a smile. "The job's finished. I didn't expect to be here this long. I shouldn't have stayed this long." He glanced restlessly down the valley again. "So. Are you coming?"

"Yes." Jeremy stood up as straight as he could. "I'm coming."

"Good." Dan boosted Jeremy onto Ezra's back. "I'm leaving early," he said. "You better not tell your folks."

"I won't."

Nobody was pumping on the bicycle frame as they plodded past. Jeremy looked up at the brown hillside and looked away quickly before they could go green. He had thought that would never happen again. But maybe it could. Anyway, tomorrow he'd be gone.

Ezra broke into a jouncing trot, and Jeremy had to grab the saddle frame as the pony headed for the barnyard and the water tub there.

"Mr. Greely," Dad called from the porch.

Jeremy stiffened. Dad sounded cold and mad, like the day Jeremy had made the fields go green.

"We want to talk to you."

Mr. Brewster stepped onto the porch behind him. Rupert and Jonathan followed, with Mr. Mendoza, Sally Brandt, and the Deardorf boys.

Mr. Mendoza had his deer rifle. They all looked angry.

"My brother got into town last night." Sally's voice was shrill. "He told me about this scam he heard about back in Pendleton. Seems this guy goes around to little towns pretending to be a surveyor for the Corps. He buys stuff with Corps vouchers."

"We searched your stuff." Ted Brewster held up a fist full of white. "You carry a few spare letters, don't you?" He opened his hand. "You're a fake."

The white envelopes fluttered to the dusty ground like dead leaves. Stunned, Jeremy turned to Dan, waiting for him to explain, waiting for Dan to tell them how they were wrong, waiting for him to remind them about the water.

"Dan?" he whispered.

Dan looked at him finally, his head moving slowly on his neck, and Jeremy felt his insides going numb and dead.

"Mother gave you dried apples." Jeremy swallowed. "Dried apples are for birthdays."

For one instant, Dan's gray eyes filled with pain. Then he looked away, turning a bland smile on the approaching grownups. "I heard about some bastard doing that." He spread his hands. "But I'm legit."

Dad took one long step forward and smashed his fist into Dan's face. "He described you." He looked down at Dan sprawled in the dirt. "He described you real well."

Dan got up very slowly, wiping dust from his face. Blood smeared his chin. He shrugged. They took him into town, walking around him in a loose ring. Jeremy stood in the road, watching the dust blow away on the hot breeze. When the last trace of dust blew away, he put Ezra into the barn and climbed up onto the rimrock. He didn't come down until dark.

"I wondered about that guy," Rupert sneered as they got ready for bed that night. "Federal survey, huh? They don't care about us, out here. I don't know how anybody could believe him."

"Hope is a tempting thing." Jeremy's mother leaned against the doorway. She hadn't scolded Jeremy for running off. "If there was any water around here, no matter how deep, someone would have drilled for it a long time ago." Her voice was tired. "I guess we all just wanted to hope."

Jeremy threw himself down on his mattress without looking at her.

"I'm sorry," she murmured. "I'm sorry for us, and I'm sorry for him, too."

"They'll hang him. I heard 'em talking."

"Shame on you, Rupert. You don't gloat about a man dying."

Jeremy buried his face in the pillow. I hate him, too, he thought fiercely. Why couldn't have Dan been what he said?

"They're gonna hang him," Rupert whispered to him after Mother had left. He sounded smug. "No wonder that jerk wanted you to help him. You're too dumb to figure out he was a fake."

Jeremy pressed his face into the pillow until he could barely breathe. If he made a sound, if he moved, he'd kill Rupert. Rupert might be almost sixteen, but he'd kill him. Somehow.

Rupert was right. They were going to hang Dan. He'd seen it in their faces when they walked up to him. They hated Dan because he made 'em see that the government, the Army Corps of Engineers really didn't care about them.

Like Dad hated him for making him see what it used to be like. And would never be again.

Jeremy breathed slowly, listening to the house tick and creak as it cooled a bit. He kept hearing Dan's sad-bitter voice. *You do what it takes to stay alive. Sometimes you don't like it much, but you do it.*

Dan hadn't lied to him.

Jeremy must have fallen asleep, because he woke up from a dream about the woman with the black hair. Was she part of the *we* that had turned into *I*?

Rupert snored, one arm hanging over the side of his mattress. The sloping roof held the day's heat in and tonight no breeze stirred the hot, still air. Dan would be in the church. In the empty storage bin in the cellar. The one with the bolt on it. Jeremy sat up, heart pounding. The house creaked softly to itself as he tiptoed down the stairs.

"Who's up?" His father's spoke from the bottom of the stairs.

"Me." Jeremy froze, clutching the railing with both hands. "I . . . had to pee," he stammered. It was a feeble lie. The pot in the bedroom was never full.

"Jeremy?" His father bulked over him, a tower of shadow. "It's late. I just got back from town." He ran a thick hand across his face. "You liked Greely."

"I still like him." Jeremy forced himself to stand straight. "He's not a bad man."

His father grunted, moved down a step. "He's a parasite," he said harshly. "His kind live on other peoples' sweat. There's no worse crime than that."

"Isn't there?" Jeremy's voice trembled. "Who's going to share with him? Who's going to let him have a piece of their orchard or pump from their well some? He was just trying to live, and he didn't hurt anybody, not really . . ."

"He lied to us and he stole from us." His tone dismissed Dan, judged and sentenced him. "Get back to bed. Now."

"No." Shaking, Jeremy clung to the railing. "If it doesn't help the crops, it's bad, isn't it? Nothing else matters to you. Nothing."

His father's hand caught him hard on the side of the head. Jeremy fell against the railing, hot pain spiking through his knee as he sprawled at his father's feet.

All by itself, the firefly popped into the air between them, glowing like a hot coal.

With a hoarse cry, Dad flinched backward, his hand clenching into a fist. Jeremy stared up at his father through a blur of tears. "It's not evil. I'm not an abomination. Is it so wrong to know what things looked like?" He cringed away from his father's fist. "Don't they count?"

His father lowered his fist slowly. "No," he said in a strange, choked voice. "They don't. It doesn't count, either, that a man's just trying to stay alive. I . . . I wish it all did. I sure as hell do." He stepped past Jeremy and went on up the stairs.

Jeremy was right. They'd locked Dan up in the church basement. Yellow light glowed dimly from one of the window wells along the concrete foundation, the only light in the dark, dead town. Jeremy lay down on his stomach and peered through the glassless window. Yep. Mr. Brewster sat on an old pew beside the wooden door of the storage unit, flipping through a tattered hunting magazine by the light of a solar lantern.

He looked wide awake.

Jeremy looked at the sky. Was it getting light? How long until dawn? He leaned over the rim of the well. Mr. Brewster wasn't going to fall asleep in time.

Mr. Brewster didn't know about the makings. Probably didn't anyway. Cold balled in Jeremy belly, so bad that he almost threw up. Bigger, he thought. Bigger would be scarier.

The firefly popped into the air two feet from Mr. Brewster's magazine, big as a chicken.

"Holy shit!" The pew rocked and nearly went over as Mr. Brewster scrambled to his feet.

Nails biting his palms, Jeremy made the firefly dart at Mr. Brewster's face. It moved sluggishly, dimming to a dull orange. Oh, God, don't let it fade. Sweat stung Jeremy's eyes.

Mr. Brewster yelled and threw his magazine at it. His footsteps pounded up the wooden stairs, and a moment later, the church door thudded open. Jeremy lay flat in the dust as Mr. Brewster ran past him. The ground felt warm, as if the earth had a fever. Shaking all over, Jeremy listened to the footsteps fade.

Now!

He scrambled down through the window. A fragment of glass still stuck in the old frame grazed his arm, and he landed on a chair. It collapsed under his weight with a terrible crash. Panting, Jeremy scrambled to his feet. He struggled with the bolt on the storeroom door, bruising his palm. It slid back, and he pushed the heavy door open.

Dan sat on the floor between shelves of musty hymnals and folded choir robes. The yellow light from the lantern made his skin look tawny brown, like the dust. Dried blood streaked his swollen and bruised face.

"Jeremy?" Hope flared in Dan's eyes.

"Hurry." Jeremy grabbed his arm.

Dan staggered to his feet and followed Jeremy up the steps, treading on his heels. Someone shouted as they leaped from the porch and Jeremy's heart lurched. "That way." He pointed.

Dan threw an arm around him and ran, half-carrying Jeremy as they ducked behind the dark Exxon station. They scrambled under the board fence in the back, lay flat while someone ran and panted past. Mr. Brewster? Gray banded the eastern horizon as Jeremy led Dan across the dusty main street, listening for footsteps, stumbling on the rough pavement. They turned left by the boarded up restaurant, cut through a yard full of drifted dust, dead weeds, and a rusting car.

Jeremy had left Ezra tethered behind the last house on the street. The pony gave a low, growling whinny as they hurried up. Dan stroked his nose to quiet him, his eyes running over the lumpy bulges of the pack.

"It's all there, food, water, and everything," Jeremy panted. "Even the machine. It's not a very good job. I don't know how to fix a pack. The ground's pretty hard along the river, so you won't leave many tracks. Willow creekbed'll take you way south. It's the first creekbed past the old feed mill. You can't miss it. Nobody lives out that way. No water."

"I thought you were coming with me." Dan looked down at him.

"I was." Jeremy looked at the old nylon daypack he'd left on the ground beside Ezra. "I changed my mind."

"You can't stay now." Dan grabbed his shoulders, hard enough to hurt. "They'll know you let me out. Jeremy, what will they do to you?"

"I don't know." Jeremy swallowed, remembering his father's voice on the stairs. "I just got to stay," he whispered.

"You're crazy. You think you'll make peace with your father?" Dan gave him one short, sharp shake that made Jeremy's teeth snap together. "You have real magic in your hands. You think that's ever going to matter to him?"

Jeremy couldn't speak, could only shake his head.

"Hell, my own choices haven't turned out too good. Who am I to tell you what you have to do?" Dan wiped Jeremy's tears away, his fingers rough and dry on Jeremy's face. "Just don't let them kill your magic." He shook Jeremy again, gently this time. "He needs it. They all need it." He sighed. "I'm outta here. Keep making, Jeremy." Dan squeezed Jeremy's shoulder hard, grabbed Ezra's lead rope, and walked away down the creekbed in the fading night.

Jeremy stood still, the tears drying on his face, listening to Ezra's muffled hoofbeats fade into the distance. He listened until he could hear nothing but the dry whisper of the morning breeze, then he started back. He thought about cutting across the dun hills and down through the riverbed to get home. Instead, he walked straight back to town.

They might have been waiting for him in front of the church — Mr. Brewster, Sally Brandt, Mr. Mendoza and . . . Dad. Jeremy faltered as they all turned to look at him, wishing in that terrible, frightened instant, that he had gone with Dan after all. They looked at him like they had looked at Dan yesterday, hard and cold. Mr. Brewster walked to meet him, slow and stifflegged, and Jeremy wondered suddenly if they'd hang him in Dan's place.

"You little, crippled snot." Mr. Brewster's hand closed on Jeremy's shirt, balling up the fabric, lifting him a little off his feet. "You let Greely out. I saw you. Where's he headed?"

"I don't know," Jeremy said.

Mr. Brewster hit him.

Red-and-black light exploded behind Jeremy's eyelids, and his mouth filled with a harsh, metallic taste. He fell hard and hurting onto his knees, dizzy, eyes blurred with tears, belly full of sickness. Mr. Brewster grabbed him and hauled him to his feet again and Jeremy cringed.

"Knock it off, Ted."

Dad yanked him away from Mr. Brewster. "I lay hands on my kids. Nobody else."

"He knows where that bastard's headed." Mr. Brewster breathed heavy and fast. "You beat it out of him or I do."

"He said he doesn't know. That's the end of it, you hear me?"

"You talk pretty high and mighty," Mr. Brewster said softly. "Considering you had to beg for help last winter. Seems like you ought to shut up."

Jeremy felt his father jerk, as if Mr. Brewter had punched him. He felt his father's arms quiver and wondered if he would let go, walk away.

"Seems like we all pitched in, when mice got into your seed stock a few years back," Dad said quietly.

Mr. Brewster made a small, harsh sound.

"Come on, Ted. Let it go." Sally's shrill exasperation shattered the tension. "While you're standing there arguing, Greely's making tracks for Boardman."

"We got to split up," Mr. Mendoza chimed in.

"Let's spread." Mr. Brewster glowered at Jeremy. Abruptly he spun on his heel. "I bet the bastard headed west," he snarled. "We'll go down the riverbed, cut his tracks." He stalked off down the street with Mr. Mendoza.

Sally Brandt pushed tousled hair out of her face, sighed. "I'll go wake up the Deardorfs," she said. "We'll spread north and east. You take the south."

He felt his father's body move, as if he had nodded. Jeremy stared down at the dust between his feet, tasting blood on his swelling lip, heart pounding so hard it felt like it was going to burst through his ribs. He felt Dad's hands lift from his shoulders, tensed as his father moved around in front of him, blocking the rising sun. But all he did was to lift Jeremy's chin, until he had to meet his father's eyes.

"I thought you'd go with him."

Jeremy looked at his father's weathered face. It looked like the hills, all folded into dun gullies. Not angry. Not sad. Just old and dry.

"If we find Greely, we got to hang him," Dad said. "Right or wrong, we voted, Jeremy."

"I was going to go." Jeremy swallowed, tasting dust. "You had to ask for food. Because of me."

His father's face twitched.

Without warning, the firefly popped into the air between them again, pale this time, a flickering shadow in the harsh morning light. Jeremy sucked in his breath, snuffed it out as his father flinched away from it. "I'm sorry," he cried. "I didn't mean to make it. It just . . . happened. It makes Rita Menendez laugh. I won't do it again ever."

"Do it again." His father's hand clamped down on Jeremy's arm. "Right now."

Trembling, afraid to look at his father's face, he made the firefly appear again.

His father stared at it for a moment. With a shudder, he thrust his fingers through the firefly, yanked them back and stared at them. "It scares me," he whispered. "I don't understand it any more than I understand this damn, never-ending drought." He looked at Jeremy suddenly. "You scared the pants off Ted. He's not going to forgive you for that. I don't think everybody believed what the Reverend had to say, but enough did, son."

He sighed. "I don't have any good answers. Maybe there aren't any — not good ones." He met Jeremy's eyes. "I've got to look south for Greely," he said. "Which way do you think he'd head? Down Willow creekbed — or by the main road to La Grande?"

Jeremy hesitated for a moment, then straightened his shoulders with a jerk. "I think he went down the main road," he said and held his breath.

His father shaded his eyes, stared at the dun fold of Willow creekbed in the distance. "There aren't any good answers." He sighed. "I'll look for Greely on the main road," he said.

CELILO

Dan Greely limped slowly eastward, along the old highway. The empty bed of the Columbia river dropped away on his right, a huge gash of cracked clay and weathered gray rock. The Pipeline gleamed dull silver, half buried in the middle of the riverbed in this stretch. The Drylands lay at his back, The Dalles ahead, down the riverbed, hidden by the high walls of the Columbia Gorge. A semi roared past, a single rig, maybe a local making up with a convoy. Not much traffic. Dan wiped sweat and grit from his face, shaded his eyes against the glare of the setting sun. Those were the old falls, up ahead. Already. He lowered his head and limped on. It had been a long time since he had been back here.

Those ledges of stone looked the same, as if the heat had dried up time in this place, preserved it, like the shriveled carcass of a coyote he'd found out in the Dry once, a year old or a dozen years. He sneaked a glance at the dusty ledges of the long-dead falls.

Someone stood on the edge, where the rocks jutted out over the deepest part of the riverbed. Dan caught his breath, thought he saw the flutter of black hair on the hot wind.

Amy was dead. Long dead. The figure was gone, had been nothing but a shimmer of heat, he told himself, a trick of mind and memory and heat. He wrenched his eyes away from the falls and his foot turned as a rock rolled beneath it. His pack pulled him off balance and he hissed through his teeth as his weight came down on his bad knee. The sudden searing pain caught him by surprise, kicked his feet out from under him. Tires blurred by in a rush of motion, inches from his face as he sprawled onto the crumbling asphalt.

Brakes screeched and doors slammed. "Hey, you all right?" Footsteps scraped on sandy asphalt. "I damn near ran over you."

"My knee." Dan breathed shallowly, sweating.

"Let's see." A man squatted beside him, lean and weathered brown. "Jesse, come take a look, will you? You got the touch for this sort of thing."

A woman joined him, older, with a lined, sun-dried face and a thick braid of gray hair.

"I twisted it some days back. Just now . . . stepped wrong. Or something." He sucked in a breath as the woman squatted beside him and began to prod and twist his knee gently. "That hurts."

"Might be just a sprain." She didn't relent with her probing. "Might be you finally tore something. Can't tell with joints." Her faded shirt flapped in the wind as she shrugged and rocked back on her heels. "A splint's the best you can do. Get off it and give it some rest. It'll get better or it won't." She said it resentfully, as if Dan had asked her for a handout.

Well, he hadn't asked her for anything. "Could you folks give me a ride into town?" he said through clenched teeth. Although what he'd do there if he couldn't stand or walk, he didn't have a clue.

"You heard Jesse." The man shook his head, slapped dust from his faded jeans as he stood. "You can't walk around like that. You stay a couple of days with us, rest that knee up, and I'll give you a ride into town come market day. Maria won't mind."

"Hell she won't, Sam." The woman tossed her braid back over her shoulder. "Maria has enough trouble feeding you all as it is. He can stay with me, since you're going to be stubborn. Renny just left with a convoy and won't be back 'till next weekend. I've got space."

She was speaking over Dan's head as if he was deaf or a car-hit dog. "Thanks, Ma'am," Dan said and he made his voice humble and polite. He didn't feel polite. The weight of that pain scared him. What if he *had* torn something? What then? "I appreciate it," he said, and he did, never mind her attitude. You took what was offered and said thank you. Or you died.

He took the man's offered hand, and he needed it to get up, even without his pack. As soon as he started to put weight on his knee it buckled. His belly sour with fear, he leaned on the man, made it to the cab of the truck and onto the patched seat. They squeezed in beside him, smelling of sweat and dust. He didn't want to be stuck here, so close to the falls and the past.

"I'm Sam Montoya," the man said. "This here is Jesse Warren." He chuckled. "She barks but she don't bite."

"I'm Dan Greely. From La Grande." Not recently, but it was a name to give.

Dan braced himself against the dash, trying to spare his knee, as the truck lurched down off the highway, onto a dirt track. He clenched his teeth against the pain as they bounced and jolted up out of the Gorge. Vertical ridges of gray rock rose on their left. On their right, the Columbia bed looked like a dry wound in the earth's crust. With a groan of gears, the truck heaved itself over the rim and out onto rolling land.

"Darn ethanol don't got no oomph," Montoya grumbled.

Jesse didn't say anything.

Dan stared out at dusty soaker-hose fields, recognizing the leaves of the ultra-engineered soybeans pretty much everyone was growing now. If they weren't growing biomass bushes. Dead, dun land separated the rows of beans, dotted with sparse clumps of tough grass. A dustdevil twisted across a rocky draw, stirring the tumbleweed skeletons. Water for crops meant you had something. If you didn't have it, you found something that the people with water wanted.

No one gave anything away. Not anymore.

So what did this man want? He would want something. Dizzy and a little sick from the truck's jolting, Dan closed his eyes. He didn't like not knowing the price in advance.

The truck turned off on a narrow track that led back toward the river-bed, stopped finally in front of a small, weathered house at the very edge of the Gorge. Rows of soybeans surrounded it, and a gray barn sagged behind a tumble-down pole corral. Dan slid cautiously down from the truck cab. The steel cube of a Corps water meter jutted up beside the porch.

The Corps of Engineers controlled all the water now. There were no more private wells, not since the Groundwater Mining Act had passed. Here, it came from the enormous, buried Pipeline that protected all that was left of the Columbia River. Dan let Montoya help him up the sagging steps. It felt almost cool inside the house. The main room was small — a table, a few wooden chairs, and a wood stove made up the furniture.

Montoya pulled out a chair. "Sit down and I'll bring your pack in."

It felt really good to sit still. Dan looked around. This was an old house — almost a shack — cobbled together out of dried-out, gray wood and warped, ancient sheets of plasterboard. Two lean-to bedrooms opened into the main room. That was it. Dan eased his leg up onto a second chair.

"This'll help with the swelling. I'll wrap it later." Jesse draped a wet cloth across his knee.

Dan's skin twitched at the cold wetness soaked through his jeans. He leaned forward to fold it across his kneecap. It had been some time since he'd been in a house with water from a tap. Out in the Dry, in a land without water meters, they cleaned dishes with sand, watered plants one at a time, with a bucket and dipper. The magic tricks and stories he had to offer, the gossip from the last settlement, earned him a mug of water, some food if there was any to spare, and a bed.

It was a risk to come back here, but he'd run out of choices. It was getting worse out there. He touched the sodden cloth on his knee, watched a crystal drop fall to the wood floor. He'd make out all right here, he told himself fiercely. His knee would get better.

"Water?" Jesse plunked an orange plastic pitcher and three glasses down on the table.

You got used to being thirsty, didn't think about it. Until someone offered you water. "Thanks." Dan took the glass she handed him, made himself drink it slowly. Politely.

"You headed for The Dalles?" Montoya thumped his pack down on the floor, and picked up a glass.

"I don't think the Corps is hiring." Jesse refilled his glass. "No other jobs."

"I'm not looking for a job." Not with the Corps, that was for sure. This time, it was easier to drink slowly. Pipeline water. He drank it anyway. "I'm a magician. And a storyteller. I was on my way into town to try a show."

Screened by the table top, he'd pulled the handkerchief out of his pocket, folded into a tiny, tight roll, and had tucked it between his palm and thumb while they were looking at the water being poured. Time to start paying for his stay here. He let them notice his empty palms as he gestured, waved his hand over the pitcher, and shook out the handkerchief with a flourish, as if he'd just pulled it from the spout.

It was smooth. Montoya whistled.

Jesse grunted. "You had that rag in your hand."

"You ought to do pretty good in town. Not too many can afford wireless service. Costs too much." Montoya set his glass down, winked at Dan. "I'd part with some dried pears or a bag of beans for a show like that. A lot of folks would."

"If you've got any pears to part with." Jesse scowled at him, tugged on her braid. "Water bill's due this week, remember? You got to pay that, first."

"We can cover it. We did okay with the early beet crop." Montoya touched her arm lightly. "Take care of our friend here, Jesse. Maria's gonna be mad if I'm not back by dark."

"She'll be scared, is what she'll be." Jesse watched him leave. "Sam's always too ready to help." She threw Dan a hard look. "Maria's got another little one, and they barely got by before that."

Dan sipped water, his pain turning into anger again, dry and bitter as the dust on his skin. "Out in the Dry, people don't have too many kids," he said softly. "Not for long anyway."

Jesse stared at him for a moment, her face still, empty of expression. "I've got to weed, now that it's cooled off some." Her chair scraped on the floor as she stood.

That had been stupid. Dan listened to the screen door bang behind her, his lips tight. She could throw him out. He stuffed the handkerchief back into his pocket. Montoya had even brought in his stick. Dan bent for it, listened, heard nothing but wind and the distant croak of a crow. What if his knee didn't get better? He fought the pain as he made his way across the floor. Yeah, he could get around if he had to. Barely. The dizziness caught up with him again, and he leaned against the doorframe of one of the bedrooms, sweat crawling slowly down his face.

A dresser and a double bed took up most of the small room. Paintings had been pinned to the plasterboard walls. Watercolors? Dan risked a limping step into the room. A river twined across a dozen sheets of paper, full of graygreen water. The Columbia? The painted banks were a blur of greens and soft browns. Had it really looked like that once?

A glint of gold caught Dan's eye. A necklace hung from the corner of a picture frame on the dresser. Dan picked up the chain, twined it around his fingers. It felt like real gold. A thick amber bead hung from the fine links, a tiny fly embedded in its golden depths. Dan looked at the picture. A woman stared up at him through a windblown tangle of dark hair. She was smiling, but her eyes looked reserved. Private.

She looked a little like a younger Jesse.

"Curious?"

Dan's hand twitched and the necklace fell with a tiny clatter.

"I though your knee hurt." Jesse stood behind him, hip cocked against the doorframe.

"It does." Dan tried to control his flush. "I was looking at your paintings."

"Uh huh." Jesse's eyes measured him. "That's Renny," she said. "My daughter." She held out a couple of newly split and peeled twigs. "I'll put a splint on that knee for you." She bent to retrieve the necklace. "Stay out of my room."

"Yes, ma'am."

Montoya showed up next morning. Dan was sitting at the table, polishing a tricky double-lift and little-finger-break combination for a sandwiched ace trick.

"How's the knee?" Montoya set a plastic jug down on the table.

"Better." Dan touched the bandage Jesse had made from what looked like a torn sheet. The stick splints helped. "Take a card." He offered Montoya the pack, then dealt the two black aces face-up onto the table top. "Five of diamonds." He slipped Montoya's five openly between the aces. With a flourish, he picked up the three cards, placed them on top of the pack and tapped it square. "Now, sir, your five of diamonds has vanished." He spread the top two cards.

Only the black aces stared up at them, and Dan heard Montoya grunt. "Let's see if I can find them for you." Solemnly, he spread the pack face-down across the table. The two red aces winked face-up from the middle of the spread, a single card sandwiched between them. Without a word, Dan reached for it, flipped it over.

"My five." Montoya picked up the card, turned it over his thick fingers. "Pretty neat." He gave Dan a slow smile. "You do that good, magician."

"It's just a trick, Sam." Jesse stood in the doorway, skinny arms crossed, brown dirt staining her hands.

"You're right." Dan gathered up the cards. "It takes two little maneuvers that I don't let you notice, and I set the pack up first."

"We must seem awful stupid." Montoya tapped the deck of cards. "Gawking like we do. Thick-headed."

"You got a better idea?" Dan shrugged and tucked the cards away, knowing he should keep his mouth shut. "It's an honest trade. I take the time to learn how to make it look good, you get to be impressed for a minute or two."

"I didn't mean it that way," Montoya said mildly. He cleared his throat. "You get your bill from the Corps yet?" he asked Jesse.

"Nope. I can't pay it until Renny gets in, anyway. I'm short." Jesse scowled at the plastic jug on the table. "How come you've got milk to waste?"

"I wasn't plannin' on wasting it. I thought we'd drink it, if you'll get us some cups. We got our bill yesterday." He leaned his arms on the table. "We got a foreclosure notice."

"Foreclosure?" Jesse scowled, spilled drops of milk. "You're not that far behind, Sam."

"We are now." Montoya's smile vanished. "The Corps hiked the rate again. Re-tro-*ac*-tive." He dragged the syllables out. "The Columbia Association is behind it. That means we're gonna owe more for the last six months. The beans ain't gonna cover that, no matter how good the crop comes in."

"They'll cut you off if you don't pay." She handed round the cups of milk, frowning. "Renny can lend you the scrip to pay off the hike."

Montoya shook his head, frowning. "Sara Dorner showed up this morning, all upset. It's not just me. They're doing it to everybody between The Dalles and the Deschutes bed."

"You sound like you think there's something we can do about it." Jesse put her cup down.

"We can stick together and stand up to the Association!" Montoya stared into his cup. "If we don't, if we don't hang on, we'll dry up and blow away like the dirt, blow right on out into the Drylands. Or into the camps." He stood up. "I got to get going. Think about it, Jesse."

"You can't fight them," Jesse yelled after him. "Why don't you listen to Maria and take care of your own family for a change?" She whipped around to glare down at Dan. "Why didn't you tell him that it's no use?" she snapped.

Dan shrugged. The milk was warm as blood, rich and goaty. How long since he'd tasted milk? Out in the Dry, people didn't have too many milking animals. What you coaxed out of the ground, you mostly ate yourself. When they had it, they didn't trade it for card tricks. He shifted his weight, stretched his leg tentatively. He could walk, even if it hurt. If he took it slow, he could get around. Another day, he thought. And he'd move on.

Through the window, you could see clear down into the old riverbed and the falls. He hadn't noticed it yesterday, but it had been getting dusk. Dan sucked in a breath as he spied a tiny figure standing on the worn lip of the cliff, just like yesterday. A kid, he told himself. Playing. He jumped as Jesse leaned over his shoulder.

"That's old Celilo Falls," she said. "My grandmother grew up on the Warm Springs Reservation. She used to tell me stories about the falls. All the tribes used to fish here." She stared down at the dry ledges. "She talked like she'd been there herself, watching the men spear salmon from the platforms. She couldn't have been that old." She laughed shortly. "Hell, maybe she was. I don't know."

Jesse turned away. "They drowned it all, you know. Way back in the old days. When they built The Dalles dam. She said the Salmon People kept it safe. When I was little, she told me that one day, the water would go down and it would all be there, just like in the old days." Jesse laughed.

"When the reservoir started going down and they finished the Trench Reservoir and started the Pipeline, I used to sit here and watch the rocks show a little more every week. That was when I was pregnant and not sure just how I ended up that way. Sometimes I thought I could almost see them — up there on the platforms, stabbing the fish with their long spears. I was just hungry, I guess, and a little crazy. Hadn't been any salmon in that river for years." Jesse plunked a heavy pot down on the table. "There's nothing out there but dust. Here's the rest of last night's beans, if you're hungry."

She sounded angry, like she was sorry she'd said so much. Dan looked out the window again, but the figure had vanished from the ledge. Jesse was old enough to remember water in the riverbed. Dan couldn't do it, couldn't imagine that enormous ditch all full of clear water, millions of gallons of it.

Amy had been able to see it. *This place remembers*, she had said, the first time she'd gone out on a patch crew. The super had let her bring him along, little though he was. You *can see how the river used to be when you stand up here*, she had said. Amy would have recognized Jesse's watercolors.

"I know what the Association is up to," he said.

Jesse turned and looked back at him, the empty milk jug in her hand.

"They want your land," Dan said harshly. "They're in bed with the Corps. They can bring in crew labor from the Portland camps, make more money farming beans and wheat than they can get from selling you water."

"That seems like a lot of trouble for the Corps, when all they have to do is send out bills right now." She frowned.

"It's getting more expensive to mine water. And protect it." Dan shrugged. "I bet the Association gives the Corps a kickback, once they take over here. Gang labor's cheap and permanent. They're using it in the Willamette Valley. The Association owns a lot of land it got back on water-foreclosure. You got to buy everything from the boss when you work on a gang, and pretty soon, they own you."

Amy had signed them on. He had been ten, and Amy had been desperate, scared by how close they'd come to dying as they hitched north from California. He remembered that — how she was always scared.

"Profit." Dan looked out at the dead falls. "They've got the water. They can farm the dirt cheap."

"You worked on a gang," Jesse said.

"Right here. The Association provided contract grunt labor for the Pipe. When I was a kid." The silver glitter of the Pipe down in the dusty bed hurt his eyes.

What's going to happen to you? Amy had cried, when she had started getting sick and couldn't work her shift anymore. *I told Mom I'd take care of you.*

"You're not going to beat the Association," he said.

"I'm not planning to try." Jesse turned her back on him.

Jesse was in the field, cleaning silt out of the feeder tubing, when Montoya drove up next afternoon. Dan sat on the porch, shelling dry beans for market and counting the crop rows, figuring yields. The dry pods crackled between his palms. Jesse didn't have enough land under hoses to get by. Good thing that she had a trucker daughter to bring in scrip. The necklace was back hanging on the picture. It would be worth a lot in, say, Portland. If he wanted to do that again. Steal. He tossed a handful of pale, pebble-hard beans into the pan. He needed to get out of here. Now. Too many ghosts.

Dan nodded to Montoya as he climbed out of the truck. Maybe he could talk Montoya into giving him a ride into town. He could get a hitch there.

"Lo, Sam." Jesse came around the corner, wiping sweat and dust from her face.

"Sara Dorner came over this morning," Montoya said, without preamble. "A couple of Association people came out to make an offer on their land. They offered Matt and Sara a job, too."

"Let me guess." Jesse tossed her tube-brush onto the porch. "Matt shot 'em."

"Nope." Montoya sighed. "But I guess he did cut up rough, threw a few punches. They took off before he could get around to using the rifle. Sara's pretty upset, afraid they'll be back to arrest him."

"Matt's a short-tempered fool." Hands on her hips, Jesse glared at Montoya. "I bet Maria's real happy about you being in the middle of all this."

"They'll get around to us pretty soon, so I guess we'd better talk to the Association folks. Jesse?" Montoya spread his hands. "They got to see we're all together on this. Otherwise they're gonna pick us off one at a time."

Jesse glared at him, gave Dan a quick, hostile look. "All right." Her shoulders sagged suddenly. "I'll come be a warm body for you, Sam, but it's not going to work."

"It will if we make it work. You got to believe that." Montoya touched her arm. "That's all we got."

Jesse shook her head without answering.

"How about you?" Montoya turned to Dan. "Like Jesse says, we could use warm bodies. After market, I'll give you a ride west as far as Chenowen."

As if he'd been reading Dan's mind. "All right," he said.

"Thanks."

Dan met the man's dark eyes. "You know, if you make this work, if you bring everybody together . . ." He paused. "They'll just shoot you."

Montoya said nothing and his eyes didn't waver.

"I'll get my stick." Dan turned away.

The Dorner place was way south, at the fringe of the irrigated land. A trailer house sat crookedly on the concrete blocks, surrounded by fields of genetically engineered sugar beets, destined for the ethanol stills. The dark green beet tops drooped in the heat, revealing the black-and-gray network of soaker hose and feeder lines between the neat rows.

"They're shut off," Jesse said.

"Looks like it." Montoya stared at the beet rows and shook his head.

The Association didn't have to come out personally to shut off water. The Corps controlled the meters from The Dalles. All of them. Dan braced himself as the truck bounced through sun-hardened ruts. The hot wind whipped the dust away from the tires, riffled the drying tops of the beets. Once they went down, beets didn't come back. The dark roots looked too small to be worth much. By tomorrow, the Dorners would lose the crop.

Montoya pulled the truck up beside a flatbed and a scatter of battered pickups. Tethered to a decrepit wagon, a bony Appaloosa swished its tail at flies. Twenty or thirty men and women milled in front of a sagging wire gate. The wind snatched at their clothes, fluttering shirttails like faded flags.

"Hey, Sam," someone called out.

"Carl's just finishin' up the pipe," a small, round-faced woman said.

Dan followed the looks. A crooked line of old, galvanized irrigation pipe led from a pile of freshly dug dirt down the slope and out of sight. Someone had the tools and technical skills to cut into one of the Corps' big feeder lines, then. As he watched, water bubbled out of a joint in the old pipe, darkening the ocher soil like spilled blood. Someone cheered, and, in a moment, everyone was cheering.

They really didn't know the Association very well. The pipes belonged to the Corps. They'd just stand back and let the Corps deal with it. Dan leaned against the fender of the flatbed. Jesse stood on the far side of the crowd, arms crossed, watching the celebration. She looked up suddenly and their eyes met. Her lips crooked into a faint smile, sardonic and intimate at the same time.

Dan looked away, flushing.

"Here they come." A lanky kid perched on the flatbed's cab, pointed.

"They must've been waiting for us to do something," a woman said.

Someone had tipped them off about this little demonstration, Dan thought. Men and women sidled together, bunching up as a van growled toward them, raising a flaring tail of dust. *Columbia River Association* glared from the sides in red letters.

"Where's Matt?" someone called out.

"Safe. Sara's with him. And Tom."

Dan watched the guns come out — old hunting rifles, some shotguns, and a few pistols. The van pulled up in a swirl of dust. Three men got out, wearing the Association's short-sleeved khaki uniforms. Not one of them carried a weapon.

Dan watched the crowd notice that. He watched the rifle barrels waver and the pistols disappear into pockets again. Folks thought they were the first ever to stand up to them. The Association would send people who knew how to handle a crowd. They always did.

"I'd like to talk to Matthew Robert Dorner." The shortest of the three stepped forward. His tone was friendly, like he'd just dropped by to chat.

"He's not here!" someone yelled belligerently, and the crowd murmured, closing in more tightly.

"Look, folks, I'm not here to pick a fight with you." The short man sounded tired. "We're down here to oversee water distribution for the Corps, that's all. They've got enough on their plate keeping the Pipeline in operation." He took his cap off, wiped his face on his sleeve. "You know how far the water table in the Columbia Aquifer's dropped in the last twelve months? In about five more years, we won't be able to pump from it at all. Every drop you use will have to come from the Trench Reservoir and the Pipe. The price of water is going to go up fast, starting now." He turned slowly, his eyes moving from one dusty face to another. "Most of you are hardworking folk. Don't cut your own throats for the sake of the ones who aren't. There's only so much water, folks. That's it. Beginning, middle, and end of story."

The wind rustled through the wilted beet tops. Men and women traded sidelong looks, shuffled their feet in the dust.

The Association man cleared his throat. "Water piracy is a big-time felony. You draw a lot of federal years." He looked over their heads, up into the hard blue sky. "You can get the death penalty, depending on how much you hurt folk down-flow. I know you folks are upset. It's tough, watching someone you know go under. I suppose, since I didn't actually see anyone hole that pipe, I could just patch it, write it up as a materials failure."

Slick. Dan stretched his aching knee gently. The man was putting himself on their side, just one of the thirsty, fighting the drought like everyone else. Underneath his smile, he was letting them know they couldn't win. He'd do a smooth card trick, Dan thought sourly.

He watched the eyes shift some more, feet scuff up more dust. They were listening to the ugly echoes of felony and *death sentence,* deciding they could meet the rate hike somehow, and that Matt was a reckless fool, not worth risking the family for. Nobody took risks for anyone else anymore. You had enough risks of your own. Dan leaned against the hot metal, waiting to see who'd sneak away first.

"We could maybe understand your rate hike." Montoya stepped out of the crowd, thumbs tucked into his belt. "We know it costs a lot to feed all those Corps people while they keep the Pipe flowing. And we gotta pay Canada for the water that feeds the Rocky Mountain Trench. We know all that. It's this *retroactive* bit that's hard to swallow." His smile looked weathered, as old as the cliffs. "We've given you whatever you asked for, worked ourselves 'till we drop to pay off your water. Matt 'n Sara ain't no lazy bums. They work as hard as any of us, and they could make the hike. They can't make the hike you laid on the last six months of water. None of us can." He tilted his head, his eyes on the Association man. "Seems kind of . . . well . . . coincidental, you offerin' to buy 'em out like that. You in the land business now?"

"That was charity." The Association man's voice had lost a bit of its smooth tone.

"Was it?" Montoya frowned, appearing to consider. "Seems like you could'a waived the *retroactive* hike for charity. Matt 'n Sara work as hard as any of us. If they go down, I figure we're all gonna go down. Where are we gonna go? Since I don't think we have any good options, I guess we'd better figure something out."

Dan heard the responsive murmur, even though Montoya's tone had been quiet and reasonable. The bodies shifted again, edging closer now. They were a crowd again, not just a bunch of tired, worried men and women ready to slink away and take what they could get.

The Association man felt it, too, and threw Sam a quick, hard glance, before his face smoothed out. "Hell, I told you I'm not here to start a fight." He gave them a rueful smile, like he was sorry they couldn't be friends. "If you don't pay your fees, or if you cut into the pipes, the Association's gonna come down on you hard and legal. Backed up by the Corps."

"Fine," someone hollered from the back of the crowd. "We'd rather deal with the Corps. They don't want our land."

"Have it your way." The man shrugged, turned his back on them.

His two silent watch dogs followed him, their backs stiff. Someone cheered as the van lurched down the slope. That started them all cheering again, milling around, slapping backs and hugging, like they'd really backed the Association down.

Montoya was in the center of it all, but as if he felt Dan's attention, he looked up and their eyes met. His were bleak in spite of his smile. He knew what was coming. Dan turned away and headed for the pickup, leaning hard on his stick. As he rounded the front of the flatbed, he stopped. Jesse stood on the far side, talking to a thickset, bearded man with the pale skin and tattooed left arm of a convoy trucker.

". . . she picked up a ride east, figures she'll get herself into a long-haul convoy back there," the man was saying. "She says she's got enough saved for a down-payment on her own truck. I don't know why she didn't come tell you yourself." His tone was a shade too jovial. "Just short on time, I guess."

"That isn't any reason." Jesse's face was stone.

"Hey, come on, now." The trucker scuffed his feet in the dust, trying hard to keep his cheerful tone. "I hate to lose my partner, but you know she's always wanted her own rig, her own routes. I figure she'll be back, Jesse. Come spring, maybe. You'll see."

"We both know Renny's not coming back, but thanks, Jim. Thanks for telling me." Jesse turned away, walked past Dan as if he wasn't there.

Her face looked faded and slack, as if all the life had drained out of it. Dan watched her start down the dirt track, stumbling a little, moving stiffly, like an old woman. The reset of the crowd was catching up now, still wound up and full of themselves. They climbed onto the flatbed and the parked trucks. Jesse was still in view, but no one asked what was wrong, no one ran after her. Dust puffed up from under her feet, whirled away on the dry wind.

Montoya asked, when he finally made it back to the truck.

"She started walking home." Dan stared through the window at the reviving beets. "Your wife didn't come along."

"Nope." Montoya started the engine.

"What's she going to do, after the Association puts you in prison or kills you if they can't?"

"I told her it wouldn't make no difference, if they were gonna kick us off the land anyway." He gripped the wheel. "We make it together or we don't make it. I don't think the Corps' in on this. We got to get them to look at what the Association's up to. We're all scared, but we'll stick together on this."

"You think so?" The truck lurched down the track, shrouded in dust. Dan caught glimpses of the riverbed up ahead, and the dry scar of the falls. "People don't risk what they got. Not anymore. They don't give anything away. My sister and I begged our way up from California. I wasn't so little that I don't know how she paid for what they gave us. This togetherness stuff is a dream. They'll walk away and leave you for the Association, soon as they get pushed hard."

"I'm sorry," Montoya said heavily. "About your sister. And you." He gave Dan a brief look. "But I think you're wrong. You gotta believe in something."

Dan looked away, a fist of pain clenched in his chest. "I stopped believing a long time ago."

"I know. You could try again," Montoya said quietly. "Not everyone is like the folk you met."

Dan kept his eyes on the dun land passing. "I can't." A vulture turned in the dry vault of the sky and he wondered what had died. "I . . . did some things I'm not proud of. If I stay around here . . . I'll probably end up in prison."

Montoya was quiet for a long time. "I thought card tricks was a tough way to make a living out in the Dry." He looked sideways at Dan. "Better than what you were doing?"

Dan shrugged, his lips tight.

"Some day, you're gonna have to stop running, son."

"From prison?"

"From yourself."

Dan kept his eyes on the patient vulture and Montoya didn't say another word during the trip.

Dan woke to darkness and the sound of wind. It took him a minute to get his bearings, to remember the feel of the narrow bed in Jesse's house. The east wind was booming down the Gorge. Sand and dust rasped against the walls. Dan rolled onto his back. Something had awakened him. A dream? His chest ached and he kicked the sweaty sheets aside.

A board squeaked, and light glimmered in the main room. Jesse? Dan raised himself on one elbow. She had come in just before dark, dusty and silent, and had vanished into her room without speaking to him.

The bedroom door creaked, and Jesse walked into his room, a small, solar lamp in her hand. The dim yellow glow streaked the room with shadows. She wore nothing but an oversized T-shirt, and her hair cascaded down her back and over her shoulders, coarse and gray, standing out from her head as if charged with static. Here eyes looked enormous, full of shadows.

"Are you okay?" Dan sat up, gooseflesh prickling his arms. She looked like a ghost.

Jesse set the lamp down on the table without answering, stripped the shirt off over her head, and dropped it onto the floor. Her skin was brown, lighter where her clothes had covered her, and her flesh looked lean, tough, dried onto her bones. The soft light outlined the flat ridges of muscle in her abdomen, pooled shadow between her drooping breasts, made her cheekbones stand out sharply.

She leaned across the bed and ran her hands lightly down Dan's sides. "What is it?" Dan asked, his mouth dry.

She shook her head once, and the ancient bedframe creaked with her weight as she slid one leg across his thighs. Aroused and uneasy at the same time, Dan put his hands on her hips, felt her shiver.

She leaned forward, kissed him hard. Her teeth bruised his lips and Dan pulled her down against him, desire flaring inside him like a flame. We are both lost, he thought. They made love fiercely, silently, flesh straining against flesh. Her eyes were dark and opaque in the dim light, focused inward even as she clutched him.

Her answer to Renny.

Afterward, she slid off him and knelt on the edge of the bed, face turned to the black rectangle of the window. "I knew it was going to happen," she said softly. "I knew she was just going to walk away from me one day."

Dan searched for words that would have some kind of meaning, found nothing. He touched her arm, but she pulled away from him, shook her head.

"I drove her away. I could have taken off, on my own. Gotten by all right. But I had a kid. A daughter. I sweated every water bill. I loved my daughter. And I . . . hated her, too. A little." She stood, shadows streaking her face.

He reached for her hand, but she slipped away from him, out into the darkness of the main room. He heard her door close softly and firmly. He turned off the fading lamp, got up and limped to the window, drafts tickling his bare chest.

Outside, the sky was black, starless. Dan listened to the wind roaring down the Gorge. Out in the Drylands, it would be whipping up dust, sending sheet lightning shuddering across the sky. You died in the dust storms. If you couldn't find shelter.

Dan didn't go back to sleep. The wind kept him awake and he could feel Amy out there on the lips of the falls. *I hated her, too. A little*. Had Amy felt that? Tied to a little brother? Dan sat on the rumpled bed, listening to the wind, waiting for the night to end. This place was full of ghosts and yesterday. If he didn't leave now, they'd trap him here. And he'd never escape.

As soon as it was light enough to get around without stumbling over things, Dan fixed his pack. He filled his jug from the kitchen tap, trying not to think about how soon they'd shut off her water, now that she couldn't pay. He slung the pack over his shoulder, water from the jug trickling coldly down his arm. His knee hurt, but he could manage.

The sun was coming up. The door to Jesse's room stood open and harsh light streamed across the neatly made bed. The threadbare T-shirt lay in a heap on the unrumpled quilt. "Jesse?" Wind rattled a loose shingle. "Jesse, you in here?" Renny's picture had vanished, but a glitter caught his eye. The gold necklace glittered on the floor in a scatter of bright gold. He picked it up, started to put it on the dresser.

His hand hesitated. Never again. He had made that promise years back. Payback for the gift of his life. Slowly his hand closed over the gold and he thrust it savagely into his pocket.

And now you can't come back here, a small voice whispered in his head. He ignored it as he limped out of the house.

The pack weighed a ton, and the rough track down to the highway made his knee hurt. Not much traffic this early. He limped along, leaning hard on his stick. Sooner or later, someone would come along. Ten miles to The Dalles. He could catch a ride to Portland, maybe, at the truck plaza there.

Thin clouds had moved in from the west, turning the sky a cheating gray. The hot wind whipped dust in his eyes, tugged at his clothes. Dan heard an engine and stuck out his thumb. This one stopped and Dan smothered his reaction as he recognized Montoya.

"Leaving?" He leaned out the window.

"Yeah." Dan felt the hot, heavy weight of the necklace in his pocket.

Montoya got out, leaned against the fender. "The Association didn't waste any time," he said. "They started showing up last night, quiet-like, offering folks jobs. Supervisors. Gang foremen. Good-paying jobs, I hear. They arrested Matt Dorner." He looked up at the weathered of the Gorge. "I guess you were right."

He looked . . . defeated. "What job did they offer you?" Dan asked harshly.

"Nothing."

They wouldn't. They knew who their opposition was here. Dan looked away. If Amy had knocked on this man's door, they might have made it. Both of them. It hadn't happened that way, but it could have.

"There's another way," he said. "Go to the Corps headquarters, down in Bonneville."

Montoya just looked at him.

"The Corps was supposed to run the whole Pipeline project — they run all the federal projects." Dan shrugged. "The Association started out as a civilian contractor working for the Corps, but they had enough political clout to finally edge the Corps out. Not that the Corps is likely to be any better than what you've got," he said bitterly. "But they don't want your land. The general there . . . Hastings . . . he got the Association rammed down his throat. I don't think this retroactive stuff is legal." He shrugged again. "If it's not . . . General Hastings might help you out. Just to cut the ground out from under the Association."

"General Hastings." Montoya said the name slowly. "How do you know this?"

"I . . . worked for the Corps. After . . . my sister died." He couldn't make himself meet Montoya's eyes. "I was a surveyor's assistant. You go talk to Hastings."

"I tried that." Montoya shook his head. "Back when I first heard rumors about a rate hike. No one would talk to me."

Maybe not. Hastings didn't like hicks much.

"Come down there with me." Montoya's eyes glittered, hard as obsidian. "You know this man. Talk to him. Tell him to listen to me."

"I can't do it."

"You told me. I'm asking you for this, Dan. I'm asking you to do it."

No one had ever asked him for help. Dan turned his back on Montoya, stared out at the dry, dead falls. No ghost today.

"What do you see?"

Dan flinched at Montoya's hand on his arm. "Nothing." He shook off Montoya's hand. "You can't really change anything. Not today, not tomorrow, not yesterday. The Corps laid off all their civilian employees a few years back. Including me. I took some things with me when I left Bonneville, valuable stuff. I stole it, because I wasn't going to beg any more. I went around in the Dry pretending to survey for wells that were going to go in. I tricked people." He stared at Montoya, feeling dry and utterly empty inside. "So don't ask me to be a hero for you."

"So that's it." Montoya stared up at the Gorge rim, his face etched like the rocks. "You weren't surveyin' when I picked you up."

"Yeah, well, I got my mind changed. By a kid." Dan looked away. "I figure he's dead now."

"An honest trade, you told me. Entertainment for you knowin' how."

"I'm not staying." He hoisted his pack. "If you care about your wife, your family, you need to stay out of this."

"I'm in the middle of this because I do care about them," Montoya said quietly.

A big semi came growling around the bend, heading into The Dalles. It slowed with a hiss of brakes. "Yo, Sam." The bearded trucker who had delivered Renny's message stuck his head out of the cab. "You okay?"

"Yeah," Montoya called out. "You going to Portland? He needs a lift."

He didn't sound angry, he just sounded tired. "I'll get my pack," Dan said. He shook off a dull sense of regret. "Thanks." He grabbed it, then had to look out at the falls, one more time. He wasn't coming back here. Not ever. So he could look.

And she was there. Amy. Up above, staring down at him.

Celilo Falls, eddy in time, coyote-corpse of yesterday. Dan stared at her, sweating. She was real, like when that kid with magic in his hands had summoned her. If he looked down the bed would he see a patch crew working on the Pipe? Maybe see a skinny kid with black hair standing down there, looking up into the sun, looking up to see what his sister was doing up there?

The road ran almost level with the top of the old falls along here. It was a mirage, he told himself. A crazy trick of light and memory. On the ledge, Amy leaned out over the drop that had bruised her face purple and broken her neck.

The cheating, cloudy light made the stones glow and her black hair streamed over her shoulders.

"Hey," the trucker called. "You comin' or not?"

A rock rattled down the cliff face.

"Amy!" Dan yelled, but the wind snatched the words from his mouth. He scrambled over the cement barrier, heard Montoya shout something behind him. He stumbled and skidding down into the riverbed. The wind was worse down here, full of grit, filling his eyes with tears.

Panting, groping for handholds, Dan scrambled up the ledges that made up the falls. Amy was right above him, so close, so real. Could you hear a ghost's shirt flap in the wind? Dan's fingers slipped, his skin shredding on the gritty stone. He wasn't close enough. In a moment, she would fall past him, arms spread, like she was trying to fly.

Above him, she took the last step, poised at the edge, body starting to can t outward . . . "Don't!" he screamed. "Goddamn you, *don't!*" He got his feet under him, lunged, pain spiking up his leg. His fingers touched cloth, clenched tight, and he fell hard, knees scraping on the rock, heard a cry, felt her sprawl beneath him — no ghost, no ghost — warm under his hand, against his face. Alive.

Thunder boomed overhead, dry and hollow. Dan lay flat on the stone, panting, face buried against a cotton shirt, arms clasped around warm flesh, hard ribs.

"Dan? What . . . the hell?"

Dan's heart lurched and he raised his head slowly. The hair was gray, not black. The wind tangled it across her face, and she pushed it out of her eyes with a faltering hand. "Jesse," Dan said numbly. "You were going to jump."

"No." She looked away. "I don't know."

Her eyes held the same dun emptiness that filled the Drylands.

"Don't do it," he whispered.

"What do you care?"

He fumbled in his pocket, still breathing hard, sweating with the throbbing pain in his knee. Thunder boomed like cannon over his head as he pulled out the necklace, held it out. "I stole this."

"Keep it." Her loose hair stuck to her face, veiling her empty eyes.

"I watched my sister jump off this ledge," he said thickly. "I think she hated me a little, too. Because she got stuck with me." He saw her flinch and look down at the rocks below.

"Don't do that to Renny," he said.

The trucker had left. Sam Montoya leaned against the fender of his pickup, watching them.

"If you let me stay on." He laid the necklace beside her knee. "I figure I can make enough with the card tricks in town or down in Bonneville to make up the pay hike." He started to climb down, careful of his knee.

At the bottom, he leaned his forehead against the face of the cliffs, waiting for the pain to ease off some. Jesse was climbing down after him. Something stung his cheek, cold and wet. Water? Dan saw a thin, dark streak on the rock face. Another drop stung his face. Water was seeping over the falls. Had it actually rained upstream somewhere, or was the Pipe leaking? Dan looked up.

Amy knelt on the edge. It was her, this time, not Jesse. Her lips moved, shaping silent words.

I'm sorry?

Dan felt another drop on his face, like a tear. "I love you," he whispered.

She faded and vanished as Jesse reached the bottom.

"You can stay if you want." Her smile was crooked and frail. "I've got a lot of space." She pulled the necklace from her pocket, stared at it for a moment, then fastened it around her neck. "Looks like Sam's waiting." She shaded her eyes. "I bet he'll give us a ride back up to the house."

"Yeah, he probably will." Dan found his stick where he had dropped it sliding down from the highway, and straightened. "He probably will." Dan looked up at the ledge once more but it was empty. He knew it would be empty. Step by painful step, he climbed back up to the highway with Jesse.

THE BEE MAN

Nita Montoya's brother sold her when she was fifteen — to the Bee Man who came around sometimes to sell honey to the field hands. At least, that's what her other brother, Ignacio, called it. *Selling.* Alberto had slapped him and they almost started fighting, even though Ignacio was only two years older than Nita and a lot smaller than Alberto. Mama screamed at them both, and they stopped, but their bitterness scorched Nita, made her want to hide. There was no place to hide in the camp unit they lived in.

"She's a good girl," Alberto told the Bee Man. "She works as hard as any boy and she minds real good, even if she can't talk."

The Bee Man was old. His curly hair had gray in it, and his long face was lined and folded, brown as old leather. Alberto turned to look at her, and Nita flinched. He was mad. His anger hurt her, like the ache in his back hurt her when he came in from working the bushes, like Ignacio's hating hurt her. Like Mama hurt her. Nita drew a line in the dust with her toe, wishing that she didn't have to feel their anger and their aches. Alberto was mad because the foreman had tried to put his hands under Nita's shirt, back behind the machine shed. Nita rubbed out the line, remembering the time she'd gone to the outhouse late and the foreman had been back there with one of the women. When he'd trapped her behind the machine shed, put his hands on her, his hot sticky excitement had been scary, but it had made Nita's skin prickle with strange feelings.

She had run away when the foreman touched her, but Alberto had seen them. Now he was mad.

"You go with the man, Nita," Alberto said to her, too loud and too slow, the way he always talked to her, as if she couldn't hear. "You're going to live with him now. You mind him." He wasn't looking at her any more. He was looking at the jug of honey in his hands. The honey looked yellow as pee.

"Come on." The Bee Man smiled at Nita. "You carry these, all right?"

Nita took the pole he handed her, balanced it across one shoulder. It was a hollow piece of plastic pipe. More jugs — mostly empty — hung from each end, bowing the pole in front and behind, making it bounce as Nita walked. She followed the Bee Man down the dusty lane that led from long rows of units to the main road that led through the ag camp. Dust whirled away from their feet, and Nita's shift stuck to her sweaty back.

The Bee Man felt . . . quiet. She studied the curve of his shoulders and back, bent beneath a heavy pack. His hair straggled down his neck in loose curls. He felt like the fields, dry and dusty, like the wind that never stopped blowing.

It wasn't a happy feeling and it wasn't a sad feeling. It was just . . . quiet. Nita relaxed a little as they walked across the sunbaked valley floor, toward the brown humps of the mountains. The bushes crowded the road on either side of them, their scratchy, upright branches holding in the heat. The valley was flat as a plate, and the salt crept up out of the ground, making white crusts on the bush stems, coating everything with gray powdery dust.

"They used to grow grass here, in the old days," the Bee Man said suddenly. "Not for hay. Just for seed. It was cooler then. It rained. People had so much water that they grew grass in their yards, just to walk on. This whole valley was green."

He didn't look at her, just talked. Nita walked a little closer behind him, so she could hear his words.

"This is all tamarisk. Used to be a weed." He flicked the dusty branches of the bushes that reached out above the racked asphalt of the road. "They engineered it to tolerate salt. And it's tough. So now we pipe seawater over from the coast and save what sweet water we have left for drinking. Never mind that the salt kills the land."

He made it sound like the fields weren't a good thing. Mama, Ignacio. And Alberto worked in the fields, weeding the little bushes, cleaning the soaker-hoses, and cutting branches for the grinder. Magic turned the ground up bushes into food. So Alberto said. What would you do without bushes? Nita wondered about that. Maybe this man remembered the old days. He didn't look that old though.

Papa had told her about the old days, when the riverbeds had been full of water like a cooking pot, when the rains had come soft and gentle and all the time. Nita didn't like to think about Papa. Preoccupied, she nearly poked the Bee Man in the back with her pole as he stopped.

"You stay here." He shrugged out of his pack. "I'll be right back."

He said the words too loud, like Alberto did, be he smiled at her again. Nita nodded, watching him drape a flimsy white scarf over her head. They were at the edge of the fields now. The empty land rose up in front of them, folded and rocky, streaked brown and dirty gray, dotted with a few dusty trees that still wore green leaves. She had never been beyond the fields before, and the bare land looked gray and empty.

Clumps of spiny thistle, tufted with purple blossoms, clustered at the edge of the field. Nita watched the Bee Man bend over a piece of tree-trunk standing in the shade of a twisted oak. There weren't any other trees around, and the heat beat at her. A water jug hung from the pack frame. Nita reached for the jug, sneaked a look at the Bee Man.

The air around him shimmered like heatwaves above asphalt, and Nita heard a low hum. It sang peace. It sang a song of fullness, of enough to eat, of comfort and no fear. She put the jug down, took a step closer, eyes on the humming shimmer.

It felt so peaceful. She hummed the sound in her throat. What would it be like to feel that way, always? She hummed louder, felt some of the song's peace seep into her as she crept closer. The Bee Man's head was wrapped in the scarf. It was so fine that Nita could see his face through the folds.

The air around him was full of . . . bees. They landed on his shoulders and on the flimsy cloth, patched his faded shirtsleeves like brown fur, filled the air with their soft comfort-song. Nita watched him reach into the hollow piece of treetrunk. It was full of bees. They crawled across the backs of his hands, flew up to land on his scarf and on his shirt. She'd never seen so many bees in her life — just one or two at a time, crawling around inside the yellow squash blossoms in the little garden they watered with part of their ration, or with water bought at the public meter.

"What are you doing here?" The Bee Man straightened with a jerk.

Nita flinched at the stab of his fright. The bees felt it, too. Their soft song turned harsh, and they swirled around his head like summer dust.

"Go back to the pack," the Bee Man said sharply. "Right now! Run! Ow!"

He winced as a bee stung him. They were angry now. She hummed louder, trying to block out their shrill, painful note, groping for the tone of comfort. That was it! A hair lower, she found it, sang it to the bees, pitching it against their harsh sound. It spread slowly through the swirling cloud of bees, lowering their angry song, gentling it.

Humming, she watched bees land on her bare arms, crawl up the front of her shift. They tickled, but their bodies looked velvety soft. *Peace,* she hummed. *Comfort.* And she stroked one of the black-and-brown bodies delicately. A hand brushed the bees gently away, and Nita looked up with a start. She had forgotten about the Bee Man.

"Come away now." He was frowning, but he wasn't angry. "We'll let them settle down."

He was pleased with her. Pleased! Afraid to breathe, afraid she'd shatter this precious moment, Nita followed him back to the pack.

"I'm glad you like bees." The Bee Man smiled at her. "The last kid I hired was scared to death of them."

Nita looked down at the dust as he pulled off his scarf. She wanted to ask him about the bees and their song, but the words stuck in her throat like they always did.

"I'm going to lose this hive." The Bee Man shouldered his pack, his pleased feeling fading. "The tamarisk doesn't need my bees. They come from cell cultures, so they don't have to bloom, and the salt's killed off most of the native plants. I'd move the hive if I had a place for it, but the wild-flower bloom in the hills is bad this year."

The dusty wind blew through the Bee Man's words. Nita let him walk ahead as they climbed into the hills, threading their way between straggling oaks with drooping dusty leaves and tall, tall firs. They walked for the rest of the afternoon. It was a long walk, up into the dry, folded hills of the hills. The dust didn't burn up here. It was just dust, but you could still taste salt on your lips. They followed a cracked, curving road that led past a cluster of houses, a church, and a boarded-up store, sitting on the edge of a narrow creekbed. The street was empty and Nita didn't feel any people.

"You can still pump water from some of the deep wells up here in the coast range," the Bee Man said. "So a few people still farm up here —veg-etables mostly. This is Falls City, where they hold the market on Sundays."

Alberto and Ignacio went to the market in the valley occasionally, and sometimes Mama went too, but Nita had never gone. She followed the Bee Man up the dry riverbed; it was hard going now, and she was tired. She couldn't remember walking this far in her whole life. You only went as far as the fields, and then you came home. The riverbed was full of rocks and evening shadows, and they had to climb around an old waterfall. The honey jugs bumped and banged, and the pole snagged on the rocks. The Bee Man held out a hand to her, offering help, but she pretended she didn't see it. If she worked it right, people would forget she was there, and then their feelings didn't bother her so much.

"Almost home," the Bee Man said at last. He turned down a narrow streambed that led up into the slope above the larger creekbed they'd been following.

Small green plants with waxy leaves grew between the rocks under their feet, and a few firs spread shadowy branches above their heads, turning the bed into a tunnel of twilight. Nita paused. Bees? She heard them, saw them streaking down into a narrow crack in the rocky fence of the bank. They sang a different song, this time. Louder. Harsher. Curious, Nita went closer, trying to catch the new note.

"Nita, don't!" the Bee Man yelled.

Bees erupted from the crack, whirling toward her like a gust of dark wind. Nita cried out at the first stings. She dropped the jugs and tried to run, but the pole tripped her. Bees swarmed over her, burning like fire as she clawed at them.

Then the Bee Man was slapping at them, hissing through his teeth as the bees stung him, too. He wrapped his scarf around her head, yanked her to her feet. Sobbing, Nita stumbled blindly along in his grip as he pulled her into a run. Hot pain spread across her skin as the Bee Man dragged her up the stream bed.

"Keep running!" he panted in her ear. "Just a little more and it'll be all right . . ."

They were running uphill now. Rocks stubbed her toes and Nita fell again. This time the Bee Man didn't make her get up. She curled herself into a ball, face pressed against her knees, afraid that she would hear the bees following her, humming loud, humming angry as Mama.

"Here, now. Here, this'll help." The Bee Man was back, unwinding the scarf from her face, coaxing her to sit up.

Nita sucked in her breath as cool wetness soothed the hot burning. Mud? She touched the tawny smears he was dabbing onto her dark skin. It was mud, and it helped.

"I'm sorry. I should have warned you about that damn nest, but I didn't think." The Bee Man dipped more mud from the plastic bowl in his hand. "They call them killers for good reason. The whole nest'll come after you, and, if it happens, you run. That's all you can do. If you don't, you can get enough stings to kill you." He grunted. "They came up from South America, a long time ago. From Africa, before that. They do real good in the Dry, but you can't work with 'em and they don't give much honey, anyway. I would have taken out that nest a long time ago, but it's way back in the rock." He combed a dead bee out of Nita's tangled hair. "You're not swelling anyway, so you'll be alla right, I guess."

Nita looked down at the bee, too full of pain to even nod. It didn't look any different than the honey bees. Killers. That felt right. It matched their ugly, violent song. Nita shivered, fear crawling up her spine. She knew the killers' song now.

The Bee Man set down the bowl and stood up. Nita watched him disappear into a tent made out of faded green plastic. Rock shelved out above her head to make a shallow cave that breathed cool, damp air on her burning skin. They were on a flat space, like a rocky shelf above the streambed. In the thickening darkness, Nita could barely make out a big, blackened cook pot on a ring of stones, and a stack of chopped branches. A light went on inside the tent, making the green walls glow.

"Those killer stings hurt. I still jump and I hardly even notice the honey bee stings any more." The Bee Man ducked out of the tent, a jug in one hand and a small solar lantern in the other. "This will make you feel a little better, anyway." He poured pale, golden liquid into a plastic cup.

Dry with thirst, Nita gulped at the liquid. It wasn't water. It tasted sweet, with a faint honey smell, and it felt bubbly on her tongue. She held out her empty cup hopefully.

"Not too much, or you'll have a headache in the morning. This stuff has some kick to it." He filled her cup half full of the bubbly honey-water. "There's plenty of water. Bees showed me a little seep-spring back in the rock. It hasn't dried up yet." He nodded at the cool darkness under the overhang. "If you're hungry, there's bread and some dried fruit in that basket. Not fancy, but edible. I was going to hire another boy at the market," the Bee Man said slowly. "Alberto asked me to take you, instead."

He was afraid, she realized suddenly. Of her? Nita swirled the last of the honey-water in her cup, frowning a little. Why should this man, taller than Alberto, be afraid of her?

"Water's in that jug there, drink all you want. You can use this sleeping bag." The Bee Man stood suddenly and picked up the honey-water jug. "Don't wander off, okay? You could get lost, and you can die of thirst, even this early in the year." He paused in the doorway of the tent. "Damn it, Alberto," he muttered. "We're even. I'm never going to live this down."

He was afraid. Afraid. What did he mean, anyway? Nita crossed her arms against the first hint of evening chill, pressing her forearms against the new, tender swell of her breasts. Her body felt strange, as if it wasn't really hers anymore. The Bee Man's scared feeling had to do with that. It had a prickly edge that made Nita think of Alberto, when he and Theresa Santorres went for their evening walks with their arms around each other.

Nita wriggled into the sleeping bag. She didn't want any food. The honey-water had filled her stomach and softened the worst of the pain. The Bee Man moved around in the tent, talking to himself, a few low words she couldn't quite make out. It was getting cold, like it always did at night. She pulled the thick fabric of the bag up over her shoulders. It smelled like the Bee Man, like honey and sweat and dust.

It smelled strange. She sniffed the dry, night air, missing the familiar smell of the crowded unit, in spite of the hurting anger that filled it. They had lived there almost as long as she could remember. Since Papa died.

I'll kill the bastard, next time he touches her, Alberto had snarled. *And they'll hang you. You're gonna get us all fired, and what will we do then?* Mama had said that, arguing with Alberto, hissing and angry, after they thought she was asleep. It had been Mama who had made Alberto ask the Bee Man to take her. A hard lump closed her throat, and Nita made a small, choked sound that tried to turn into a sob.

"You hurting?"

She had forgotten his presence, and the Bee Man's touch made Nita jump.

"Easy, now. Gently. Bad dreams, maybe?" He stroked her tangled hair hesitantly. "Things can look pretty dark, your first night away from your folks," he said, and he felt like he was remembering. "We'll get along fine," he said as he got to his feet. "If you have any more bad dreams, you call me, hear?"

Nita nodded. He didn't feel so scared now. He felt peaceful, like the bees. She fell asleep, comforted by his quiet song.

The Bee Man woke her before dawn. They left the narrow streambed and climbed up into the dry hills, their shadows stretching ahead of them, thin and spindly on the dusty ground.

"We'll gather firewood later." The Bee Man broke a limb from a fir with a dry, brittle snap. "I don't know how much longer the forest's going to last. It's too dry for seedlings to make it, and the old trees give in to beetle damage and die. At least the land's still alive up here. Flowers still bloom. Stuff grows along the bottoms of the old streambeds and in the low places here a little water seeps up. We're killing the land, down in the valley," he said. "If the rains came back tomorrow, it would still be a desert down there."

Nita looked at the dying trees. The Bee Man's words blew through her, dry and dusty as the wind, full of gray shadows. She hadn't ever thought of the land as something that could be alive or dead. Land was just . . . land. Dust or rock or bushes. Nita stopped. Two bees crawled over a small spike of fuzzy purple flowerlets that grew from a crack in the rock. Out here, all by themselves, the bees' song was faint and hard to hear, but it comforted her. Nita scooped them gently from the flower. They buzzed in her closed hand, confused, not angry yet, searching for the vanished sunlight.

"I thought you'd be scared, after yesterday." The Bee Man looked over her shoulder.

He was pleased with her again. His pleasure warmed Nita, drove away the gray chill of his talk about the dying land. Nita opened her hands and the bees zoomed away.

"There's a wild nest at the top of this slope," the Bee Man said. "I figure we might as well take it, now that the honey-bloom's over." He pulled two of the flimsy scarves from his pack, handed her one. "You always wear this veil, hear?" He draped it over her head, tucked it carefully into the neck of her shift. "Stings on your arms hurt. But you get one too close to your eye and you can go blind."

The cloth made it hard to see, but Nita could hear the bees' song as they got close. They darted in and out of a broken stump, singing contentment. She sang with them as the Bee Man built a small fire where the smoke would drift over the nest. The bees swirled up, confused by the smoke, angry as the Bee man chopped into their dead treetrunk home. Nita hummed the harsh note, changing it, soothing the hive's distress until the comfort-hum wrapped her, thick as the warm honey-smell rising from the folded layers of golden comb inside the trunk. Fascinated, she leaned over the opened nest. Pulpy white larva filled some of the cells and others had been closed with waxy brown caps. She could see pale, half-formed bees beneath some of the caps.

"I hate to strip the nests like this, leave them to starve." The Bee Man sighed as he brushed bees from a sticky slab of comb and sealed it into one of the plastic pails they'd brought with them.

So this nest would die? Nita stared at the shattered trunk. Brown bits of broken comb and golden honey stuck to the splintered wood and the bees settled on their ruined nest in a dark layer. Their song would end, because she and the Bee Man had smashed through the wood and taken the comb? When the Bee Man touched her shoulder, Nita jerked away from him.

"Nita?" The Bee Man followed her into the shade of a dying pine. "What's wrong?"

Nita shook her head, wanting to tell him that it was wrong, that the bees' song shouldn't die. The words wouldn't come. They stuck in her throat, hard and hurting. A bee landed on her hand, sipping at the sticky honey coating her skin. Nita closed her hand over it, crushed it. Slowly, she opened her hand, dropped the dead bee into the dust at the Bee Man's feet.

The Bee Man sighed. "That nest would have starved out before the next rainy season. It wasn't big enough to make it through the dry months. I take their honey so that we can eat. I take out the killer bee nests that compete with these." He stared down the slope of the hillside. "Down in the valley, we grind up those test-tube shrubs, digest them into sugars and grow wheat cells or soybean cells or even orange juice-sacs in tanks. So we eat and we survive, but nothing else can grow down there. Just bushes. We can never go back to the way it was. We're killing the land to stay alive." He shook his head bitterly. "You keep running, and all you can do is stay one step ahead of the Dry."

It had hurt him to take the wild nest, too. He loved the bees. Nita reached out suddenly and touched his hand.

He started a little, as if she'd pinched him, but then he smiled at her. "Let's take what we've got and call it a day," he said.

They went out every day to harvest a careful share of comb from the Bee Man's hives and to strip the small, wild nests they'd found. The sparse flowers had dried up in the hot sun that seemed to get hotter every day, and no more honey would flow until next spring, he told her.

"I've never seen anyone handle bees like you," the Bee Man said more than once. "I wish I had your talent with 'em."

He was pleased with her.

When they took shares from the Bee Man's hives, she sang them comfort and they buzzed gold and black and brown around their heads as they cut the slabs of storage comb free, leaving the larvae-filled cells behind. When they took the wild nests, Nita sang them a gentle song that was full of the Bee Man's sadness at taking their honey, and the bees settled onto their comb in a dark, quiet layer.

The Bee Man talked to her. He told her how the bees lived, how a worker danced to show the other bees where flowers grew, and how the hive knew when to grow a new queen. He taught her how to live with the bees, how to melt comb into liquid honey and cakes of valuable wax, how to let the bees show her the tiny water seeps, what to eat and not to eat, how to survive in the dry hills.

He told her the names of the flowers; yellow bells and shooting stars down in the crevices, where water seeped up from the winter rains; lupine and desert parsley up high, where it was drier; fescue and wheat grass in tough, dusty clumps up on the ridges, where trees still cast a little shade. He didn't feel scared any more, and that pleased Nita. He felt warm inside, peaceful as bee song.

His song and the bee song blended, seeping through the years of silence that filled her up, like water soaking into a field. When she was little, before Papa died, she had talked. Nita listened to the Bee Man's words and wanted to tell him how the bees sounded. He loved the bees, but he didn't hear them. She was sure of it, and his not-hearing surprised her.

But the words still wouldn't come.

One afternoon, they walked clear down to the edge of the fields to check on the tree-trunk hive where they'd stopped on Nita's first day with the Bee Man. The hive was gone, replaced by plowed brown dirt and the dusty green tufts of newly planted bushes. Soaker hoses gleamed in the furrows like basking snakes.

"They just ran the machines right over it." The Bee Man shaded his eyes, squinting against the harsh light. "I should of moved it, never mind whether there were enough flowers up there for another big hive. Too late now."

He didn't talk much as they walked back up to the camp. His shoulders drooped and his toes dragged as he walked, raising salty dust that hung behind them in the still air. That evening, they melted the week's small take of comb. Nita strained out dead bees and larvae, watching foam and liquid wax swirl on the surface of the simmering honey. The Bee Man was still sad, and she sat down beside him, close enough to feel the warmth from his arm against hers. He looked at her as she touched his hand, and smiled, blinking a little, as if he'd been thinking about something else and had forgotten that she was there.

"The fields keep catching up to me," he told her. "Stick the plants in the ground and kill the ground with salt water. I don't know." He stared into the red glow of the coals beneath the iron pot. "It scares me, what we're doing. I keep moving on, but it's always right behind me. The Dry. The salty fields. It doesn't pay to look back." He rubbed his face.

"My father was a hard man," he said. "There was only his way to do things, so I took off when I was about your age. I was lucky. I ran into an old beekeeper, who taught me about bees. After awhile, my father didn't seem so impossible anymore, so I want back." He laughed, a short, bitter note that made Nita wince. "They were gone. Dad, Mom, the whole town. The Dry had moved in, eaten up the fields, filled the streets with dust. I don't know what happened to my folks. Someone told me that they went back east to find a cousin, and someone else told me that they went to Portland. I never found them. Maybe they're dead." He shook his head slowly. "It doesn't pay to care too much. One day you turn around, and everything's gone. Like that hive."

Nita took his hand in hers, wanting to tell him that the bushes and the Dry were just *things* — just salt and plants and dry land — not killers that could chase you. He started to pull his hand away, then closed his fingers around hers, tight enough to hurt.

"You're a good listener." He got stiffly to his feet and lifted the honey pot from the fire. "I thought I was doing Alberto a big favor by taking you on, ruining my reputation in the bargain. I guess my reputation's still shot," he said, and laughed.

Nita didn't understand, but she smiled, too, because he was warm inside again, like the bee song.

Nita woke in darkness that night, struggling up from nightmare to the dry rumble of thunder higher in the mountains. Lightning flickered across the horizon and Nita clutched the sleeping bag around her. Thunder made her remember the gunshots. She had been playing in the yard when they drove up. They had carried guns in their hands, had called her father by name.

Thunder boomed again and Nita sat up with a gasp. Cold wind gusted through the camp, shaking the tent, and the thunder cracked again. Hard drops stung Nita's arms and face. Rain? She stumbled to her feet, but already the shower had moved on, riding the cold wind down the streambed. Lightning glared, searing Nita's eyes with the stark image of the tent, woodpile, and the pot of cooling honey. Then the darkness rushed in again, thick as dirt on a grave, pressing down on her, smothering her. Shivering, Nita slipped into the tent.

The air smelled like plastic, honey, and the Bee Man; thick and comforting. He lay on his side, wrapped in a tangled quilt. The soft rasp of his breathing filled the tent, and he stirred, murmuring in his sleep as Nita curled up beside him. The thunder rumbled again, but it didn't scare her this time. Maybe it was raining, somewhere. Nita closed her eyes and fell asleep to the soft murmur of the Bee Man's dreams.

In the morning, Nita woke with the Bee Man's arms around her. His breath tickled her neck, and the warmth of his body against her back made her breasts feel tight and tender. She wriggled closer against him, felt him wake up.

He murmured something, still half asleep, and his arms tightened around her. Nita felt the stir of of his desire — like Alberto and Theresa — felt an echo in her own flesh. It took her by surprise, made her skin go cold and then hot. She pressed back against his warmth full of a strange ache that came from everywhere and nowhere, centering between her legs like a second heartbeat.

The Bee Man's eyes opened and he sat up, pushing roughly away from her. "What are you doing here?" he asked in a harsh, funny voice.

Scared. He hadn't felt scared like that in a long time. Nita scrambled to her feet. He was staring at her, frowning, all muddy and mixed up inside, like a pan of wash water after the whole family has used it.

"It's all right." He forced a laugh. "You just . . . surprised me. That's all." He stared at her for the space of several heartbeats, then began to talk again, too fast. "This is market day, remember? We're almost out of beans, so we'd better get started if we want to get there before the best stuff is gone." He stopped, looked at her again. "It's all right," he said.

Nita ducked quickly outside.

It wasn't all right. The Bee Man's fear clogged the air as he strung full honey jugs together and loaded cakes of wax into the pack. He didn't look at her, didn't talk much. Nita kept her eyes on the ground as they made their way down the riverbed to town, hurt by his feelings, unable to shut them out. She didn't know what she had done to scare him.

She felt the market as they climbed out of the riverbed, a babble of feelings like people shouting all at once inside her head. Alberto had never offered to take her along when he went, and Nita was glad. Ramshackle booths roofed with frayed and faded plastic crowded the parking lot of the old high school. The Bee Man's muddy fear was almost lost in the clamor of so many people. Nita stayed close behind him as they threaded their way between the piles of greens and carrots, old clothes, oily machine parts, and battered electronics that formed the dusty aisles. If she closed her eyes, she would be lost, drowned in the blare of noise.

They unloaded their packs, set out the cakes of wax and the jugs of honey at a corner of the old gray school building, in a strip of shade. Nita squatted with her back against the wall while the Bee Man traded honey and wax for hard bread, beans, dried fruit, or grimy government scrip that you could trade for water or use in a government store. People called the Bee Man David. They laughed and joked with him, while their eyes slid sideways to look at Nita. They all looked at her. Some of them looked at her body, all hungry. Others looked from her to the Bee Man and got mad, like Alberto had gotten mad at the foreman. Nita hunched against the wall, dizzy and trapped.

The Bee Man didn't look at her at all. Nita closed her burning eyes, trying to shut out the stares and the crowd noise. When she opened them again, Alberto was standing in front of the neatly lined-up honey jugs. "Hello, Nita," he said in his too-loud, too-careful voice.

Nita looked past his thick shoulders. Mama was walking up the crowded aisles.

"How are you getting along?" Alberto was asking the Bee Man. "I haven't seen you for awhile."

"Okay." The Bee Man turned a jug of golden honey slowly between his hands. "But I'm thinking of moving on again, so I guess Nita ought to go back home with you."

Nita stared at him, Mama forgotten for a moment, stunned by his words. He wanted her to go, wanted it with an intensity that took Nita's breath away, made her feel sick and empty inside. Nita's lips moved, silently shaping the word to ask him. *Why?*

"You see?" Alberto turned to Mama, his temper flaring. "I told you this wasn't going to work."

"It's not Nita's fault," the Bee Man said. "It's nothing she did or didn't do." He looked past Alberto, straight at Mama. "She's just a kid. You take her home, and you keep her there. Let her grow up."

"Don't you talk to me like that. " Mama shouldered past Alberto. "You think I don't know what you're saying? You think I kicked my daughter out, sent her off to whore, maybe? Well, you think about what it's like for us, mister. If we get kicked off the farm, where do we go? To one of the camps, to live on hand-outs with the no-good and the drifters? What do we do? Alberto said you're a nice man, that you'd take her." She clenched her fists, glared at the Bee Man. "You want to blame someone, you blame her father — you blame Sam. We had a good place, a good farm. It wasn't much, but we took care of ourselves. And our kids." Her voice trembled.

"He left me with the children to feed. So, now we got to scratch in the dust, bow to some strutting little rooster of a foreman who sniffs around my daughter like a dog after a bitch in heat! You want to blame someone, you blame Sam. Not me. Not my son!" She spun on her heel and stalked away, pulling her sun-scarf up over her gray hair.

"I apologize," Alberto said between clenched teeth. "For my mother." He had gone pale under his weathered tan. "Nita, get up. Let's go." He reached past the Bee Man, grabbed her by the arm.

"Wait a minute." The Bee Man caught Alberto's wrist. "What happened to her? Why can't she talk?"

"She just stopped." Alberto looked away. "She looks like Papa," he said. "It's scary, how much she looks like Papa." His face twisted. "Mama didn't mean that Papa walked out on us. It wasn't like that at all. Papa was organizing a water strike, up in The Dalles. That's where we lived. Two men drove up to the house one day and shot him, right in the yard. Just shot him down in cold blood. Nita was right there with him. She saw it all."

Run! Mama had screamed, but he hadn't run.

The Bee Man was mad, now. Not scared any more. Mad. Like Alberto. Like Mama.

Nita twisted out of Alberto's lax grip and ran. The Bee Man shouted something, but she closed her ears to it, dodged around a pile of vegetables. Green squashes went flying and a woman screeched at her. Nita ducked her head as she darted through the forest of shoulders and hips, pursued by flashes of surprise and irritation. Her eyes ached as she ran, dry as the riverbed.

The Bee Man followed her. In the breathless heat of late afternoon, Nita heard him call her name as she climbed up a narrow, twisting creekbed high in the folded mountains. Too late, she looked back and saw the footprint she had left in a damp patch of creekbed clay. The thunder that had awakened her last night had meant rain somewhere higher on the slopes, and the runoff had come, quick and violent, down this bed.

She hadn't thought he would follow her. Nita shrugged her small pack higher on her shoulder and scrambled upward, toward the rim of the creekbed and drier ground where her tracks wouldn't show. On the other side of these hills lay the sea. The Bee Man had said so. The full water jug that she had taken banged her shoulder painfully. He called to her again, his voice hoarse, as if he had been shouting for a long time.

"Nita? Come back! You can't just run away like this. You'll die out here."

Not true. Nita ducked down into the hollow left by a wind-felled tree. The tilted mass of roots and sunbaked dirt roofed the torn earth, and she crouched in the cool shadow, catching her breath. She would live with the bees. The Bee Man had showed her how. The bees would find water for her. They would sing to her with the sound of the Bee Man's peace. Nita swallowed, her throat tight, peeking down into the creekbed.

He wasn't down in the creekbed. He had climbed the bank, too, appearing only a dozen yards away, circling around a rocky outcrop. Nita squeezed deeper into her hiding place, holding her breath.

"Nita?" He cupped his hands around his mouth, looking up the creekbed as he shouted. "Damn it, Nita. Don't do this!"

Anger.

It wasn't his anger that she was hearing. Nita's arms prickled with the memory of burning stings. Killers. Afraid to move, she peeked between the twisted roots of the old tree. There they were — a little farther along the side of the streambed. Nita's heart beat faster at the sight of the bees darting in and out of a broken treetrunk. If she had gone on a little more, she would have walked right into them.

"Nita?"

She flinched, her heart leaping. He was right beside her, on the other side of the roots. Nita squeezed her eyes closed, trying to make herself small, trying to become invisible, like she'd done in the unit, trying to hide.

The Bee Man wasn't mad anymore, but he was still scared. Nita opened her eyes a crack. Papa had been scared like this, the day the men had come. Run, Mama had screamed, but he hadn't run. He had looked at Nita, afraid, had scooped her up, tossed her behind the old pickup, where the men with the guns couldn't see her.

The Bee Man hadn't seen her. He had walked past her hiding place, was starting to climb down the side of the creekbed. Nita sucked in her breath, fear squeezing her. Rocks and pebbles, loosened by his feet, bounced down the slope. A few of them hit the killer bees' treetrunk. Their song rose a notch and a small cloud of bees swirled into the air. The Bee Man saw them.

He looked, but he didn't stop. He couldn't hear their song. He didn't know that they were killers. She scrambled to her feet, her head full of their harsh warning. In a moment, he would be too close.

You can die from too many stings, he had told her. "Stop," she whispered, but he didn't hear her. More bees swirled into the air, humming anger, humming death. "Stop!" she screamed.

He heard her, twisted around, his surprise flaring bright as lightning. A rock slid out from beneath his foot, and he staggered, struggling to stay on his feet. More rocks slid and he gave a cry, falling backward, rolling down the slope in a shower of dirt to slam into the killers' tree trunk.

The killers boiled out of their nest. Nita cringed at their harsh song. *All you could do was run*, he had said.

"Run!" she screamed.

Hands covering his face, the Bee Man tried to get to his feet. He fell again and stared crawling away from the nest, too slow, too slow, yelling something as the bees swarmed over him.

The stings hurt him. It had hurt Papa to die.

Nita dropped her pack and scrambled down the slope. A killer stung her face. Their harsh song hammered at her and they settled on her, stinging, stinging, stinging. Nita stumbled, clawing at bees on her face, slapping at them, struggling with her fear.

Run! Mama had screamed. *Why didn't you run? I hate you! I hate you! I hate you!*

The bees would kill the Bee Man.

"I hate you!" Nita screamed with Mama's voice and rage flared up inside her, hot as flame. *I hate you!* Fists clenched at her sides, barely feeling the stings, she sang with the killers, louder and stronger, until her song was the killers', until they hummed her note. Then, she lowered it, gentled it.

Slowly, reluctantly almost, the dark cloud of killers lifted, thinned away, back to their tree trunk. Nita scrambled down the slope. The Bee Man lay curled up in the dust and she clutched him, terrified that he wouldn't move, that he would lie still and silent under her hands, like Papa had. She gasped in relief as he sat up, clutching at his leg.

"My ankle," he gasped. "I thought . . . I hope it's just twisted. Nita?" He wiped sweat out of his eyes, his face swollen with stings as he looked at the nest. "How did you do that? How did you drive them away?"

Nita licked her lips, struggling with stony words. "I . . . hear . . . their song," she whispered. "I . . . sang with them."

"You hear them?"

Abruptly, Nita leaned forward, kissed the Bee Man on the lips. For a moment, he crushed her against him, fingers digging hard into her back.

"Don't." He pushed her away.

"You're scared," Nita whispered. "Of me."

"I'm not . . ." he began. Stopped. Sighed, and pulled her against him. Gently. "I know what people think . . . about you living up here with me. I don't give a damn what anyone says, but I didn't know . . . how I was going to start feeling. He stared down the dry creekbed, his face folded into harsh lines. "You can't afford to care like that anymore."

Scared. Of her. Nita sighed, feeling hollow inside, sick with the stings, or maybe from her rage-song to the bees. She touched her face, the face that reminded Mama of *that* day, every day, felt tears and mud beneath her fingers, the lumpy swelling of stings. "I was going to go live with the bees," she said. "By myself. I can do that."

He was struggling with his fear. Nita waited, all still inside, like an empty hive.

The Bee Man took a long, slow breath. "It scares me, how I feel about you. I'm forty and you're a kid, and that scares me some, too." He gave her a sideways look. "Can you feel me, too? Like you feel the bees?"

She nodded. Fear and desire, and under it all, beesong peace, like a layer of golden honey. A stalk of tiny, white blossoms poked up from the rocks at Nita's feet; shooting stars, coaxed into quick bloom by the shower. Nita bent and picked it. Up on the bank, the killers sang their harsh song and she shivered, tasting fear of her own. "It's all right," she said. "You don't have to run always."

"It's a lot safer to run," the Bee Man said, but he took the stem of flowers from her and tucked it into her hair. "Will you tell me what the bees sound like?" he asked her softly.

"I will." She took his hand.

This time, he didn't pull away.

THE DRYLANDS

CHAPTER ONE

The crowd was bigger this afternoon. It grew every day, spreading like a dark cancer across Michigan's dry lakeshore. Waiting. For them. In the lead transport truck, Major Carter Voltaire clutched the side for balance, eyeing the crowd through the view-slit cut into the protective siding. They hated him, that mob. They hated the tired men and women riding with him. Because they were Corps, because they wore uniforms. Cold anger twisted into a knot in Carter's guts. Every day they gathered on the strip of dusty ground between Lakeshore Drive and the sudden drop-off that had been the shore of Lake Michigan once but wasn't anymore — not by five miles or so. When the troop trucks got closer, they'd start throwing stones.

"Heads up." Carter's dust mask blurred the order. "Get ready for rocks." Gray lakebed mud caked their suncloth coveralls, cracking off in ugly scales as they moved. The salt in the dust burned the eyes, burned the lungs. Breathe enough dust out here and your lungs would never be the same, mask or no mask.

Just so those stone throwing assholes on the lakeshore could drink. Rumor blamed the latest ration reduction on the Corps. Carter's lips tightened. What did it take to get it through their thick skulls that there wasn't any more water? Sure it wasn't enough, but "enough" water didn't exist anywhere anymore. At least there was something in the pipes. After the bastards got done throwing the day's quota of rocks and insults, they could slip back into the refugee camp, or hit the welfare taps, and get a nice drink of water. Courtesy of us, Carter thought sullenly. Courtesy of the Corps. Because the Corps had built most of the Rocky Mountain Trench Reservoir and the Great Lakes Canal system. Without the water it brought down from the blessed wetness of the arctic tundra, Michigan would be a lot farther from its old lakeshore than it was.

He could hear them now, not chanting, just growling. Like animals. Carter's teeth snapped together as the truck dropped into a rutted, dried-out sinkhole. "Get ready to hit the deck," he yelled. High sides had been added to the flatbed trucks the Corps used as crew transport. It protected them from the worst of the rocks. But it was only medium-weight plastic board and it wouldn't stop a bullet. Carter touched the Beretta at his hip, reassured by its weight. All officers went armed. An armed guard went out with every crew, carrying a laser-sighted M20. Carter shaded his eyes, stomach churning.

You were always nervous, coming in. Running the damn gauntlet. His crew braced themselves against the lurch and sway of the truck, watching through the slits or staring at each other, waiting for the rocks. They joked about it in the barracks — toss a little black humor around. No one was joking today. It was getting to all of them. Working conditions were bad enough on the lakebed, and this shift had been hell. They'd slid around in sticky mud, had mired a dozer to the seat in a sinkhole trying to get that purification intake in on schedule. The CO was going to be pissed.

In the five years he'd been posted here, he'd built how many new intakes? Lake Michigan's sullen, scummy beach receded farther out every year. Too late, he thought bitterly. We stopped doubting the global warming thing. Just too damn late. On the lakeshore, a young, black man danced out from the edge of the crowd, waving his arms, yelling something. Gave them the finger.

Yeah, we get the drift. Carter shifted his stance, touched the Beretta.

The level beams of the setting sun turned the dust haze to gold. Carter shaded his eyes, but the dust had blurred individuals into a faceless mass. It got into your soul, the dust. Ate it away, the way it ate your lungs. The setting sun reflected back from the glass of the Chicago towers, blinding him, making the black panels of the solar arrays stand out like the wings of crouching demons.

"Shit. Look at 'em." Lieutenant Garr spat over the side of the truck. He had been the one who mired the dozer, and he was still touchy. "I kinda wish one of 'em would try something big." He jerked his head at Suarez, who had the M20 today. "Blow a couple away."

"Cool it, Lieutenant." Carter rubbed a hand over his face, knowing exactly how Garr felt. The Beretta hung like a lead weight on his belt. "We could lose."

"Me, I'd go for the grenades." Garr grunted, made as if to spit again and didn't. "Even with bone grafts, Abado's never gonna be happy with what he sees in the mirror."

Corporal Abado had driven the dozer — until he stopped a brick. The protective sides didn't deflect everything, and brick did a lot of damage if it hit in the right place. Like your face.

"If I was doin' it, I'd just shut off all the welfare taps." Garr jerked a stiff finger across his throat. "They can't pay for it, let 'em die. Who the hell do they think keeps the water running? Shit, turn it off."

"Ease off," Carter snapped. Yeah, he felt the same way sometimes, but this kind of talk didn't help morale at all. And it was bad enough. They hated you — the civilians — and you ended up hating them back. Every time a new water cut came down, the Corps took the blame. Keepers of the water? Yeah, sure, Carter thought bitterly. Maybe you just had to hate *something*, just to stay sane.

He'd lost three men this past year. Shot dead by snipers, two of 'em. Simons died when they blew a pipe. Shrapnel had gutted him and he bled to death before they could get him in.

The truck slowed. Willy, their driver, had a lot of practice running brick alley. He took it in slow enough so the troublemakers had time to get out from under the wheels if they hustled, but fast enough that not too many rocks got over the sides. They could see the faces now; black, Latino, and white. The cheap masks hid gender and the lakebed dust turned them all into the same gray color. It was as if the drought had done what laws had never quite achieved. It had blurred color and gender lines, turning everyone into one gray, sexless race of thirst and rage.

Carter took a deep breath, a hot bubble of anger pressing against his ribs. He was tired of living in a damn cage, tired of getting screamed at, tired of rocks and snipers. *We didn't make it stop raining*, he wanted to scream at them.

The first chunk of concrete clanged against the truck's fender and Willy sped up slightly. "Incoming!" Clutching the bed wall, Carter squinted through the view-slit. The other two trucks were right behind, practically on their bumper. More rocks. He ducked as something *whammed* into the plastic armor. Almost home. A few dozen meters and they'd be through the gate, safe once more inside the chain-link and razor-wire fence around the base. Safe inside their cage.

The cheap dust masks muffled the shouts, turning them into the ugly, unintelligible barking of animals. A bottle arched over the side of the truck and smashed against the wall. Glass fragments and wetness stung the exposed skin of Carter's face and his heart skipped a beat. No smell of gasoline or organics. No feel of a chemical burn. The puddle on the warped floorboards was yellow. Piss? A security details rolled the big gates open. "Everybody clear the area immediately," a burly captain bellowed through a loudspeaker. "This area is off-limits to civilians. Clear it immediately. I repeat . . ."

Now the crowd would back off, closing in behind the trucks to chase them through the gates, hooting and howling, throwing the last barrage of stones and garbage. It had become a warped ritual.

The crowd stirred suddenly, bunching into thick knots. The wall of faces and bodies parted and a battered little VW charged through, raising a plume of dust behind it.

Heading straight for them.

"What the hell?" someone yelled behind Carter. "Watch it, Willy!'

He was trying. The truck veered, but it was like an elephant trying to dodge. The right front wheel slammed into a sinkhole with a crash. Bodies went flying, slamming into the armor walls, bouncing around like so many dolls. Carter clutched his view-slit, muscles screaming as the truck tried to shake him loose. The van was almost on them . . . Murphy was down and God knew where his rifle was. The van was aiming for the rear of the cab. Trying to blow the fuel tank? It could be loaded with plastic. Carter yanked his Beretta out. Had to aim one-handed, cowboy shot. The truck swerved again, slamming him against the side, nearly tearing his grip loose. He had seconds. Sun on the windshield . . . he squinted. Couldn't see the driver. *Now!* He squeezed the trigger, emptying it at the oncoming car, firing as the windshield dissolved in a glittering shower of glass. Got you, Carter thought, and the anger in his chest blossomed hot and sweet in his throat. Got you, you bastard.

The VW swerved wildly, sideswiping the truck with a groan of rending metal. For a moment the two vehicles locked and Carter looked down through the smashed windshield, into wide, surprised eyes in a small face, a dusty blue tee shirt splotched dark with blood. Then the big truck seemed to shake itself free and they were past, roaring for the gate and safety. Behind them, the car rolled slowly over. One wheel spun briefly and then it exploded with a *whump* of burning fuel. With a howl, the dusty mob surged forward, screaming, hands reaching to tear them apart . . .

"Carter? Hey, Carter, wake up."

Carter bolted upright, gasping.

"Hey, it's okay. It's just me."

"Johnny?" The room came suddenly into focus — walls, bed, his room on the base. Johnny stood in the doorway, looking worried. "I-I'm awake." Carter ran a shaking hand through his hair. "It's all right."

"Like hell." The mattress dipped as Johnny sat down on the end of the bed, his freckled face still worried. "You can get some pills from the doc, you know. Hell, I take 'em." He laughed, coughed. "You sleep good."

"Yeah, maybe I'll do that." Carter glanced at the bedside clock. Six AM and just getting light. The Chicago Riot was weeks ago. The burned-out rubble of the camps and the looted distribution centers had been bull-dozed into trucks and dumped out on the lakebed. The unclaimed bodies — so damn many bodies — had been buried.

A kid. Carter tossed the tangled and sweaty sheet aside, rolled to his feet. He'd shot a kid. He'd looked ten. Maybe twelve.

And it had felt so good. To pull that trigger.

"What's buggin' you, man?" Johnny lit a cigarette. "The inquiry? They cleared you. You got a commendation."

"It's just the heat." He leaned on his dresser, staring out through the dusty glass at the blare of heat and light.

"Don't shit me." Johnny blew smoke at him. "Spill it."

"I don't know." Carter shrugged. "It just seemed so . . . pointless you know? So many people died. And I . . . started it. You know?"

Johnny was shaking his head. "You are a *case,* you know? You're responsible for the drought, aren't you? I forgot. You stopped the rain, didn't you? You dried up all the farmland and the forests and cost all those poor people their jobs, didn't you? Damn, you are some kind of bastard."

"Ah, cut it out." Carter shrugged, laughed. "Okay, I'll stop."

"Hey, I know it was bad, man." Johnny's face had gone serious. "It looked like all of Chi was burning to the ground in the news. I figured you guys were all dead. You didn't start it and you can't end it, and you know it." Johnny crushed the end of his cigarette out on the heel of his boot. "The refugee camps are getting bigger, the experts say it's not gonna rain, and those people in the camps, the ones who've lost everything, they're gonna take it out on you. They want all the water they can drink and they're gonna kill to get it. They're enemies now," he said softly. "They're not on our side any more."

"Dammit, we're all on the same side." It had taken two brigades of the 82nd Airborne and the 75th Rangers to deal with Chicago. And they had dealt with it, in spades. The South Side and the camps looked like the aftermath of a war; burned-out buildings, scorched piles of rubble. He looked beyond the vicious thorns of the wire perimeter fence, out to where water shimmered in the lakebed. Scummy, salty, precious water — the dying lake seemed to exert some kind of strange magnetic power. The Chicago refugee camps had been the biggest in the country, as if the lake had attracted all the rootless people for a hundred miles in any direction, had drawn them into the shadow of Chicago's soaring towers and self-contained arcologies. It had attracted darkness with them — pulled in the frustration, the despair, and the rage that made people want to lash out, to break something, anything.

"Funny, how we both ended up serving water." Carter kept his eyes on that distant shimmer. "Priests of the new religion, Johnny?"

"Speak for yourself." Johnny laughed. "I'm divorced, not celibate. Just ask Amber. I think my ex is keeping count."

"You know what I mean." But Carter smiled in spite of his mood. Johnny could do that.

"If you mean water is power, you're a tad slow figuring that one out." Johnny levered himself to his feet. "You know, you're not much fun, Lieutenant Colonel Voltaire. I came here to celebrate your promotion and transfer, and you're not doing a very good job of celebrating. You've got a hangover is all. Get a shower and let's get some breakfast. That's an order." Johnny grabbed Carter's robe from the end of the bed, threw it at him. "As a member of the Water Policy Committee, I'm your boss, remember? Hell, I'm a *god*. Hop to it."

"Yes, sir." Carter gave him a mock salute and headed for the bath room.

Johnny was almost right — about his being a god. This had been a fancy hotel once, and now the officers had their own showers. Carter shivered as he stepped under the feeble spray of tepid water. Too early for the solar panels to have warmed up the tanks. Yeah, Water Policy decided who got the water, and how much. But it was up to the Corps to get it there, keep it running, and defend it. In the old days, the Corps had been a bunch of engineers. They had built levees and designed dams and were mostly civilian employees. Carter wondered if any of them had ever gone armed. Maybe after the hurricanes flattened New Orleans back at the start of the century. Not otherwise. He banged the soap into its tray and turned the spray back on to rinse off the lather.

It had taken presidential emergency powers to condemn private water rights in the first place, and that had nearly triggered a revolution right there. Afterward, no one could agree on who should administer the water, so . . . they had redefined the Corps. Water Policy might not be a bunch of gods, but they answered only to God, and the Corps answered only to Water Policy. Which made Johnny a member of the most powerful body politic in the US. No, that was no surprise at all — not if you knew Johnny. A few people made the mistake of not taking him seriously, writing him off as nothing more than a rich man's spoiled son. That was a serious mistake. When Johnny wanted something, he didn't kid around. It was no accident that he was the youngest member of Water Policy. When they were kids, Johnny had said he was going to be president. When he got older, he'd realized that Water Policy had more power. Ever since the Middle East fiasco, the presidency hadn't been worth much.

He'd done it. Water Policy. As young as he was.

Shaking his head, Carter hit the dryer and raised his arms to let the stream of warm air evaporate the moisture from his skin. Beneath his feet, the last of the water gurgled into the recycle filter for tomorrow's shower.

You tried not to think about that too much. "So you make the decisions and everyone gets pissed at *us*." He raised his voice as he pulled on his uniform. "Want to explain that to me?"

"You turn off the taps, not us." Johnny stuck his head through the doorway and grinned. "We keep our hands clean. What's the beef? Somebody tell you life was fair or something?"

"I'm just griping." Carter sighed, haunted by that damn dream. The Corps could call in whatever force was deemed necessary to maintain and protect waterflow; regular Army, Marines, the Air Force if they wanted it. "We could probably nuke Washington," Carter said. "If we really needed to."

"Only if we told you to do it."

Johnny sounded like he thought he was kidding. Carter sealed the front of his coverall. "We've walked all over the Constitution and the Bill of Rights," he said bitterly. "You know, it bothers me sometimes. It bothers me a lot, but the numbers work, Johnny. We *make* them work." If he had said this to the mob on the lakeshore, would any of them have listened? He shook his head, still damp with recycled, reused water. "Hell, all I want is to get the job done and to keep my people from getting hurt while we do it."

"Which you will, of course, do with flying colors." Johnny grinned. "You're just the type of officer the Army loves, Carter."

A hint of needling in Johnny's tone? Carter looked up, but Johnny was smiling, his expression casual. "I don't know about that," Carter said slowly. "But I'll do my best. This transfer was a surprise. It's not the normal rotation." He shrugged. "I've heard that the Columbia Riverbed has its own share of troubles."

"Hey, it's not bad out there." Johnny slapped him lightly on the back. "That's my district, remember? The locals around The Dalles are mostly soaker-hose farmers. You get tough with them and they'll fall into line." He winked. "Of course, I'll have to keep a close eye on you."

"It's a long way from San Francisco."

"Hey, we're supposed to be mobile. Besides, I can do what I damn well please." Johnny squinted into the mirror, running a hand over his carefully cut, sandy hair. "How can anyone with your black hair burn and peel like you do?"

"Wrong genes, I guess." Carter shrugged. "All the melanin ended up in the hair and not the skin. Let's go get breakfast." He ushered Johnny out into the hall.

The original carpeting had been left in place when the building had been renovated into a Corps base. Its rich magenta pile was worn in the middle, faded to a dull red. Along the edges, however, the rich color glowed, clashing with the drab pastel yellow that had been used on the walls. Some

Army shrink had probably decided pale yellow was an uplifting color. Carter thumbed the elevator button. It was working this morning. The elevator was a privilege of rank — when it worked. Even with the solar arrays, you didn't waste power. The car dropped fast enough to leave Carter's stomach somewhere behind.

He *had* drunk a little too much beer last night. It had been awhile since he and Johnny had hung out together. Oh, they'd talked on the phone or exchanged emails. But they hadn't really spent any time together, not for a lot of years now. Then, all of a sudden, Johnny had showed up — stranded by some canceled meeting and the iffy airline schedules — and they'd had a long weekend to catch up.

It hadn't been the same.

Which wasn't too unexpected, considering that they'd been pursuing their own lives for the past several years. But somehow . . . it *had* been unexpected. And uncomfortable. Something had changed between them and Carter wasn't sure what it was, or when it had happened. So he had drunk more beer than he should have. He felt bad about that change. "You were pissed at me," he said as they stepped out into the old hotel lobby. "When I wouldn't quit the Corps and come work for you and Water Policy. How come?"

"Do you really need to ask?" Johnny paused in the middle of the lobby, ignoring a trio of privates who saluted Carter and hurried past. "I was a compromise appointee and I know it. I was Trevor Seldon's bright young son, the hotshot rising-star economist, picked to satisfy the young Republicans with money. I'm not too popular with the Committee, even now. If I fuck up, I'm screwed. I wanted you to watch my back."

"I didn't exactly back you up when we were kids," Carter said, a bit surprised by Johnny's intensity. "You mostly dragged me along kicking and screaming. I was always scared shitless we'd get busted."

"Hey, maybe that's why I needed you," Johnny said lightly. "You kept be from getting in too deep, you and your conscience."

Only it had been Carter who had gotten in too deep, and it had been Johnny's money and his dad who had saved Carter's ass. "I'm sorry," he said awkwardly. "I just don't think I'd be much help working for you. I'm not the political type."

"Hell, let's drop it. It's water under the bridge." Johnny shrugged and gave him a crooked smile. "I'm where I want to be and you're happy with your Corps."

Yeah, maybe. Carter looked up as a captain with an MP insignia walked toward them across the lobby. Security. Carter returned his salute irritably. "What's up, Captain?"

"Were you planning on going outside, sir?" The captain nodded at the gasketed, revolving door that led into the main compound.

"No. We're on our way to breakfast."

"Fine, sir." The man nodded. "Just stay inside, please, until we give the all-clear. We got a possible sniper up in the old tower across the drive."

Not another one. "I thought the city was going to let us drop that thing," Carter growled.

"There's some sort of hang-up on the demolition permit." The captain's thick blond brows drew into a single line above his scowl.

"What's up?" Johnny was looking from the captain to Carter.

"Snipers." Carter jerked his head. "You get a clear shot into the compound from that old office building across Lakeshore. We've been trying to get permission to tear it down, but the city's dragging their feet. I think the mayor's son-in-law owns it. Anyone hurt?" He turned back to the captain.

"Negative, sir." He shook his head. "No shots, just a report of movement. We've got a sweep team over there now."

It hadn't ended, the rage that had erupted into the riot. It had simply gone underground, smoldering like a fire beneath the surface. No mob along Lakeshore anymore. Now they were dealing with snipers and homemade bombs. You checked with the sentries before you walked out into the compound, and you didn't stand too close to your window after dark. Every piece of equipment on the lakebed required an armed guard at night. He would be glad to get out of here.

A small commotion erupted behind them. Carter turned. Medics were pushing a gurney fast down the hallway that led from the underground parking. A uniformed figure lay on it, and IV bag swinging from the pole. Carter hurried over, recognizing the major who trailed the medics. It was Renkin, his replacement.

"Someone planted a bomb." The major's lips were pale and a smear of blood marked his cheek. "They got in past the guard last night. It was wired to the number-two dozer."

Lieutenant Garr lay on the gurney, his face white beneath his dark tan, the front of his uniform dark with blood. "What about Rogers?" Carter asked softly. She drove number two. His jaw tightened at Renkin's headshake. "Didn't you check out the equipment?" He watched Renkin flinch. "Didn't you have them *look*?"

"The equipment is under guard." Renkin's face darkened. "Sir." He glared past Carter. "That guard is posted twenty-four hours a day. He's up for court-martial, as far as I'm concerned." Renkin slapped salty lakebed dust from his coverall. "He must have been asleep. He let that bastard walk right past him."

Renkin was too worried about maintaining his unit efficiency record. Carter stared at the man. Extra equipment checks took time.

"It wasn't my fault. Sir." Renkin was breathing hard. "You wouldn't have done any better. You think that promotion means something, don't you? You're a little display for the media, because the media thought we came down to heavy on those animals. So the Corps promotes a few extra people — just to show that we're pleased with ourselves, that we didn't do anything we're ashamed of. And you get tapped, *Lieutenant Colonel* Voltaire. But I'm no floor show. I'm still out there in the dust, so don't give me shit, you got it?" He stomped on after the gurney.

"Whoa." Johnny came up behind Carter. "What's eating him?"

"He got two people killed." Carter looked down the hall, but the gurney had disappeared into the med unit. Garr had looked bad.

Wheels creaked and another gurney followed the first. The team pushing it wasn't hurrying. Carter looked away from the sheeted form, throat tightening. Rogers. He smelled burned flesh and his stomach twisted. She talked to that damn dozer as if it were alive, and she could make it dance. She never mired it, no matter what kind of shit she got sent into.

If he had been out there this morning, she would be alive. He flinched as Johnny's hand landed on his shoulder.

"Knock it off, Carter. That jerk was in charge, not you."

"He was right, you know. About the promotion." Carter watched the second stretcher follow the first down the hall. "It was a media message."

"Christ." Johnny snorted explosively. "That still doesn't make it your fault. Cut yourself some slack, Carter. You aren't responsible for the entire world. I hate to break the news to you."

"Excuse me, sir." The MP was back. "It's all clear. You can go out any time."

"Good." Johnny nodded. "You got the guy?"

"We got him." The captain saluted Carter, pivoted, and marched back to his post at the lobby desk.

We got him. He was dead, whoever he had been. No questions about that. Carter turned away as the gurney bearing Roger's body disappeared down the hall that led to the morgue. He had heard the grim tone of satisfaction in the captain's voice and he felt it, too. Revenge. Who cared whether the guy in the tower had a rifle or if he just some dried out drifter with the poor sense to camp out there?

An eye for an eye.

It was in all of them, that cold, deep rage. You saw it in every pair of eyes around you. The world was drying up and they were all scared of dying, all hating the planet that was killing them.

You couldn't make the planet bleed.

"I've got to go check on Garr," he said to Johnny. "You go ahead and get breakfast. I'll catch up with you."

"Want me to come along?"

"No. Thanks." Carter shrugged off Johnny's hand. "I'm going to be the CO at The Dalles." He stared down the empty hallway. "I'm not going to let this happen there."

"You won't." Johnny's eyes glittered. "I have faith in you. You'll do exactly what you need to do."

For a moment, Carter hesitated, a little taken aback by Johnny's intensity. But that was Johnny's turf. Maybe, finally, he was starting to care about the people he was in charge of. That would be a good thing. Carter hurried down the hall to find out how badly Garr was hurt.

CHAPTER TWO

The ride was a bad one. Nita Montoya sat stiff and straight in the seat of the decrepit Winnebago as it groaned around another bend in the road. Twilight was falling, and the air reeked of cheap perfume. A bottle must be leaking somewhere in the jumble of black-market items that filled the rear of the RV. Beside her, clutching the wheel, the man reeked of lust. Rachel squirmed in Nita's lap, fussing, her face screwed up, fists waving.

"Easy, love." She bounced her daughter gently on one knee, watching the dark, bearded driver from the corner of her eye. Andy, he had said his name was. He was a trader, doing the little town markets, selling black-market clothes, electronics, pharmacy-labeled medicines and cosmetics. He had offered her a ride this afternoon and she had accepted, because she was tired, and she had a long way to go yet. He had felt all right, then.

"You sure you want to chase after this old man of yours?" His grin turned into a grimace as the old RV tried once more to lumber off the narrow, broken road. "Anyone who'd walk away from a sweet thing like you ain't worth it. I make a pretty good living, doin' the markets. These dryland hicks can't trade for squat. You wouldn't believe what I can twist 'em out of."

Asshole. "I think I'll get out pretty soon." Nita hugged the fussing Rachel to her chest. "She's going to cry like this for a long time."

"No problem." His smile revealed his yellowed, uneven teeth. "I don't mind kids."

He was lying. A darkness had been building inside him for the last hour — a gathering storm charged with sex and threaded with the red lightning of violence.

She felt it. Since she could remember, Nita had felt all of it; Mama's pain, Ignacio's anger at the dusty world, and Alberto's terrible resignation. Joy, lust, fear, anger. The world around her shrieked with the noise of humanity. It had driven her into herself as a child, the more frightening because the adults in her life hadn't understood. It wasn't until much later that she had learned why, that she was a freak. *Unique, a mutation,* David had said, trying to be kind. *That's how the species evolves.*

Unique was another word for alone.

The Winnebago was slowing. The dark storm inside this man was about to break. Nita sucked in a quick breath, stifled by the stuffy air, struggling with the urge to fling the door open, leap out with her daughter and run.

She could die without her pack and her water jugs. They would both die. Rachel was screaming now, back arched, feet kicking. "Easy, love, Rachel, it's all right." Feeble words — they didn't touch the fierce brilliance of her daughter's distress. But they covered the motion as she tucked her struggling daughter into the sling she wore across her chest and slid her hand into her pocket. The switchblade clicked open. This close to him, she felt the hot ache of his erection, couldn't help but feel it. The RV was edging off the road. Nita swallowed and leaned toward him, her throat dry with this storm. "We're getting out now."

He started to laugh, then flinched as the blade pricked through his shirt. The RV swerved and the muscles in his arms bulged, corded tight with fury. Rachel shrieked. Teeth clenched, Nita tried to keep her hand from shaking. I will kill him, she told herself. If he moves. This decision made, her hand steadied. He made a small sound in his throat as she edged the blade deeper, his rage collapsing into fear.

"Stop now and turn off the engine. Keep your hands on the wheel."

He did, and sat very still as she reached behind herself to open the door. He was all fear now. Perhaps he believed she would stick the knife into him, kill him anyway. As he would have done? Disgust clenched her belly. She groped behind the seat, awkward with the weight of Rachel in the sling and swung her pack one-handed out the door. It thudded onto the dusty asphalt, the tied-on water jugs bouncing. Carefully she backed out of the door. "If you come after me, I will kill you," she said.

"You bitch." His lips trembled. "I'll get you. You little tramp."

She slammed the door and stepped back, clutching Rachel to her. He might have a gun in the RV and who would know if he shot her, left her here? He could run her down with the RV. Only fields lined the roads, lines of sugar beets hugging the buried soaker hoses, nowhere to hide. Stupid! His emotions had filled her head and made her stupid. Nita shoved the now-useless knife into her pocket, slung her pack onto her shoulder and ran, cutting across the fields, toward a small clump of struggling trees in the distance. Behind her, she heard the Winnebago's engine growl and then catch. Rachel hiccupped and cried as Nita pounded through the dust between the rows.

A house! She hadn't noticed the shack tucked into the shade between the old, weary trees. Sagging and weathered, tethered to the black wings of solar panels, it would belong to the beet farmer. It night save her. If he was afraid of witnesses. Yes. The Winnebago roared on up the road, raising a choking cloud of dust that stung her eyes and coated her throat. Panting, she staggered to a halt.

"Are you all right?" A figure limped out of the deepening dusk, an old man with wispy white hair. "That was Andy Belden's rig, wasn't it? The trader?" He stopped in front of her, weathered and stooped, only worry clouding the deepening darkness. "He's a slimy bastard. Gonna get himself hung one of these days. Or shot. Did he . . . did he hurt you?"

"No. No, he didn't." Nita tried to laugh, but it wanted to come out a sob. "I just decided to walk."

"It's too dark for walkin'. You come inside now. My name's Seth." His smile seemed to lighten the darkness. "I got an extra bed for you and the baby, and I'd love the company."

His worry was soft against her mind, like gentle winter sun. "Thank you." Nita let her knees begin to tremble. "I would be very pleased to stay."

The house was pleasant inside. The front room held a table and cupboards, besides the old sink with faucets that probably didn't work, a propane stove, and painted cupboards that shone white and spotlessly clean in the light of the small battery lantern he turned on. A shirt hung from the back of a chair and a Bible lay on the scrubbed table top. He ushered her into a small, adjoining living room. A sofa, upholstered chairs, and a woodstove and a china cupboard crowded the small space. Curtains hung at the windows, striped with darker fabric at the edges where the sun hadn't bleached out the blue-flowered print.

"You sit," Seth told her. "Stew's almost done. I'll bring you a glass of water."

Nita sank into one of the oversized chairs. Rachel was hungry, groping at her shirt. She looked around the small room as she lifted her shirt and tucked her daughter's small warmth against her. A woman had done this, Nita thought. Her absence ached in the dustless surfaces and unused feel of this room. The glass shelves in the china cupboard were filled with small, china animals; dogs, horses, ducks, even a white goat with curly horns and a golden bell around its neck. Hers she thought. Her picture stood on the shelf. It had to be her — a respectful space around it made it the centerpiece of this unused room. Nita studied her as Rachel nursed. She had a wide smile, but a subtle sadness clouded her eyes. In the picture she was young, with only a few gray hairs in her dark curls.

"Here we are." Seth appeared in the doorway, a tray in his hands. A blue ceramic pitcher stood on the tray, flanked by two matched glasses. "I thought we'd do it formal. I never use these." He set the tray down on the table. "How's the young one?"

"She's fine." Nita watched him pour a silver stream of water into the glass, her throat tightening. You were always thirsty out here in the drylands. You put it away in the back of your mind, ignored it, until someone offered you a glass of water. And then, suddenly, you were dying of thirst. She picked up the glass, forcing herself to drink it slowly. It tasted so sweet, water. No, not really sweet — honey was sweet. It tasted of life. "Thank you." Nita set the empty glass down. "For the water. For letting us stay."

"Like I said, I get lonely. Leah was always proud of this room." He gave the picture a quick smile, as if she was listening to him. "I don't use it much, and that would make her sad. She'd be pleased to see me use the pitcher, too. I gave that to her for our twentieth wedding anniversary. Bought it in Portland."

"It's lovely," Nita said. His grief was new and sharp, but the love beneath it had an old, weathered feel to it. The last of her tension drained away, leaving her tired. Secure.

Seth was watching her over the rim of his glass, legs crossed, eyes sharp and dry as the land outside. "You on your way somewhere?" He leaned forward to tickle Rachel's belly. "Or on your way from somewhere?"

"To somewhere." It wasn't quite a lie. "We're on our way to The Dalles." She settled the sleepy Rachel more comfortably on her lap. "David — my husband — heard of a job there."

"The Dalles, huh? What kind of a job?" Seth leaned forward to refill their glasses.

"Working for the Corps. Pipeline work."

"Yeah?" His sparse eyebrows rose. "I heard there's trouble up that way. Trouble about the Pipe. Hope he got his job. Where you from, anyway?"

"The Willamette Valley, west of Salem." Nita stirred uneasily. She knew the questions that were coming, knew them too well. She didn't want to hear them from this man's lips, but Rachel had fallen asleep, and her sleeping weight pinned Nita to the chair.

"All the way from the Valley? That's some hike." Seth whistled. "How come you got stuck on your own? Seems like this David of yours'd be worried about his wife and kid on the road alone. There's not a whole lot o' law outside the big towns like The Dalles, Bend, LaGrande. Lot can happen out here."

Nita's lips tightened. "I . . . haven't heard from David." She said the words because they had to be said, had to be faced every morning with the silent, rising sun. "I couldn't go when he got the word about the job.

Rachel was too little and it was honey flow season. We were bee hunters. We'd have missed the harvest if we both left. So I stayed on until it was over."

He was supposed to have sent word when he got settled. He had planned to come back for her, if he could. For four months she had waited. Nita stroked Rachel's sleeping face, listening to the murmur of her daughter's small dreams. "We hunted bees way up in the coast range," she said and heard the defensiveness in her tone. "It wasn't like we had a cell phone or anything. Messages get lost all the time."

He heard it, too, and his sympathy was like the soft hum of bees on the still air. "Yeah, messages get lost." He picked up the tray and got stiffly to his feet. He didn't tell her that people get lost, too. He didn't have to.

"I'll go dish up the stew," he said and put out a hand as she started to rise. "You stay put. When I got the table ready, you can put her down on the bed."

Nita blinked back teas as he shuffled out of the room. A lot of dusty miles lay between their tent in the mountains and The Dalles. Andy and his stormy violence wasn't the worst she could meet out here. It was easy to die in this dry land. But it wasn't his death that haunted her dreams. Nita stroked a wisp of hair back from Rachel's face. *She looks like you*, David had said, and he had been afraid. He had always been afraid of her deep down inside. Ever since he had understood what she was — that she would know how he felt. Always. It's all right, he had told her. I don't mind. And part of him didn't. Part of him was happy when she translated the bees' soft song for him, told him how the hive was content or nervous or happy. Part of him liked it that she knew when he needed a touch, or love, or a little private space.

And part of him feared her.

He wouldn't look into that shadow, wouldn't face it. But it had always been there. After Rachel's birth, it had grown darker. He had been full of a nervous restlessness, like the bees before they swarmed.

She looks like you.

It was easy to die here. It was easy to walk away, too. The drylands ate yesterday. They buried it in dust, dried it up, and blew it away.

"Think you can put the little one down?" Seth stuck his head through the door.

"I think so." Nita scooped Rachel gently into her arms and carried her into the tiny back bedroom. Seth didn't seem to have noticed her tears. Nita laid her sleeping daughter on the bed and wiped her face on her sleeve. "You're not like me," she murmured. "You're normal." *Normal.* The word hurt her.

Rachel whimpered softly in her sleep — she would look like Nita, yes, and like David, too. "I love you," Nita whispered. She tucked the spread around her daughter and tiptoed out of the room.

Seth had cleared off the table and spread a flowered tablecloth across it. He had set out thick, white china and a cut-glass bud vase full of golden grass stems. "You get sloppy, living alone." He ladled bean and vegetable stew into a bowl. "I'm glad I got an excuse to set a proper table."

Nita took the filled bowl with a smile at the spotless room, but something was wrong. A stiff uncomfortableness had replaced his peace.

"This is great." She spooned up stew and smiled. "You're a wonderful cook."

"Thanks. It's garlic does it. You can't never get too much garlic in a dish." He put the pot back on the small propane burner and sat down. "You know, if you want to hang around until tomorrow afternoon, I can give you a ride on into Tygh Valley. You could likely find someone heading north on 197, who could get you closer to The Dalles."

He was lying to her. Why? Nita's earlier sense of safety began to leak away. "We're close to 197, then." She made her voice light. "I wasn't sure."

"Yeah, you're close." Seth put his spoon down, eyes fixed on his stew, as if a fish had suddenly jumped in the middle of his bowl. "We got a good weekly market there. Folk come in from all around. Few weeks back we had some excitement." He poked his fork tines into a thick cube of squash. "Some guy come through doing magic tricks. Cards and stuff, but more than that." He looked up suddenly, frowning. "He made stuff . . . appear. Frogs and butterflies and such. Out of the air, like. It was a gadget, he said. Little black box." He reached for his water glass, took a long swallow. "Good thing for him. Couple of us kind of got him aside, eased him on out of town. He got the message real quick, and beat it."

"What kind of message?"

"That folk around here don't have no sense of humor when it comes to that kind of thing. You know, a lot of weird stuff happens in the Dry." He held his glass up, stared into its crystal depths. "Kids get born strange. Some folks say it's the water or the dust." He shrugged. "The Reverend, he says it's the devil. Rev says we've killed the land with our wickedness and now its ghost is rising up, looking for vengeance. It's taking over our children, right in the womb, turning 'em evil. You got to stop it 'fore it gets out of hand."

There was something hot and hard running through the softness that she had felt before — a shining thread, like a thin stream of molten metal. It frightened her, that hot thinness. It was aimed at Rachel. He had overheard her in the bedroom. Nita put down her spoon. "You're wrong," she whispered.

For a moment, he looked her in the face, his eyes dry and pitiless as the sky. The hot-metal feel of him burned her so that she clutched the tabletop to keep herself from leaping to her feet. The knife felt heavy in her pocket but it didn't reassure her. Not this time.

Seth looked down suddenly, and the hot glare faded. "I don't know." His voice was unsteady. "Leah and I, we had three kids. They all died. She said it was the will of the Lord, Leah did. That it was God's choice. Maybe, but a little bit of her died with each of 'em." He looked at her, looked away. "I believe in the Rev," he said slowly. "He's a pure man. I believe God speaks through him. When he holds out his hand, the dust storm ceases. But . . . I don't know. The Robinson boy was a good kid — but when he touched someone, they . . . glowed. Like colors in the air, all around. He said you could see sickness that way. Leah tried to stop 'em when they started to throw stones. He got away. The Rev said she was a weak vessel, that God would punish her. She died a month later." He picked up his fork again and ate a cube of squash. "It was my fault," he said and guilt beat in him like a second heart. "I should have taken her home. I knew they were gonna do it."

"I'm sorry," Nita whispered. The stew tasted like dust, but she ate it, spoonful at a time, afraid to reject his food, afraid, period.

She helped Seth with the dishes, hiding her fear. He told her that he got up early to soak the beets before it got hot. The scary part of him was watching her, waiting for her to go to bed first. Nita smiled for him and shut the bedroom door tightly behind her. No lock, but she jammed the back of the single chair beneath the doorknob. *Don't tell people what you can feel.* David had told her that years ago, when he had first understood. *"Different" scares people, he had said. Scared people can hurt you.*

Rachel's diaper was wet and Nita changed it, wrapping the wet one up in the plastic bag from her pack. No time to let it dry and air out now. She sat down on the edge of the bed with the switchblade in her hand. Listening.

Part of Seth grieved for that boy, and for his own dead children. But another part of him was forged from that hot, molten ugliness. She heard his footsteps in the hall, soft and careful. Nita held onto her knife, fear a stone in her chest. The doorknob turned gently. The chair creaked a little and skidded an inch or two across the wood floor. Silence. Nita held her breath, heard only the rush of blood in her ears. She watched the single window, waiting for a face to appear, for the glass to smash in.

Silence.

Perhaps . . . just perhaps, the grieving part of him had coaxed his body to sleep. She didn't dare hope, but . . . perhaps.

Silence.

After a long time, when the house had creaked and groaned itself to sleep, she gathered up her daughter, her pack, and her water jugs. Heart pounding, she climbed through the window. No Seth. The moon was up high enough that she could see to walk along the cracked asphalt of the county road at the edge of the fields. She fished the map from her pocket and spread its creased folds out on the moonlit asphalt. Yes. If she took this road, it would bring her to 197 well north of Tygh Valley. Nita refolded the map, slid her arms through the pack straps, and tucked Rachel into her sling. An owl screeched thinly as she started walking, and fear lurked in the darkness behind her, nipping at her heels.

CHAPTER THREE

C arter fought the wheel of the little car he'd drawn from the Corps' Portland motor pool. It was a new electric model, and light enough that the wind kept pushing it off the highway. The Columbia Gorge would make a great wind tunnel, he thought sourly. Sheer vertical walls of black rock rose on his right. The dry Columbia bed yawned on his left, like an ugly wound in the Earth's crust. Wind towers stood in silver ranks, their long blades turning briskly, scouring energy from the wind. Those were the Corps' towers. They powered the pumps that pushed water through the Pipeline. You couldn't see the Pipeline itself — the six immense pipes lay buried like veins beneath the riverbed. Another truck convoy thundered past him on the left — triple trailer rigs doing about eighty — and the car tried once more for the ditch.

A ramp was coming up. Arms aching, sweating in spite of the laboring air-conditioning, Carter fought the car off the highway. *Rest Area*, a blue highway sign proclaimed. The ramp curved gently toward the towering cliff wall, ending in a small roadside parking lot. It wasn't much of a rest area, but at least the wind wasn't so bad down here. Carter slammed the car door, his sweat springing out in earnest in the dry heat. The asphalt lot was empty except for a big semi rig parked at the far end and a lanky man with a tail of blond hair sitting in the narrow strip of shade cast by a bank of vending machines. Carter headed for one of the three pay-toilet units beside the machines, very conscious of his uniform.

He had a new CO to meet and no time to change, or he would have been in civies. You didn't wear a uniform off base, not if you were traveling alone. The blond guy didn't seem to notice, or he didn't care, anway. Carter pulled the door shut after himself, baking in the plastic oven despite its reflective coating. He held his breath as he unzipped. These new composters were supposed to be odorless, but something was sure wrong with this one.

The week was not going well. He'd come in three days ago, expecting to meet up with Johnny. But Johnny wasn't in Portland. He had been called back down to the regional office in San Francisco for some kind of emergency meeting. So Carter had kicked around Portland on his own, seeing what sights the city had to offer. The refugee camps in the old suburbs didn't do much for the atmosphere. They reminded him too much of Chicago.

He glowered at the heavily caged vending machine. It offered water, pop, and a few snack items. Carter stuck his debit card into the slot and a plastic pack of water thunked into the tray. Sun-hot. Grimacing, Carter poked the attached straw through the plastic and took a swallow.

Beyond the parking lot, the sheer cliff wall of the Gorge towered over the ruins of a stone building. The stone was grooved with the traces of a long dead waterfall. This must have been a park once. Someone had tacked a laminated postcard to the splintered remains of an old signpost. The colors had bleached to yellows and greens in the sun, but you could just make out a waterfall, yeah. Carter squinted at it, then lifted the card carefully. *Multnomah Falls.* The brittle cardboard cracked as he read the caption on the back, and the card came away in his hand. Carter stared at it, not sure what to do with it. He finally managed to wedge it under a thick splinter of wood. Johnny would laugh at him, but someone had put it there.

He had looked forward to a few days with Johnny. Golden-boy Johnny. Carter shook his head, smiling, remembering. Johnny had been king of the private school they'd both attended, and Carter — forever on the outside — had watched him operate with a resigned envy. It had turned his universe upside down when this star picked him to hang out with. At eleven, he already knew how the world worked. It didn't work like this, except in fairy tales. His mother was the live-in housekeeper for old man Warrington and everybody knew why the old man paid his tuition to the school. He'd figured Johnny needed backup and so he'd made a wary trade — friendship for his fists when needed.

Johnny had dragged Carter with him into every inside clique and hadn't asked for anything . . . *anything* . . . in return. That had turned the school's little universe upside down. Which was probably the joke that Johnny had intended in the first place.

But by then they had become real friends. Carter blinked, sighed, found himself staring at the crumpled water pack in his hand. He spiked it into a trash can, turned . . . and froze.

In front of his eyes, the cliff face wavered and changed. A silver tail of water fell down from the rocky lip, exploding into white mist in a shallow basin far below. Ferns sprouted from the rocks and emerald grass covered the shady ground between trees.

The postcard — that was it — only it was *real*. For the space of three heartbeats, Carter stared at that green vision. Then — it vanished. Only dust and water worn rock remained above the dry hollow that had once been ringed with ferns. "Mother of God," Carter said out loud. The falls stayed dead and he looked around, half embarrassed by his exclamation. The lot was still empty. The blond man was leaning on the rail that edged the parking lot. He was staring at the falls, ignoring Carter.

Fatigue, Carter told himself. Stress. Better watch the driving. He started for the car, uneasy, more disturbed by his momentary vision than he wanted to admit. He had never hallucinated in his life. And there had been a strange feeling of . . . reality to that brief vision. As if it wasn't a vision at all, as if, for an instant, he had stepped back through time into the green, unbelievable past. He unlocked the car door.

"Hey, soldier? Hang on a minute."

Carter stiffened, turned, saw the blond man limping toward him. He leaned on a stick and his legs looked crooked, as if they didn't bend just right. He was wearing a faded shirt and worn jeans, and his long, sunbleached hair was tied back into a thin tail. He looked as if he might be about Carter's age, maybe early thirties, but it was hard to tell. His tanned face had the lined, sundried look of a drylands native.

"You heading east?"

"To Bonneville."

"Can I get a ride? I was hitching in the truck, but the guy sleeps afternoons and I'm not sleepy." He gave Carter a crooked grin.

He didn't look like much of a threat. He was a head shorter than Carter, slender and wiry. "Sure." Carter reached inside and popped the car's hatch-back. "Put your pack and your stick in back. This thing's got as much room as a tuna can."

"Thanks." The stranger stuck out a hand. "My names' Jeremy. Jeremy Barlow. I appreciate the ride."

"I'm going there anyway." Carter returned Jeremy's firm grip. His hands were misshapen, the joints thick and ugly, and he handled his pack clumsily.

"You coming from Portland?" Carter started the car and took the eastbound ramp.

"Yeah." Jeremy shrugged. "Looking for a job, but jobs are tight and there are a lot of things I can't do too well." He held his hands up briefly. "Rawlings keeps saying that the depression is over, but I think he's talking for the next election. So I guess I'll hit the road again."

"The president has been saying that things are looking up since the last election. The line still seems to work, don't ask me why. Or he thinks it does." Although if Johnny was right about the Alliance breaking up, that might not be enough to get him through the next election. Carter and the car ducked as another triple rig roared past. "What do you do? On the road?"

"I'm a magician. I do a few card tricks and stuff." He looked at Carter, a hint of a smile at the corner of his mouth. "Don't run off the road, okay?"

A tiny dragon appeared on the dashboard in front of Carter. Its green scales glittered in the sun and it glared at Carter with ruby eyes. Abruptly it reared back, snorted a tiny tongue of flame, and vanished.

"Good thing you warned me." Carter stared at the spot where the dragon had stood. "Holo projector?"

"Yeah." Jeremy held out a small, gray box. It resembled an ordinary notebook except for the lens at one end. "It fools people."

"I'm impressed. That's a damn sophisticated gadget. You're some electronics whiz."

"Not me," Jeremy said a shade too quickly. "I got it from this old guy. Now there was a whiz, alright."

Stolen? Well someone had done something pretty marvelous. "This seems to be my day for visions," Carter said lightly. "I was looking at that old waterfall beside the rest area and, for a moment, I could see it just like it must have looked back before the Dry. With water. Green." He shook his head, pierced by unexpected longing. "It was . . . beautiful."

"It was." Jeremy was looking at him, his expression enigmatic. "You're not from around here, are you?"

"I just flew in from . . . the Midwest." Carter let his breath out in a sigh. "It's something — seeing the country from the air. The Pipeline feeds tundra water into the Missouri, so the Mississippi drainage isn't too bad. They still do a lot of soaker hose farming there. Biomass crops, mostly. But then you cross the Missouri, fly on over Colorado, Wyoming . . . and all of a sudden, it's dead. You look down from the airplane and you see desert."

"The Drylands." Jeremy's tone capitalized the word. "That's where I was born. You can live there, but you got to live by the rules. There's only so much water. Out there, they take the extra babies and the ones who aren't perfect, and they leave 'em out somewhere. In the dust."

"You're kidding."

"No, I'm not kidding." Jeremy stared through the windshield, rubbing his crooked hands gently on his thighs. "If you don't do it, maybe your next real dry summer, you get to choose who dies then. There's only so much water. It's another world out there, Carter. Sometimes you make ugly choices. It makes it worse that you can see the way it used to be," Jeremy said softly. "You catch it out here — a flash of yesterday once in awhile." He looked over at Carter, the faint grin quirking the corner of his mouth again. "No, you weren't going crazy."

"Glad to hear it." That vision had been so damn real. *Bonneville*, a green sign proclaimed. *Next Three Exits.* "We're here."

The highway curved out and around and now he could see the dam. Bonneville Dam. It stretched across the dry riverbed like a gray wall, broken by the silver arches of a pumping station. Solar arrays spouted like black wings from the top, aimed by their computers at the setting sun. "You want to come to the base?" Carter asked Jeremy. "They might be hiring civilians."

"Maybe later." Jeremy nodded. "It's been awhile since I've hit the big Bonneville market. I usually do pretty good there. You can drop me at the next exit, if you would. You stationed here?"

"No. I'm on my way to The Dalles." The dam was so big. This close, it loomed like a vast cliff. Carter pulled off at the exit ramp and went around to get Jeremy's pack from the hatch. "Come by the base, if you get up there. Maybe you could at least do some shows for the personnel."

"Maybe I'll do that." Jeremy slung his pack over his shoulder and picked up his stick. "I'll be along. I stick to the highway towns out here."

"I imagine the little rural communities are pretty slim pickings."

"It's not that." For a moment, Jeremy's face was grim. "They don't like magic out in the drylands. Thanks for the lift. Good luck in The Dalles." He raised one crooked hand in a salute and walked down the ramp.

Carter pulled back onto the highway, puzzled by Jeremy's comment about magic. Local traffic cluttered the lanes here in town; pickups and the little electrics, even older hybrids and a few bio-diesels. Below the highway, new silocrete buildings and haphazard shacks cluttered the shelving slope of the old riverbed. Solar arrays sprouted from every rooftop and the ubiquitous wind towers lined the riverbed. Up ahead, a ramp exited left, to curve down behind the dam itself. The turreted castle of the Corps gleamed in the level beams of the setting sun. This was it. Carter slid the little car in behind a rickety old bio-diesel pickup with a goat in the back and turned off onto the ramp. The buildings of the Corps headquarters huddled on the south side of the Pipe, up against the inner wall of the old dam. Rec or mess halls, apartments for enlisted and officers, a playground with a pair of basketball hoops — so normal — but Carter felt a sense of foreboding as the shadow of the dam swallowed him.

He had to slow to a crawl as he zigzagged through the anti-bomber barriers. The Green Beret on the gate ran his ID through the computer and didn't crack a smile until after Carter's thumbprint had cleared. By then, a corporal had appeared to escort him to General Hastings' office.

Tight security. All security had to be tight these days, but it didn't do anything for Carter's mood as he followed the corporal's brisk pace. Administration was inside the dam itself, in the space that had once been taken up by the huge turbines and generators. Carter's sweaty uniform dried quickly in the cool, conditioned air as he followed his guide through a set of gasketed doors and down a long corridor. He looked at the pastel yellow ceiling, imagining that vast bulk of concrete squatting above his head. It gave him the willies. Uniformed men and women wearing the Corps insignia passed him and saluted, but Carter caught their quick, surmising glances. New kid in town. He wondered what rumors had gone around.

"In here, sir." The corporal opened a door marked *General Hastings*.

Inside, a cluttered desk with a computer and two plastic chairs stood on a nondescript magenta carpet. A large framed photograph hung on the wall above the desk. It looked like an old photo of the dam. White water poured through the spillway, and the cliffs of the Columbia Gorge glowed with greenery beneath a gray sky.

"Hard to imagine, isn't it, sir? All that water, running right over our heads?" The corporal grinned.

He couldn't really imagine it, but it didn't help his growing claustrophobia to try. Carter suppressed a shudder as the corporal ushered him into the inner office. "Lieutenant Colonel Carter Voltaire reporting for duty, sir." He saluted and stood at attention.

The thickset man with the square face and general's star didn't even look up from his screen. Carter waited, listening to his own breathing. Bad start? The small office looked as shabby as the corporal's cubby. The carpeting was worn and the furniture looked like refugees from a flea market. The Chicago base was luxurious by comparison. A large vid screen covered one entire wall. Pictures stood on Hastings' cluttered desk; a flat photo of a smiling young man in dress greens, holo cubes of a woman holding a baby, and a blond boy leaning on the handlebars of a new bike. Carter stared at the man in the dress greens. I know him, he thought, but the name eluded him.

"At ease, Colonel." Hastings looked up at last, extending a stiff hand. "Welcome to the Columbia."

He didn't sound very welcoming. "Thank you, sir." Carter returned the general's strong grip. "My orders, sir."

"I already looked at the file." Hastings took the hardcopy, tossed it onto his desk and crossed his arms. "Tell me what you're going to be doing up in The Dalles."

A test? "My unit is responsible for maintaining the Pipeline in our sector, including the diversion complex where the Klamath Shunt splits off to the south, sir." Carter could feel blood seeping into his face. "I've reviewed the flow reports for the last year, along with maintenance records and the tech namuals for the Pipeline and the Shunt complex. I understand the requirements for the system and the mechanics of its operation, sir." I did my homework, General. Screw you, too.

"I *hope* you understand the mechanics." Hastings' expression didn't thaw. "I hope you also understand the importance of maintaining the Pipeline flow. The Ogalalla aquifer has been pumped out, and the Columbia aquifer will be too low for cost-effective pumping in less than a year. That means the Pipeline *is* the water source for most of two states."

"Yes, sir."

"I wanted someone with more years," Hastings said coldly. "The Dalles isn't the place for an inexperienced CO, no matter how much of a hotshot you were in the riot."

Carter flushed. "My name was added to the promotions list very recently. Sir."

"I didn't ask you, Colonel." Hastings stared at him with distaste. "I just hope you can handle the situation. Because of the Shunt valves, The Dalles sector is particularly critical to the function of the Pipeline. We've had some local unrest there lately, including acts of sabotage against the Pipe. The integrity of the Pipe must be protected, no matter what the cost. Do you understand me, Colonel?"

"Yes, sir."

"Good." Hastings nodded. "Your predecessor, Colonel Watanabe, was murdered. Did you know that?"

"Yes, sir." Hell, everyone knew it, just like everyone knew who'd fired the first shot in Chicago. "Has anyone been charged yet, sir?"

"No, but we know who was behind it. The same terrorists who are sabotaging the Pipe." Hastings was watching him closely, his blue eyes sharp and wary. "They call themselves the Columbia Coalition. A man named Dan Greely heads it. Watch out for him."

"Yes, sir."

"You can get whatever else you need to know from your second in command, Major Delgado." Hastings waved a dismissive hand. "Sandusky can drive you up there. Report into me when you're settled."

"Yes, sir." Carter saluted smartly and marched out of the room. Great. This was about as bad a start as you could manage.

Corporal Sandusky was waiting in the outer office, his expression carefully neutral. "If you'll come with me, sir." He cleared his throat. "I'll drive you to The Dalles."

"Fine." Carter let his breath out in a rush. "I've got a Portland car."

"You can give me the keys." Sandusky held out a hand. "Is your luggage in the car?"

"Just a carryall and a duffel bag." He'd shipped the books and the few items too heavy to carry.

He followed the corporal back outside. It was already getting cold, as the daytime heat radiated away into the dry air. The corporal didn't say much as he transferred Carter's bags into a motor-pool electric Chevy. It was dark beyond the yellow glare of the base floods. Scattered lights gleamed like a small galaxy across the black gulf of the riverbed. In the old days, the cities had blazed with light. People had squandered it the way they had squandered water — had decorated with it, put up displays of color and dazzle. Not anymore. Electricity cost and the national power curfew cut all power at 10:00 PM local time.

The small galaxy of Bonneville disappeared behind them as Sandusky turned onto the highway and stepped on the accelerator. "Tell me about Colonel Watanabe." Carter spoke into humming silence.

"A routine patrol found him by the Pipe. Shot in the head at close range, sir. They figure it was a setup. Rumor had it that the colonel got too close to the Coalition, sir."

"You think they did it? This Coalition?"

"Who else?" Sandusky shrugged. "They're the enemy around here, sir. A couple of our guys got shot out on patch detail. Hicks picked 'em off with a thirty-ought-six. Bastards. Excuse me, sir." Sandusky threw Carter a quick, nervous glance in the rearview.

"Yeah, they were bastards." Carter looked out the window. Darkness filled the Gorge, so thick you could cut it. You could feel the high walls on either side, holding in the darkness, squeezing it down around you. Violence. Maybe you found it anywhere you found water. Maybe you couldn't separate one from the other. Carter shook himself and took a deep breath of the cool, conditioned air. "What about this Dan Greely person?"

"Don't know much about him, sir," Sandusky said briskly. "He bosses the Coalition, and I heard he's an ex-con. Guess it tells you something about the hicks around here — who they pick to run the show." He snorted. "The general won't let him on base, so he doesn't bother us any."

Being an ex-con didn't necessarily mean much. He'd come damn close to being one himself. Carter struggled against a growing sense of foreboding. Hastings wanted to hate his guts and he was walking into what sounded more and more like another Chicago.

"Sir?" Sandusky whipped the Chevy around another car. "I heard about the riot, sir. I just want to say . . . you guys sure kicked ass. Sir."

"Yeah, we kicked ass." Carter stared out into the darkness.

"Those campies are real scum. The hicks are about as bad, just so you know. Sometimes I think we ought to just go down the whole damn river-bed, run the troublemakers out into the Dry." Sandusky slapped the steering wheel for emphasis. "Let 'em make trouble out there."

Carter looked at the shaved back of Sandusky's head. "It wasn't just the camps." He closed his eyes, remembering briefly the equal weight of his rage and the Beretta. It was as if all the darkness, despair, and rage generated by the shriveling, dying land had trickled slowly to the lakeshore, like a dark, ugly oil spill around the feet of the towers. He had been the spark that had set if off. "It was all of us." Carter sat forward, peering at Sandusky's young face in the rearview. "It was the towers and the base and the camp. We were all ready to start killing each other. So we did it, and the Corps came out on top, because we had the guns and the organization. Everyone else was just killing. It was hell, and it just happened. Let's drop it, Corporal."

"Yes, sir."

Sandusky shut up after that. He didn't understand. He probably saw the world in black and white, Carter thought. That was how you had to look at it, sometimes. Them and Us. Because you had a job to do and shades of gray could make it hell.

He must have drowsed for awhile, because the next thing he knew, they were at The Dalles gate. If anything, this one was better defended than Bonneville. Which said a lot about the situation, Carter thought sourly. The guards positively gleamed — they'd been expecting him. Wearily, Carter returned the razor-sharp salutes. He was the Old Man now, and everybody had to show for him. He stifled a yawn as Sandusky finally pulled the car up in front of a residence block. Security lights shed a yellow glow on the apartments. Ugly boxes, reflective siding and windows defended them from the sun.

Sandusky led him to the front door of the second unit from the end. A gusty wind pushed dust and trash down the concrete street, whirled grit into Carter's face. Beyond the apartments, he could make out a bulking wall of deeper darkness. The Dalles dam? Like Bonneville, the Corps base seemed to have been built at its foot.

Sandusky was fumbling with the door. A dying geranium sulked in a pot on the narrow, concrete porch. A door opened somewhere and Carter heard a woman's laughter before it slammed shut again. The wind buffeted the geranium, yanked at his uniform.

"Is it always like this?" Carter shielded his face.

"Windy, you mean? Yes sir. It either blows up or down the Gorge. Down is usually worse, sir." Sandusky picked up Carter's carryall and pushed the door open. "Here you are, sir."

Carter stumbled over the threshold, blinking in the sudden glare of the florescent ceiling lights. The door was gasketed to keep dust out and cool air in. Sandusky grunted as he yanked it closed behind them.

"Anything else, sir?" He flicked on a small air conditioner set into the wall and saluted without meeting Carter's eyes.

"No, I guess not. Thanks for the ride."

He shouldn't have been so short with the kid. You couldn't blame him for being curious about Chicago. Carter looked over the two-room suite. It was smaller than what he'd had on the lakebed. The main room held a wide sofa bed, two upholstered chairs, and a big screen video. A refrigerator/single burner stove combo and sink had been fenced off into a kitchen by a Formica-topped breakfast bar. Doors led to the bedroom and a tiny bathroom, which was equipped with a digester toilet and a self-contained shower cabinet.

It looked impersonal without his books and his sound equipment, like a cheap motel room. Carter took his carryall into the bedroom, trying not to wonder if this had been Colonel Watanabe's quarters. The warm, dry air smelled of disinfectant. The clock said ten. Midnight, Chicago time. He flopped onto the double bed that nearly filled the small room, still bleary from his nap in the car. What he needed right now was a beer, a shower, and about eight hours of uninterrupted sleep.

Someone knocked at the door.

Now what? Carter stomped across the apartment and jerked the door open.

A civilian stood on the threshold, dressed in jeans and a faded denim shirt.

"Welcome to The Dalles, Colonel." The stranger walked past him as if Carter had invited him in. "I know it's late, but I thought I'd better drop by and introduce myself." He waited while Carter closed the door, smiling wryly. "I'm Dan Greely. You're Carter Voltaire, yes?" He extended a hand. "Welcome the The Dalles, Carter."

Carter kept his hand at his side, wide awake now. He looked the tall, lanky man over. Greely had weathered brown skin, dark eyes, and brown hair streaked with gray. Carter placed him in his forties. No sign of a weapon. "You're the leader of the sabotage ring here," Carter said deliberately. "What the hell are you doing here? Who gave you a pass?"

"If you mean the Coalition, we aren't behind the sabotage," Greely said. "I think we're on the same side, Colonel."

"That's not what General Hastings told me."

"No, it wouldn't be." Greely grimaced. "That's why I wanted to introduce myself in person. There isn't much . . . official communication between the Corps and the Coalition right now. Hastings hates my guts, to put it bluntly."

Carter crossed his arms, a bit impressed by this guy's cool. "Tell me why I shouldn't call the MPs?"

"You could do that. You could even make a trespass charge stick, because I *am* trespassing. I didn't come in through the gate." A grin flashed and faded on his face. "That's it, though. If you could get away with anything else, Hastings would have locked me up long ago."

Carter tugged at his lip. "You showing off for me? Or what?"

Greely's expression sobered. "I'm here because *we* want to find out who's sabotaging the Pipe, too. We don't want to take on the Corps, or stop the water. We're a bunch of farmers who're trying to keep crops alive long enough to make harvest. Someone's sabotaging the Pipe, but it's not us. Colonel Watanabe knew that, too. He listened to us."

"Colonel Watanabe's dead," Carter said softly.

"Yeah." Greely held his eyes. "Think about that, okay? Think about this, too; What the hell do we gain by cutting off our own water? Don't let Hastings sic you on us. It's the wrong trail."

"I guess that's for me to decide," Carter said. This guy had balls. Carter lifted the phone and called base Security. "I have an unauthorized civilian in my quarters," he snapped. "I want an escort for him." He cradled the phone and faced Greely's wary stare. "I'll tell you this much," he said slowly. "I'm the CO here, which means my people and the Pipeline come first. But I'll make up my own mind about things. If you want to cooperate, come talk to me. I'll listen to you."

Knuckles rapped briskly at the door. "Base Security, sir." The grizzled sergeant's face was expressionless as Carter opened the door. "You have an unauthorized civilian, sir?"

A retreaded Green Beret? They made up the bulk of MPs these days. "Escort this man off the base, Sergeant," Carter said coldly. "I want him to go through the gate in exactly the same condition he is in now. And then you tell your CO that I expect to see him here in ten minutes."

"Yes, sir." The sergeant's salute was precise. "Ten minutes, sir. This way," he said to Greely and his tone was absolutely neutral.

Greely looked over his shoulder. Gave Carter that crooked smile. "Glad to have met you, Colonel. If you want to talk to me, leave a message at the government store in town. I don't have a phone."

"Greely." Carter waited until the man met his eyes. "Any more killings will screw everything up."

"I'd like to give you a guarantee, Colonel." Greely paused in the doorway, his expression grim. "We're trying to stop this. Think about Watanabe, okay?"

Yeah, he was thinking about Watanabe. Carter watched the clock, frowning. The sergeant's commanding officer, a young captain, arrived in exactly five minutes. He left ten minutes later, his back ramrod straight. No one in Security was going to sleep well tonight, Carter thought grimly. Not until they'd found the hole Dan Greely had walked through.

"Sir?" This time, the man at the door was a major, dark haired, with a long face that gave him a Saturnine air. "Major Delgado reporting, sir." He saluted. "I understand you had trouble here, tonight?"

It hadn't taken him long to get dressed and over here. Carter gave him a point or two for that. "A trespasser," Carter said. "At ease, Major. Come in." He stood aside, tired and twitching with tension now. God, what a beginning. "Security's dealing with it."

"Security had standing orders to arrest Greely any time he turned up on Corps property," Delgado said tightly.

"On what charge?" Carter eyed the major. "Trespass?"

"Yes, sir." Delgado's eyes glittered.

Carter shook his head, too tired to deal with any more of this tonight. "We'll talk about it tomorrow," he said. "In my office at oh-nine-hundred. I don't want to be disturbed any more tonight, unless it's a major emergency."

"Yes, sir." Delgado saluted, his spine still rigid with anger. "Tomorrow, sir." He marched out of the apartment, his stride parade ground stiff.

No one else knocked. Frowning, Carter stripped out of his sweaty clothes. Dan Greely had sounded sincere. Which might make him nothing better than a damn good used car salesman. He tossed his clothes into the corner and flopped naked on the bed. Two votes against Greely — Hastings and Delgado — and the situation felt more and more like another Chicago. The bottom line was he didn't know squat about what was going on here, and he'd better start fixing that first thing in the morning. Carter grabbed for the sheet, way too wired to sleep, and was out before he'd pulled it all the way up.

CHAPTER FOUR

The shrill beep of the alarm jerked Carter out of sleep just as he took aim at the sun-bright windshield of the VW. Groggy, he reached for the alarm . . . and nearly fell out of bed as his hand missed the nightstand that wasn't there. The adrenalin rush woke him up fast.

He was in The Dalles, not Chicago. The nightstand was on *that* side of the bed. He slapped off the alarm. Four-thirty. He blinked at the glowing red digits. Five hours should have been enough, but it felt more like ten minutes. Carter threw back the sheet and stumbled to the bathroom. Day one as Old Man on this base. Time to start getting a feel for what the hell was going on here, and judging by last night, he'd better do it fast.

He wasn't sleepy anymore. He turned on the water, gasping as cold hit his skin. Lousy insulation on the storage tanks. Carter made a mental note to get on Building Maintenance's ass. No one needed a cold shower to start the day.

It was still dark as he left the apartment and walked quickly through the yellow-lit streets. He turned right, feet crunching in gravel. He'd memorized the layout here. Lights glimmered on his right — enlisted personnel housing according to the map. Toys cluttered the grass-carpeted front yards — bikes and three-wheelers, a battered doll lying spread-eagled beside the sidewalk. The base was closed here, as in Chicago; you lived on post. Inside the cage. It was hard on the families.

Headquarters was a long, low, concrete building, ugly and functional. The duty sergeant showed Carter to his office and gave him a quick tour of the layout. His office was about as shabby as Hastings', Carter decided. Flow reports in hardcopy lay neatly on his desk, waiting for his signature. Carter leafed through them quickly. No problems, but he would know if there'd been any problems. A map of the Pipeline covered one wall and a blowup of The Dalles sector covered another. Veins, Carter thought as he studied the blue tracery. Those veins made him uneasy. *I wanted someone with more experience,* Hastings had said. Hastings could go take a flying leap. But those veins carried the lifeblood of this damn, dusty here-and-now. Cut them, and a lot of people would suffer. Die. How close to a war *were* they, out here?

Carter turned around at the sound of a cleared throat.

"Sir." A gray haired sergeant with the wiry build of a jockey slauted. "Sergeant Willis, sir. Anything you need?"

This would be the topkick — the senior NCO. The duty sergeant had called him, and probably Delgado, as well. The new CO was up and roaming around. "Everything's fine, Sergeant." Carter looked around at his cramped office. "Notify all the COs that there will be a staff meeting at oh-seven-thirty," he told Willis. "Right now, I need coffee. And some breakfast."

"Yes, sir. I'll take you over to the dining hall," Willis said.

"Ten minutes." Carter turned to the computer to take the pulse of the Columbia riverbed. It was interesting that Delgado hadn't arrived yet. Perhaps the duty sergeant hadn't called him after all. Or had Willis ordered him not to? Carter frowned at the numbers on the screen in front of him. What did Willis have to say that he didn't want Delgado to hear? He would listen during his tour. He'd listen very carefully.

The sun was well up as Willis showed him around the base. A light wind brushed Carter's face but it was going to be hot, later. Half asleep this morning, he'd forgotten sunscreen. Bad move. He had dark hair, but his fair skin never tanned. The dusty street ended at the vast wall of the dam. "This was a power company dam." Carter looked up in awe at the enormous intakes that yawned like cave mouths in the stained concrete. "It never stored an acre foot of water for ag or drinking."

"I guess they had plenty of water back then, sir." Willis shrugged. "We wouldn't be so tight now if the Trench Reservoir had been built sooner."

True. Carter remembered his momentary vision of the waterfall. How could you worry about water when you looked at that every day? By the time the federal condemnation of private water rights had finally made it through the courts, it had been almost too late. Not that it could have kept the climate from changing, or the seas from eating Florida and much of Los Angeles, but it would have helped. If they'd started sooner, the Trench might be full clear to capacity. Now — if Johnny was right, and Canada shorted them on the tundra water — it might never fill.

"The O club's down there, sir." Willis nodded. "We use it as the officer's mess. Enlisted mess is the 101 Building — that green monster down there. The exchange and the drill hall are across the street. This is Main. The

MEQ is down there." He pointed south, down the street Carter had walked up in the darkness.

"How tight is it on base?" Carter asked. He watched Willis think about his answer.

"It's tight." The corporal's eyes flicked away.

"How tight?" Morale mattered. These were his people now.

Willis frowned, clearly picking his words. "The kids've gone, so my wife and I took a single-bedroom unit."

"You're entitled to more."

"Yes, sir." Willis nodded. "There's two families sharing the three-bedroom unit we had, sir." Willis cleared his throat. "Colonel Watanabe authorized extra air conditioners, sir. For some of the units."

He was waiting to see how Carter would react, or maybe Delgado had pulled the extra units. "Good move," Carter said and watched Willis not show his relief. Carter shaded his eyes, squinting into the harsh sunlight. The gray wall of the dam zigzagged across the dusty gouge of the riverbed. The Corps buildings and residences clustered on the Oregon side, sheltered by the concrete wing of the dam. Firs and a few thirsty maples shaded the dusty streets. An old spillway had been converted into a tunnel that led to the west gate. Beyond the dam, the spidery span of a highway bridge arched over the riverbed. People still used it.

He watched a bright-blue semi pull a triple trailer across the bridge. Beyond it he could see The Dalles. Metal-sided warehouses and a couple of ancient wooden grain elevators baked in the sun. Fruit, Carter remembered. And wheat. That was what people had grown around here, back when the river was full of water. Now they grew drought tolerant soybeans and sugar beets, all dependent on those blue veins full of water buried under his feet. Wind vanes turned steadily, ranked along the shelving banks like strange, metallic trees. The wh*omp-whomp-whomp* of their turning created a constant base note beneath the sounds of the day. Carter had a feeling he was going to get tired of that sound very quickly. Parallel strands of bright-orange wire fenced the compound on all sides, strung four inches apart on six-foot poles. Carter approached it cautiously.

"Don't touch it, sir. It'll knock you cold." Willis stepped up beside him. "It could kill you if you got tangled in it. A cut strand or a ground activates an alarm."

It hadn't stopped Greely, Carter thought sourly. Security better have found that hole. He stared at the orange wire, tired with a weariness that went beyond the physical. Why couldn't the people on the other side of that wire understand that only so much water existed? "Where do you keep the coffee?" Carter asked.

"This way, sir."

"Not today." Carter shook his head. He needed to know how his people ate, too. That mattered. "We'll hit the enlisted mess."

The noise level dropped by an order of magnitude as Carter walked through the door. The CO. It didn't quite get silent, but he felt the eyes as he picked up a tray at the end of the serving line. The mess was open, he noticed. Families could pay and eat here. Which meant that the food situation locally wasn't good — or at least it wasn't a good idea to shop locally. The families sat on one side of the hall, the active duty personnel on the other. Not many families this early. A very young woman with an infant in her lap was trying to hush a complaining three-year-old girl.

"The colonel opened the mess, sir. You got to go to Bonneville to buy a lot of stuff, these days." Willis held out a plate for scrambled eggs. "Gas costs over ten bucks a gallon out here."

Which most of the lower grades wouldn't be able to afford. "Why can't you shop in The Dalles?" Carter filled a mug with coffee — or what passed for coffee these days. "Local attitude?"

"It's not bad, sir." Willis stressed the words slightly. "The colonel opened the mess before we closed the base. You don't have much choice outside of the local market or the government store. The locals don't live so good, either."

This man didn't hate the locals, anyway. Why did Delgado? Carter picked up a glass of orange juice. Maybe that was why Willis hadn't included him this morning. Carter had a feeling that Willis was doing a bit of subtle propagandizing: *The situation doesn't have to be this bad. How about it, boss?*

They were all asking, every man and woman on the base. How about it, boss? How are you going to handle things? Carter felt the weight of those silent questions as he picked up his tray and turned away from the line. Then the child threw a bowl onto the floor with a clatter and launched herself into a screaming temper tantrum. The whole room went silent. The woman's face was red as she tried desperately to silence her daughter, and now the baby was crying. Carter looked away, straight into the agonized face of a Corporal across the room. Dad. Scared that Carter might just get pissed and close the mess.

It was tough for the enlisteds.

Carter waited until the woman looked up, then caught her eye. "Kids," he said, and smiled.

The food wasn't bad. Soy eggs and bacon, but who ate the real stuff these days. Johnny, he thought wryly. Maybe not even him. The orange juice was real, even if it was grown in a cell tank. Time breathed down his neck now. The staff meeting was coming up. Carter ate fast and pretended he wasn't aware of the inaudible and collective sigh of relief as he left the mess.

Delgado and Captain Arris, Security's CO from last night, waited for him in his office.

"There is no breach in the base perimeter." Arris's eyes were locked on Carter's left shoulder. "Sir."

"How did a civilian get in here?" From the corner of his eye, Carter watched Delgado scowl.

"I don't know, sir." Arris's face was stone. "No excuse, sir."

Shit on that. Families lived on this base and this could turn into a war zone any day. "Go find it," Carter said gently.

"Yes, sir." The captain saluted, spun on his heel, and marched out.

"I could have found out, sir." Delgado studied the ceiling. "If we'd arrested Greely."

"We don't play that way, Major," Carter snapped. Easy, he told himself. He needed this man, whether he liked him or not. "I'm going to be feeling my way around for awhile," he said, making his voice warmer. "The general warned me about Greely, and I'll keep my eyes open. If he's behind this, we'll get him."

"I hope so, sir." Delgado didn't sound convinced. "Just watch yourself, sir. They shot Colonel Watanabe in cold blood."

He needed to look into the evidence there, find out what had happened. Not now. The clock on the desk glared at him. "We've got a staff meeting in five minutes," he said. "Afterward, you can give me a tour." And tell me about Greely, Watanabe, and what you think is going on here, he didn't say.

The staff meeting was everybody's chance to size up the CO, and Carter's chance to take their measure. Operations, Communications, Pipeline Maintenance, Base Support, MPs, and even Battalion Aid; they all gave Carter a brief evaluation of their situation. It wasn't as bad as he had expected, and he felt a cautious relief as he listened. Tension here, yes, and hostility toward the locals, but morale seemed to be solid. Sabotage — aside from the two sniping incidents — had been limited to shooting out the guts of the wind turbines or busting the solar arrays that powered the pumps. The chief surgeon reported that stress levels on the base were within normal parameters for a low-threat combat zone. This wasn't a war. Yet.

That feeling was borne out as Carter toured the rest of the base. The comments he overheard were that the locals weren't too bad as a whole, but there was an open hatred for the few terrorists who had been doing the shooting. No, it wasn't a war yet, and he was going to make damn sure it didn't end up one.

It was midafternoon before he got a chance to tour Operations with Delgado. This was the nexus of the job — the air-conditioned heartbeat of their sector of the Pipeline. Carefully protected from dust by a double set of doors and an autonomous air-filtration system, the room was a maze of electronics. Inset terminals lined the four walls and the long stations that ran down the center of the room. Screens glowed with multicolored schematics, blinking numbers in green and amber monitoring water flow, turbulence, temperature, and pipewall stress. One entire wall was covered with a detailed topographical map of The Dalles sector of the Pipeline. Uniformed men and women sat at their stations, faces intent.

"This is the readout on the main flow." Major Carron, who had been conducting the tour, stopped beside a bank of four monitor screens.

"Everything is within normal parameters, sir." A small, red-headed lieutenant saluted, her eyes sweeping Carter with one quick, appraising glance.

"Tell me what you're doing." Carter leaned over her shoulder.

"Monitoring flow turbulence, sir." She pointed. "These screens give us a veiw of the Pipe's interior wall via optical fibers. Those screens give a readout from the flow sensors. An increase in turbulence means a leak. A sudden decrease indicates a failing pump, sir. The water backs up into the sumps."

"You see a lot of pump problems?"

"Yes, sir." The lieutenant's face was expressionless.

Courtesy of the locals. The lieutenant wasn't going to say it.

Carter frowned. Apart from the main Pipeline, The Dalles sector was responsible for the first miles of the Klamath Shunt, a major diversion that led down through the Klamath Aqueduct to augment the output of California's vast desalinization plants, watering the fertile Sacramento Valley. Turbulence and wear on the Pipeline was intense at the enormous valve complex of the Shunt. The Corps also monitored every local diversion line, every branch, and every individual tap line. Consumption was recorded by individual ration meters, but the Corps kept flow data on every line, no matter how small. If piracy was suspected, the flow rates could be retrieved and reviewed for evidence of a tampered meter or an illegal tap.

Diversion and branch lines were big enough to require leak monitoring. Carter prowled the Operations room, checking line codes against the big map, getting a feel for what water went where and how much. To his casual eye, it seemed like the local farmers used a lot of water. Carter resolved to look up some of the production stats for the high farmland in the Gorge, then compare it to what was coming out of the Willamette Valley, say. You didn't have the right to be wasteful. Not any more.

Carter jumped as a beeper went off. It snapped heads up from monitors, stiffened shoulders.

"Leak," The red headed lieutenant called from her station.

"How bad?" Carter leaned over her shoulder.

"Flow turbulence in the ninety-second subsector indicates a third stage leak, sir, with a priority rating of twenty-three point four percent."

The weary hours spent with the manuals and briefs were paying off. This was a small leak, possibly too small for a spotting crew to find on a chopper sweep, possibly a waste of their time when they might be needed elsewhere. Carter scowled at the numbers, aware that Delgado and the lieutenant were waiting for some kind of decision. The question was whether to send out a crew or not. Wasted crew hours would reflect poorly on the efficiency rating of the sector, but the leak might get worse if it went unpatched. Eventually it might graduate to a second stage leak with some measurable loss of flow in the lines. That would be bad for the farmers downflow, and bad for his record.

"Do we go?" Delgado asked.

Carter glanced at the map. Damn. Subsector 92 was clear out at the far end of their territory, near the west edge of the John Day sector. "Right away," he said. "Draw an APC from the motor pool." The teams had been using the standard 4x4s for patrol, but after Chicago, he was damned if he'd send people out in soft-skinned vehicles.

"With a gunner?" The glitter was back in Delgado's eye.

"Self defense only." He raised his voice slightly. "I don't want any accidents."

"Yes, sir." Delgado saluted, his face expressionless again.

Carter looked around the room, registering both the positive and negative reactions to his order. "Keep me posted." He turned back to the lieutenant. Carson, he read from her uniform. "Page me when the leak is patched."

"Yes sir."

She looked relieved. He wondered why. The order for self defense only? Carter looked at his watch. It was late. He sighed, smelling his own sweat, wishing for a shower and a few peaceful hours to relax and assimilate the day. Those hours would be better spent going over reports. No time to relax yet. The wind tugged at the loose fabric of his coverall as Carter left the building, and the level beams of the setting sun edged the rim of the dam with gold. A crumpled candy wrapper skidded along the concrete sidewalk, bounced over the low curb and into the street. Three lanky young enlisteds in khaki shorts crossed at the end of the street, laughing and talking loudly. The tall black kid in the middle carried a basketball, spinning it lightly on his fingertips. Showing off. Carter smiled as the kid flipped the ball easily to his buddy. It was cool enough for a pickup game now. Carter felt a little wistful.

He wouldn't have much time for basketball for a while. He turned down the narrow alley between two storage buildings. This was a natural shortcut to his quarters, and the buildings cut off the infernal wind. It was quiet, already dark with evening shadow. He passed a door and heard it open. Turning, he caught a glimpse of fast motion behind him, then someone slammed into his back and sent him stumbling forward. A hard forearm clamped across his throat, cutting off his air. Carter stabbed backward with his elbow, felt it connect. His attacker grunted hoarsely.

Carter twisted, lungs burning, stabbed back over his shoulder, aiming for eyes. Black spots wavered in his vision as someone grabbed his hair, yanked his head back and sideways. Carter caught a glimpse of red hair, a face. He gasped as the choking arm relaxed beneath his chin, sucked in a desperate lungful of air and something else, a cold, stinging nothing that numbed his lips and throat, numbed his chest, soaked upward into his brain and downward into his knees.

Floating, weightless, Carter watched the pale wall of the shed slide past him as he fell into a dark, cool, blackness.

CHAPTER FIVE

H eat woke him, searing heat that glared red through his closed eyelids. Thirst. He opened his eyes, squeezed them shut as light and pain lanced through his skull. Stones grated beneath his cheek. He was lying facedown in the dust. The alley . . . vague memory of a choking arm . . . darkness. Where was he? Carter got his knees under him, got halfway to his feet. Dun land and *light*. It began to revolve slowly and he lurched onto hands and knees again, retching bile onto the sunbaked clay between his palms.

The spasms eased finally, leaving him sweaty and shivering. Memory was coming back, slowly and in pieces. Cautiously he eased himself back into a sitting position; this time, the land stayed still. Empty hills stretched away on all sides, streaked with afternoon shadows. No road, no buildings — just dirt, sun, and rock. The shivering had stopped, and Carter wiped vomit from his chin, trying to think through the fierce ache in his skull. Someone had grabbed him right off the base and had dumped him out here. Nice going, he thought bitterly. Great start. Great security. He was naked except for his shorts. He touched his arm and winced. From the look of the sunburn, he'd been out here for a long time.

Here. Fear tightened his stomach and dewed his face with sweat. Where the hell was *here?* The dun, dead land marched away on all sides of him, broken by tilted bands of rock and gray clumps of struggling sage. Empty. He swallowed, his mouth dry as the ground. The riverbed and the highway could be in any direction.

He had better choose the right one.

He straightened, examining the horizon. The sun was setting beyond the shoulder of a mountain peak. West. So that was probably Mount Hood, unless the people who had jumped him had hauled him an awfully long way to dump him. Which they could have done. Better to assume he wasn't that far from the riverbed. It would be north. That way. Carter shaded his eyes. Walk that way and sooner or later he'd hit a road, a house, something.

Question was . . . would he reach it in time?

Carter clenched his teeth and staggered to his feet. He owed someone for this. For a moment, he swayed as the world revolved briefly, then it steadied. So far, so good. He had a couple of hours of daylight yet. People lived out here even if it didn't look like it. He'd see lights even a long way off. Carter picked out a thumb-shaped lump of rock to the north, fixed his eyes on it so he wouldn't wander, and started limping toward it.

It was tough going. His head stopped hurting after awhile, but thirst tortured him. He tried to chew some of the dusty sage leaves, but the stems cut his mouth and made him feel thirstier than before. His back stung. When he touched his shoulder, blisters burst beneath his fingers, spilling sticky fluid. He must have been unconscious in the sun for hours. Bastards.

Twilight was a blessing when it fell. An early moon rose, three-quarters full, shedding enough light to get by. It was harder to find north, but he managed to identify the Big Dipper, found the pole star and used that. The pleasant cool turned cold quickly. Before long he was shivering. And the landscape didn't change. He could have been walking in place. Going in circles.

Somewhere, he thought, they were laughing at him, sitting around, drinking beers. He clutched at that thought, squeezing hard rage from it, and for awhile it kept the cold and thirst at bay. Then a sharp piece of obsidian sliced his foot and tripped him onto his knees. He clutched at a rocky outcrop and hauled himself to his feet. His arm hurt and he touched the bend in his elbow gingerly. In the colorless moonlight he could just make out a dark bruise. Someone had shot him up with something. To ask him questions? For a moment the ache in his head intensified, and he had a vague memory of a voice.

Carter forced himself to keep going, limping badly now, barely able to swallow. Step by painful step, he kept going, feeling slippery blood on the stones beneath his cut foot. He started fuzzing in and out of consciousness, saw Johnny watching him with a smile, but his mouth was too dry to yell at him. Then Johnny turned into the kid in the VW, and Carter wanted to ask him what he'd meant to do, when a thin cry banished his ghost, bringing back the night and the cold and the pain.

The sound came again, like a baby crying. Coyotes? Wild dogs? Carter looked around, barely able to stay on his feet, searching for something he could use as a weapon. The moon had been so bright earlier, but it was dim now. Or maybe the darkness was thicker. The coyote or dog baby-cried again. Close. His foot slapped down hard, jolting his teeth together. A road. He stared at the pavement beneath his feet. Then something moved in the darkness behind him, coming at him. The coyote? Carter reached down to scoop up a rock, staggered, the moon wheeling overhead, his balance gone..

The road slammed against his hip and shoulder, knocking the breath out of him. It didn't hurt. It should have hurt. Hands grabbed him and he swung a fist, remembering hands holding him down, a voice asking, asking, asking through the pain in his head that tore him apart. He swung again, blindly.

"Hey, knock it off." High pitched voice. A hand locked around his wrist. "I'm trying to help you, okay? Take it easy."

Carter stopped fighting as his vision cleared. He was lying on his back on a road. The moon floated overhead, casting its pale light.

"What are you doing out here?" A woman knelt beside him, a thick, dark braid dangling over one shoulder. "What happened to you?"

His tongue wouldn't work right. He tried to ask for water, managed a noise, at least.

"Hang on."

She walked away and Carter struggled to his elbow, afraid suddenly that she would vanish, like Johnny, like the kid. But she reappeared in a few moments, a plastic jug and a cup in one hand, lit by the small, solar lantern in the other. She set the lantern down and water gurgled as she tilted the jug. The sound made him tremble.

"Here." She slid an arm beneath his shoulders. "Take it slow, okay? Or you'll just throw it all up, and it's all I have until we get to The Dalles."

He forced himself to sip the water when he wanted desperately to gulp it down. Nothing had ever tasted that good. She refilled the cup and he emptied it again. "Thanks," he gasped, finally able to speak. "Thanks a lot."

"I'm sorry if I scared you." She tilted her head and the lantern light burnished her skin to dark copper and pooled shadow beneath her high cheekbones. "I called but you didn't hear me."

"I thought I heard a coyote," Carter said. She was young. Twenty, maybe, dressed in faded jeans and a patched denim jacket. Hispanic, with a wide face and dark, tilted eyes. "I'm glad you weren't."

"Me, too. I'm Nita Montoya," he said gravely. "How did you end up out here? You might have died. Who did this to you?"

"My name's Carter Voltaire." He started to add that he was with the Corps, caught the words in time. Not out here. "I don't know who dumped me out here." He pushed himself into a sitting position. "But I'm sure going to find out."

"Not tonight." She touched his arm lightly, then got to her feet. "I'll bring my stuff here. I've got some extra clothes that might fit you."

She left him the light. He listened to the reassuring sound of her foot-steps, the crackled of the dry sage. In a few minutes she reappeared, lugging a frame pack and carrying a bundle in her arms. "You don't have to be afraid of the night," she said as she laid the bundle on the ground. "Don't blame the land. It isn't evil."

"I'm not . . ." He stopped. "Yeah, I guess I am." He hunched his shoulders, winced as the blistered skin puckered. "It's so damn big. And empty. You could die out here and nobody would know."

"That's true." She sat down beside him and reached for the pack. "But you can die anywhere. I know what lives out here." A smile warmed her voice. "I know what can eat me and how to avoid being eaten. Towns scare me," she said softly. "People can be so full of ugliness."

Ugliness? Carter thought of Chicago. "Maybe, but it still bothers me. All this dead emptiness."

"Empty yes, but not dead." That smile glimmered in her voice again. She pulled a tight roll of fabric from her pack, shook it out. "You'll find life in the cracks, even if you don't see it; mice, insects, the tough weeds, even flowers. This shirt should fit and maybe the jeans. They're David's. My husband's." She handed them to him.

He reached for the clothes and sucked in a harsh breath. His sun-burned back had stiffened while he sat, and it felt as if his skin was splitting open.

Nita knelt behind him with the lantern, hissed between her teeth. "I didn't realize it was so bad."

Carter winced as she ran her flingers lightly across his shoulders. "I was out in the sun for awhile."

"Yes, you were." She fumbled again in her pack and took out a small plastic tub. "This will help. You're bad all over, but your back is the worst."

"No kidding," he said dryly. Even the cool touch of the salve hurt like hell. "What are *you* doing out here in the middle of nowhere?"

"It's not the middle of nowhere." The smile warmed her voice again. "We're not too far south of The Dalles." She capped the tub and tucked it back into the pack. "I'm on my way there. To meet David. He works for the Army." She reached for the shirt. "I'll help you. You'll be warmer."

"What's his last name?" Carter gritted his teeth as he eased his arm through the shirt sleeve. "Maybe I know him."

"You're from there?" Hope leaped in her voice. "David Ascher. He's in his forties, with curly brown hair. It's just going gray. Do you know him?"

"I'm sorry." Carter buttoned the shirt, grateful for its warmth. This David was bigger than he. He'd have to use something for a belt. "Is he a civilian?" He tugged the jeans on.

"Yes." Her shoulders slumped. "You're still shivering. You can wrap my sleeping bag around you."

He was shivering, although he didn't feel particularly cold. That was probably bad. Teeth chattering, he zipped the too-large jeans, wondering what they'd used on him. They. The enemy. He wondered if it was Greely.

Nita draped a patched sleeping bag around his shoulders. "David has to be in The Dalles." She spoke softly, as if she was talking to herself. "I'm sure he's there."

Carter looked at her more closely, seeing tears in her eyes. She wasn't sure at all. "Where are you from?" he asked her gently.

"West of Salem," she said. She lifted her chin. "We hunted bees in the mountains."

A thin cry made Carter jump. A baby? That's what he'd heard and not a coyote? Incredulous, he watched her lift an infant from the bundled cloth. "You walked all the way from Salem with him?"

"Her." Nita sounded amused. "This is Rachel. I hitched a lot and yes, I walked. How do you get around where you come from, anyway? Go back to sleep, sweetheart." She rocked the baby gently. "You're not really hungry."

She had walked all this way with her child in her arms. Carter felt a small, hot anger for the man who had left her to do that.

She lifted her head suddenly to look at him, her expression defensive. "The bees were dying," she said sharply. "We couldn't make it trading honey any more, and we had to do something. A friend told him about this job with the Corps."

"Listen, I'm with the Corps, in The Dalles. I'm the new CO." Carter watched her face, half expecting hostility. "I can check on David for you. If he ever worked for us, I can find the records."

"Could you do that?"

"Yes." She was almost beautiful when she smiled like that. "I owe you a lot more than that."

"No, you don't." She seemed genuinely surprised by his words. "Out here, you don't just turn away. It could be you, tomorrow. Remember that, okay?" She smiled. "Pay me back that way."

"I will." The sleeping bag seemed to be helping. The shivering wasn't so bad. "I don't understand this world," he said. "And I need to. Fast."

"Why?" She tugged at her braid, tossed it back over her shoulder. "Why is it so important?"

He didn't have the words to explain. He had a feeling this land had rules that he didn't know yet, and if he didn't learn them in time . . . he'd make the wrong decision.

And end up with another Chicago.

"You'll be all right." She took his hand in hers. Fingers closing firm and cool around his.

"I hope so." He looked restlessly northward, into the darkness beyond the lantern's yellow pool. "People have to be out looking for me. You don't have a cell, do you?"

"A phone?" She sounded amused. "You need to rest. We'll just wait. I don't have any extra shoes and your feet are a mess. Someone will come by and we'll get a ride. People still drive on this road. It's nice and clean. Lots of traffic."

As if her words had conjured it, the distant sound of an engine broke the silence. Someone. Carter staggered to his feet, wincing at the pain.

"Not yet." Nita clicked off the lantern. "Get down." She pulled him off the asphalt, into the sparse sage. "Out here, at night, you want to know who is driving before you ask for a ride. Sometimes it matters, Carter." She tucked her sleeping daughter against her side.

"How are you going to know who's driving in the dark?"

She didn't answer, but he crouched beside her, nervous now. The engine growled suddenly louder. Twin cones of yellow light splashed across the landscape, picking out rocks and sage, casting stark shadows. Carter blinked, momentarily blinded by the light. The car was a 4x4, going slowly, as if the driver was scanning the sides of the road.

Nita's hand closed tight on his arm and Carter pressed himself against the rocky ground, infected by her caution. The car cruised by. The turreted castle gleamed on the door, illuminated by the backsplash of the headlights. With a whoop, Carter starggered to his feet. For an awful moment he thought the car would drive on down the road, disappear into the darkness. "Here," he yelled. "I'm here!"

Brake lights glowed and flashed into white backup lights. With a growl from the transmission, the car backed toward him. It stopped and a uniformed man sprange out. "Colonel? Is that you?"

Delgado's voice. "Yes! Major." Carter limped forward. "Am I ever glad to see you."

"My God, we all thought you were dead, sir." Delgado grabbed him by the shoulders, eyebrows rising as he took in Carter's clothes. "I was expecting to find a body. What happened?"

"Somebody jumped me on the base." Carter leaned against the car, his knees shaky again.

"Are you hurt?" Delgado caught his arm and opened the door. "Sit down, sir. Should I call for an ambulance?"

"I'm just dehydrated. And sunburned." Carter sagged gratefully onto the car's front seat and grimaced. "I don't do so well, hiking barefoot."

"Greely really screwed up this time." Delgado's tone had gone cold. "He didn't figure on us finding you in time. You out there — freeze!"

He dropped into a half crouch, yanking his pistol from his unsnapped holster.

"Don't," Carter yelled. "She's with me." God. Carter ran a shaky hand across his face as Delgado holstered his weapon. "Nita, it's okay. She helped me, Delgado. We'll give you a ride into town."

"I don't mind walking." Nita stepped cautiously into the light. She was clutching Rachel tightly and her dark eyes were wide. "I expected to walk."

"I'm sorry, Nita." Carter held out a hand. "A ride's the least I can do. You're out of water, remember? Because of me. Major, put her stuff in the back."

"Civilians don't ride in Corps rigs," Delgado said, but he said it under his breath, bending to drop the Chevy's rear gate as he did.

Reluctantly, Nita handed him her pack and empty jugs. Rachel had waked and was fussing, waving tiny fists. "I don't know," Nita said, and her eyes followed Delgado.

"Come on." Carter tried to ease her nervousness. "Get in. I'll worry about you out here by yourself."

"I get along out here a lot better than you do." But she gave him a faint smile.

Delgado was calling in to the base to let them know that he'd found Carter. "I want to get you into the infirmary pronto." He pocketed his cell and put the car into gear.

"What makes you think Greely was behind this?" Carter clung to the dash, trying to keep his blistered back off the seat.

"Who else, sir?" Delgado glowered at Nita in the rearview mirror. "There's a car missing. I figure Greely wanted to make it look like you'd walked away from a breakdown and got lost. Quite a coincidence that she happened to run into you."

"I ran into her," Carter snapped. "I can almost remember one of them. It'll come to me. Eventually."

"It'll be Greely. I know that guy."

In the rear seat, the baby was crying in short, breathy bursts of noise. "Is she all right?" Carter twisted painfully to peer over the back of the seat.

"She's just upset." Nita looked pale and tense in the glow of the panel light.

"Are *you* all right?" Poor kid. Delgado had scared the crap out of her.

"I'm fine." She shook her head impatiently. "Will you let me out on the edge of town, please?"

"I owe you more water, at least." They were speeding down a long hill now, and Carter could see the twinkle of curfew-exempt lights in The Dalles, although the base was still invisible. A few lights had never looked so good.

"We can take you to a motel. I'll pay for a few nights. That'll give me some time to check on your husband."

"No." She held her daughter close, eyes on Delgado's back. "I appreciate it, but no thank you. You can let me out here," she said as they reached the bottom of the hill.

Delgado pulled over to the side of the road with a screech of brakes. He jumped out and went around to the rear of the car, dumping Nita's pack unceremoniously onto the ground.

"Wait a minute." Carter flung the door open and struggled to his feet.

She had tucked her daughter into a cloth sling across her chest. The baby was quieter now, whimpering softly. With a deft twist she shrugged the pack onto her shoulders.

"Wait." He had a feeling she would vanish and he'd never see her again. "How do I get in touch with you? About your husband?" That was the talisman, the magic charm that brought the smile back into her eyes. "I've got to give you your clothes back, too," he said quickly.

"I'll come to the base, okay?" She touched his hand lightly. "I'll ask for you."

He watched her walk away into the dark, light-headed and dizzy with exhaustion and dehydration. He wondered who the hell David Ascher was, and why he had left her. And he found himself hoping he didn't find that name in the Corps personnel files.

"Come on, Colonel." Delgado put a firm hand under his elbow. "You got a date with the infirmary, sir. You look like you're gonna pass out."

CHAPTER SIX

You're damn lucky Delgado found you in time." General Hastings' face filled the screen on Carter's desk. "I'd file charges against Greely's bunch tomorrow, but that damned judge Lindstrom won't issue a warrant. He's been on the side of the Coalition since day one."

"There's no hard evidence that the Coalition was behind it." Carter kept his tone as neutral as possible. "Someone got onto the base with a forged pass. The guard went through our file of local troublemakers, but he couldn't make a positive ID. It wasn't Greely. Believe me, I stuck the photo right under his nose."

"He wouldn't be at the wheel." Hastings' snort was contemptuous. "He's not stupid."

Carter shut up. No point in continuing this discussion. It might well have been some stooge of Greely's. But Greely had called Carter the day after Delgado had brought him in. He'd been upset — worried that Carter would blame the Coalition. And he'd been ignorant of the circumstances of the kidnap incident . . . or a damn good actor. Another player here? Who? Carter sighed. "I saw one of 'em. I wish I could remember him clearly enough for an ID."

"Me, too." Hastings' face enlarged, as if he had leaned closer to his terminal pickup. "I wish I knew what they were after. It'd give me a better idea of what we can expect around here."

Carter had a feeling that Hastings wouldn't have grieved much if they'd ODed him in the process. Tough luck, getting stuck with this bastard, but he'd survived Hastings' type before. Do your job well, keep a low profile, and pray you got transferred out before you collected too many poor evaluations.

"I assume you've dealt with your security problem."

"Yes, sir." Which was a flat lie. Arris still couldn't find Greely's goddamned hole. Carter's back was itching again and the need to scratch made him sweat. His skin was peeling off in sheets and the bloody itching never stopped. "That kidnap bothers me," he said slowly. "They must have guessed that the broken down car would put someone on my track the minute you put a chopper into the air." Delgado had been right about that stunt. Carter shook his head. "They also had to figure that I'd walk north, heading for the riverbed. If I did, I was bound to cross that road. People use it all the time. It was a better than even chance that someone would find me." Carter scowled at the fading bruise of the injection site. "I don't think they meant to kill me."

Hastings grunted.

"We had another sabotage attempt last night," Carter continued doggedly. He reached for the hardcopy report of last night's incident. The skin between his shoulder blades itched and he willed it to stop. It didn't stop. "One of the patrols scared them off. The shaped charge they left behind would have punched a pretty good hole in the Pipe. Quite professional. I need more people," he said bluntly. "I've got everyone putting in extra duty hours already. We can't keep this up."

"I can't give you any more." Hastings looked down at his desk. "Anything else to report, Colonel?"

"General, morale is going downhill fast. These doubled patrols might stop the sabotage, but I'm running everyone ragged." He had hired civilians to help with the mess and housekeeping, but attrition was high. Working for the uniforms didn't make you very popular in town.

Hastings was scowling. "I sent in a request for more troops and got turned down. Water Policy is soft-pedaling. Probably because of Chicago." His stare was accusing. "A lot of people thought we overreacted there — thanks to the damn media." His lips twitched as if he wanted to spit. "If you start a war in The Dalles, Colonel, you're on your own."

Thanks for nothing. Carter clenched his teeth against the need to scratch. Johnny was going to be in town tomorrow. He'd ask him if this Water Policy line was on the level. The same ugly darkness of Chicago was starting to seep in here. Us and Them. Carter realized he was scratching his shoulder, yanked his hand away. "Sir?" He drew a deep breath. "I've talked to Greely," he said. "I'm going to meet with the Coalition leaders this afternoon."

"Are you crazy?"

Hastings wasn't reacting any better than Delgado had. "No, sir. If we're going to keep a lid on things, we have to do some talking. Or we *will* have a war on our hands." He hesitated, gauging Hastings' frown. "I might pick up some critical details, sir."

"You might get yourself killed this time. You're underestimating Greely. He is the Coalition."

"Believe me, I'm not underestimating him."

"Aren't you?" Hastings' expression was hard. "He worked for the Corps as a civilian employee, back when he was a scruffy kid. It was my first year here in Bonneville. He's bright, all right. He worked up to surveyor's assistant, then he ran off with some pretty expensive equipment. He played a scam all over the eastern half of Washington and Oregon, pretending to be a Corps surveyor. He took what he wanted and paid people off in fake Corps scrip. This is the con man you're dealing with, Voltaire. Don't get too wowed by that golden tongue. He's had a lot of practice."

Huh. Carter frowned down at the hardcopy scattered across his desk. That might put a new twist on things. "I still need to go."

"It's too dangerous."

"Are you ordering me not to attend this meeting, sir?" Their eyes locked.

"Hell, no." Hastings' face receded, as if he had leaned back in his chair. "It's your sector. You're the CO. You get to screw up on your own, but you'd better keep Watanabe in mind. He got soft on the Coalition, too."

"So I hear." Carter saluted crisply. "Thank you, sir." And go to hell.

The screen blanked, and Carter leaned back in his chair, sweating in spite of the air-conditioning. Hastings had made it clear. Fuck up and it was Carter's ass on the line, not his. He picked up the report of last night's sabotage attempt, tossed it back onto the desk. It wasn't that hard to punch a hole in the Pipe, and the local pumping stations were easy targets. These bastards could wear them out playing hide and seek. Things were tense between Corps and locals, but not impossible. Not yet. But it was only a matter of time before some tired, edgy trooper shot an innocent local by mistake. That could blow it, good.

His back was driving him nuts. Carter unzipped his coverall and reached for the analgesic cream the doc had given him. It didn't work as well as Nita's salve had, he thought sourly. She had never come to the base, but no David Ascher had ever worked for the Corps. Maybe she found him somewhere else, or maybe she just moved on. Carter tossed the tube back into his drawer and slammed it shut. He'd meant to ask around for her in town to return the clothes, but he hadn't had the time. No, he hadn't made the time. He hadn't wanted to hear that she'd found her husband. It was almost time to leave for the Coalition meeting. Carter pushed her face out of his mind and put in a call for Delgado. It would be good to see Johnny tomorrow. Maybe he could put this mess into some kind of perspective.

*

The meeting was held in a house. It stood back from the two lane highway that wound up the side of the Gorge on its way toward Dufur and on southward, and had once been one of several suburban residences built close together on the steep hillside. A satellite dish gleamed on the roof. The houses on either side were dark, although Carter thought he caught the glimmer of a dim light in one upstairs room. Candle or lantern? It was half an hour past the power curfew. As they drove up, Carter made out the remains of a flagstone patio beside the house. Skeletons of yard furniture rusted beneath the eaves, their plastic webbing shredded to colorless fringe.

"I don't like this place, sir." Delgado set the brake hard.

"You'd rather we were meeting in a church?" Carter said easily. "If they're going to shoot us, they could do it there just as easily."

"Not funny, sir." Delgado frowned. "I know this crowd, remember?"

"Yeah, I remember." He rubbed his shoulder blades against the seat back. "I think we're safe enough. If the Coalition is behind the sabotage, they're being too careful about covering their tracks to blow it so openly. It's on the record where we are and who we're meeting." Neither of them was armed. Delgado hadn't liked that at all, and he'd thought about coming alone. But Delgado, with all his hostility, was a different perspective. He wanted that perspective.

"Wait a minute." He put a hand on Delgado's arm as he started to get out. "My job is to keep the water running, and I don't want to spill any more Army blood to do it. The Coalition may not like us and vice versa, but if they're not behind the sabotage, we need them. You will keep your opinions to yourself, tonight. Am I understood?"

"Yes. Sir."

"But I want you to listen to every word and give those opinions to me afterward. Got it?"

"Yes, sir," Delgado said grimly.

They climbed the sagging porch steps cautiously. Light seeped through the thick curtains at the windows. The house faced west, so the curtains were heavy enough to shut out the afternoon, sun, faced with sheets of silvery mylar. The warped boards of the porch creaked loudly under their feet and the door opened.

"Colonel Voltaire." Dan Greely stood in the doorway, silhouetted by the light. "I'm glad you came." He held out his hand.

"This is Major Delgado," Carter said as he returned Greely's brief, firm grip.

"We've met." Greely withdrew his hand smoothly when Delgado ignored it. "Everyone else is here." He stepped aside. "Come in."

A wooden table occupied one end of the long room, opposite an old sofa and two upholstered chairs. A cluttered desk stood against the wall with a battered laptop. Carter wondered if they had hacked the Corps cloud. The Dalles didn't have a wireless server. Faded wallpaper boasted a ghostly memory of flowers, and the carpet was worn but clean. Three women and three men sat at the table, their faces stark and shadowed in the light of two solar lanterns that hung from an overhead chandelier. They were all in their forties at least. One woman looked older, her face lined and etched by wind and sun. Her wispy hair was gray and she alone smiled. The others seemed about as thrilled with this party as Delgado.

Carter tried to file names with faces as Dan introduced the four soaker-hose farmers and two town merchants who made up the decision-making core of the Coalition. The air in the room felt stuffy, charged with tension. Carter sat down, and after the briefest hesitation Delgado took a seat, too.

"Water?" Greely carried a plastic pitcher to the table and began to fill the empty glasses in front of each person. Everyone drank, or at least sipped a little, their expressions formal. A ritual? Carter drank some of the cool water and lifted his glass in a sort of salute. Delgado stared straight ahead, his own glass untouched.

"So how come you're here?" One of the farmers sat forward, thick arms bulging under the tight sleeves of his tee shirt. "You Army people don't give a crap about us."

Nice start. "We do give a crap, or I wouldn't be here." Carter set his glass down. Harold Ransom; he dredged the name from Greely's introductions. A beet and soy farmer. "We need to talk. This sabotage is hurting everyone and it's not going to bring one more drop of water down the Pipeline, or make it one cent cheaper."

Silence settled over the table as Ransom's face reddened. "You really think we're doing this? Cutting our own throats?" He half rose, muscles cording in his arms. "We're the ones going thirsty. Not you. You bastards keep cutting our ration and I've seen *flowers* growing on that damn base. You think we're that dumb, do you?"

"I don't know if you're dumb or not." Carter shrugged. "If you're not, then help us catch the people who *are* sabotaging the Pipe."

"You ain't really looking." Ransom snorted. "You've already decided it's us."

"*I* haven't decided anything. Yet."

Ransom made a rude noise.

The gray-haired woman cleared her throat. "I've got three rose bushes in my garden, Harold. I'm willing to spend water money on them. I don't see why Army people can't grow flowers, too," she said gently. "It doesn't mean they're stealing it."

Ransom grunted.

"Colonel Voltaire's willing to talk to us." Greely leaned forward. "That's a start. How long do you think our crops are going to last if someone wrecks the Pipe and all the water stops tomorrow?"

"That's not what's bothering me," Ransom growled. "Down in the Valley, they arrested those folks who wouldn't pay the new water tax, remember? Sent 'em to prison and took their land. We're gettin' set up for that, and you bet the Army'll get their cut. You're awfully damn hot to be buddies with the uniforms." He glared at Greely. "You gonna get a cut, too? For keeping us quiet?"

"Knock it off, Harold." The gray-haired woman's voice wasn't gentle this time. "Try thinking for a change."

The hose farmer grunted again, but he looked away.

Sandy Corbett. Carter studied her and she noticed, gave him a brief sharp look, then turned to the others. "Dan's stood out in front around here for longer than you've been growing weeds," she said in a crisp, clear voice. "He's paid a stiff price for doing it, too, which is more than I can say for you, Harold Ransom. We've all got an interest in stopping this sabotage stuff before it gets worse. Yes, we've been blamed for this. What do you expect? We've been giving Bonneville trouble for years, and doing it quite well, too." She smiled and a dimple showed in her dry, weathered cheek. "This time, people have been killed." Her expression sobered. "So what if they're Army? It could be one of us next time. Whoever is doing this does not have our best interests at heart. Maybe we can work together with the Colonel here and maybe we can't, but we won't get anywhere if we pick a new fight every time he opens his mouth."

"Okay." Ransom shoved his fists into his pockets. "I'm done, Sandy. I'll shut up."

Carter cleared his throat, watching the eyes shift his way. "Water's tight," he said. "Mexico's screaming about its water share falling off. The media doesn't have the story yet, but there's a possibility that Canada may pull out of the Alliance. If that happens, we're going to face a major short-fall. All of us. That's why agricultural rations have been cut lately — to keep the Alliance in one piece." Bless you, Johnny, for keeping me in the loop, Carter thought. The men and women around the table were listening to him at last. Carter met the eyes that didn't shift away from his — every-one but Ransom and a merchant whose name had slipped past him. I know you folks are tight," he said slowly. "There's nothing the Corps can do about that."

"I don't know." Sandy Corbett looked troubled. "I keep hearing that the valleys aren't getting cut — that they're getting the water you're taking away from us."

Carter had been waiting for this accusation. "They aren't getting cut as badly." He watched them bristle. "I called up the numbers. A lot of water goes down the Klamath and Willamette shunts, but that's where the production is." He opened the folder he'd brought and took out the sheaf of hardcopy he'd printed up that afternoon. "Take a look for yourselves." He handed around the pages. 'We're pulling our maximum share out of the Trench Reservoir. Per acre-foot of water, the Sacramento and Willamette valleys are leading you in production by a factor of fifteen percent." He paused, waiting as they turned pages. "Those numbers count," he said flatly. "A lot of people have to eat."

"So do we." Ransom tossed his copy down. The white pages spilled off the table, fluttering to the floor. "The valleys are all big ag-plexes, growing biomass." His lips twisted. "They're growing salt-tolerant stuff for the tanks and I'll bet you ain't counting the seawater they mix into the irrigation lines, either."

"I figured in the seawater. They still get fifteen percent more production for every gallon of sweet water they use. Why don't you put in biomass shrubs up here?"

The silence slapped him in the face. Wrong thing to say. Even the Corbett woman looked angry and Greely was staring at the tabletop.

Ransom pushed his chair back with a scrape that shattered the silence. "You uniforms really don't give a shit. I'm wasting my time." He spat.

The glob of spittle landed on the toe of Carter's boot. From the corner of his eye, Carter saw Delgado stiffen. "Hold it," he barked.

For a moment they all froze. "I'm sorry." He kept his eyes on Ransom's face. "I'm new here. Tell me why biomass won't work for you. I'm asking."

The heavyset farmer hesitated, chewing his lip, scowling at Carter. He glared at the door, hunched his shoulders. "Takes three years to get a decent first crop," he said harshly. "And you don't really make much unless you got access to cheap seawater. We don't. You gonna feed my kids for three years while I wait to harvest? We don't have no savings. Not after we pay your damn water bill. Yeah, I can buy a start on credit from Pacific Bio. Then they'd own me, just like they own the clone-stock, and they'd own my land. You think I'll ever get free of that debt, Mr. Corps man? You checked to find out who really owns the Valley? Huh?"

"I will check." Carter frowned. "What about government loans or a subsidy?"

Ransom's laugh was bitter.

Hell, it had been a stupid question. Carter rubbed his face wearily. "The welfare camps ate it all. There wasn't any extra money."

"It's not just the wait or the loans to buy clone-stock." Sandy Corbett spoke up. "They're using seawater to irrigate down in the valleys because it's cheap to pump in from the coast and the clones can take it, but the salt builds up in the soil. You go look at that land," she said softly. "Nothing grows there but the clones. The salt kills everything else. Once you start growing bushes, you can't stop. Once you start growing them, the land dies."

"Amen," someone murmured.

Carter nodded. He'd been down in the Valley. He'd noticed the salt crusts, but after Michigan's bed, it had seemed normal. He hadn't really looked at the land. "I'll do what I can to keep your water from getting cut any further." Carter looked at the wary, sundried faces one by one. "That's all I can promise, and you're going to have to help me stop this sabotage. I can't argue for more water if we're losing it to leaks."

"We've been trying to catch the suckers." Another of the hose farmers spoke up. "Dan's organized some patrols, but there's a lot of Pipe out there."

"And your soldiers shoot at us," Sandy Corbett added with a frown. "It's dangerous to go anywhere near the Pipeline any more."

"They're under orders to return fire only."

"You'd better check on that," she said tartly.

"I will. We have to work together on this." Carter ignored Delgado's restless movement of protest. "I'd like to use civilian and Crops patrols on the line. My people are wearing out. It would take some of the pressure off them if we could coordinate our efforts."

"It's funny." Sandy Corbett frowned into her glass. "In a town as small as The Dalles, you hear everything. You know who's in bed with whom and who's sneaking around where they shouldn't be." She turned the glass slowly between her fingers. "No one knows who's behind the sabotage. We should know."

"So it's not local?" Carter frowned

"No." She shook her head. "But whoever they are, they know this part of the country awfully well."

"And why are they doing it?" Carter frowned down at the papers stacked in front of him, listening to their silence. "I'll do what I can." He shuffled the papers back into his folder. "I hope we can work together on this thing."

"I think we've made a start," Greely said.

"We have, indeed." Sandy Corbett stood up, pushing hair back from her square face. "I figured Bonneville was going to stick us with a real bastard after Mike got murdered." She gave Carter a smile and stuck out her hand. "I'm glad we pulled you."

Her smile was warm and genuine and he returned her firm grip. These people might be telling the truth. As they saw it. He was offered more hands, shook, and was given murmured farewells from everyone except Ransom, who had left the room silently and by himself. Greely waited for Carter on the porch. It was full dark now, and the wind was picking up. "I'm impressed." Greely grinned crookedly. "You handled Harold, and Harold isn't easy to handle."

"You didn't give me much help," Carter said shortly.

"You're right, I didn't." Greely sighed. "You heard Harold. He thinks I've sold out and he's probably not the only one. You didn't really need me." His grin flashed briefly. "You were doing fine on your own."

In spite of his light tone, Ransom's accusation had clearly stung. This man didn't fit the picture Hastings had painted. "I was serious about running civilian patrols," Carter said slowly. "They'd have to operate under Corps NCOs, though. Do you think you can organize it?"

"I'll try." Greely frowned. "We've had some ugly incidents around here. Uniforms aren't too popular."

"Neither are locals, on my side of the fence," Carter said dryly. "I'll have my officers pick level-headed people for the mixed patrols."

"I can tap people who'll behave themselves. I think it's worth trying." Greely sighed. "You have to understand the situation here. We fight every day just to stay alive. We fight drought, dust storms, debt, and bad crop prices. We don't know how to stop fighting any more." He ran a hand through his graying hair. "Me, I'm tired. I'd like to get through this without any more bloodshed."

"Amen," Carter said.

Greely gave him a quick look.

"Do you ever see yesterday?" Carter looked down the hill, toward the riverbed. It was invisible in the darkness. "A glimpse of how it used to be?"

"No." Greely sounded puzzled. "That would be a hell of a vision." He was silent for a moment, his eyes, too, on the distant, invisible riverbed. "I don't know if I'd want that kind of vision," he said slowly. "I don't think I'd want to really know what we've lost."

"Hastings told me you worked for the Corps," Carter said bluntly. "He told me you ran a scam out in the Dry, pretending you were a Corps surveyor."

Greely didn't answer and Carter watched the man's weary profile.

At last he sighed and faced Carter. "Yeah, I did that. I was twenty." He looked down at his hands, turning them slowly palm up. "I stole uniforms, gear. I went around pretending that I was surveying for a new shunt line. I'd been begging for most of my life and I was tired of begging. I hurt a lot of people." He let his hands drop slowly to his sides, his eyes steady on Carter's face. "I gave people hope and then I left it to die. I went to prison for it, finally. A lot of years later. When it was convenient for General Hastings. I spent three years behind bars, and while I was there, a good friend of mine got shot. We'd been organizing a water strike here in The Dalles. He had a wife and three kids. If I hadn't been in prison, Sam might not have died." He shrugged heavily. "Or maybe they would have killed both of us. I guess I'll never know."

"Pick your teams," Carter said. "And we'll set up a schedule. You can reach me at the base any time. I'll leave word at both gates."

"Thanks." Greely held out his hand and Carter clasped it.

Delgado was waiting for him beside the stairs, just out of their sight. Eavesdropping? Carter clicked on his flash as he went down the steps. "What's your opinion?"

"They're stringing you along, sir." Delgado sounded sullen. "They're setting you up, like they did Watanabe." He spat. "That dude is slick."

"Hold it." Carter put out a hand as Delgado opened the car door. "How come you hate these people so much?"

"I don't hate them. Sir." Delgado stood stiff and still

"I don't want to request your transfer," Carter said slowly. "But your attitude is going to cause problems. If we don't clear this up right now, it goes in tomorrow."

"You want to clear things up, sir?" Delgado's eyes gleamed in the light from the flash. "I'll clear it up for you. My brother was here at The Dalles." He spoke so softly that Carter could barely make out the words. "He was out chasing a leak last fall — on his own, because we were only running two to a spotter crew back then and his buddy had gotten sick. Some hick picked him off with a thirty-thirty. He crawled a half mile through dust and rock to reach the highway, almost made it before he bled to death. Sonny was nineteen. He was the first one the hicks got."

"I didn't see his name on the report," Carter said.

"Mom remarried. Sonny was my half brother. Sonny Espinoza. He went into the Corps because I was in it. He was a kid, sir. He wasn't even old enough to drink."

"I'm sorry."

"You think they're decent folk, just because they talk nice to you. You want to believe Greely 'cause he spins a sweet line. They'll kill you in a second if they think it'll get 'em more water. That's all that counts for them. And we're in the way. That's how they see it. We're the enemy."

Delgado slid onto the front seat. "Why don't you worry about your own people instead of the hicks?"

"That's enough, Major." Carter flushed. "I'm doing this *because* I care about my people. Go on back to the base. I'm going to walk."

"You sure you want to walk, sir?" Delgado's face was cold. "If you meet any hicks, they may change your mind for you about how nice they are. You'd better ride, sir."

"Drive back to the base, Major." Carter stepped back as Delgado gunned the engine and pulled away from the house. Easy, he told himself as the car's taillights vanished around the corner. Delgado's attitude was understandable, even if it was out of line. It was the crack about taking care of his people that had stung.

It wouldn't have bothered him if he were sure of himself here.

Damn it.

Carter started down the hill, walking fast. The major was going to get a transfer. Immediately. He had reasons for his feelings, but cooperation was their only hope, and he had no business being here. If the Coalition wasn't behind the sabotage, who was? Bitter locals, Carter guessed, no matter what the Corbett woman thought. Revenge. Carter made a mental note to check on local bankruptcy and foreclosure records. Maybe something would click. And what about Dan Greely? Carter let his breath out slowly. *I gave people hope and then I left it to die*, he had said. He'd heard shame in those words.

Debris skittered dryly across the asphalt. To the west, the town was almost completely dark. Electricity came from the few operating nuclear plants, from wind or solar batteries, and it cost a lot. Without energy, Carter thought bitterly, civilization rolls back a thousand years or so. Technology had ground to a crawl as the Middle East's oil went up in vast funeral pyres and the hydroelectric dams went dry. The economy had tottered into the Crash.

The moon was up now, low enough on the horizon to be blocked by the rim of the Gorge. Carter could just make out the gray mass of the concrete ramp that led to the highway bridge. He walked slowly, paying attention to the night noises, using his flash as little as possible. Delgado had probably been right about the risk. He'd been trying to prove something to Delgado — or had it been to himself? Carter grimaced. He should be safe enough. Most of the trouble had come from soldiers and locals mixing at local bars. His route bypassed town, and the truck plaza was no danger. Truckers stayed out of politics.

Delgado had let Nita off somewhere around here. He wondered if she was still in The Dalles. Six semi rigs bulked darkly in the plaza lot and lights gleamed in the windows of the old motel where the truckers stayed. The riverbed yawned beyond the motel, a vast trench of deeper darkness. In the old days they had shipped wheat down the river on barges. Big boats. That was a weird image — a river of water as a highway.

A small noise brought Carter to attention. Footsteps? He slowed. Yes. More than one person, and they weren't trying to be quiet anymore. Carter put his head down and walked faster, listening hard. He might make it to the gate if they thought he hadn't noticed them.

The footsteps broke into a run. "Get him," someone yelled.

Carter ran. The gate wasn't impossibly far away, but he was panting after only a few yards, his salt-damaged lungs burning with each labored breath. He risked a quick glance over his shoulder. Three of them, and they were catching up. Too late to try for the truck plaza. Carter veered off the asphalt, running down into the rocky scrub that flanked the road. His only hope was to lose them, but the rising moon flooded the ground with light. Gasping, Carter stumbled into the dark mouth of a huge culvert that ran beneath the high berm of the interstate. No hope of losing them and he hadn't gone armed to the meeting. They must have seen him.

Black darkness filled the culvert. Carter crouched against the concrete wall. A figure skidded into view and Carter struck hard, his fist sinking into the man's belly. He was small and went down easily, retching and gasping as he rolled in the dust. The other two were right behind him. They spread out to flank him. Kids. Carter's throat tightened. They were just kids. He backed warily, keeping them both in view. One of them — a skinny boy with a ponytail of dark hair — edged into the mouth of the culvert, a baseball bat cocked in his hands. Carter dropped into a crouch, his belly full of ice, glad of the wall behind him. The other kid had a knife. If they knew what they were doing, he was dead.

"Fuckin' uniform, you lookin' for action, huh? We'll show you action." The skinny kid rushed him.

Carter ducked the bat's swing with an inch to spare and heard a dull crack as it hit the wall. The impact jarred it out of the kid's hands. As he grabbed for it, Carter chopped him at the base of the skull. The other kid was on him, knife flashing as he slashed at Carter's face. Carter chopped his wrist aside, grabbed it, spun and used the kid's momentum to throw him hard and clean. The knife clattered somewhere and the kid hit the ground flat on his back with a grunt of pain.

Panting, eyes stinging with sweat, Carter picked up the bat. Cautiously he bent over the ponytailed kid he'd chopped. The boy's eyelids were fluttering and his fingers twitched as Carter touched him. He looked about fourteen. Carter tapped the cracked bat lightly against his palm. The third kid had vanished, but the one he'd tossed was picking himself up out of the dust. Tangled hair hung across his face and he kept his eyes on the bat in Carter's hands. He didn't doubt that Carter was going to swing at him. "Next time, lay off," Carter said. "You hear me?"

The kid never took his eyes from the bat.

"Take care of your friend. And get out of here." Carter jerked his head at the ponytailed kid, who was up on his hands and knees. He backed toward the base end of the culvert mouth, the gray moonlight showing him that he had a clear path. Another shape moved as he neared it, and a blade glinted. Carter took a quick step forward, the bat swinging up.

"Don't!" The shadow retreated into moonlight, became a woman with one hand raised against the bat's swing.

"Nita?" Carter lowered the bat, hands shaking with the knowledge of how close he'd come to hitting her. "What are you doing here?"

"They meant to kill you." The switchblade in her hand gleamed.

"I know." He glanced behind him.

"They took off."

Carter listened, hearing only wind and a tiny, rodent scuffle. "You're still here? I thought you'd found your husband when I didn't hear from you."

"David wasn't in your files, was he?" She hung her head, her face hidden by loose hair.

"You didn't find him," he said gently.

"He's not here. I don't think he ever got here." She clicked the knife closed and slid it into her pocket. "I think I've asked everyone in town. No one remembers him."

"I'm sorry," he said, hearing the inadequacy of the words. He looked beyond her and saw a rumpled sleeping bag spread out in a small hollow. "You're not camping here, are you?"

"The kids don't bother *me*. I don't wear a uniform." Nita squatted beside the sleeping bag as her daughter stirred and whimpered. "It's free." She picked her up. "It's as good a place as any."

Her face looked thinner than he remembered. The pale moonlight accentuated her high cheekbones, filling her dark eyes with shadow. Something had changed in her face. He had seen strength there before, a confidence that was missing now. Her loosened hair clung to her face in dark wisps as she bent over her daughter. She looked . . . defeated.

"I still owe you," Carter said softly. "And I need to return the clothes you lent me. Why don't you stay with me for a day or two? You can have a shower and catch your breath. It's a genuine offer, okay?" He smiled. "No price tag. No strings."

She looked up at him, finally, frowning as if she were going to refuse. Then her daughter whimpered again and she sighed. "Thank you." Her shoulders drooped. "I think I'll take you up on it. Just for a night or two, all right? Until I decide where to go from here?"

"You can stay as long as you need to."

Carter helped her gather her belongings, keeping an eye out for the kids. They reminded him way too much of the lakeshore. He picked up Nita's pack as she tucked Rachel into her sling. "I'll feel a lot better when we're inside the gates," he said, but he wondered if it was any safer in there.

CHAPTER SEVEN

Waiting outside the base's ugly wire gate, Nita wondered if she was making a mistake. She had meant to move on, go down the river-bed to Bonneville; maybe David had gone there. But she was tired. Rachel whimpered and Nita hugged her. Carter was talking to a uniformed soldier just inside the gate. The man held an ugly rifle and he didn't like her. The gate itself scared her. There were two gates, actually, all steel mesh and razor wire, one on either side of the small, square building where the soldier was now tapping keys on a terminal. The soldier was like the gate, all razor-sharp barbs of hostility.

Nita looked away from the glinting, thorny gate. Razor wire had fenced the ag-plex where she had grown up. A drifter had tried to climb it one night, drunk or just desperate. Nita remembered the blood that had soaked his clothes and darkened the dust beneath his tangled, slashed corpse. She shook herself, angry at her own weakness. The past week had left her fragile, full of darkness and childish fears. Carter had offered a clean place to sleep, and this was just a wire gate, nothing more. He was waiting for her. Nita tossed her head, picked up her water jugs, and marched past the razor-wire soldier.

"You'll have to carry this when you go in and out." Carter offered her a small plastic card. "You can't get past the gate without it. Are you all right?"

He was concerned. "I'm just tired." Nita reached inside the neck of her shirt, fished up the small bag that held her few remaining pieces of scrip, and tucked the card into it. "Thank you," she said. He was also nervous. His feelings radiated strongly, unmistakably, at this close range. She looked around, jumpy in this strange place, reacting a little to his ner-vousness. Houses lined the dusty street, bathed in yellow light from lamps on tall poles. So much light! "It looks like a city," she said.

"It's like a town. A small one," Carter said. "The base where I was stationed in Chicago was a lot bigger. This way." He turned abruptly onto a narrow walk that led up to one of the buildings.

It wasn't too bad. Fewer people lived here than in The Dalles, so it wasn't as noisy. Carter had unlocked the door and Nita followed him inside, blinking in the sudden light. The luxury of the room took her breath away. Curtains hung at the window, made of rich, glossy cloth. A thick carpet covered the floor. She touched the padded arm of a sofa, feeling a little dizzy. "The foreman at the ag-plex lived like this," she said aloud. "We used to peek through the windows when he wasn't around. We kids thought it was heaven."

"It's just a basic, Corps apartment. No frills."

She had embarrassed him for some reason. Nita bit her lip. The last of her self-assurance was evaporating in the face of this luxury. She was lost here, out of her depth. No, it was David who was lost. Carter was speaking and Nita forced herself to pay attention to his words.

"You and your daughter can sleep in the bedroom," he was saying. "That'll give you some privacy. The shower's in here. I'll get you a towel." Carter bustled around as he talked, covering his discomfort with motion.

Nita put Rachel down on the soft, wide bed, hoping she'd stay asleep for a little while longer. The shower was in a small white room along with a toilet and a sink. Incredible. Nita peered through the glass doors, feeling as if she was trapped in some crazy dream. "How do you work this?" she asked.

"Haven't you ever used a shower before?"

He sounded so *surprised*. The giggle escaped in spite of herself. "We used a pail." She shook her head. "When the water got too dirty, we poured in on the beans. Where did you grow up?"

"Western Pennsylvania." Carter looked away. "Outside of Pittsburgh."

"It's all right." Puzzled Nita groped for the source of his discomfort. "There was a shower house on the ag-plex, but it cost too much for us kids to use it. Then I went to hunt bees for David and we lived in a tent, up in the hills. Does that bother you?"

"No, no, it's not that." Carter laughed awkwardly. "I guess I took some things for granted. I mean, water's tight, but even in the suburbs, even on a welfare card, you get time in a public shower. The water gets recycled," he said quickly. "It's not wasted."

"I never lived in a city. That's all." Nita gave him a tentative smile. "You do things differently there. I grew up in the Dry. What do I push, or turn, or whatever?"

He showed her the lever that turned the water on and told her that it was on a timer and would go off by itself after a few minutes. Then he retreated, closing the door tightly behind him. Nita stripped off her shirt and jeans and stepped into the plastic cabinet. When she turned the lever, water fell down on her like rain, but gentle and warm. It ran sensuously across her skin, funneled down between her milk-heavy breasts, over the flat curve of her stomach, and into the dark hair between her legs. Nita shook her head and smiled as water spattered the cabinet walls. She unbraided her hair, let the water wash through it, and combed the squeaky wet strands with her fingers.

It was wonderful. She wanted to stay in there forever.

The water shut off all too soon. Regretfully, Nita dried herself, careful not to drop any of the water onto the floor where it would evaporate and be wasted. In the bedroom, Rachel was beginning to fuss. Nita pulled on her clothes hastily and opened the door. Carter was hovering in the doorway to the bedroom, eyeing Rachel, his indecision humming in the air. He wasn't used to babies. Nita slipped past him and scooped Rachel into her arms. "I'm sorry." She lifted her shirt, letting Rachel find a nipple. "She really is a quiet baby, most of the time."

"That's all right." Carter was carefully not looking at her breast. "Do you need anything else? I put a glass of water by the bed."

Aha. "We're fine." Nita smiled for him, trying to make him feel easier. "Thank you for letting us stay here," she told him.

His eyelids flickered. "Good night," he said and closed the door softly behind him.

He had offered her sanctuary and now he wanted her. Men. Nita sighed and shifted Rachel to the other breast. Did he think that would horrify her? She smiled. How old did he think she was, anyway? She had a child. She shifted Rachel to her other breast, the smile lingering. He was honest, this man. He had been honest about his fear, out in the darkness. She liked him for that. Lying down, she curled around her daughter, pulling the quilt over them both. She was tired, but sleep brought dreams of David hit by a truck on the highway, his throat slit by a thief, or torn to pieces by feral dogs.

Those dreams weren't the worst. The worst were the dreams where he walked away, and never looked back as she called and called.

Rachel whimpered.

"It's all right, love, it's all right," Nita murmured. But it was not all right. She closed her eyes against the stinging tears and concentrated on her daughter's primitive, hunger-satisfied content.

Nita woke suddenly, wondering when she had fallen asleep. She had dreamed, but she couldn't remember it. David again? Throat aching with dream tears, Nita eased herself off the bed, tucking the quilt and pillow around Rachel. It was dark in the room, but light from the tall lamps outside seeped in through the windows. Nita peered out The world looked dead, colorless and gray. She tried to swallow the lump in her throat, but it wouldn't go down. It was so easy to die in this dry land.

David had loved her. She had felt his love for her, warm as his body against hers at night. She had felt the dark shadow of his fear, too; she had had no choice but to feel it. The darkness and the silence pressed around Nita, closing on her like a fist It made her feel more alone than she had ever felt before — even on that long ago day when she had run away from Mama and Alberto forever.

David had come after her then. He had searched for her and found her, alone in the Dry. And she had told him why she had run, because she had understood at last that he loved her.

The first, faint shadow of fear had been born then, on that day. If only . . . she had kept silent.

If only.

Nita leaned her forehead against the thick, cool glass of the window. The dream-tears made a hard lump in her throat and that emptiness outside threatened to drown her, suck the life out of her. Slowly Nita became aware of Carter. He was awake, too, silent in the other room. He wanted her, and, beneath his desire, he felt sorry for her. Because he thought David was dead? Strange man; honest enough to admit that he was afraid, upset because she had never used a shower, angry at himself for his own feelings. He cared about her.

The emptiness beat at the window like a dark wing, trying to get in. Nita edged away, reaching for the bedroom door. It creaked a little as she pushed it open. Carter heard it and knew she was there. Nita took a single step into the room, her heart beating fast, his desire flickering through her like heat lightening. He lay on the sofa that he'd pulled out into a bed, watching her, just visible in the light that seeped in through the windows. He wasn't sure yet why she was there. But he hoped.

She smiled, invisibly in the dark. The darkness crouched at Nita's heels and she closed the door against it. He didn't say anything as she came to stand beside him. She took off her shirt and dropped it onto the floor, hearing the soft hiss of his indrawn breath, aware of his gaze on her skin, hot as noon sun.

"I told you no strings." His voice was husky.

"I heard you. Hush now."

David had never come to this town. He had been afraid of her, afraid of what Rachel might be. Darkness lurked on the other side of the flimsy walls. Nita closed her eyes briefly and touched the smooth skin of Carter's shoulder. He shivered, propped on one elbow, face turned up to her. Nita ran her fingers lightly across the dense curl of his hair, traced the jut of his cheekbones beneath his pale skin. How could you live in the sun with skin so white? She touched his lips lightly with her fingertips, her heart beating fast now, a hot, sweet ache between her legs. When he reached up to tangle his fingers in her loose hair, she slid onto the bed beside him, losing herself in the quick, searing heat of his lips and tongue, twining her legs with his. He rolled onto her and she arched beneath him, breathless with his desire and hers, too. She locked her legs around his narrow hips, moving with the rhythm of his body, riding the tight, soaring spiral of their mingled passion. The bright nova of his coming burst inside Nita and she cried out as he swept her along with him.

His small twitch of reaction told her what she had done — called David's name. She twisted away from him, burying her face in the pillow. The tears came at last, unstoppable. Because she had hurt him. Because he wasn't David.

He pulled her gently against him, cradling her face against his chest, stroking her damp hair back from her face. There was no anger inside him, only warmth and a little sadness. "I'm sorry you didn't find him." He traced the curve of her cheek with a gentle fingertip. "Part of me isn't sorry," he said, and the sadness showed in his smile. "I was afraid I was never going to see you again." He kissed her gently and Nita tasted the salt of her own tears on her lips. Then he looked down, startled.

"I'm sorry." Nita wiped at the trickle of milk on her breasts.

Surprised, Carter touched one dark nipple, watching beads of white swell, combine, and trickle down the dark curve of her breast. "Does that always happen?" he asked, fascinated.

"Usually." Nita smiled through her tears. "Sometimes it's worse. Be glad Rachel was hungry tonight."

"I didn't know that." Carter met her eyes, his own face gentle. "Tell me about yourself," he said. "Anything. About David, if you want to."

"Tell him about David? She wanted to talk about David; she wanted to tell Carter how much she loved him, how he had been a sanctuary of safety and comfort after a childhood of confusion and hurting silence. She needed to tell him so that they would both know. Nita drew a shaky breath. To tell him that, she would have to tell him why David was afraid. She closed her eyes briefly, thinking of Seth and his molten violence. "I was born right here in The Dalles," she said. "We had a soy farm, I guess. My father . . . was killed when I was little. After that, we went to live with my brother Alberto on a bush farm in the Valley. I didn't mean to come back here."

"I'm sorry."

"About my father?" She studied his face because he was sad again. "Don't be." She turned his hand over and traced the lines in his palm. "An old woman I knew claimed she could read your future in your hand. I never knew my father." She laid his hand down and covered it with her own. "He got shot in some kind of water war. Mama never forgave him for getting killed and leaving her. When I was little, I thought it was my fault, her anger." Nita sighed. Ghosts inhabited this town. Hurtful ghosts. "She was angry because she had loved him and he had died. I didn't understand until it was too late," Nita said. "I think I could have loved Mama if I had understood."

Carter's hand closed tight on hers. "I don't remember my father either. He died when I was a baby. My mother never remarried." He lifted one shoulder in a jerky shrug, restless suddenly, his hazel eyes dark as copper in the dim light.

A wound here? Something he didn't want to talk about anyway. Nita lifted his hand, kissing his fingers gently.

"I met a woman who reminded me of you earlier tonight." Carter changed the subject abruptly. "She talked about the land as if it were alive, as if we could kill it. The land mattered to her. I can't feel that," he said. "It just looks like dirt and rock to me."

"You have to know how to look."

"Can you show me?" he asked softly. "I think it would help me understand the farmers."

"Yes," she said. He wanted something so much here. She wondered just what it was. "We'll go up into the hills, and I'll show you."

He pulled her close again, his breath warm against her face. "You did a crazy thing, you know, coming into that culvert tonight. You could have gotten hurt."

He was asking her something and she wasn't sure what it was. "They meant to kill you," she said and shut her lips tightly, afraid he would ask her how she knew.

In the bedroom, Rachel whimpered. Relieved at the distraction, Nita got up quickly. She would not tell him. She didn't want to feel it ever again; that gathering shadow, the darkness behind the smile and the reassurances.

Rachel wasn't really hungry. Nita tucked her between them and she smiled, eyes fixed on Carter's face as she nursed. She wasn't sleepy, either. "Sometimes she just likes to play," Nita said, resigned. "Maybe because it's cooler, nights."

He didn't mind. He smiled at Rachel's smile and poked a finger into her palm so that she could grab it. He was shy — pleased when she grinned and drooled at him.

Nita wasn't sleepy either. It was as if Rachel had infected the with her wakefulness. So they talked. She told him about the big ag-plex where she had grown up — about weeding the neat rows of special tamarisk bushes while the grown-ups pruned the branches to feed the digester. She told him about the dust and the cool mud around the soaker hoses, about the white crusts of salt that formed on the bush stems, stinging the cuts on your hands and prickly on your tongue. She didn't tell him about the foreman and his hands, behind the shed, or about Mama's bitterness, Ignacio's stifled rage, or Alberto's resignation. She couldn't.

He told her about growing up in the walled suburban enclave. Son of a housekeeper in the world of the rich. The darkness lay there — a wound that was deep and old and ugly. He tiptoed around it, not close enough to give it away, and she didn't pry. He told her about his friend Johnny, who had given him entrance into this luxurious world that she couldn't even begin to imagine. He worshipped this friend, or owed him a debt that went as deep as the wound, was maybe part of the wound.

She wasn't sure that she liked this friend.

Night was fading into dawn, brightening to morning. Rachel slept, finally; head turned to the side, fist by her mouth, drowned in a murmur of dreams. I love you, Nita thought, and felt her heart contract. Outside, voices. Army people walking by, on their way to do whatever they did here. "Why did you go into the Army?" she asked Carter.

"Hm?" His eyelids fluttered — he had been almost asleep. "Oh." He yawned. "Because the Corps was looking for officers at the time, so they paid me to go to school." He frowned, not sleepy anymore. "I liked it," he said. You know where you stand in the Corps. Your status is very carefully and precisely defined. You don't have any questions about who you are." He looked to the window and the morning voices beyond. "I hope they got the officer they wanted."

"They did." She touched his face. "They got more than they paid for."

He frowned, then shrugged and smiled for her. "I've got to go to a reception this afternoon. Johnny — the friend I told you about — invited me." His smile grew warmer. "I'm not going to be at my best."

"You don't have to be at your best." Nita rolled lightly off the mattress, came around to his side of the bed, and leaned down to kiss him. "You should be tired today." He reached up for her and she slid onto him, drowning doubts and the past in the vivid here-and-now of skin, and sweat, and love.

CHAPTER EIGHT

The reception was for Johnny — some kind of private party. It was the first time they'd gotten together since their near miss in Portland, but this wasn't Carter's first choice of situation. He grimaced as he parked his car, wishing that they could be hanging out somewhere over a couple of beers. He wanted to tell Johnny about Nita. Maybe he just wanted to listen to himself try to explain to Johnny how he felt.

Then maybe he'd have a clue.

He slammed the door and locked it. The house was on a narrow street that overlooked the public market and the main streets of The Dalles. It was big, with a fresh new coat of paint. Carter stifled a yawn. He had gotten about two hours of sleep — not nearly enough, but too much if you wanted to look at it that way. He smiled. Nita and Rachel had been asleep when he'd left to review the night's flow reports and the morning's business.

Nita. He paused on the wide, railed porch, staring blindly at the old warehouses that lined the riverbed's edge far below. Her black hair had veiled the pillow and she had smiled a little in her sleep when he had kissed on the cheek. He had felt . . . Carter shook his head impatiently.

The door opened. "You going to stand out here all day?" Johnny grinned at him, casually elegant in a loose shirt and linen slacks. "So I'm sorry I missed you in Portland, already. Stop sulking out there and come on in."

"I'm not sulking. I'm asleep." Carter let Johnny sweep him through the door, grinning. "I was sorry to miss you, too."

"We'll connect sooner or later." Johnny slapped him on the shoulder, but his grin seemed a bit strained. "Better yet, we'll go down to San Francisco and do the clubs." Johnny held out his hand to a tall, dark-haired woman. "Meet Gwynn. She's giving this party. She owns the government fuel franchise for The Dalles."

"It's a living." She held out a hand to Carter, smiling. "Although I'd much rather live in San Francisco. When are you going to invite *me* down to do the clubs?" She gave Johnny a smile. "Glad to meet you, Colonel."

"I'm glad to meet you, too." Carter returned her light squeeze of greeting. "Thank for letting Johnny drag me along here."

"Oh I would have invited you anyway." A dimple showed at the corner of her mouth when she smiled. "Let me get you a glass of wine?"

"Thanks." Carter watched her walk gracefully away. Johnny's current lover?

She was the type of woman Johnny fell for — tall and elegant. They always reminded Carter of Amber, Johnny's ex-wife. Although he was never going to say *that* out loud. Twenty-five or thirty men and women milled in the long, well-furnished front room. A few of them browsed the laden table set up in front of the windows. The rest clustered at the far corner of the room, watching some kind of performance. A burst of clapping and laughter greeted Carter.

"A magician. The guy's pretty good." Johnny jerked his head at the crowd. "Gwynn hired him off a streetcorner down in Bonneville. Here's your wine." He took the glass from Gwynn's hand and kissed her lightly and proprietarily on the cheek. "When the show's over, Gwynn can introduce you around."

"So what brings you to The Dalles?" Carter asked as he wandered over to the buffet table with Johnny. "Gwynn?" He gave Johnny a sideways look. "Or business?"

"Actually, I wanted to see you. Gwynn and I are old news. I think she likes you, by the way." Johnny smiled, but a serious tone underlay his light words. "I want the lowdown on what's going on here. Hastings has been putting in some heavy troop requests. I want to hear your side of it before we shell out." He took Carter by the elbow, steering him toward the far corner of the room. "What's happening here?"

"Nothing, yet." Carter sipped his red wine. It tasted like real stuff — not a cheap tank grown blend. Gwynn must make good money on her fuel franchise. "The troop request is real, Johnny. I was planning to lean on you. We've got a sabotage situation that's escalating fast, and not enough people to deal with it. We need more bodies."

"That's bad." Johnny frowned into his own glass. "Like I told you — Mexico is getting restless. That means there's no extra water to play with. If someone blows a big hole in the Pipeline, the valleys dry up."

"So give us more people." Carter watched Johnny's face, struggling with rising frustration. Johnny wasn't hearing him. This was Johnny Seldon, member of Water Policy. The friend you could reach. Not this guy. "Hastings said he got turned down."

"He did. I can't do it, Carter." Johnny smiled a smooth, seamless smile. "Chicago scared a lot more people than you. Military force to protect water flow was a hot issue, and the media would love to go after us again."

"You think I don' t know that?" Carter drained his glass, trying to hold on to his anger. "Damn it, Johnny, we're going to have trouble if we don't get extra people."

"I don't think you understand." Johnny lowered his voice. "No one has more power than we do — not even the president — but it's not a sure thing." His eyes glittered in the light from the window. "You better believe we know it, even if we pretend to be so civic minded and above it all. The country amended the Constitution once to create Water Policy. They could do it again and take it all away. That amendment only passed by a hair-thin margin."

And a lot of people had claimed it was rigged. "So the Committee's going to play to the media?" Carter set his glass down on the windowsill very gently. "And we can go to hell?"

"Come off it, Carter. You're talking like I'm the enemy." Johnny sighed and sipped his wine. "Look, I've got a little leverage, even if the old boys think I'm still in diapers. I'll try, okay? Now I've got to go socialize. I'm Gwynn's major attraction this afternoon — and I need to feel some people out about things." He rolled his eyes. "This job is twenty-four hours a day."

"Thanks, Johnny." Carter touched his shoulder lightly.

He wanted to feel hopeful, but he simply felt depressed. He'd known Johnny long enough to know when Johnny was sweet-talking his way out of trouble. Oh, Johnny had that tone down pat. And he'd just used it, promising to look into Hastings' troop request.

So Hastings wasn't going to get his troops and Carter was on his own. Dan Greely's volunteers looked better and better. Carter retrieved his glass from the window, wanting more wine, wanting suddenly and intensely to get drunk, go back and get into bed with Nita and pretend this wasn't happening. It hurt that Johnny had used that voice on him. He could have just said no, up front. Too bad, buddy. I've got my own row to hoe. Carter could've understood that. Carter shook his head.

A waiter offered a tray of full glasses and whisked away Carter's empty one. He wandered back to the buffet table, looking for Johnny and not finding him, scanning the grazing crowd. He knew some of them — or knew who they were, anyway. They were the upper crust of The Dalles; the professionals, the business owners, the owner of a small trucking firm. Only a couple of farmers, as far as he could tell. No one from the Coalition meeting, not that this surprised him.

"Colonel Voltaire." A very tall, dark-haired woman in a suit wandered up. "How nice to meet you. I'm Amanda Morrisy." She offered him a long-fingered hand. "I'm with Pacific Biosystems."

"Nice to meet you." Carter wondered how she had known his name. Johnny? "I didn't know Pacific Biosystems had an office in The Dalles."

"We don't." Her smile was cool. "I'm in town looking for contract business. She made a face. "Without much success, I might add. I find a lot of resistance to biomass crops along the riverbed."

"So I've heard." Carter returned her firm grip. He had to look up to meet her gaze. "Why do you think that is?"

"These marginal farmers are always conservative and closed minded." She shrugged. "You have to ram every change down their throats. It doesn't matter if it will benefit them or not; if it's new, it's bad."

Carter kept his expression neutral, remembering the Corbett woman's face at the meeting. "I hear that the salt-water irrigation in the Valley does a lot of damage."

"It would be a wasteland if we didn't use seawater in the mix." She shrugged. "The old crops would be too expensive for anyone to buy and US food reserves are down to about thirty-six hours' worth." She was still smiling and her tone was polite, but her eyes had gone cold and sharp. "I don't see how anyone can seriously criticize a system that produces a very good and consistent yield."

"I wasn't criticizing." Carter smiled politely and edged toward the table.

"I want you to know how much we appreciate Corps support." She followed him. "We depend on the water that comes down both the Klamath and Willamette shunts, and by augmenting it with seawater, we make it work that much harder for all of us. It would be cost effective to pipe seawater up the Gorge you know." She smiled. "Once, this was highly productive farmland. You do a fine job here, you know?"

"We do our best." Carter gave her a thin smile. She was after something. "Excuse me." He reached for a plate. The magic show was over and people were heading for the table en mass. He wasn't really hungry, but it gave him an excuse to put bodies between them.

"She's feeling you out. They'd like to have you in their pocket, too." The low voice at his elbow was familiar. Carter turned, looked down at the small man with the thick tail of blond hair. "So you're the magician from Bonneville." Carter smiled. "I should have guessed. Jeremy, right? Jeremy Barlow."

"That's me." Jeremy gave Carter one of his crooked grins. A small green frog appeared on the tablecloth beside a bowl of mixed nuts. It stared up at them for a moment, throat pulsing, then leaped onto a cheese plate and vanished. Behind them, someone squeaked in surprise.

"That is some gadget." Carter shook his head as Jeremy surreptitiously pocketed his projector. The frog seemed to have bought them some space at the table, and from the look of innocence on Jeremy's face, Carter suspected that had been his intention. "What did you mean?" He lowered his voice. "About Pacific Bio's pocket?"

"What I said." Jeremy reached for a small sandwich, picking it up carefully with his thick, clumsy fingers. "They own a lot of politicians — they pretty much run California, and I guess they weren't too ethical about how they got that job. Now they're after what they don't already own in Oregon. Or so I've heard." He bit into his sandwich.

"Where did you hear this?" Frowning, Carter balanced his plate lightly on his fingers. "I haven't heard it."

"Maybe you don't listen to the right people." Jeremy picked up another sandwich, then frowned at it. "I ride with truckers a lot."

"Truckers stay out of politics."

"Yeah, but they don't miss much. You can't stay out of something unless you know where and what it is, and they make sure they know it all." His lopsided grin came and went again. "I believe them." All trace of a smile vanished from his eyes. "I move around a lot. I've been down in California and back east. Pacific Bio owns a lot of ag land. They own the people who work it." He looked at the half-eaten sandwich in his hand, put it down. A shiny black fly appeared on it, large as Carter's thumb. It took off, zoomed in a tight silent circle above the sandwich, and then popped like a soap bubble. "It's tough trying to fight the Dry," Jeremy said softly. "You plow your soul into the land, because it's the only way you can keep yourself hanging on, keep watering, and weeding, and praying you make harvest this year." He looked up, his eyes as dry and blue as the sky. "When you lose that land, when you walk away from it, you leave your soul behind."

"Poetic, but hardly true." Morissy leaned over Carter's shoulder, smiling. "If we contract to grow biomass on someone's land, we don't buy the land. We don't need the taxes. We simply offer a contract that covers our investment in cloned bush-starts and equipment. The farmer still owns the land. He sells to us, and we pay him. Simple transaction."

"Except that they owe you for the bushes. And they owe those taxes." Jeremy shrugged. "Debt can be a pretty heavy chain to drag." A glowing insect popped into the air between them and vanished abruptly.

Morisy flinched. "Did you contract some land to us and then regret it?" Her smile had gone tight. "Is that what's bothering you?"

"No." Jeremy picked up his plate with the uneaten sandwich on it. "My father never contracted our land. It died, and so did he. It wasn't your fault." He gave the Pacific BioSystems executive a slight bow. "Maybe I'll see you in The Dalles," he said to Carter. "Take it easy."

"They have to blame someone." Morrisy gave Carter a wry, conspiratorial smile. "You much catch a lot of it, too. You'd think we'd engineered the climate change just so we could make a buck."

"Yes." Carter looked after Jeremy. "We catch a lot of that." Maybe that's all it was — a sourceless anger and darkness, like in Chicago. Blame for no reason. If that was true, nothing he did in The Dalles was going to help. He frowned.

Dan Greely had made that anger feel pointed and personal. So had Sandy Corbett. And Nita, who had never stood in a shower. *When you walk away, you leave your soul behind.* Had one of them shot Delgado's' brother and Mike Watanabe? Harold Ransom, or the Corbett woman, or even Greely? It wasn't at all impossible. Where the hell could you stand in this mess?

Carter felt a tiny click as the stem of his wineglass snapped. He stared numbly at the small blossom of crimson on his palm.

"Hello." Gwynn paused on her way across the room, two full glasses in her hand. "What did you do?"

"I cut myself." Embarrassed, he grabbed for a napkin. "I'm sorry about the glass."

"Never mind about the glass. Come on." She took him firmly by the elbow, smiling over his shoulder at Morissy. "I've got a first aid kit in the kitchen."

Carter followed her through a swinging door and into a large, bright kitchen. A big sink was set into a center island with a polished granite top. Stainless steel appliances hummed and copper pots and pans hung from wrought-iron hooks overhead.

"Wash your hand." She pushed him toward the sink. "I'll get something for it. You know, I was about to rescue you from Pacific Bio's clutches. You didn't have to get so dramatic." She winked at him over her shoulder as she rummaged in a cupboard.

"I didn't . . ." He stopped, felt himself blushing. The wine had gone straight to his head after his sleepless night.

Gwynn reached for his hand, patted it dry with a clean napkin. "I suspect she's feeling you out for a deal. You're the new water lord in town. The only reason she came to this party was to meet you."

Carter stared at her, feeling stupid. "I don't have the authority to make any flow changes."

"You might have the General's ear. If you don't, don't worry. She won't bother you much longer." Gwynn laughed, reached up and touched his cheek lightly. "What desert island did you grow up on? The Corps controls the *water*, remember? These little deals . . . get done."

Carter leaned slightly away from her touch. "I've never paid much attention to politics," he said stiffly.

"Oh, you're too wonderful." And she stood on tiptoes to kiss him lightly, briefly on the mouth.

"I should be getting back," he said, and she made a face at him.

"So soon?" She smoothed a strip of tape over the shallow cut on his palm. "Just because my wineglasses bite?"

"I've got things to do." He moved toward the door, feeling utterly out of place here. "Uh, thanks for having me."

"Any time." Her eyes sparkled with amusement. "I'll have to give you a chance to drink my wine without incurring serious bodily injury."

"Sure." He edged toward the door.

"Fine." Her smile widened. "That's a promise then. How about next Friday?"

A waiter saved Carter by coming in to ask about more wine. Gwynn had to go down into the basement to show him and Carter used the opportunity to escape. The crowd had thinned out in the main room; people were leaving. He didn't see Johnny anywhere, and felt a pang of disappointment. He had probably assumed that Carter had already left, and had left himself.

A set of French doors that opened onto a small side patio stood ajar and Carter went out that way. He'd parked the car on that side of the house. He closed the doors behind him and took out his cell phone to give Johnny a call, see where he'd taken off to.

Johnny was out here, standing in the shade under the eaves with Morissy. The Pacific Biosystems suit was tapping her index finger lightly on her palm, her shoulder's stiff with authority. Johnny's posture was . . . defensive. Carter's toe caught a loose stone, and at the sound they both turned.

"Carter?" Johnny's laugh was too bright. "Where did you run off to? I thought you'd gone."

"We'll get together later, Johnny." Morissy gave Carter a cool smile. "Nice meeting you, Colonel, however briefly. Perhaps we can get together another time." She walked briskly around the corner of the house and disappeared.

She looked pissed. Carter caught Johnny's arm as he started from the doors. "Wait a minute." He caught Johnny's flicker of irritation, ignored it. "What was that all about?"

"A little offer of sex." He smiled at Carter's reaction. "They're always fishing for a price, but that ain't it. She wasn't happy about my turn-down. I saw you in the kitchen with Gwynn." His smile carried the faintest trace of a leer. "She has the hots for you, my friend. I can tell."

"Are they leaning on you?" Carter asked softly. "Pacific Biosystems?" Water Policy members, with a life term, top pay, and no permissible business connections, were supposed to be beyond corruption. But water was power, Gwynn was right. "Johnny, I get the feeling something's eating you."

"It's not." Johnny took a deep breath. "Look, Carter, do you have any idea of the responsibility we have?" His voice had gone hushed and his face had gone pale, except for twin spots of color on his cheeks. "I was the boy genius economist — the bright and shining new star in the world of water and money — so now I have the real stuff. The real power. But you know me." He grinned, a feeble stretch of his lips. "Sometimes I get . . . a little over the top."

"Don't I know it." Carter gripped his arm hard. "How many times did we nearly get busted? What are you telling me?" His voice sobered. "Are you in trouble?"

"No." Johnny's face firmed and he smiled — a real smile this time, if a bit rueful. "I got a little drunk at a party and . . . did some things that might have been misinterpreted. Morissy misinterpreted them in spades. I'm not for sale." He met Carter's eyes. "Not now, not ever. But she's being . . . awkward."

"Blackmail?"

"No, nothing like that." Johnny laughed, half angry. "I don't put stuff into email or on paper, for that matter, give me a break." He started down the graveled yard, toward the street and the parked cars. "No, it's a nuisance, is all. The media could pick it up and throw rocks, but they won't break any bones. I wasn't kidding about Gwynn, you know." He looked back over his shoulder. "She and I parted friends a long time ago. She's a very hot lady, Carter. With money."

"She's very nice."

"You got someone already?" Johnny's eyebrows rose. "You never could play poker for shit. When did this happen?"

"Someone I just met, Johnny." He tried to make his voice casual. "Nita. Nita Montoya."

"Latino?" Johnny's eyebrows rose as they reached the cracked sidewalk. "Well . . . congratulations, I guess. Is this, like, long term?"

"God, I don't know, Johnny." Carter heard the irritation in his voice, couldn't help it. "You tell me. Listen, I've got to get back to the base. Can I drop you somewhere, or do you have a car?"

"You can drop me at my motel." Johnny followed him to his car. "Tell me how you're settling in up there."

He didn't tell Johnny much, but Johnny for once didn't seem disposed to talk so that was fine. The swirling undercurrents of the party had left him uneasy, full of misgivings. You could be tempted. Anyone could be tempted. Gwynn had certainly been fishing this afternoon. He wondered what Morissy had on Johnny. Something, for all his disclaimer. When the time was right, he'd ask again, and maybe Johnny would tell him. But this wasn't the time, and Johnny was vague about when they could get together again. Maybe tomorrow, he told Carter. If he didn't have to bolt out of town suddenly.

It was late in the afternoon as he drove back to the base. The slanting beams of the sun touched the dusty land with gold and reflected from the random window in bursts of fire. He had checked in by phone and everything was quiet at the base. No trouble on the Pipeline. No one had even yelled at him as he drove the Corps car through town. Maybe he could keep this situation under control. Maybe it wasn't another Chicago. Carter returned the guards' salute as they waved him through the gate, anticipation stirring in his belly and groin.

He wanted to tell Nita about the party, hear her reaction. She had such a different perspective on this world. He wanted to tell her about Jeremy and his frog on the table. He might laugh. He had never seen her laugh, and he wanted to do that, suddenly — make her laugh. He parked in front of his apartment and hurried up the walk. Whatever would or wouldn't work itself out between them, he wanted to see her *now*, to put his arms around her, bury his face in her hair and breathe the soft musky scent of her skin. The door was locked. He unlocked it and pushed it open. "Nita?"

Her name echoed through the apartment. He knew even as he shut the door. The sofa had been closed and the sheets lay neatly folded on it. He looked anyway, surveying the empty bedroom and bathroom.

She had not left a single trace of her presence behind, except for the folded sheets and the towel she had used. He picked it up, a lump heavy in his gut. Her scent rose faintly from the thick folds.

He threw it into the laundry hamper and tossed the sheets in after it.

Not strings attached, remember?

Part of him refused to believe it. She had a pass. She could walk through the door any minute.

She wasn't going to. He knew it as surely as if she'd left him a note. She *had* left him a note — in the folded sheets and the empty apartment.

He wished now that he'd stayed at the fancy, freshly painted house. He wanted to get drunk with Johnny, tell him about Chicago and how it was his fault. And Johnny could tell him why Pacific Biosystems thought they could own him and they could laugh about it and maybe cry, like a couple of teenagers who couldn't hold their liquor.

He didn't call Johnny. He needed to go down to Operations and look over the flow reports himself, never mind that Delgado had already done it.

He needed to review the day, check things out. He needed to think about the party gossip, and Dan Greely, and how they were going to put civilians on patrols without too many headaches. He walked through the apartment once more, checking to see if she'd left anything behind.

She hadn't.

He didn't slam the door on the way out.

CHAPTER NINE

Nita looked around Carter's apartment as she braided her hair. In the bright light everything looked too sharp, too vivid. It made her head ache. She tied off the end of her braid with a thin, silk ribbon David had given her.

Last night, alone in the darkness, it had been so easy to believe that he had walked away.

In the harsh light of day, she wasn't so sure. Anything could happen. A man could break his leg and spend weeks healing in a farmhouse somewhere. He could run away and then change his mind. "I don't know," Nita whispered. The word sounded as loud as a shout in the silent apartment. She bent and yanked the sheets from the sofa bed. The faint scent of their lovemaking rose from the cloth as she folded them, and she bent her head, pierced by the memory of last night. I came in here because I was lonely, she told herself. That's all it had been — a midnight need for comfort.

If that had been true yesterday, it was a lie now. She bent double over the armful of folded sheets, a stone of pain in her belly. "I love you, David," she cried. "I do."

On the bed, Rachel woke with a hungry cry. Nita threw the folded sheets onto the floor as Rachel began to wail. "Not your fault, love." Nita calmed herself as she went to pick up her daughter. "I'm angry at me, not you. Have your breakfast and then we'll go."

This was where David would come to find her, so she would wait for him for awhile longer. But not here. Nita stared at the wall as her daughter nursed. She couldn't stay here. She didn't dare. When Rachel was finished, she repacked her pack, filled her water jugs, and tucked Rachel into her sling. Standing in the doorway, hand on the knob, she looked around at the empty rooms. She had spent one night here; less than twenty-four hours.

It felt familiar — as if she had lived here for days. Weeks. Nita thought about leaving Carter a note, but what could she say that wouldn't be a lie, or be misunderstood? She bit her lip. Silence was best; he would understand that message. It was a message she had to give him.

And herself.

Nita yanked the door open and walked through it, out into the hot, dusty wind. A different guard was at the gate, a woman about Nita's age. She eyed Nita suspiciously, but without the razor-wire feel of the man yesterday. She despised Nita a little, and Nita wondered why. She lifted her head, holding out the pass Carter had given her. It wasn't until she had walked halfway down that dusty road that led to the truck plaza and the highway that she realized that she still had the pass; the guard hadn't asked for it. Nita held it on her palm, half tempted to toss it into the dusty weeds that lined the road. But a part of her wanted to keep it, and she tucked it carefully into the pouch around her neck, trying to ignore the small prick of her guilt.

If she was going to stay in The Dalles for awhile, she would have to find a job. She was running out of scrip. Hitching the pack higher on her shoulders, tickling Rachel's belly until she smiled and gurgled, Nita plodded through the afternoon sun toward town and the stores there. Maybe one of them had a job open.

"I'm sorry." The round-faced, balding manager of the government store was genuinely apologetic. "I wish I could give you some kind of job." He leaned on the counter, surrounded by aisles of controlled items: liquor, beer and wine, cigarettes, candy, a small meat counter, and shelves filled with other small, water-expensive luxuries that the government had loaded with restrictive taxes. "Have you tried Laurel, the manager down at the market? She might have a job for you cleaning out the booths or something."

"I tried her." Tired to the bone, discouraged, Nita shifted Rachel's sling higher on her shoulder. There were no jobs in this town. She had been up and down the main street, asking at every store and fuel station, not just the market. "She's got a kid working for her."

"Oh yeah, her nephew." The manager frowned, scratching at the brown spots that speckled his bare scalp "Things are real tight in town, what with the water cuts these past two years. The district supervisor's been making noises about closing this store. Crazy, I say, because the nearest government store'll be Bonneville, but hell, no one's got scrip to spend except the truckers. All they buy is booze, and they're mobile anyway. I had the news on this morning. Italy and Greece are blowing up the refugee boats coming over from Africa — just sinking 'em. Can you believe it?" He shook his head. "Hell, what's happening to us? You'd think our humanity's drying up with the water. Look, I got about an hour before closing." He scowled at the clock on the wall. "You can polish the front windows for me and sweep out the back room. I've been meaning to get around to that for a week now. I can pay something for it."

It was a handout — because of the news story. "Thank you," Nita said. She'd take a handout.

"You're looking for a job?" A man had come in from the street, tall and lanky with dark, graying hair.

"Hi, Dan." The manager lifted a hand. "Nita here's been trying to find something, but you know how it is. Dan Greely knows everyone." He nodded emphatically. "If anyone can find you a job, he can."

He was already regretting his offer of the sweeping job. Nita was too discouraged to be angry.

"I heard a woman was in town, looking for her husband. Is that you?" The newcomer leaned against the counter beside her.

"David Ascher. He was supposed to have a job here. He's about your height." She looked up, frowning. "He has curly black hair, only it's starting to go gray." The faint flicker of her hope died easily at the man's headshake.

"I'm sorry. I haven't heard of him. I might be able to help you out with a job, though," he said thoughtfully. "I had a man working out at my farm. He left about three months ago, and I need some help. It's field work, but I have an extra room in the house. All I can offer you right now is board and a share of the profit — if there *is* any profit this year."

Nita considered, watching the man from beneath her lashes. The offer felt genuine, but the ride to Tygh Valley had made her wary. The man's graying hair and his lined, sundried face put him in his forties, maybe more. About David's age. He was staring at her, examining her face with a searching intensity that made Nita uncomfortable.

"Don't I know you?" He sounded uncertain. "What's your name, again?"

"Nita. Nita Montoya."

His eyes narrowed. "You're not . . . Sam Montoya's daughter, are you?"

His sudden tension brought her head up. "Yes." She eyed him warily. "He died a long time ago."

"I know." The man's voice has hushed, muted by a flood of emotion. "I knew Sam. I even remember you. You must have been about four, last time I saw you."

She had been five and a half on the day the men had come to kill her father. Nita took a step backward as Rachel began to whimper.

"Well, I'll be." The manager leaned over the counter, clucking with delight. "Sam's youngest. I heard the name, even, but it didn't click. He was a good man, your dad." He nodded, light glancing off his spotted scalp. "We miss him, eh Dan?"

"Where did you go?" The man named Dan spoke as if he hadn't heard the manager, as if he and Nita were the only people in the store, or the world.

She took another step backward, suddenly wanting to run, to put distance between herself and this stranger's frightening intensity. "Mama . . . took us to live with my brother Alberto. Down in the Willamette Valley." The door was right behind her. "Thank you for offering to let me sweep," she told the manager. "I think I'll check one or two other places first." She escaped, the door banging shut behind her, out into hot, dusty safety of the street.

He followed her, stretching his long legs to catch up, his determination like a hot breath on the back of her neck, making her want to run.

"I'm sorry if I upset you. Nita? Want to slow down for a minute, before we both get heat stroke?" He sounded plaintive. "I won't bite. I promise."

"You didn't upset me. Oh, all right, you did." Nita stopped suddenly. She couldn't outrun him, and it was too hot even to try. "I hadn't really thought about it . . ." She wiped her sweaty face on her sleeve, groping for words. "That people here would have known my father, I mean." The town and the dusty yesterday that she remembered were two different worlds. "It just . . . took me by surprise."

"I'm sorry."

He was. "Don't be. It was a long time ago." His name was Dan Greely, she remembered. "Mama never mentioned you." She heard the accusation in her tone, watched his eyes flicker.

"I'm not surprised." He sighed and pushed hair that needed cutting out of his eyes. "Maria never liked me much. She blamed me for Sam's death."

Grief? His emotion struck Nita like a blow.

"How is your mother?" he asked.

"She died three years ago." Rachel's sling was rubbing her shoulder and Nita tugged at the knot, uneasy again. This man remembered her father much better than she did and after twenty years, he still mourned him. "A spray plane crashed into the residence compound at the ag-plex. Alberto died, too," she said. "I don't know where Ignacio is. He took off."

"I'm sorry," Dan said softly. "Poor Maria. She never made peace with Sam's choice. I don't think she ever understood how much that choice cost him."

Nita sneaked a look at his face, studying the weathered profile. "I don't really know what you mean," she said. "Mama never talked about The Dalles at all." Except to blame her husband for dying and Nita for living.

"I was serious about needing a hand in the fields," Dan said slowly. "I've been spending too much time with politics lately and the beans are suffering. I can't guarantee that you'll get much more than a place to live out of it, what with the recent water cuts, but you and your baby are welcome, if that suits."

She wanted to say no and walk away from this man and the ghosts he raised, but she was tired. If she and Rachel were going to eat, she had to find a job. Already she was losing weight and Rachel's fussing suggested her milk was failing. Nita sighed, liking the quiet feel of this man, ghosts or no ghosts. She felt no darkness in him, no threat. The ghosts would be everywhere, now that people knew who she was, she guessed. "I'll take it." She hitched the sling higher on her shoulder. "I've never worked beans, but I've worked bushes. I know how to pull weeds and run a soaker-hose system."

"Great." His smile warmed her like sunlight. "I'm glad to share with you. I'll put the word out about your husband. I know a lot of folk around here. How old is your baby?" He tickled Rachel lightly under the chin, smiled with her drooly smile.

"This is Rachel. She's six months old." Nita had the feeling that she had made a good choice, had found a place to wait for David.

Or hide from Carter?

She shook her head to banish that thought. "I appreciate the job."

"I appreciate the help." He held out a hand. "Why don't you give me your pack? Rachel looks like quite a load on her own. My truck's parked at the market. I was just on the way home."

CHAPTER TEN

Stomach tight, Carter marched down the long hall that led to Hastings' office. He hadn't been back here since his first day on the riverbed, and the vast bulk of the dam still oppressed him; making him sweat in the cool air. He had received a preemptory summons from the general this morning. No explanation, just an order to report in person.

Either he had fucked up in a big way or something was coming down, too big to risk to email or the phone. Corporal Sandusky wasn't in his cubicle. Carter paused outside the general's door to straighten his uniform and run a hand through his hair. He wasn't sure which possibility worried him more.

"Enter." The general's growl answered his knock. "You made good time." He looked up as Carter entered and jerked his head at the big wall map of the Pipeline. "We got trouble."

"What kind of trouble, sir?" Carter braced himself.

"Orders from the top. We have to increase the flow in the Colorado Diversion line by three percent. Mexico filed a petition to the UN — whining about its share again. Hastings grunted. "Personally, I'd tell them to shut up and be glad we let them in on any of it at all." He grunted again. "This time, the EU sided with China in the UN Water Committee. So the greedy Mex bastards get what they want."

Carter didn't remind him that Mexico had contributed one third of the monumental construction cost for the Trench Reservoir in the Rockies and the Pipeline system itself. He frowned, doing the numbers fast in his head. The increase would come from the Trench, because Mexico got its share of tundra water via the Colorado and Rio Grande aqueducts, and they had their origins in the Rocky Mountain Trench Reservoir. The Trench was already supporting its maximum outflow. "Where is the water going to come from?" Carter asked, knowing the answer even before the general spoke.

"It's going to come out of the Columbia's share. Every drop of it."

Carter whistled a low, resigned note. "That means another big cut in everyone's water share."

"Not everyone," Hastings said grimly. "We can't reduce the volume going into the Klamath and Willamette shunts without causing major crop losses. I've been ordered to keep their flow at current levels."

Cater stared at his commander. "If we maintain the Shunt flows," he said flatly, "the residents between the Deschutes bed and the Willamette bed are going to get slashed. Local water use is already cut to the bone, sir. I've spent hours looking at the numbers. It's going to finish off the soaker-hose farmers." Ransom was going to love this.

"I see you understand what we're likely to encounter," Hastings said dryly.

"The local situation is going to blow sky high," Carter said grimly.

"It's your job to keep the lid on." Hastings tossed his pen onto his desk. "I've filed a demand for support troops. Combat units. Maybe this time we'll get some action out of those whipped dogs in Water Policy." He gave Carter a cold, evaluating look. "I hear one of 'em's your buddy."

"John Seldon's an old friend, sir," Carter said stiffly. "It stops there."

"We're going to need tanks when this news breaks."

That could well be. Carter stared at the wall map, thinking fast. "I'd have to look at the numbers again, but we should be able to divert flow from the Great Lakes canal into the Trench to pick up some of this short-fall." He frowned, struggling to recall the use equations. "The Missouri and Mississippi systems were operating on a comfortable margin when I left Chicago. They could trim it."

"That's for Water Policy to decide." Hastings shrugged. "Give me the numbers and I'll look at them. If you haven't missed something, I'll pass them along upstairs." He looked sharply at Carter. "Don't waste time grieving for the farmers along here, Colonel. They're a damned inefficient bunch."

It was true. Biomass crops would dramatically increase the final per-acre food yield along the riverbed if Pacific Biosystems pumped in seawa-ter. He thought about the Corbett woman's face when she talked about the dying Valley. And Jeremy's assessment. Carter let his breath out in a sigh. "When is this reduction scheduled to go into effect, sir? I need time."

"You don't have any time. The UN came down hard on this. We got a forty-eight-hour notice." Hastings got to his feet and paced restlessly across the room. "Water Policy is trying to impress the media. Save the Alliance. Nice line. Your buddy's looking for hero status, Colonel. We get to do the dirty work." He glared at Carter. "Any protest we make is going to come after the fact."

Carter groaned and rubbed his face, thinking hard. "We'll have to change the flow rates gradually or the turbulence will tear any weak spots wide open. Even so, people are going to see their flow cut before we have a chance to notify them." Then the shit would really hit the fan. "Is there any way to stall on this?"

"Nope." Hastings picked up a piece of hardcopy, waved it at him. "It's our baby."

Carter scowled at the wall map of the Columbia system, the blue veins that carried life to the dry, brown land. "Sir?" Carter cleared his throat. "Why did you deny my request for Major Delgado's transfer?"

Hastings' eye narrowed. "Why did you request it?"

"His brother's death has affected his judgment where the locals are concerned." Carter chose his words carefully. "He's an excellent officer otherwise, but I think he needs to be stationed somewhere else." With this cut coming down, Delgado's inflammatory attitude could be the spark that started something.

Hastings was scowling at him. "I know about the major's brother. Yes, he's bitter, but he's been here for a long time. He's had a lot of experience with local politics, and he came up the hard way. You need his judgment."

Carter felt himself flushing. "Sir . . ."

"That's my final decision, Colonel."

"Yes, sir," Carter said stiffly. Damn it. "I'd better go get my people working on this."

The flat photo of the man in dress greens had been moved. It stood beside Hastings's terminal screen, as if he had been looking at it. It clicked suddenly — who he was. "Captain Hastings," Carter said in surprise. "I knew Doug Hastings as O.C.X. We all liked him — he was a good man." And a general's son? That had been a well-kept secret. "Where's he stationed now?"

"He's dead." Hastings picked up the photo. "A retaining wall came down and took out his whole crew. A bad design, approved by an officer who didn't know his ass from a hole in the ground."

Carter stiffened. "I realized that I'm short on experience, sir. I keep it very clearly in mind."

"A pretty speech." Hastings' expression didn't thaw. He put the photo down and straightened it carefully. "Doug should've gotten a purple heart. We're in a war. We're fighting drought and the hicks, all over the damn country. He should've gotten a medal. You better get going before all hell breaks loose." He didn't return Carter's salute.

Now he knew where the hostility came from, anyway. Carter walked slowly back to his car, relieved to escape the looming weight of the dam.

He was sure as hell on his own — and it occurred to him to wonder if Delgado wasn't reporting back directly to the general.

As he left the complex, he called Delgado and told him to pull all the programmers back on duty. He didn't explain why. Hastings was right to worry about eavesdroppers. All he needed was to have someone spread the word that the Corps was about to cut off the water. He'd need those tanks then. He might need them anyway. The wind had started up again, blowing hard from the east, hazing the air with dust. Dust devils twisted along the floor of the riverbed. The Chevy's seals were shot and dust seeped into the car. Carter pulled on his goggles and punched in the number Dan had given him.

"Deschutes government store," a cracked voice answered. "Bob here."

"Hello." Carter raised his voice to be heard over the roar of the engine. "I'm trying to reach Dan Greely. He gave me this number."

"Probably. He don't have a phone." There was a pause and Carter heard distant voices, as if the man was talking to someone with his hand over the phone. "Who is this?" he finally asked.

"Colonel Voltaire. Dan asked me to get in touch with him."

"He's not here." The voice had gone flat and cautious. "If I see him, I"ll give him your message."

"Listen, it's important." Carter kept a tight rein on his rising anger. "Please get the message to him — ask him to come to the main gate at the base. I need to talk to him right away. They'll let him in."

"If I see him, I'll sure tell him."

"Send someone out to find him." But the line had gone dead. "Damn." He tossed the phone onto the seat. The suspicious old fart. If Greely didn't show, he'd have to send a detail out to look for him, and that could be misunderstood. Carter clutched the wheel and concentrated on keeping the Chevy on the battered road. Chicago was leaning over his shoulder and he needed to talk to Johnny. Right now. There had to be another way to handle this water shuffle. He felt as if he were tiptoeing across a mine field — one misstep and it would blow up in his face. It was not a pleasant feeling.

When he reached the lower gate at The Dalles, the corporal on gate duty came out to the car instead of waving him through.

"Colonel?" He saluted. "I got a call from the east gate, sir. There's a visitor waiting for you. A Mr. Greely, sir, a civilian."

That had been fast. The old fart had given Greely the message after all. "Thanks. Have someone escort him to my office." Carter drove on through the gate, worry knotting his gut.

He stopped by his apartment — to get the dust mask he'd forgotten this morning, he told himself. The empty rooms mocked him as he retrieved it from the kitchen counter. Part of him kept hoping she'd come back, coming up with reasons for her disappearance. He had looked for her at the weekend market, but hadn't seen her. He slammed the door behind him and headed for Operations.

Greely was waiting in Carter's office, examining the big wall map of the riverbed. An alert young private watched his every move.

"We locals aren't very welcome here," Greely said as Carter walked in.

"We uniforms aren't very welcome in town. You can go," he told the private, and switched on the office air conditioner.

"I heard you had some trouble out near the truck plaza last week." Greely looked concerned. "I'm glad you didn't get hurt."

"Do you know everything that goes on in town?"

"Pretty much." Greely shrugged. "I also heard that you didn't do any more than you had to." Greely leaned against the wall beside the cool breath of the air conditioner vent, his expression thoughtful. "Those kids could have hurt you. Killed you even. You might have been justified in beating the shit out of them. At least."

Carter reached for the insulated carafe on the end of his desk. "I guess I just don't feel so justified anymore," he said slowly. "Water?"

"Thanks." Greely watched Carter fill two glasses. "Those were highway kids. They stick to the convoy routes, come and go with the truckers. Sex earns 'em a ride and some food. Sometimes their parents are dead, some of 'em come from the camps or from families that broke up drifting."

He took the glass Carter handed him and drank the water down in sharp, quick swallows, as if thirst was something he couldn't quite control, or as if he'd never really gotten enough water to drink in his life. Jeremy drank like that, Carter remembered. He had noticed at the party. "Were you born in the Dry?" he asked.

"L.A." Greely put the glass down. "I spent a lot of time out in the Dry, though. Too much time."

Carter took his glass, filled it again, and handed it back.

"Your kids were out to settle a score. A rough customer beat one of the boys to death a couple of weeks ago." Greely stared into his glass. "A uniform, the rumor goes. Bob said you needed to talk to me right away."

Carter set his glass down very carefully. "Trouble's coming. We have to reduce the Columbia flow by nearly four percent in a little less than forty-eight hours. I didn't know about this until this morning."

Greely frowned, his face lined and tired. "I could say that you were stringing us along the other night. I could say that any promises you make are worth so much dust." He lifted a hand. "I believe you." He met Carter's eyes. "I think you're as much on our side as you can be. But I'm not going to be in the majority, Voltaire. Why this reduction?"

He listened without interruption as Carter repeated what Hastings had told him. "So the valleys get the water." Greely's shoulders slumped. "I'd get strung up for saying it, but you're right about their production rate being better than ours." His lips tightened. "They can do it because it's all ag-plexes and they mix with seawater. You heard all this the other night. So." He faced Carter, his eyes narrowing thoughtfully. "You and I have to make some fast plans if we want to keep a lid on this riverbed."

"What if the Coalition backs the cut?"

"Can't happen." Greely shook his head. "Yeah, Sandy and I kind of organize things, but we don't run the show. The Coalition has a lot of members, and Ransom is pretty close to your average hose farmer as far as attitude goes."

"Great." Carter rubbed his eyes, a headache building at the back of his brain. "Got any other ideas?"

"Maybe." Greely frowned. "Sandy and I might just yell about this, whip everyone into a nice frenzy, and head out to the Shunt for a big, noisy, demonstration."

"Are you crazy? That's just what we want to avoid."

"What we need to avoid is bloodshed." Dan's expression was grim. "There's no way the folks here are going to accept what you're doing. They're going to scream, and they need to scream. I want the media to come hear them scream. It's their families who are going to suffer from that reduction, not their credit balance. This isn't a chess game, Carter." His voice had gone low and hard. "People are going to lose their land, they're so close to the edge now. Do you know what happens if federal ag credit forecloses on you? If you're lucky, you get a job hoeing bushes in the Valley — but bushes don't take much labor. If you aren't lucky, your kids grow up as campies, or hit the highways with the truckers. Some kind of protest is going to happen. We've got cool heads in the Coalition. They aren't all Ransoms, and they'll help me and Sandy maintain some kind of order. If you help, too, maybe we can at least keep anyone from getting killed."

"I hear what you're saying, Dan," Carter said quietly. "I know it's not a game. I think I do know what's at stake. For all of us."

"Yeah." Greely held his gaze for a moment. "Maybe you do at that." He looked at the wall map. "It's got to happen at the Shunt. The media won't show up unless we give them something tasty. A threat to the Klamath Shunt is a threat to the Sacramento Valley. That'll bring them running. Besides," Greely gave Carter a lopsided grin. "The Shunt is a long way from town. Some folks won't be able to get there, and others will use that as an excuse not to show."

"I can't risk the Shunt."

"I told you, it's not a chess game." Greely looked down at his hands, his face etched with weariness and years of sun. "We'll do this with or without you. The only way you can stop it is to throw barricades across every access road and try to block the riverbed. You'll be dealing with small groups, then, and a lot of those groups are going to be following the hot-heads. There's going to be shooting. If we organize this thing, the Coalition has at least a chance of keeping it under control."

If he let this happen and the Shunt itself took damage, he was dead. "I could call the MPs right now." Carter hung onto his temper with an effort. "Even if we can't make anything stick, we could hold on to you for a day or two."

"What are you after?" Greely met his glare without flinching. "When you cut the water, there's going to be trouble. It might not happen at the Shunt, but it'll be bad. I thought that's what you wanted to stop? This protest will give folks a chance to scream and yell, blow off some steam." He ran a hand across his weathered face. "You've got no particular reason to trust me, Voltaire. I know it." He sighed. "We can do this together, or we can do it from opposite sides. You choose."

Stubborn bastard. Carter frowned. If he trusted this man, if he was sure, he'd risk it. Because the plan made sense. But he wasn't on Greely's side, he was in the middle. Carter stared through the window, seeing sun baked dust, remembering how the sun had flayed his naked back. Greely could have dumped him out there. He had no evidence either way.

"All right." Carter laid his palms flat on the desktop. "We're going to have riot gas up there. If anyone breaks through our line or makes a serious try for the shunt bunker, we're going to use it and come down hard on the crowd. That's the best I can do, Dan. You'd better keep your people under control, because I cannot risk the Shunt."

"Sandy and I know some dependable folk." Greely was clearly think-ing hard. "They're good at keeping a crowd peaceful without making it obvious. I'll see if I can keep some of the hotheads out of this. What about the uniforms?"

"My people won't start anything. I'll put in extra officers to make sure they stay in line." Carter shrugged at Dan's dubious expression. "It better work," he said. "Or you'll be dealing with a new CO out here."

"Thanks." Greely got to his feet. "They're good people, the ones who are going to go under." He looked away briefly. "I'd better get going if I'm going to set up a reasonable demonstration in forty-eight hours."

"I'll look into that kid's death," Carter said as Greely started for the door. "And I'll make it clear that any violence against civilians in town or elsewhere is going to mean serious trouble."

"Thanks." Greely turned back suddenly and held out his hand.

Carter returned his grip, saying a small prayer that he was reading this man accurately. "Good luck. To both of us."

"You're letting Greely set you up," Delgado growled when Carter informed him of the plan.

"He's right. This water cut is going to mean some kind of confrontation." Carter stared at the quiet bustle of Operations, seeing that blue tracery of life in his mind. "Even you agree with him on that. What do you want to do? Trade shots with the locals from the riverbed?" Yeah, he probably did. "Greely thinks that this project will act as some kind of safety valve, and I think he might be right. It's all a matter of where and when, not whether."

"You do it his way, sir, and they'll tear the Shunt apart. I say we arm everyone, wait until they show up, and round up the lot of them."

"That'll get the shooting started," Carter said grimly. "I didn't say we were going to do it Dan's way exactly." Trust was a luxury he couldn't afford. "We're going to have armed troops inside that Shunt bunker. If we're lucky, we won't even need the gas. If there's a serious threat to the Shunt, we open fire." And that would end any chance of peace between the Corps and The Dalles.

Delgado's eyes glittered. "That's a good plan, sir."

How many lives would it take to satisfy Delgado's hungry ghost? "We are going to shoot only as a last resort." Carter stared at the major. "There will be no provocative action taken by any enlisteds or officers during the protest. None. I am holding you personally responsible for that, Major. Do I make myself clear?"

"Yes, sir." Delgado saluted.

Delgado was too sure that the locals were going to start the riot he wanted. Carter stalked out of Operations, worry churning in his gut, wishing he was equally sure that Delgado was wrong. Outside, the wind scoured the riverbed beneath the velvet blue of the dry, twilight sky. Carter looked eastward, finding the faint glitter of the first star low on the horizon. It was a planet, not a star. Saturn? Mars? He couldn't remember. He had forgotten to ask Greely about Nita. Wearily he headed toward the mess hall, praying that he and Greely really were on the same side.

The dry eye of the planet winked at him and, in the distance, a coyote pack raised a shrill chorus to the night.

CHAPTER ELEVEN

D an and the Coalition had managed to come up with an impressive number of people on short notice. Carter leaned against the hood of the parked truck, watching the crowd mill in the blazing sunshine. The afternoon was windless for once, and dust hung in the air, burning his damaged lungs.

Hands Off Our Water! The crude signs had been lettered in blood red paint. *Uniforms Get Out! This Land is Our Land!* He couldn't see the expressions from this distance. Here at its mouth, the Deschutes bed was wide and rocky. The crowd had spilled over from the highway, but so far they had stayed behind the tape barricade that the Corps had erected. But he didn't have to see their expressions to know what their mood was. A man and a couple of women were leading chants: *Army out, it's our water*, and *Water water everywhere, how come the Valleys get our share?* In between the chants, the crowd murmured with the sound of a big animal growling low in its throat.

This was different from Chicago. In Chicago, the violence had built up like gas pocket in a mine — odorless, invisible. The explosion had come suddenly, violently. Maybe Greely was right, and the yelling would bleed off some of that deadly power. Maybe.

They were chanting again. The media was here, just as Greely had wanted. Reporters with vid-cams stalked the fringes of the mob, angling for dramatic shots. Carter's lips tightened as he walked the line they had set up, clapping shoulders, speaking to his officers and NCOs. They were all nervous. This wasn't what they had signed on with the Crops to do. They were water people, trained to maintain the Pipeline. They weren't combat troops. They were welders and flow specialists, dozer drivers and surveyors. "Let them yell," he said to one of his sergeants. The man was wire-tight, and Carter put a hand on his shoulder. "Barking dogs aren't so likely to bite."

"Yes, sir," the sergeant said, but he didn't sound convinced.

They were wearing the new-issue riot gear — helmets, Kevlar cover-alls, rock-shields, and stun wands like cattle prods but with a lot more oomph. Riot gear must be a growth industry, Carter thought bitterly. Gas masks dangled from every belt. He had parked the convoy of government vehicles in a rough line about twenty yards in front of the silocrete dome that housed the complex Shunt valves. Inside the Shunt bunker, a carefully selected detail crouched, armed with laser-sighted M20s. If civilians got past the trucks, they had orders to open fire. And it would all go to hell after that. Carter shaded his eyes against the glare.

Lava rock, eroded by ages of wind and water, stuck up out of the riverbed clay in long ridges. They reminded Carter of dirty molars jutting out of a bare jawbone, like the horse's skull he and Johnny had unearthed in the meadow behind Johnny's family compound one summer afternoon. The sun was still well above the horizon and the riverbed held the heat and dust like a bowl. Here and there, umbrellas stuck up above the crowd among the signs, casting tiny pools of shade.

On the slopes above the rocky sides of the gorge, green leaves shimmered in the sun — sugar beets. Carter took a hand-held amplifier from the back of a truck. *They're desperate*, he had told his officers this morning. *They're scared for their kids and their homes.*

It was hard to keep that in mind as the crowd chanted and growled.

"Tell us." The florid-faced Ransom bawled from the front rank of the crowd. "Tell us why you bastards decided to cut off our water?"

"We're not cutting off your water." Carter kept his voice calm and reasonable, but his hand amp boomed it out over the riverbed, harsh and loud. "We have to send more water down to Mexico or the Alliance goes down the drain. And then Canada can legally short us. Then you'll really see water cuts."

"Screw Mexico," Ransom bawled. "Don't feed us this Mexico shit. You're taking our water to feed those damn bush farmers. It was on the news. You cut us four and a half percent. You know what those numbers mean? They mean that our kids are gonna go hungry. Or do you care?"

Damn the media. It sure had been on the evening newscasts, was all over the internet, and he would give a lot to know who'd leaked it to them. Carter unclenched his teeth with an effort. "This cut means that you're all going to have a hard time," he said. "Some of you are going to lose your farms. I wish that there was something that the Corps could do, but there isn't. If the water doesn't go down the Shunts, a lot more people are going to have a hard time — the people who depend on the valleys for their food. If the bushes die, they go hungry. Their kids go hungry. We've got to get the maximum use out of every gallon of water. Numbers count. It's damned tough, but they do."

"At least he'd not jerking us around," a man yelled from the crowd. "He's saying it like it really is."

"Sounds like shit to me," a sarcastic voice rang out. "Feels like, smells like it, too." A ripple of muttering and nervous laughter ran through the crowd.

The laughter didn't relieve any tension. If anything, that sarcastic voice had cranked it tighter. "You've got real complaints." Carter raised his voice. "But you're picking on the wrong people. Yeah, we carry out the orders. We reprogrammed the valves that reduced your water, but we didn't make the distribution decisions. Water Policy did that, and right now we're looking at some numbers that may change things, let us bring in water from the Great Lakes to make up the difference. But right now, we have to do what they tell us to do."

"So what?" The sarcastic voice yelled again. "You gonna send us to Washington to talk to the Committee? You think we really believe you're looking at numbers? None of you care about us as long as you eat. So I say we do something about that."

The crowd roared approval, drawing together like an animal crouching for the attack.

There he was — the voice — a ginger haired man with a square, calculating face. Carter tensed. He knew that face, had a sudden, cloudy memory of an arm beneath his chin, choking him. "Violence gets you nothing," Carter yelled over his speaker. "If you wind up in jail, if there's no water in the Pipe, what the hell have you gained?"

"Won't matter then, will it?" Red-hair faced the crowd, arms raised stiffly, fists clenched. He had to be wearing a mic and a hi-tech amp because you could hear his voice all across the riverbed. And that voice was like a whiplash, charged with energy, crackling with power and anger. "Yeah, go ahead and listen to the uniforms," he yelled. "Let's shuffle on home like good little citizens. We can sit in our houses and behave while our crops wilt and our kids die. Or we can make those fat cats in Washington listen. We can hurt 'em where they're hurting us, right? If they're hungry enough, they'll pay attention. Let's do it!" he howled. "Smash those valves. Let the bushes wilt this time."

A rock banged off the fender of a truck. Another starred the windshield of Carter's Chevy. The crowd surged forward, individual voices lost in the mob roar. Dan's people were trying. You could see them, like rocks in a flood; men and women grabbing at people, shouting, forming little whirlpools in the slow forward surge of the crowd. He spotted Greely near the center. He was holding his own, slowing people down, but it wasn't enough.

"Spread out," Carter ordered. "Hold the line. Don't break."

They had to stop the crowd well in front of the trucks. His people were moving forward, protected from the scatter of rocks by their shields. Out in the crowd, the redheaded man swung a fist and one of the dissenters went down. The first people hit the line and Carter heard screams. Those stun wands hurt. You blew it, Dan, Carter thought. Time to stop this. Now. Carter headed for the truck where they had set up the gas launchers. A windshield shattered, spraying him with bits of glass. Carter ducked, searching for Dan again in the milling chaos. He'd disappeared. Dust drifted in choking clouds, obscuring the struggling bodies. The line was being forced back, pushed toward him and the trucks. His orders had been to launch the gas if the line gave. Carter grabbed the comm. Link from his belt. "Wilson? Captain?" Nothing but static. What the hell had happened?

They were on him; a struggling line of swinging wands and riot sticks, still backing. The locals were using fists mostly, no gunfire, thank God. A couple of them had gotten hold of riot sticks. Dust blinded Carter, filling his eyes with tears. A corporal staggered backward and collided with him, half stunned, clutching his face where a stone had hit. Blood gleamed on his fingers. Carter got an arm around him and stumbled for the launcher, fear cold in his gut. If they got past the trucks, they'd have to open fire. A stone hit him in the back and he tripped, pulled off-balance by the corporal's weight. A bearded man loomed suddenly out of the dust, a riot stick swinging for Carter's face.

Carter flung up his arm, bracing for the blow.

A uniformed shoulder slammed him aside as the soldier pivoted into a high, straight-legged kick. The local took the blow just under his sternum, and went down gasping. "Are you all right, sir?" The soldier grabbed his arm, hauled Carter to his feet.

She was a short, stocky woman. "Thanks, Private — Wasson." He read the name from her uniform pocket. "Take him and follow me," he gasped, shoving the dazed corporal at her.

"Yes, sir." The square-faced woman grinned, but her eyes looked scared.

He ran for the truck with Wasson right behind him.

"Permission to open fire, sir?" Delgado emerged from the dust. "They're through the line, sir."

"Why the hell didn't they launch the gas?"

"Wilson said you called, sir, told him to hold off."

Carter chopped off his words with a savage gesture. "Do it."

"Sire, they're too close." Delgado's eyes burned with suppressed triumph. "It's too late to stop them."

"*Now!* Help them," Carter snapped at the private. "Drop the canisters along the Deschutes edge of the crowd." What little wind flow would carry it back over them.

The Corps people who didn't get their masks on in time were going to get a dose, too. No help for it. The *whump* of the gas launcher echoed across the riverbed, and Carter heard the first packed yells as the white clouds billowed up. People staggered drunkenly as the gas hit them, going down onto hands and knees, sprawling sideways as they tried to stand. The stuff knocked out your sense of balance, left you flat on the ground, retching with dizziness. It wasn't much fun. Some of the gagging figures on the ground wore Corps suncloth, but things were starting to break up. A media vid-cammer was down on the ground with the locals. Carter felt a sour satisfaction as the man retched.

"Get our people up here and then start picking up the locals," Carter ordered. "I want to talk to Wilson *now*." If Delgado was lying — if he'd interfered with the launch order — he'd face a court-martial and to hell with Hastings. "We'll pick up only the locals who were doing the actual fighting. And I want Greely here. Let the rest go. No rough stuff, Major." They'd salvage what they could out of this mess.

"Yes, sir." Delgado saluted and vanished into the dust, his expression carefully neutral.

Carter went looking for Greely, angry and hurting from the stone bruise on his shoulder blade. It had been damn close. The crowed had blown up fast. Greely had underestimated them, or had overestimated the Corps' power. Or it had been a setup.

Carter scanned the scattered bodies still retching into the dust. Greely wasn't on the ground. He wasn't among the sullen locals being loaded onto a truck. The medical team was already on the scene and Carter went to get a report on injuries.

He kept an eye out for Greely as he secured the bunker and made sure that the soldiers didn't get too zealous or too rough about rounding people up. He did see Sandy Corbett; she was helping some of the gas-struck. Ironically, the gas had hit the people in the rear of the demonstration hardest — the people who had hung back from the fighting. At least Harold Ransom had breathed gas. If anyone deserved it, he did. He kept a sharp eye our for Red-hair, but he had vanished, too.

It could have worked, it might have worked, if that bastard hadn't gotten started. He had been damned good at getting the crowd hot. Coming wired for sound had been clever. Everybody had heard every word. A media copter lifted, and Carter groaned inwardly. Ratings ought to be real high tonight. His were going to be pretty damn low.

The whole afternoon had been a disaster for everyone except the media. Carter fought a rising sense of discouragement as the sun set and darkness crept down the riverbed. They had arrested twelve locals. Besides an assortment of minor injuries a private had gotten his jaw broken when he was hit in the face with a riot stick. Carter's people were sullen, angry that they hadn't been able to settle the score. Half a dozen had breathed gas, and Delgado radiated righteous vindication. Wilson had cleared him. Someone had played a sophisticated game with the electronics. That was some serious sabotage, not the stuff of dirt farmers. Corps communications were supposed to be un-hackable. Carter had to think about that.

An insider? Delgado himself?

At least nobody had started shooting. Greely had managed to keep the rifles at home, he'd give him that much. Carter detailed extra security for the Shunt dome. They'd have to keep a twenty-four-hour armed guard there, he thought wearily. He didn't dare trust his electronic security anymore. That meant more duty hours and less sleep for everyone. And the plan to use locals on patrol was laughable now. The trucks were pulling out, heading back for the dam. Where the hell had Greely got to? He was looking real bad right now. Carter's shoulder twinged as he backed the Chevy around and followed the last truck up the access road to the highway. He should have tapped someone to drive.

He drove one-handed, taking it slow. Back at the base, he'd have to report into Hastings. He was not looking forward to that conversation. Carter eased the car around a bulge in the Gorge wall. He wanted Greely to tell him why it hadn't worked, and he wanted that explanation to be damn good.

The moon was up. It turned the riverbed into a wasteland of gray shadow, sterile and alien in the cold light. A blot of darkness bulked at the edge of the bed. Carter took his foot off the accelerator, slowing even more. A side road took off from the main highway here, a narrow dirt track that meandered down into the riverbed from a gap broken through the rusting guard rail of the interstate. He could just make out a car parked close against the bank, almost invisible from the highway. It looked like a Corps vehicle.

If it was, it shouldn't be here.

Carter reached for his phone, then snapped it closed. They could be listening. Carter drove on around the curve of the Gorge wall and then pulled over to the side of the highway, out of sight of the parked vehicle. He killed the headlights, and climbed out.

It was quiet and already cold, the wind just beginning to stir for real. His footsteps rasped on the gritty asphalt, loud in the silence. He unsnapped his holster and drew his Beretta. After climbing over the guardrail, he worked his way cautiously down the slope, testing every foothold on the steep bank.

Four figures stood in a tight cluster behind the concealed vehicle. Three of them wore Corps coveralls; the fourth was a civilian. Carter crept closer, hugging the deep shadow cast by the bank, placing his feet carefully on the eroded soil. Two of the soldiers held the civilian by the arms. The third soldier stood in front of him. He hunched forward suddenly and Carter heard the meaty sound of the blows. The civilian reeled, coughed, and sagged to his knees. They hauled him upright again and the third man drew his fist back.

"That's enough." Carter thumbed off the Beretta's safety and straightened. "This is Colonel Voltaire. Attention!"

The uniformed trio froze, faces turning in his direction.

Delgado? Carter squinted in the moonlight. "Major! What the hell is going on here, mister?"

"We were on our way back with this prisoner, sir." Delgado kept his eyes fixed on a point to the left of Carter's shoulder as Carter approached. "He tried to escape, sir."

"Did he?" Carter kept his weapon in hand as he turned to the two men holding the civilian.

The man's hands were cuffed behind him. Greely. "Sit him down and get the cuffs off him," Carter said through tight lips. "You two — you're confined to quarters until further notice." He faced Delgado. "Get these men back to the base. I want you in my office tomorrow morning at oh-nine-hundred sharp."

"Yes, sir." Delgado's face was stony.

The two enlisteds had eased Greely to the ground. Delgado bent and unlocked the cuffs. Stiffly and silently the three men climbed into the car. The engine roared to life and the headlights came on, washing the rocky ground with yellow light, making the blood on Greely's face shine wet and crimson. Carter squatted beside him, keeping an eye on the car as it backed up the slope toward the highway. "Are you badly hurt?"

"I'll live." Greely touched his mouth tentatively, then wiped his bloody fingers on his jeans. "I'm glad you happened along."

"Those three are going to regret this," Carter said flatly. "What happened?"

"I was trying to break things up and someone hit me from behind." Greely touched the back of his head and grimaced. "I woke up on the floor of the car. What happened at the Shunt?"

"We used the gas. I don't think anyone got killed. The situation went flat to hell." Carter drew a deep breath. "Did you set me up?"

"No." Greely looked him square in the face. "I didn't." His shoulders sagged. "I thought we had things under control. People were mad, but it was the media they wanted to reach."

"They sure got the media's attention."

"As a bunch of crazy hotheads. That doesn't do us any good. I'm sorry, Carter." Greely leaned his forehead against his raised knees. "I thought it would work. I guess I'm slipping."

"Too late to cry about it now," Carter said bitterly. "Who is that red-headed bastard, anyway? We didn't pick him up and he sure started things going to hell."

"I don't know him," Greely mumbled. "He sounded like a pro to me. I was on my way to shut him down when I got hit."

"He sure did a professional job. I don't think he was working alone either. Sit still." Carter got to his feet. "I'll bring the car down here for you."

Sandy Corbett had said she thought the saboteurs were outsiders, he remembered. He hadn't taken her very seriously at the time. Carter thought about it now as he eased the car down the narrow track. Working for the Coalition? Possibly. Working for someone else? Who? Good question. Carter pulled up beside Greely and set the brake. "Do you know that redhead's name?"

Greely shook his head as he slumped into the front seat.

Carter remembered that face. From the abduction? He wasn't entirely sure, and the more he tried to remember, the less certain he was. "Will you find out who he is?" Carter asked as he climbed into the car.

"I'll . . . try." Greely was leaning back in the seat, eyes closed.

More blood matted his hair, and he looked bad. Both eyes were swollen nearly shut and he looked pale beneath the blood and darkening bruises. Carter whistled softly. "We need to get you to a doctor."

"Could you give me a ride home?" he mumbled. "I'll be all right."

"You could have a concussion."

"Don't think so." Greely tried a laugh, coughed, and grimaced. "Been here before. Cracked ribs, maybe. Nothing worse."

He directed Carter up a winding road that led east from the Dufur highway. A narrow track took them to the rim of the Gorge, then led them east toward the Deschutes bed and the site of the day's disaster. To their left lay the Gorge, a yawning space of empty darkness. The Washington side was a landscape of darkness beneath the starry sky.

"Old Celilo Falls is down there," Greely said as they bounced along the rim. "It's a good place for ghosts." He caught his breath as a bad stretch jolted him. "Turn here."

The headlights splashed back from rows of low-growing bean plants, one of the high-protein soy clones, probably. The faint track they were on ended in front of a decrepit old house. The weathered siding showed a few traces of long-ago white paint and the porch sagged drunkenly. Carter helped Greely up the warped steps, supporting most of his weight.

The inside was sparsely furnished. Carter clicked on the solar lantern that hung from a wire above a rickety table. Its yellow glow revealed an ancient woodstove, the table, a couple of battered chairs, and not much else. The poverty depressed him. Two doors opened from the main room. One was closed. Through the other, Carter saw a bed and caught a glimpse of colorful pictures on the walls.

"Thanks for the ride." Greely sank onto a chair, breathing harshly. "We had a good plan. I sure thought it would work."

Carter found a clean rag hanging on a hook beside the sink and wet it under the tap. "Here." He wrung it out and handed it to Greely. "I want to believe you," he said slowly. "That it wasn't a setup."

"It wasn't." Greely folded the cloth and held it against the back of his head, his face tight with pain. "I swear it."

"I'm going to have trouble with General Hastings." Carter looked around, frowning. "I may not be able to deal with the Coalition after this. You're not living here alone, are you? You sure you're going to be all right?"

The closed door opened suddenly. "Dan?" The woman in the doorway yawned, as she combed tangled black hair back from her face.

Nita. Carter stared at her, his stomach knotting. So that was how Greely had heard about his encounter with the kids. "I guess you'll be just fine," he said. "Hello, Nita." He turned on his heel, starting for the door.

"Wait a minute!" She caught up with him on the porch, grabbed his arm.

He shook her off, numb inside. "I don't have time."

"Carter, stop it." She leaped down the steps and blocked his path to the car, illuminated by the light from the open door. "Tell me what happened to Dan. Why are you so angry?"

She had been right there, out in the Dry, with her water and her comfort. Sweet coincidence, Delgado had said. Oh yes. "What were you trying to find out for Greely?"

"No." Her face went pale. "It's not what you think."

"You don't know what I think."

"You think I betrayed you — that I'm an enemy. I didn't," she whispered. "I'm not. How can you think that?"

"Weren't you hunting for this husband of yours? You don't seem to be looking too hard," he said savagely.

"I *am* looking. Dan offered me a job working his beans, and that's what I'm doing here. I have to live somewhere, Carter. I . . . I couldn't stay with you. I should have told you before I left, but I was . . . afraid."

He looked away from the anguish in her face, hesitated for one instant. Because he wanted to believe her.

He shoved past her.

"Carter, wait!" she cried. "Please?"

The headlights caught her as Carter backed the car around. She stood on the porch steps, stiff and still, her hands clasped tightly. Delgado had been right after all.

He drove fast back along the gravel road, bouncing and bucking over the ruts and stones, but he couldn't outrun the hard fist of pain in his belly.

CHAPTER TWELVE

Dan was holding a towel to his face when Nita came back into the house. "Trouble?" he dabbed at his lip.

"I don't know." Carter was so wounded. She hadn't meant that to happen. "Here. Give me that." She took the bloodstained cloth from Dan's hand, teeth on edge. He hurt. A lot. "Who did this?"

"Uniforms." Dan groaned as she began to clean the blood from the cut on the back of his head. "The protest got violent after all. It's a good thing you weren't there."

He'd been disappointed when she had refused to go. *We need people who will keep their heads*, he had told her. *The more the better*. It was because she was Sam Montoya's daughter, Nita thought resentfully. Sam had done this kid of thing with them, so he wanted her to be part of it, too. She wasn't part of it. She didn't belong here. Now Carter was pissed at her. Damn them both.

"Hold still," Nita said as Dan flinched. She frowned at the reddened towel. "The cut on your scalp doesn't look too bad. Do you have anything I can put on it?"

"There's some stuff in the cabinet over the sink." Dan leaned his head in his hands. "I don't know if I can go through this again."

"Go through what? Getting beaten up?" She couldn't help but share his pain. Nita jerked open the cabinet door and picked up a tube of antibiotic ointment. That stuff cost on the black market. In fact, Dan had quite a supply of very expensive and hard-to-get medical supplies on the shelves. Interesting. She took down a pair of surgical scissors. "This ought to do it. You don't really need stitches. Try hard to hold still, okay?"

"This is a repeat of twenty years ago." Dan hissed softly between his teeth as she snipped hair from around the lips of the ugly gash. "Back then the Columbia Association was squeezing the water, trying to run the farmers off so they could repossess their land. The Corps was on our side back then. We beat the Association, but barely." He sighed. "People got killed in the process. I don't want to do it all over again with the Corps. I'm too damned old for this."

"Then let someone else do it."

"That's what I told your father. Last time." Dan looked at her, squinting through the eye that wasn't swollen completely shut. "He was the reason we won. Sam kept everyone together, even when it was tough, even when people were getting beaten up and shot. Folks believed in Sam. If it hadn't been for him, everything would have fallen apart. We'd all be in the camps."

"Why are you telling me this?" Nita filled a bowl from the tap and began to rinse out the towel.

"Sam was my friend," Dan said softly. "I want you to know."

So he had to tell her right now — because he might have died tonight? Because he knew that he might die soon? As her father had died? It was too much, on top of Carter's wounded anger. "Do you want to know what I remember about my father?" Nita twisted the towel, wringing red water into the bowl. "I remember when the men came. He could have run . . . he started to run. But I was in the yard. So he didn't run. He grabbed me up and threw me behind our old truck. So I'd be safe from the bullets, I guess." The gunshots had hurt her ears, louder than thunder. "His blood got on my dress. He fell down right beside me." She looked Dan in the face. "Mama never forgave me," she said deliberately. "Because he could have run. Because I was alive and he was dead. Because she loved him and he loved this damn town more than he loved her. Here." She shoved the cloth at Dan. "Hold this on your face. It'll help the swelling. But you know that, right?"

"I'm sorry." Dan took the cloth, all muddy inside. "I was in prison by then. When I got out, Maria was long gone. I'm so damn sorry, Nita."

Nita turned her back on him, trembling suddenly. She had never told anyone about that day, not even David. This man remembered Sam Montoya. "I am not my father, Dan. Don't ask me to be." She fled to the darkness of her room to bury herself in the vivid, wordless immediacy of her daughter's dreams.

Rachel woke Nita with the sun, insistently hungry. Nita nursed her, then stripped off her wet diaper and laid her on the floor on her back. Rachel laboriously rolled herself onto her stomach, face wrinkled with effort. Nita smiled as her daughter rocked herself onto her hands and knees. "You're so determined," she murmured and smiled. Rachel flopped onto her chest, protesting. "Soon enough," Nita soothed. "You'll be crawling all over the place." She stroked her daughter's dark, wispy hair and went out to bring in the diapers.

They had dried stiff, stained yellow, too soiled to use again without washing. Nita sighed and peered at the brownish water left from rinsing the bloody towel last night. She dumped it into the big plastic pail by the door. She would have to use fresh water, and take it all out to the kitchen garden afterward. Carter had been so shocked, when she had told him about washing in a pail. It hurt to think about Carter. At least she had water for washing here. The price for sleeping in a bed was diapers. Out in the fields, Rachel went naked.

Dan was waking up. Nita pressed her lips together as his pain seeped into her thoughts. Why me? she thought bitterly, wishing once more that she had been born normal.

Like Rachel.

Normal. Nita filled a plastic mug from the tap, her throat dry with Dan's thirst. Mug in hand, she hesitated in the doorway of the bedroom. Pictures hung on the walls, glowing with color in the bright morning light.

"You're a mind reader," Dan said, and didn't notice the flinch she couldn't quite conceal. He tried to sit up, but eased himself back down with a groan. "The first day is hell," he said.

The sheet had bunched around his waist. His stomach and chest were purple and green with bruises, his face swollen and ugly. It looked worse than it felt and it felt bad enough.

"Nothing's broken." Dan had noticed her expression. "I bet I look like shit, but I'll be all right in a few days."

This had happened to him before. Often enough that he knew the healing schedule. Nita put the mug down on the table beside him, wondering if her father had been beaten up like this and how Mama had felt when it had happened. "I'm sorry," she said stiffly. "About last night. I was . . . in a bad mood."

"You were right." Dan sighed. "I've been levering you. I wanted you to be your father. I guess it scares me that I might be too old to handle this all over again." His smile turned into a grimace of pain as he propped himself on one elbow. "It's ironic. I was pissed when Sam started trying to drag me into things. I'd been wandering all my life, and this place didn't seem any different than any other town that I'd been through. It isn't. I guess. But Sam made a place for me here, and I've been here ever since." He met her eyes. "I'll quit levering you. If you want to take off, I have a bit of scrip put away. I can pay you some wages, at least."

And go where? "I'll stay," Nita said.

"I'm glad." Dan reached for the mug. "I'm glad you're here. I'm not sure I could handle a trip to the sink yet."

"Ignacio was always getting into fights," Nita said. "But never this bad." Her older brother had translated Mama's bitter anger into violence. Nita took the empty mug from him, frowning. She had never asked Ignacio if he felt people the way she did. By the time she had understood it enough to ask, Ignacio was gone, driven down the road by his angry darkness.

Rachel had worked her way to the edge of the quilt and had started to complain. Nita went to scoop up her daughter, detouring into her room. "This will help," she told Dan when she came back. She plopped Rachel onto the floor again, opened the small plastic jug she had brought. "I'll have to find another hive before I can make any more," she said as she poured golden liquid into Dan's mug.

"What's this?" Dan's eyebrows rose as he sipped.

"It's honey water. I ferment it, so it's got some alcohol in it. It's good if you're sick and it helps if you're hurting."

"Maybe you could hunt bees around here."

"I haven't seen many. They've been dying." She capped the bottle. "David said it must be some kind of disease. That's why he . . . had to go find a job." A hard lump clogged her throat and she looked away, fixing her eyes on the pictures. Most of them showed a river, full of water and edged with green, like pictures Nita had seen in old books and videos. "Is that the Columbia?"

"Yep. Jesse — the woman who used to own this farm — painted those pictures. She could remember water in the riverbed, back before they finished the Trench Reservoir and built the Pipeline."

"She must have been old," Nita said, her eyes on the blues and grays and greens."

"I thought so, the first time I saw her."

Nita felt Dan's smile and realized suddenly that Jesse had been his lover. He was remembering her and the echoes of their lovemaking tickled her, softened with his sadness. She had thought David was old when she had first met him. He had been nearly forty, ancient to her young eyes. "I'm sorry," she said, knowing without his telling her that Jesse was dead.

"Me, too." Dan sighed. "She was part of the reason I stayed." He stared at the ceiling. "Sometimes I think Sam dropped me on Jesse's doorstep on purpose — that he figured we needed each other. He had a lot of insight about people — he cared, and he cared about keeping the community alive. When he died, there wasn't anyone to take his place. I discovered . . . that I couldn't walk away. I couldn't let what he did go for nothing. I guess I still can't." He turned his head to give Nita his lopsided smile. "I'm levering you again," he said. "Or maybe it's this business with the Corps. It makes me ask myself why the hell I'm still involved. Anyway, I'm sorry."

"It's all right," Nita said. "My father lived here. He was who he was, and I guess I'd better get used to it." Rachel whimpered and Nita picked her up. "The Valley's an ugly place," she said softly. "Salt from the water creeps up out of the ground and coats the bushes with a white crust. The dust stings your eyes and makes you cough. Nothing grows except the bushes. You have to go way up into the mountains to find any flowers."

"We're making things worse," Dan murmured. "We're running so hard to keep ahead of this damned drought that we can't stop. We'll never be able to go back to the way it was, even if the rains start tomorrow."

David had said the same thing. The bushes didn't need bees and the salty Valley had scared him. We scared him, too, Nita thought and settled her fussing daughter onto her hip. "The soaker hoses in the south end of the field are plugging up. If I don't get them cleared, the beans are going to wilt."

"Could I ask you to do me a favor?" Dan asked. "You can drive, right? Would you take the truck and go over to Sandy Corbett's place later? I need to talk to her, but I think she'll have to come here." He grimaced. "I'll draw you a map. The Coalition needs to start dealing with yesterday's mess."

"Sure." Nita picked up the mug. The honey water had blurred away some of his pain and he was sinking into sleep. She needed to get out of this house. Her father had sat at the table in the kitchen, had looked out the window at the dry riverbed. Maybe I *will* leave, Nita thought, but there was nowhere to go. "I'll go give Sandy your message as soon as I get the hoses clear."

The Corbett farm lay west of The Dalles, on a bench of level land above the riverbed. Nita found the gray-haired, stocky woman out weeding beets, shaded from the afternoon sun by a handwoven grass hat.

"What got into that fool colonel?" Dirt-stained hands on her hips, Sandy glared when Nita told her about Dan's beating. "Dan's the best ally that idiot has. Is he trying to cut his own throat?"

"Carter didn't do it. He brought Dan home." Nita caught the speculative flicker of Sandy's curiosity, heard the defensive note in her voice. "That's what Dan told me," she said in a calmer tone.

"Dan's too quick to forgive. Of course, that's not a bad trait, considering that he's usually smack in the middle of things." Sandy wiped her hands on her dirty jeans. "The man just can't say no to folks' needs. Your father was like that, too."

Not this again. Nita pressed her lips together, pretending to adjust Rachel's sling.

"Anyway, I'm glad you're staying out there. I worry about Dan. He takes too much on himself."

"He says that you need to meet, that you'll know who to tell."

"Oh, I'll round 'em up, although there's a couple I'd like to leave out of it," she grumbled. "I'm afraid we're in for real trouble, no matter what miracle Dan thinks he can pull off." Her weathered face crinkled into a sudden smile and she stuck out a finger for Rachel to grab. "Come sit and have a drink. I've got some scones left over from breakfast, too. No sense going back there hungry."

The house turned out to be three battered mobile homes parked in an open-sided square around an ancient maple tree. A decrepit wooden barn sagged out back. The trailers squatted on their concrete-block foundations, scabby and settled, as if they'd been there a long, long time. A thick layer of old leaves carpeted the space beneath the tree.

"Sit down. I'll bring stuff out. The place is a mess, as usual." She waved vaguely at a few old yard chairs. Old baling twine, bleached to a pale orange, had been woven into seats and backs over the battered frames. Nita spread Rachel's quilt on the crackly leaves, put her daughter down on her belly, and gave her a string of wooden beads to play with.

"Here you are." The gray-haired woman reappeared with a pitcher and two glasses clutched in one hand, a plate of thick, golden cakes in the other. "The boys are down in Bonneville, buying some new hose for the east field, and Cathy's teaching at the co-op school this week. She's got the whole brood with her." She handed Nita a glass and sat down. "I've got the place to myself today."

Nita nodded, not sure what to say, and covered her confusion with a bite of the crumbly, biscuit-like cake. An upright piano was visible through the open door of the trailer. "Do you play?" she asked.

"Some." Sandy sighed. "My hands aren't as nimble as they used to be. When I was a kid, I was going to be a concert pianist. I had it all figured out — I was going to get a scholarship, be another Van Cliburn, or Horowitz, or Huang. Oh yes, I did have dreams." She shook her head and laughed gently. "I taught your mom to play, you know."

"My mother?"

"Uh-huh. Back before she and your dad were even married. Maria loved music. She had a beautiful voice, too."

"I didn't know that." Nita looked down at the glass in her hand, trying to imagine her mother singing.

"She quit taking lessons when Alberto was born. She said she was too tired, and I guess she was, with the farm to work and all." Sandy shook her head. "You don't hear music so much anymore — not even in church. Art, music, poetry — what's happened to it? I asked Sam that one time. He said we'd had it too easy. We thought we could fix anything, that we had it all under control with our science and such. When we couldn't fix this drought, it broke something in us — our spirits, maybe. I don't know. Sometimes I think our souls are dying out with the land." Sandy shook her head, forced a smile. "You look like your dad," she said. "Did anyone ever tell you that?"

"Yes." Nita crumbled the last of her scone between her fingers. "Look, I don't remember . . . my father." How many times was she going to have to say this? Nita met the older woman's eyes. "Life was hard for us after he died. That's all I know."

"You sound a little like Maria."

"I don't blame him, if that's what you mean." Nita pressed her lips together. "Everyone wants to tell me about him. They all expect me to think of him as some kind of hero and I don't. Is that wrong?"

"Wrong?" Sandy sighed. "Maria was right in a way. Sam did put the community ahead of his own life, ahead of his family. He used to say we wouldn't make it — any of us — unless we stuck together." She poured more water into Nita's glass. "He wasn't a hero," she said, "And you're not wrong. He was just a quiet man who saw what needed to be done. He was perceptive, Sam Montoya. Sometimes you could swear he knew what you were thinking."

Dan had said that he had . . . insight. Nita's checks went hot, then cold. "I have to go." She got quickly to her feet. "I have to get back. Thank you for the water and the scones."

She drove back through The Dalles automatically, her eyes registering the road, her brain churning. Rachel fussed irritably on the seat beside her. *You could swear he knew what you were thinking.* Sandy Corbett had said it so casually. "Did you do this to me?" she whispered. A mutation, David had said. In her. But what if he'd been wrong? Nita touched her squirming daughter lightly. Father to daughter to granddaughter? "No," She whispered, but the word sounded so feeble.

When they reached the turnoff to the Corps base, Nita swung the truck suddenly onto the road. The guard at the ugly gate watched her as she parked the truck. He carried a rifle and his lust and hostility pricked at her.

"I don't see your name on the list," he said when she asked for Carter. "I'll see if I can contact the colonel."

Rachel started to cry. Teething? Or reacting to the guard? Teething, Nita told herself. She hadn't been fussy until lately.

Nita squatted in the shadow of the truck, holding her daughter tightly. "I don't want you to be like me," Nita whispered. She pulled out Rachel's string of wooden beads and dangled it above her daughter's groping fists. She would feel the anger, the lust, the broken bones. One day she would look into a lover's eyes and feel his fear. She looked like David, more like him every day. Nita blinked back tears, jumped at the clang of the gate. Carter. Nita got slowly to her feet.

"What do you want?"

"You can be angry at me." Nita straightened her shoulders. "Maybe I deserve it. But you're angry at Dan. And you shouldn't be."

"You don't know how I feel."

A thread of hurt lurked beneath his anger. "Will you come for a walk with me?" She spoke to that hurting. "Please, Carter? I need to tell you . . . about why I left."

"I can give you a few minutes." He was struggling inside, wanting to hear her, wanting to hurt her with his anger at the same time.

Nita tilted her head, hearing a hum of contentment on the hot breeze. Bees! "Here." She shoved Rachael suddenly into Carter's arms and walked away from him, following the gentle note of the nest.

A rock outcrop sheltered it in a cool crevice. Nita hummed the comfort-song to the swarm as the bees swirled up around her head. She could just get her hand into the space. Carefully she broke off a bit of sticky comb, feeling to make sure she wasn't killing brood.

"Nita, what are you doing?"

Carter's voice, and there was fear in it. Fear for her, in spite of his anger? Pain clenched in her belly and the bees felt it, their song rising and sharpening. *Gently.* She hummed it to them as she got to her feet. Calmed by her song, they trailed away as she walked back to the road. By the time she reached Carter and Rachel, only a few stragglers clung to her shirt and hair. Absently she brushed them away.

"Are you all right?" Carter jumped as a confused worker circled his head. "My God, half these wild bees are killers, Nita."

"I can tell killers from honeybees. Here." She broke off a piece of golden comb, handed it to Carter. "I only took a little. It's not a very big nest. Chew it." She lifted Rachel from his arms. "Spit out the wax when the honey's gone. The bees will find it and take it back."

Hesitantly, still angry, Carter bit into the dense, sticky chunk.

"I miss the bees." Nita dabbed a bit of honey on her daughter's lips, smiling at Rachel's chuckle of surprise and pleasure. "When the rains come, everything blooms in the hills. You have to look for the flowers, but they're there — down in the crevices where the rocks protect them, at the bottom of the old streambeds. I was like the flowers." She looked up at Carter. "I hid down in the cracks, wounded, afraid of the world. I was fourteen when I met David. I hadn't talked since I was five, and my family thought I was retarded. It was David who found me," she said softly. "He gave me space and time to grow up, to find myself. He sheltered me and . . . he loved me. It wouldn't matter, if I didn't care about you." Her voice trembled, and she shook her head. "It wouldn't even matter that I was sleeping with you. But . . . I *do* care, Carter. Don't you see? And I love David and I owe him for my life, and I don't know what happened to him. I have to find out, Carter. I need to know for sure if he's dead . . . or alive. I didn't betray you, Carter. I didn't."

"I never said you did." Carter's voice was unsteady and his anguish clouded the air.

"I didn't know Dan until a few days ago. I'm not sleeping with him." She winced at Carter's reaction. "He really is trying to help you. Don't mess things up just because I hurt you. Dan's not part of that."

"I didn't ask you if you were sleeping with him." Carter looked away, all muddy and mixed up inside. "I'd like to trust Dan, but there are a lot of men and women living on this base. They're the ones who are going to pay if I make a mistake. How well do you know Dan Greely, Nita? You've known him what — a few days?"

"He's on your side. Carter, he is."

"I'll keep it in mind." He looked back at the gate, giving in to his need to escape her. "I've got to get back. I'm sorry." His eyes avoided hers. "About the misunderstanding."

"Carter?" She closed her lips tightly. He wasn't really hearing her. He was trapped by his responsibilities, just as Dan was trapped by her father's ghost. He was walking away from her, back to his gate and the crushing weight of that place.

She could call him back. She could tell him how she knew that Dan wasn't an enemy.

Rachel started to cry, and she turned her back on the gate. I'm trapped, too, Nita thought bitterly. In her sling, Rachel kicked and fussed. "You don't feel me." Nita scooped her into her arms as the walked back to the truck. "You're David's daughter, sweetheart. He'll get here sooner or later and it'll be all right. We'll leave, go somewhere else." The words brought no comfort, none at all.

They had almost reached the truck. Nita gasped as the dusty ground suddenly shimmered. Something was wrong. She clung to Rachel as colors brightened around her. Grass? Stunned, Nita stared at the vivid green blades beneath her feet. Tiny droplets of water glinted on their tips, and the fuzzy yellow flowers swayed in the gentle wind. Spindly young trees scattered white petals across the grass and more yellow flowers swayed on long stems. Nita had seen pictures of flowers like that, tried to recall their name but she couldn't She clutched Rachel, frozen with terror and awe.

Beyond the grass and the yellow flowers, water filled the riverbed.

There wasn't that much water in the whole world. There couldn't be. Nita took a stumbling step toward it. It stretched away from her in a wrinkled gray sheet, streaked with white. The hills on the far side looked miles away and the water foamed at the foot of the dam. She saw no sign of the base.

"Carter," she cried in terror. They would be dying, all of them, buried under that gray water, *drowning*, for God's sake. She tried to run, but the access road had inexplicably moved and the ground wasn't where her eyes told her it was. Unseen humps and hollows jarred her. She stumbled, fell, twisting desperately to protect Rachel, ground slamming the breath from her body, bruising her hip. Her face was full of invisible dust and Rachel was screaming, her terror a beating wing in Nita's head. Breathless, Nita hid her face against her daughter's struggling body, surrounded by grass and flowers, wondering if she was going crazy, wondering if the world was going crazy.

Footsteps thudded on the ground. "Hey, are you all right?"

Worry pricked Nita and hands touched her shoulders.

"Are you hurt?" The hands had shifted to Rachel, as if to take her from Nita's arms.

"I . . . I'm all right." Nita forced her eyes open, then shuddered at the sight of the green grass. "No, I've got her." She clutched Rachel to her.

A man bent over her. A tail of blond hair hung down over his shoulder and his vivid blue eyes reflected his concern. Nita shook her head, not trusting her voice, wishing he would go away and leave her alone. She stretched out her hand. The grass stems didn't bend or flatten and she felt only dust and sharp gravel beneath her palm. She clenched her trembling fingers into a fist."

"Oh, shit," the man said softly.

Slowly the green landscape faded, thinning away like smoke from a smothered fire. Nita clutched the hiccoughing Rachel to her, watching the buildings of the riverbed base reappear. She looked up at the blond man. "What did you do?" she said numbly.

"Listen, I'm sorry." He squatted beside her, radiating anxiety. "It's just . . . a fancy holo projector. I was testing it. I didn't mean to scare you."

"You're lying." Nita scrambled to her feet, hearing hysteria in her voice. "You made it happen. You made me see water in the riverbed. It was so . . . huge."

"No." His distress flowered in Nita's head. "It's just a holo. I'll show you how it works." He held out a small gray box.

"That's all right," she said quickly. Because he was afraid. "I won't tell anyone," she answered his fear. "It's all right. Really. How did you do that?"

He opened his mouth to protest, then shrugged. "I'm . . . not sure." His eyes were sharp and wary on her face. "I think . . . it's a vision of the past. I just see it. Sometimes other people see it, too."

"It was so real," Nita whispered. "All those flowers, and the water . . . it looked miles across."

"You saw that much?" His eyes narrowed. "Most people just catch a glimpse, and that's if I'm standing right beside them. I was clear over near the culvert when you started running." He gave her a wary, measuring smile. "I'm Jeremy Barlow."

"I'm Nita Montoya. This is Rachel." His wariness rubbed at her. Remembering Seth, she nodded, understanding suddenly. "It really is all right. I don't think you're a freak or a demon or whatever people guess when you scare them. And I really won't tell anyone."

"I'm relieved," he said wryly.

He didn't particularly believe her. "How can you see the past?" she asked softly. "How can that be?"

"I don't know. Here." He offered a hand to help her up.

His hand was crippled, the joints thick and ugly. She noticed the stick he had dropped on the ground. His knees hurt him, now that the fear had faded. He was looking at her thoughtfully, deciding whether or not she was a serious threat.

"I could always make things appear," he said, probably deciding that it was too late to matter. "Like this." He held out his palm and a brilliant green insect blinked into life above it, settling delicately onto his fingers. "The . . . visions came later." He shrugged. "I do magic shows at local markets."

"Were you in Tygh Valley?" Nita's eyes widened. "This farmer told me about someone who did magic. He said it was a fake."

"Tygh Valley." The wariness had come back, stronger than before. "Yeah, I went through there. They weren't a very good crowd."

"They hate anything strange." Nita shivered with the memory of Seth's thin, molten ugliness. Rachel whimpered and she hugged her close. "They hate anything they don't understand, like the boy they stoned. You're right to be scared of them." She jumped as Jeremy's had closed hard on her wrist.

"You *know* I'm scared of them, don't you?" His voice was hushed, but excitement blazed behind his eyes. "You're reading my thoughts. That's how you knew I was lying about the projector. That's why you saw the river like that. You're a telepath."

"No. I don't know." His intensity frightened her and his fingers were bruising her arm. "I — I know what you're feeling," she faltered. "Scared, or angry, or whatever. I don't know what you're thinking."

"An empath. That's the word for it." He looked down at his hand and let go of her abruptly. "Sorry. It just surprised me . . . meeting someone else who's different."

Nita rubbed the marks his fingers had left. He wasn't dark inside the way the trader had been dark. His excitement had a desperate feel, like someone lost in the Dry who had finally sighted a house. A feel like thirst and hope balled up in a knot.

"I didn't hear any gossip about empaths at the market." He was watching her face. "You don't tell people, either. Do you?"

"No." Nita shook her head, trying to banish Carter from her thoughts. "I don't. Doesn't it bother you?" she asked bitterly. "That I knew you were afraid? That I know you're excited now?"

"No." He tugged thoughtfully at his tail of hair. "But it might bother some, I guess. Probably not a whole lot." He shrugged. "You can usually look at someone and tell if they're scared or mad or what have you. Most of the time."

Nita shook her head. He was so wrong.

"I didn't mean to corner you. Oh hell, yes I did." He tossed his hair back over his shoulder with an impatient jerk of his head. "I've heard all kinds of stories about kids who get born in the Dry with . . . different powers. They're always dead or over in the next town. But you're the first person I've met who's like me." He grinned suddenly. "More like me than most people, anyway. Don't you ever wonder? Why we are? Don't you want to *know*?"

"I wasn't born in the Dry." Nita shrugged the sling higher on her shoulder, looking away from his intensity. "I was born right here. I'm not sure I know . . . who I am. I haven't gotten to the why yet. I've got to go." She hesitated then nodded at the truck. "Do you need a ride somewhere?"

"No, thanks. I'm camping in that culvert. Some of the highway kids told me it was a good place. I've been doing the market in town."

"I haven't been down there for awhile. When you were on the road, did you ever meet a David Ascher, by any chance?" Nita asked as they walked back to the truck. Because she had to. "Forties, curly gray hair? He's about a head taller than you and lanky."

Jeremy shook his head.

"Oh, well." She pulled the truck door open, boosted Rachel onto the patched seat.

"I figured it was time to move on — when you guessed." Jeremy leaned on the open door. "But I think I'll stick around. I want to talk to you some more. About what we are. And maybe why." Hunger flickered in his eyes like heat lightening. "Will you come down to the market and look me up?"

"I . . . I'll try," Nita said, trapped by that heat lightning hunger. "But I don't understand. What you are trying to find?"

"Why we are." His eyes held hers, dry and blue as the sky. "I want it to matter," he said softly. "All our loneliness, everything we lose by being what we are. I want it to count. Don't you?"

"Yes," she whispered. For herself. For Rachel. It was his hunger, but it seized her suddenly, shook her to the core of her being. "I'll look for you," she said. "I promise. And I won't tell anyone that it's not your projector."

"Thanks." His brief smile lit his eyes like a shaft of sunlight and he stepped back to close the truck's door.

She had seen water in the riverbed. Nita remembered the pictures on Dan's wall as she backed the truck around in the narrow road. She had seen that river. That yesterday. Jeremy lifted a hand as she drove past him; a small figure limping back along the dusty road. *I want it to matter*, he had said. And now she wanted it too, and the intensity of that wanting frightened her.

CHAPTER THIRTEEN

"Glad I could pry you away from The Dalles." Johnny lifted his glass of wine in a toast. "I don't think I dare take a uniform out to lunch up there. I could get lynched."

"It's not funny." Carter sipped at his own wine, then set it down. "I've had to declare the town off limits to all Corps personnel." He poked at the slices of cooling meat on his plate. This Bonneville restaurant was as good as any in Portland. He hadn't eaten real beef in weeks. He set his fork down.

"It's that bad?" Johnny asked quietly.

"You're my boss. You see the reports." He picked up his wineglass and glowered into its ruby depths. "You tell me."

"By the reports, you're doing a great job. I came out here to find out what wasn't included."

"I'm sorry." Carter dredged up a smile. Even in the dim light of the restaurant, Johnny's face looked thin and strained. "I'm growling at you like you're Water Policy incarnate. There's not much to tell." He sighed. "Corps people hate locals; locals hate the Corps. It can blow any time. Any more cuts coming down?" he asked bitterly.

"Of course. But not soon." Johnny speared a leaf of blanched endive.

Of course. Of course more water cuts would happen, unless the rain came back and the whole global warming freight train reversed. Carter watched Johnny finish his salad. People around The Dalles ate mostly the high protein soybean clones. That's what they grew. And a few kitchen veggies watered with what came out of the house too dirty to reuse. A lot of 'em ended up with chronic vitamin deficiencies. The battalion's surgeon had told him it was endemic, out in the Dry. It caused a lot of birth defects, she had said. "So how are you doing?" he asked Johnny.

"Everybody loves us since Mexico backed down." Johnny grinned. "Your water-cut blues weren't in vain. Listen, I didn't come out here just to visit," he said slowly. "I heard a little . . . tidbit from my senator buddy, Paul

Targass." He wiped his mouth and tossed his napkin onto his empty plate. "There's a rumor going around that Pacific Bio's in bed with the Corps."

Carter opened his mouth to protest, but closed it without speaking. "Who?" he asked softly. "Someone at the top?"

"Don't know." Johnny shrugged. "But Pacific Bio's concentrating on their West Coast operations, so keep your eyes open." He finished his wine and emptied the bottle into his glass.

"I'm not sure I'd catch it unless someone yelled in my ear." Carter grimaced. "You're good at politics. I'm not."

"Yes, I am good at it. That's partly how I ended up where I am, and we both know it."

Yeah, Johnny had always been on top — no one had ever doubted that he belonged there. "What does Morissy have on you?" Carter asked abruptly.

"What kind of crack is that?" Johnny flushed. 'Whatever you thought you picked up at that party, you didn't. That was a matter of bedroom politics and nothing more."

"I'm sorry. I was out of line." Carter leaned back, uneasy. Johnny was drunk. He'd had most of that bottle of wine. "Take it easy. I'm on your side, remember?"

"Yeah, that's right. Good old Carter, always there to back me up. Until you decided that the damn Corps was more important."

"Oh come on, Johnny." Carter shook his head. "I wouldn't have been any use to you in politics. Moral support I can give you from inside a uniform."

"You'd have been there to watch my back." Johnny drained his glass. "It used to bug you, didn't it? When I made fun of how you hated to break the rules."

He couldn't afford to break rules. His had known that without a pricey education you went nowhere. She had paid for it on her back, never mind that old man Warrington had written the checks.

"I'm on top, Carter." The naked hunger in Johnny's eyes made Carter look away. "No one's bigger than Water Policy. And no one is going to fuck that up for me. No one."

"I don't see how they can." Carter flinched as his cell phone went off. The food he had eaten turned to stone in his belly. "Yes?"

"Colonel?" The voice on the phone sounded tinny and distant. "This is Captain Moreno, in Communications. I've got Chief of Police Durer on the line. He says it's an emergency and he won't talk to anyone but you, sir." The captain sounded nervous. "I'm sorry to interrupt you, sir but you said . . ."

"It's all right." Carter sat on his irritation. God, what now? "Patch him through."

"Hello?" A new voice boomed in Carter's ear. "This is Chief of Police Durer calling from The Dalles. It seems that I have a couple of your boys locked up down here."

"On what charges?" Carter growled. "And why didn't you talk to Major Delgado?"

"The charge is assault. And we both know there's no point in a local talking to Robert Delgado. We picked up your boys on the interstate, Colonel. They busted a kid's head with a tire iron. I think you'd better send a batch of MPs down here to collect these guys and do it quick. Before word gets around."

A kid. Great. Carter clenched his teeth. If the soldiers had committed a crime in town, they were Durer's meat. If he wanted them out of his jail, the situation was bad. "I'll send some people down right away," he snapped.

"You do that, son." Durer hung up.

Shit. Carter called Security and ordered a detail of MPs out to pick up the soldiers. By the time he got off the phone, the table had been cleared. "You sound so good when you're giving orders." Johnny grinned. "Very official."

"I'm sorry." Carter ignored the needling edge to Johnny's tone. "I've got to get back." Durer didn't like uniforms much. It might be a good idea for him to talk to the police chief in person.

"So go be an officer." Johnny flashed him a mock salute and rose. "I'll call you next time I'm in town."

Carter looked after him as Johnny walked away. Johnny was pissed. Carter stood. The restaurant had kept their water glasses filled during the meal — a touch of old-days custom that had doubtless been reflected on the bill. Carter touched the rim of Johnny's full glass. That small amount of water would matter to a lot of people. He wondered what the waiter would do with it.

From Durer's tone, Carter had half expected a mob at City Hall, but it was quiet. Carter saw to the transfer of the two bruised and sullen NCOs. They claimed that the kids had started it — that it was the bunch who hung out near the truck plaza. They'd had baseball bats, the men claimed, and they looked battered enough for it to be true.

Carter could believe it. He sent them back with Security and went inside to do his talking.

"The kid's thirteen." Durer hunched his thick shoulders, elbows planted firmly on his desk. "Look, Colonel, I'll level with you — he's one of those highway kids, yes. Anyone else could probably shoot him in broad daylight, and only a few of our upstanding citizens would give a damn. But a uniform did it. Do you get my drift?"

Durer didn't like uniforms much, but he liked the prospect of facing a lynch mob even less. "Is the kid going to live?" Carter asked.

"He's got a concussion." Durer shrugged. "I don't think the doc's too worried. You keep your tough-guys out of town, Colonel. We don't need this."

"We have to use the highway," Carter snapped. "Caught any of those rock-throwers who've been busting our windshields yet? They're using powerful homemade slingshots."

"Hey, I'm doing my best." Durer shoved a handful of papers into a battered metal filing cabinet. "I'm real short-handed."

"Yeah." Like hell. Carter turned on his heel and left the stifling office, remembering the blond kid's feral eyes in the culvert.

There was blame enough to go around here. More than enough. Carter paused outside, breathing deeply, struggling with anger. By tonight, everyone in The Dalles would know that uniforms had tried to kill a thirteen-year-old kid. And when he had the company CO Article 15 the NCOs for the tire iron, his own people would bitch because he was being soft on the locals. And Johnny was pissed at him.

He was damn tired of being everyone's enemy. Carter yanked the Chevy's door open.

"Hello, Carter." Greely sat in the passenger seat. "How come you won't see me?"

Carter hesitated for a moment, half tempted to tell Greely to get the hell out of his car and drive away. With a jerky shrug, he dropped onto the seat. "Hastings ordered me to break off all relations with the Coalition."

"Crap on that." Greely shook his head. "We need to talk, orders or no orders. It's getting worse, Carter."

"Tell me about it." Carter stared through the windshield, seeing Nita's face in the reflection of the sun on the glass. *Is Nita Montoya your lover?* "I don't think I can talk to you," he said out loud. "Even if I was willing to disobey Hastings' direct order. I keep wondering about that protest. Nice, that it happened in one place. Convenient for the media. It was convenient for whoever holed the Pipe while it was going on. We were all busy, and that leak cost me an official reprimand."

"So you think I set you up." Greely sighed. "Why?"

"Let's just say that I don't know that you didn't." Carter pounded his clenched fist very lightly on the steering wheel. "I can't stick my neck out for you any more."

"You're not sticking it out for me, damn it." Greely was angry now, too. "I thought *we* were doing it to keep people from dying around here — uniforms and locals."

"Did you ever find out the name of that red-haired agitator?"

"Bill, with no last name." Greely frowned. "He disappeared after the Shunt and no one's seen him since. I never did catch up with him. Maybe a troublemaker moving through."

"I want to believe you," Carter said softly. "I can't afford to."

"You can't afford not to."

Carter twisted the key and pumped the gas as the engine stuttered and caught. "I'm keeping an open mind. That's all I can do right now."

Greely looked at him for a long moment, then climbed stiffly out of the car. "You're shooting yourself in the foot. We need to work together more than ever. If you change your mind, leave a message with Bob, at the government store."

Carter slammed the car door and gunned the engine. Part of him agreed with Dan — it would be a hell of a lot easier if he had some kind of local cooperation. Nita might not even be there anymore. She might have moved on. What the hell did it matter anyway? Teeth clenched, Carter took the corner onto the street too fast. A middle-aged woman carrying a plastic pail had to jump for the curb and the pail tilted, spilling dark-red beet roots across the sidewalk. Carter caught her raised fist and shouting mouth in the rearview as he turned onto Second. Guiltily, he slowed the car. At the next intersection he braked to let a teenage kid push a rusty wheelbarrow across the intersection. It was full of firewood — salvaged bits of weathered lumber from some ruined building or other.

The kid looked at Carter, scowled, and spat. Carter's lips tightened and he stepped on the gas as the kid bounced the barrow up onto the sidewalk. The engine stuttered again, hesitated, then roared. Carter frowned, uneasy. The car had been fine on the trip down to Bonneville and back. He drove down two more blocks, past empty storefronts and the bar that still did business. A block farther north, the street ended in warehouses and the railroad tracks. Three blocks to his right, the weekday market filled the parking lot of the boarded-up supermarket. As Carter turned the corner, the engine coughed and died. Cursing, he reached for his cell to call Security back.

It wasn't on the seat where he had left it. Swearing softly, Carter climbed out of the car and lifted the hood.

"Hey, look who's here. One of the uniforms."

Carter let the hood fall closed with a bang. The half dozen men in the shade beneath the star-spangled marquee of the town's single theater hadn't been there a moment ago. They were young, all of them, their expressions expectant, like leashed dogs. The skin tightened between Carter's shoulder blades.

Neat setup. This was the shortest route back to the base.

Without a word, they started toward him, moving easily, hands loose at their sides. Carter looked up and down the block. The market was too far away. And he hadn't come armed. They expected him to break for the market, had fanned out to cut him off.

He ran the other way, his feet pounding on the concrete as he dodged around the corner. They followed him, silently. He didn't dare look back to see how close, his salt-burned lungs already blazing with fire. To his left, the ruins of an ancient wooden building had sagged onto the street. Carter leaped a splintered beam, looking frantically for something he could use as a weapon. They'd be armed. He cut toward an abandoned warehouse at the end of the block.

Oregon Cherry Growers the faded letters proclaimed. Carter raced across abandoned railroad tracks, his feet sliding in roadbed gravel. He could hear them pounding across the asphalt lot behind him. Gasping for breath, he flung himself around the corner of the warehouse, dodging between a rusting forklift and the peeling wall.

"This way," a voice hissed. "In here. Quick."

Carter caught a glimpse of denim blue and a man's face in a crack of darkness. He slithered between two warped sheets of metal siding. A hand closed on his wrist, guiding him into darkness. Momentarily blind, Carter bumped into something that felt like a pile of stacked cardboard. He leaned against it, his knees shaky, trying to smother the labored rasp of his breathing. Footsteps thudded outside.

"You check that side," someone rapped out. "He probably went through that hole in the fence. We'll take that. Check those doors."

Metal rattled close by and Carter tensed.

"Chained shut," the shadowy figure whispered. "The crack's hard to spot."

He knew that voice. As the sounds of pursuit faded, he squinted at the man standing beside him, blinking as his eyes adjusted to the dim light. "Jeremy?"

"I told you I might see you around." Jeremy gave him a lopsided grin. "Good thing I did. You sure can't run much."

"Good thing . . . yeah." Carter sat down hard, still gasping. "I . . . can't run . . . worked on the Michigan lakebed." He was getting his breath back at last. "Salt dust messes . . . up your lungs. I owe you."

"Yeah, I think you do." Jeremy sat down beside him. "This is kind of a bad neighborhood to wander around in. If you're wearing a uniform."

"Do tell," Carter growled. And Greely had been sitting in his car. He looked around the shadowy interior of the old warehouse, dimly lit by the afternoon sun seeping through the grimy windows. Wooden fruit crates and bales of flattened cardboard boxes towered in haphazard piles, coated with cobwebs and a thick layer of brown dust. "You're living here?" A sleeping bag, a water jug, and a scatter of cooking utensils lay on a freshly swept spot on the concrete floor.

"It's free."

"I think I'm a fool," Carter said bitterly.

"I doubt it," Jeremy said dryly. "I'm an outsider, remember? I've got nothing riding on this crazy horse race. From what I've heard and seen, you're doing pretty well with a pretty shitty situation."

A glowing insect popped into the air in front of Carter, who flinched in spite of himself. "A dragonfly?" He'd seen a picture somewhere. Fascinated, he passed his fingers through the iridescent green wings. "That's really incredible. Can I see that projector of yours?"

"Sure." Jeremy reached into his pocket, hesitated. "Or maybe no." He cleared his throat. "Professional secret. I guess I'd better be rude."

The pocket was empty. Carter could see the bulge of Jeremy's thick fingers through the worn pocket. "You don't have one." He stared at Jeremy. "I wondered how I could have missed something that advanced, how come I'd never seen that kind of holo projection before. My God, *you're* doing it."

"Sooner or later I always blow it." Jeremy shrugged. "I guess it's some kind of . . . shared hallucination or something."

He was watching Carter from the corners of his eyes. "That waterfall I saw." Carter whistled. "That was you, too? You were right there. Tell me about this stuff, will you? I've never run into anything like it."

"Yeah, it was me . . ." Jeremy dragged the words out reluctantly.

He looked ready to run. "Hey, what's wrong?" Carter spread his hands. "It's not illegal to . . . do whatever you call this. What's up?"

"Nothing." Jeremy managed a crooked smile, relaxing fractionally. "I'm never sure . . . how people will react. When they find out. Sometimes it's . . . bad."

"Bad?"

"Do you understand why it's dry, Carter? Really understand?"

"Yeah, global warming, we let too much CO_2..." He let the words trail away as Jeremy shook his head.

He knew the mechanics of water distribution better than all but a handful of people on the planet. "I think I see what you mean," he said slowly. "I guess no . . . can any of us really understand why it's happening? To us?"

"I don't understand this either." Jeremy held out his hand and the dragonfly seemed to light on it, fanning its wings slowly. "I can make the little things like this happen when I want. The visions of the past just come on their own. I don't know how, or why. People don't understand this drought and it terrifies them. They don't understand the things I do either." He smiled thinly. "Sometimes, I guess they link the two. They can get . . . a little crazy."

"Like how?"

Jeremy shrugged. "I've heard stories about other kids being born with . . . weird powers. Out in the Dry. People usually kill them. You run into a lot of superstition out there." He hunched his shoulders. "It's a god, the drought. Like it or not. And it's an ugly one. My dad used to beat me if he caught me 'making.' This drifter gave me the idea of doing the magic show thing. He thought what I did was wonderful." Jeremy gave a short laugh. "When I hit the road and tried it, I damn near got myself killed right off."

His tone made Carter shiver.

Jeremy laughed softly. "Hey, it's your fault for figuring out my scam. I'm getting careless, I guess. But I met this woman the other day. She's kind of like me. Different. She's an empath — she hears your emotions and your feelings. It's been . . . a long time since I ran into someone who was . . . different. Want some water?" He went over to his campsite, fished a plastic mug from his pack.

"Thanks. Why'd your dad beat you?" Carter asked.

"Maybe because he was scared." Jeremy shrugged. "Maybe because I was his son, and he didn't understand it any more than he understood the drought. He was afraid of the drought, too. He should have been. It killed him, finally."

"He plowed his soul into your land?" Carter said softly. "And died with it?"

"You were listening." Jeremy handed him the mug full of water. "At that party."

"Yeah, I was listening." Carter drank the tepid, musty water, watching the gathering shadows turn the stacked crates into shapeless towers of darkness. "What's it like to see the way it used to be?"

Jeremy was silent for a long time. "Sometimes I get angry," he said at last. "We could have stopped it, you know."

Carter got stiffly to his feet and went to one of the front windows. It was getting dark. He rubbed dust from a windowpane, wondering how many kids were hanging out at the truck plaza tonight.

"I'm going to walk back to the dam with you." Jeremy fumbled in his pack, then straightened with a small automatic in his hand. He held it comfortably and Carter noticed that the trigger guard had been partially removed to accommodate Jeremy's thickened fingers.

Carter looked at it. "I shot a kid once," he said slowly. "During a riot. I pulled the trigger because I was scared and mad. I thought I'd never do anything like that again." He shook his head. "Maybe there's no way to keep this mess from turning into a war."

Jeremy looked down at the gun in his hand. "When people want something from you and you can't give it to them . . . sometimes they hate you. Let's go." He slipped the gun into the waistband of his jeans. "I know a route that should be safe."

Carter slipped out the crack after Jeremy, shadows crowding his heels. The scabby towers of the old grain elevators filled the alleys between the warehouses with darkness. Carter and Jeremy followed the rusted railway tracks along the bank of the riverbed. Semi rigs slept in the truck plaza lot. Lights gleamed behind barred windows in the old motel, but Carter didn't see any kids.

They went slowly, at Jeremy's limping pace. "Your knees hurt you, don't they?" Carter asked. "I could get you some painkillers from the pharmacy at the base."

"No thanks." The smile was back in Jeremy's voice. "I tried booze and drugs once or twice when I was a kid. Things . . . get out of hand. Visually, I mean. You wouldn't want to be anywhere near me."

The wind whispered dryly and Carter welcomed the yellow wash of light from the big halides above the lower gate. He returned the guard's surprised salute briskly. "Thanks for the convoy." He turned to Jeremy. "You want a ride back?"

"No thanks. It's a nice night for a walk." Jeremy's faded shirt hung open, unbuttoned.

The light gleamed on irregular patches of shiny white scar tissue. They blotched his chest and flat stomach, ugly and visible against his tawny skin. Burn scars.

Jeremy noticed Carter's glance. "This old guy was pretty good at picking up my visions." He touched one of the scars. "He thought that if I could see water, I could find it for him. Make him rich. He . . . didn't believe me when I said I couldn't. After that, I made up the projector," Jeremy said softly.

"If you need to get onto the base, come to either gate," Carter said. "I'll leave orders to let me know. Any time."

"Thanks." Jeremy gave him a short, sharp nod. "Don't forget," he said. "People around here want something from you and you can't give it to them, either." He turned abruptly and vanished into the darkness without a backward glance.

CHAPTER FOURTEEN

The beans at the west end of the field were ripening too early. Nita's feet stirred up the brown dust of the path as she carried the yoked pails of freshly picked soybean pods back to the house. Dan thought it was because they weren't getting enough water, that a feeder line must be plugged. The beans were too immature to dry, Dan had said, so they'd have to go fresh to the local market.

"So we pick beans, love," Nita murmured to her daughter. "It beats chopping bushes."

Rachel grinned and gurgled, waving her fists.

"Glad you agree." Nita smiled, but it turned into a sigh.

Carter wouldn't talk to Dan. The town was so full of anger that it made her sick to her stomach when she went in to the market. The smart thing to do was leave before things got worse. She shifted the pole across her shoulders, wishing suddenly and intensely that she could step back across time to the hills and David and the bees. She had been safe there. Nita reached the edge of the field and walked on out to the rim of the Gorge. Far below, she could see the rocky ledges that had once been Celilo Falls.

The picture was there, on Dan's bedroom wall. Nita could believe in the river, looking at Jesse's painting of the cascading water. Jesse had been remembering; it came through in the soft colors like a whisper of the past. The paintings reminded Nita of the man she had met by the cultert — Jeremy — and her vision of the river. She had had that same sense of past.

Thinking of river water, Nita rounded the corner of the house and stopped in surprise. A battered car stood in front of the porch. She hadn't heard it come down the road, and didn't recognize it. One of the Coalition people, probably. They came and went all the time. Nita thumped the bean pails down on the proch, lifted Rachel out of her sling, and opened the door.

"I wondered who the hell was sleeping in my bedroom." A small, wiry woman looked up from the table. She had short-cropped, graying hair and the tattooed left forearm of a convoy trucker. Gold chains glinted at her throat and a half a dozen gemstones winked from the rim of her right ear. "So Danny's finally gotten tired of sleeping alone, huh? He went for a young one, this time." She looked Nita up and down as if she were a goat for sale in the market. "That his kid?"

"No, she is not." Nita flushed. "And I work for Dan. He told me I could use your room."

"Relax, honey. I don't need it." The woman stood, stretched like a cat and gave Nita a thin smile. "I'm Renny Warren," she said. "I own this farm, in case Danny forgot to mention it."

"Oh." Nita blinked. "You're Jesse's daughter."

"Yes." Renny said the word casually, but the whip-flick of her resentment made Nita wince. Closed subject.

"Where is Danny, anyway?" Off meddling as usual?"

"He's out picking beans." Nita heard the stiffness in her voice and tried to hide it by settling Rachel on her quilt.

"The kid doesn't look like him."

"Because she's not. Like I said." Nita straightened, staring the small woman in the eye. "I'm not sleeping with him."

"A wee bit defensive aren't you?" Renny patted Nita's cheek lightly.

She was enjoying this, Nita realized suddenly. She was trying hard to make Nita lose her temper. "Of course I'm defensive." Nita let go of her anger and laughed. "Everybody in town thinks I'm in bed with Dan." She smiled at the older woman. "I should wear a sign: 'I am not Dan Greely's lover.'"

"They wouldn't believe you."

"That's why I don't bother." Nita smiled and a bit to her surprise the trucker returned it. "Can I get you water? We've got beans left from last night, if you're hungry. And fresh tomatoes."

"I'll take the water. I eat a lot better than beans." Renny leaned against the table, her eyes on Nita. "I hear The Dalles is taking on the Army."

"I guess so." Nita frowned as she filled a mug. "I'm staying out of it, thank you."

"You think so? Living here with Danny?" She snorted. "I guess I'll sell this place, buy some land in the Willamette Valley." Renny sipped at her water, her expression casual. "They're irrigating a lot of new acreage down there. Bushes are a hot crop and they don't take as much labor as beans. I wouldn't need anyone year round. I could contract for seasonal crews."

Nita kept the smile on her face as she knelt to dangle the wooden beads for her daughter. She felt the needling edge beneath Renny's words. She hid a smile at Renny's exasperation. Renny was not getting what she wanted here. "Do you want me to go tell Dan you're here?" she asked sweetly.

"No." Renny laughed suddenly and set down the empty mug. "Tell him I'm in town, staying down at the truck plaza. I'll be around." She reached out to cup Nita's chin in her hand. "You're too good for either Danny or this dead town. If you get tired of digging dirt, let me know. You might make a good trucker. We could find out."

Absently tickling her daughter, Nita watched Renny stride across the yard and climb into the car. She wasn't quite sure what Renny had just offered.

She told Dan about Renny's visit as they drove down to the market.

"You never know when Renny's going to drop by." Dan's voice was neutral. "How did you get along?"

"All right, I think." Nita shrugged. "I'm not sure why."

Dan gave her a thoughtful, sideways look. "Renny's touchy," he said slowly. "We've never liked each other much. Sometimes I think the only reason she keeps the farm is that she owns it and I work for her and she likes that. I don't see much of her." He shook his head. "Have you seen my tool folder? The one that I keep in the glove box? It's missing. I might have put it down when I was working on the pump."

"I haven't seen it," Nita said absently. Dan felt sad and a little angry. About Renny? I am tired of knowing, she thought sullenly. She stared out the window at the concrete wall of the dam stretching across the riverbed. She could feel the town even before they reached the main street; tension hummed in the air like the buzz of a kicked beehive. Nita shivered and held Rachel tighter as her daughter began to squirm.

"It's early for fresh beans." Dan parked at the edge of the market lot. "We should do pretty well."

Nita settled Rachel in her sling and lifted two pails of the green bean pods from the back of the truck. Dan picked up the other two pails and they walked down the block to the market. The noise made her fingers twitch.

"'Lo, Dan." A chunky man in faded suncloth coveralls waved. "Hi, Nita. I've been looking forward to meeting you. There's space here." He waved at the asphalt beside the pile of soap blocks he was selling.

"How're you doing, Pete?" Dan set his pails down.

Nita smiled grimly at the soap vendor as she put down her pails. His lust felt like sweaty fingers on her skin. She spread out a towel with an angry snap so that Dan could pile the beans onto it. If Pete didn't knock it off, she'd kick his damn soap right into his lap. That should wilt him.

"Hi, Carl." Dan straightened as the chief of police marched up. "You look a little grim this morning. Anything wrong?"

"Maybe." Durer cast a quick, hard look at the obviously listening Pete. "Want to come along for a little ride with me? I've got something to show you."

"Sure." Dan's voice had gone flat.

Trouble, Nita thought. Durer was really upset. Rachel kicked and squirmed, her face screwing up to cry as Nita tried to sooth her.

"I'll be back in a little while, okay?" Dan stood, brushing dust from his jeans. "You don't mind staying here by yourself?"

"I know how to sell beans, Dan." Nita smiled for him. Pete was seething with curiosity and lust in about equal proportions. Nita turned her back on him and began to arrange the beans.

"See you in a little while." Dan followed Durer.

Not soon enough, Nita thought grimly. Dan's weariness hummed in the air, a weariness of spirit, she thought. He didn't want to be doing this. He was trapped. Nita tucked Rachel into her lap. Trapped by her father's ghost. "I think it's time we moved on," she whispered to Rachel, and pretended that she didn't feel a pang at the thought.

The beans sold faster than she had hoped. Dan had been right — most crops weren't quite ripe yet, and green soybeans made good eating. Dan had given Nita a list of the goods they needed and she was able to trade for most of them before noon. The three rough blocks of soap that Pete swapped her for a bowlful of beans smelled like rancid vegetable oil. They smelled like his constant, irritating lust. Nita wrinkled her nose at the bars as she tucked them into her pack. Too bad no one else had soap to trade today.

A tall, fair-haired man stopped in front of her blanket. "I'm looking for Dan Greely. Do you know where he is?"

Everyone in the whole damn riverbed knew she was living with him. Nita eyed the man. He was dressed very city. "He's off with Chief Durer," she said. "He'll come back here eventually. If it's important, you should probably wait."

"Chief Durer?" The man's eyes evaluated her. "Is there a problem?"

Nita blinked at the sudden satisfaction in the man. As if he was glad for the trouble? As if she had answered a question for him? Wariness tightened her stomach. "I don't know."

"Hell, yeah, there's trouble." Pete clucked his tongue from behind his soap pile. "Anytime Durer comes looking for Dan, you can bet your ass it's no social call. The uniforms are probably cutting up rough again. They beat up some kid last week." His eyes gleamed. "You hear about that?"

Nita squashed a fierce desire to kick the jerk. "I'll tell him you were looking," she said, ignoring Pete. "What was your name?" She smiled at him, hoping that she looked dumb and innocent. "Can he find you somewhere?"

"My name's John Seldon. I'll catch him later." He wasn't smiling, but he was still pleased inside.

Nita watched him walk away, trying to place the name. She had heard it . . . Then it clicked suddenly. Johnny. This was Carter's friend; the one he cared about, or owed a debt to. He worked for the government. So why did he want to see Dan?

She definitely didn't like him.

The sun rose higher, driving what little shade remained into hiding. Nita spread a sunscarf over her head and shoulders and leaned forward as she nursed Rachel, so that her shadow would shade her daughter. A knot of people had gathered on the far side of the lot. Nita heard laughter and applause and felt distant ripples of excited pleasure. Pete draped a dirty cloth over his pile of soap and wandered down the street to watch. Nita craned her neck, curious, but unwilling to disturb Rachel's sleep. Some kind of entertainment?

The crowd broke up after a while, scattering among the stalls, still full of laughter and good feelings. It was a nice change. Nita stretched cautiously and winced. Her right foot was asleep and her shirt was soggy with sweat beneath Rachel's sleeping warmth.

"Hi, I'd about given up on seeing you again."

Nita looked up. "Jeremy." She smiled, pleased to see him again. "Was that you, down the block? Making people laugh?"

"Uh-huh." He sat down beside her, his sky-colored eyes on her face. "I thought I scared you away, on the riverbank."

"You almost did." Rachel was waking up, hungry again, and Nita lifted her shirt, glad that Pete hadn't returned. "I haven't been hiding from you. I was at the market last week, but I didn't see you. I . . . don't like coming into town."

"I bet." His smile lit his eyes like sunlight. "Even I can feel the tension. It must be rough for you."

"It's . . . kind of wearing. Yes." It made her feel funny, talking about it like this. Sometimes David had asked her what she heard in the bees' song, but that was all. He didn't ask her about what she heard from people, or how it felt to hear it, and that silence had become hers, too. She had never really put it into words before. "You made people feel better with your show. I appreciated it." She wrinkled her nose.

"I'm good for something, I guess." His smile was crooked now.

Nit sucked in a quick breath. At the end of the block, where the street ran up into the hillside, the ground had gone suddenly green with grass. Tree branches, heavy with leaves, swayed above the roof of the supermarket. Tiny white flowers bloomed beside her, poking up through the cracks in the parking lot's surface. "It's beautiful," Nita murmured. She tried to touch one of the blossoms, but felt only gritty asphalt beneath her fingertips. Jeremy was staring at it, bitter inside. Sad. "I'm glad I can share this," she told him as the green vision faded. "I can tell Rachel how it used to be, when she's older. She needs to know. It's like you pull a moment out of the past, spread it out for us to see."

"For you, maybe." But a slow smile lighted his pale eyes and eased some of the bitterness inside him.

"Excuse me?" A stocky woman with a pack slung over one shoulder had paused in front of them. "Do you have any beans left at all?" She frowned into one of the empty pails. "I meant to stop by earlier, but I got busy talking."

"I have a few left." Nita reached for the pail beside her and tilted it to show the woman the pound or so of pods remaining in the bottom.

"That'll have to do." The woman gave her a broad smile. "I can even give you scrip."

Nita wrapped the beans in the faded piece of cloth that the woman handed her. As she started to put them into the woman's pack, she froze, hand poised in midair, her heart contracting.

"Something wrong?" the woman asked.

"Where did you get that pack?" Nita asked.

"I bought it." The woman eyed her warily. "Julio has a little second-hand store in Mosier. He comes into town for the weekend market. Is it yours? Was it stolen?"

The weight of the heavy blue cloth made Nita's fingers tremble. She turned the flap over slowly. The letters D A had been worked on it in bright green thread. Nita touched the slightly crooked curve of the D, tears burning her eyes, threatening to spill over.

"What is it? Nita?" Jeremy touched her shoulder.

"David Asher," Nita whispered. "This is David's pack." They were both staring at her, uncomprehending. "I've been looking for him." Nita spoke past the lump in her throat. "My husband. He was supposed to meet me here."

"I'm so sorry." The woman covered her mouth with her hand.

"What about the man who sold this to you?" Jeremy turned to her. "What's he like?"

"Julio Moreno?" The woman sounded surprised. "He's honest, if that's what you mean. His family has lived in Mosier forever. They grow sugar beets. Julio could tell you where he got it. I don't think the man ever forgets anything."

Nita stacked the empty pails together, gathered up Rachel, and scrambled to her feet. 'I've got to go talk to him." She tucked the squirming Rachel into her sling.

"Do you want to keep the pack?" The woman cleared her throat, her pity warm in the air. "If you'll swap me for yours?"

"Thank you." Nita emptied her pack onto the ground and handed it to the woman. "Thank you very much." She rubbed the worn fabric gently.

David had bought the cloth at the Salem market. He had taught her how to sew with that pack. It had been a hard job and she had made a lot of mistakes. There was the seam that she had resewn four times. She had thrown it out the door of their tent after the third time and David had laughed at her temper. He had picked it up, and told her to work on it another day, and they had made love in the afternoon heat. Nita's throat closed on tears as she tucked Rachel's quilt, the water bottle, and a spare diaper into the familiar folds.

Rachel started to cry irritably as Nita walked back to the truck. Dan wasn't back yet, but she couldn't wait for him. Jeremy had followed her, not saying anything as she tossed the empty pails into the truck's bed. She opened the door and felt for the keys beneath the seat. It was only ten miles to Mosier — they could be back in an hour. Dan would know it was important. He'd understand. She stared at the keys in her hand. *You should know how to drive*, David had said when she had turned sixteen. He had traded precious honey for the use of a clunky old electric hybrid and he had taught her how to drive. Nita climbed onto the seat.

"I think I'll come with you." Without waiting for her reply, Jeremy pulled open the passenger door and climbed in.

"No, thanks." Nita glared at him.

He made no move to get out.

"Fine. Whatever." Nita started the engine.

Rachel started crying hard, her face red and angry as Nita backed the truck out of the lot. Not because she feels me, Nita thought fiercely. That's not why. She drove west, past the empty car lots and abandoned shopping centers that clustered at the edges of town. Rachel finally stopped crying. Nita looked sideways to discover that Jeremy had her daughter on his lap and was making a bright-green insect hover above her face. Rachel reached for it, smiling tentatively, her face still blotchy with weeping. Nita felt a stir of gratitude, but a cold stone of fear sat in her chest, squashing the words down inside her.

West of The Dalles, one of the stark cliffs had crumbled into the river-bed. It had taken a section of the interstate with it and traffic had to turn off onto the old highway. Nita took the two-lane winding road fast. The land rose on their left, barren slopes patched with tough weeds and clumps of sun scorched grass, pierced by rocks like broken teeth. You could see the stumps left from the orchards that had died and been cut for firewood. Cherries, Dan had told her. She had never eaten a real cherry. Cherries came out of the vats, fed by the bushes that had killed the Valley and hadn't needed David's bees. A few tall poplars remained from the old windbreaks, like posts of a vanished fence. Nita forced herself to slow down, afraid of what might happen if the land went suddenly green.

It didn't go green. Jeremy made glittering butterflies and tiny green frogs for Rachel and the hills remained dead and brown.

It took less than half an hour to reach Mosier. Nita parked in front of an empty auto-body shop. Across the street, a tall white house stood up on a bank above the level of the road. Clothes hung on the wide porch, swinging in the wind, and Nita caught sight of cluttered chairs, saw the glint of glass on tables. Julio's secondhand store.

Jeremy handed Rachel to Nita without a word. Clutching her daughter, Nita climbed the steep steps that had been cut into the bank. The wide porch was crammed with clothes, old tools, china plates and cups painted in vivid colors, plastic dishes, and furniture. Some of the clothes looked as if they had been hanging on the porch for years, faded into drab pastels by the sun. Others looked new and fresh, as if they had come from a store.

"You wish some help?" A lanky man wearing a too-large denim overall stepped from the house. His left arm was scarred and twisted, but his eyes looked young, in spite of his gray hair. "You are looking for clothes, *senora*?" He smiled at Rachel. "For *la nina*?"

"No. Thank you." The words stuck in Nita's throat. Slowly she held out the pack. "This belongs to my . . . husband." Her voice trembled in spite of herself. "A woman said she bought it from you."

The man's face took on a wary expression.

"I don't mean . . . I'm not accusing you of stealing it." Nita flushed.

"I did not think you were." Julio Moreno shook his head slowly and Nita cringed at the texture of his reluctance.

"Tell me," she said.

He spread his hands. "I . . . found the pack." He looked beyond her, at the barren, brown hills. "It was away from the road, in some rocks, you know. It was empty." Moreno coughed a little. "There were bones." He coughed again. "It is easy to die in this dry land."

Bones. Nita stared at the pack in her hands, blue cloth, bought with the honey she and David had gathered, sewn in the evenings together. "Was there anything to . . . show who he was?" He? Why he? She thought in terror. The bones could have belonged to a woman.

"He wore jeans, *senora*. A shirt, blue or green. His hair was dark, I think." He shrugged, his brown eyes full of sympathy. "I put the bones in the churchyard." He pointed up the street. "That is where bones belong. Even now, when it is so easy to die."

"Will you show me?" Nita whispered. She didn't dare look at him, didn't dare look at Rachel who would have David's blue eyes and his face. Instead, she kept her eyes fixed on the pack in her hands, a wad of blue cloth that had smelled like honey and David's sweat once, smelled like a stranger now."

"*Lo siento mucho, senora,*" Moreno said softly. "I will show you."

The stone he had used to mark the grave was a stone from the hillside, gray lava rock, dusty and squarish. Nita touched it with her fingertips, feeling its coolness and its weight. It was heavy, like death. *It is easy to die in this dry land.* Nita wondered how the man whose bones lay beneath the stone had died. He had died so close to a town, so close to a road and people.

"It wasn't David," she said out loud.

Julio Moreno, head bowed, twisted arm hanging at his side, said nothing.

Nita turned away, angry at his silence.

Jeremy waited at the overgrown fence around the tiny graveyard. "I'll drive back," he said and lifted Rachel from Nita's arms.

At the truck, she climbed into the passenger side without speaking. Rachel was asleep and blessedly, didn't wake up as Jeremy tucked her onto the seat beside Nita. In spite of his hands, Jeremy handled the wheel easily. Nita stared out at the brown land as they followed the road's twists and turns through the dust. "I don't want him to be dead," she whispered, but a tiny part of her — a small place deep inside — was relieved. She leaned her head against the door, wanting to cry, wanting to weep for him. Her eyes remained as dry as the soil in the dead orchards.

The road circled around the head of a deep, cocky canyon. An old house sat down in the bottom, huge and dilapidated. A hint of majesty still clung to it in spite of its sagging roof and gaping, glassless windows. Green showed down there, the stingy, irrigated green of the present. Carefully watered rows of beans filled the floor of the canyon. As the pickup labored around a bend, Nita lost sight of the house. She wondered dully who had built it, out here in this lonely canyon.

Up on the rim again, Jeremy pulled over onto the shoulder of the road and shut off the engine. "Come for a walk," he said, and it was a command, in spite of his gentle tone.

She had no strength to refuse. When Jeremy scooped up Rachel and held out his hand to her, she climbed out of the truck. They were up above the narrow little canyon. The wind whipped at her hair, trying to tug it loose from her braid. A promontory jutted out from the wall of the Gorge like a round island of rock, connected t the land by a narrow neck. Nita followed him out onto it. The center of the promontory looked hollow, like a bowl, and the broken skeletons of old trees jutted up from the rocky ground.

Jeremy sat down with Rachel on his lap and pulled Nita gently down beside him. "I found this place years ago," he said softly. "I come back when I'm in the neighborhood."

The dry cliff top wavered to life around them. The hollow became a pond, ringed by trees whose branches were tipped with young leaves. Stiff green blades poked up through the still water and tiny flowers carpeted the green grass, white, pink, and purple. Silently Jeremy pointed. Nita turned her head and caught her breath. Beyond the rocky edge lay the river. It stretched between the carved walls of the Gorge, vanishing eastward and westward into an opalescent haze. The wrinkled sheet of gray blue water shimmered, shading into browns along the shore. She could see the highway down below here. Dozens of trees dotted the ground and the hills glowed with soft greens.

"The river is so big," Jeremy said softly. "How could anyone who lived with this ever imagine that it could be empty?" He shook his head. "It's our own fault. The Dry. I think we let it happen because we couldn't believe in it, because we had so many rivers, so much water."

He loved this lost world, in spite of how much it hurt him. His sadness blended with the sweeping curve of the river, wove itself into the green hills that would really be dry and dusty if you walked on them. Nita looked down at the ground in front of her. Flowers glowed among the lush grass stems, smaller than her little fingernail. Pink and white stars clustered with fringed blue cups. A bird fluttered soundlessly in the bushes and the branches swayed, their new leaves bright green or bronzy red. So much *life*. She was drowning in it. It filled her up in an aching rush, overflowed to spill down her cheeks as tears, dissolving the stony numbness that filled her.

"He's not dead." Nita clenched her fists, squeezing invisible dust between her fingers. "Those aren't his bones, do you hear me? I love him. I love him so much."

"It's all right, Nita." Jeremy's thickened fingers were gentle as he stroked her back. "If he died, he didn't desert you. Don't punish yourself for how you feel."

"Bastard! I didn't ask you!"

Rachel woke and began to scream. Jeremy caught Nita's wrist as she started to scramble to her feet. Teeth clenched, she tried to jerk free, but he was strong, for all his crippled hands. She slipped, gasped as she fell hard onto her knees. The pain cracked her anger and the first sob shook her. Jeremy put his arms around her and gathered her against him, murmuring meaningless sounds of comfort as she wept against his shoulder. The sobs hurt her, tearing their way out of her flesh, making her shake with their force. After a long time they finally slowed, fading into hiccoughs.

Jeremy was holding her tightly, his cheek against her hair, the warmth of his comfort gentle in her mind. Slowly she straightened. "You're all wet." She touched his tear-soaked shirt and drew a shuddering breath. "You're right," she whispered. "Part of me wants to believe that he's there, under than rock — that he didn't run away. He was so afraid — of everything that was happening." Nita choked on fresh tears. "He was afraid and because I knew it . . . I made it worse. He couldn't hide from it if I was there."

"I'm sorry," Jeremy murmured. He pulled a bandana from his pocket and wiped her face.

Rachel had stopped crying. Jeremy had tucked her onto his lap and she was sucking on her fist, staring intently at his face.

"She likes you." Nita giggled, heard the shrillness in her voice, and stopped. She touched Rachel's cheek with her fingertip. So much David's face. "What if she *is* like me?"

"What if she is?" His eyes were on hers, pale and intent. "Is that really why you think he left you?"

"Maybe," Nita whispered. "I don't know."

"You'll teach Rachel that who she is and what she is, matters. You'll teach her to be proud of herself and her gift," he said fiercely.

Need. She met his eyes, feeling it, not sure what it was that he wanted from her. "Gift?" Anger came back to her suddenly. "It's not a gift to eavesdrop on pain and lust and anger. I don't want to hear. I don't want to know." Rachel wailed as Nita snatched her from Jeremy's lap. She ran back to the truck through the green world, stumbling on the dust and rocks she couldn't see. Jeremy limped slowly after her.

"Don't be angry," he said when he caught up with her. "I know it's hard for you. It's hard for me — what I am — and my makings don't have any real value. Your ability means something. People are so far apart, even when we try so damned hard to be close. You can narrow that gap, Nita."

"No." She looked around at the flowers and the distant pond, losing herself in the sweep of the river and Gorge. She could feel peace in this place, like moisture in the air.

"It's spring," Jeremy said. "That's why it's so green. I've seen it in summer, too, but it's dry then. It looks more like . . . now. I thought you needed spring."

"Thank you." Nita touched his face, hearing loneliness in his voice, thick as layered dust. "Thank you for doing this for me. Don't ever think it doesn't have value. Please."

He took her hand between his, kissed it gently, and climbed into the truck. The land didn't turn dry and brown again until they were well below the crest.

CHAPTER FIFTEEN

I told Voltaire to keep his tough guys in line." Durer scowled over the rim of the steering wheel. "If he wants to start a war around here, he's sure doing it right."

"Take it easy, Carl." Dan grabbed for the dash as the chief of police slammed the four-wheeler through an old wash. "You do that again and we're going to have to walk back. What exactly did Sandy tell you, anyway?"

"Just that she'd found a body. The Wilmer girl." He slowed a little as they bounced down into the next wash. "She was pretty upset."

"Then how do you know a uniform's involved?"

"Sandy said so." Durer grunted. "I hope she's wrong."

He didn't think she was. Dan scowled up at the rocky wall of the Gorge above them, a sinking feeling in the pit of his stomach. Sandy didn't jump to conclusions. "Don't lay all the blame on Voltaire. I think he's trying to do the best he can, but he can't do it on his own. He's young." Dan sighed. "He's got a lot to learn."

"He's not that young," Durer growled. "He doesn't give a shit about anybody who doesn't wear a uniform."

Dan said nothing. No point in arguing with him. Carl didn't like the Corps' presence on his turf and never had. Dan wished again that the Shunt fiasco hadn't happened. If wishes here horses . . . Well, he could understand Carter's suspicions. He didn't seem like a man who trusted easily. He'd hoped that Nita could talk to him, but whatever had been between them apparently wasn't. Had to leave that one alone.

Dan fingered the faint trace of the lump at the base of his skull. It would be hard not to interpret that Shunt riot as a setup. Especially since someone had holed the Pipe while everyone was busy. He leaned back against the seat, his back aching from picking beans. His fault. He should have read the crowd better.

Where the hell had that redheaded bastard come from?

"There's Sandy." Durer hit the brakes and eased the car off the road. "She found the body while she was out looking for that damned goat of hers."

"'Lo, Dan." Sandy tried to smile, but her face looked haggard. "I'm glad Carl dragged you along. This is a little too much for me."

"Show us, Sandy," Durer said heavily.

Dan tried to catch Sandy's eye but she wouldn't look at him. She carried a blanket folded over one arm.

"Over here." She led them down a gentle slope toward a clump of spindly firs.

He could see where a car or truck had pulled off the road, and then driven down to the trees. The tracks were just visible in the dust, sharp enough to be fresh.

"Don't step on 'em, Dan," Durer growled. "I'll get Kelly to video 'em for a match. He went out to the Welsh place to pick up the doc."

The girl lay on the ground beneath the thin branches of the young firs. Dan looked away from her bare breasts and the bruises that mottled them. Dark blood streaked her pale skin. Cathy Wilmer. She'd turned seventeen last spring. The air was still in his hollow, protected from the wind. Dust motes glinted in the sunbeams, and a trick of light blurred the girl's face. Her hair was dark, long. It took him back thirty years and in a moment of vision he saw his sister Amy, lying broken in the dust beneath the dry face of Celilo Falls.

"Can I cover her, Carl?" Sandy was staring down at the girl, her face pale, jaw set. "The knife's over there." She jerked her head. "Just tossed away. It's an Army knife." Her lips twitched, then thinned. "That damn fool colonel. Why the hell did he let this happen?" She shook out the blanket with a snap and draped it gently over the girl.

Dan recognized the faded flowers on the fabric. It was the spread from Sandy's bed. He put his arm around her shoulders, feeling the tremors that shook her as he pulled her close.

"I taught her piano. She was so good." Sandy's voice cracked. "God damn him," she whispered. "Whoever did this. And Voltaire, too. I hope they blow the Pipe out from under all of them. I hope they all die."

Dan closed his eyes, holding her close, stroking her hair, hurting for Cathy, for eighteen-year-old Amy who had jumped from the top of Celilo so many long years ago. How many times could you look down on someone like this before it got to be too much and you quit trying?

The sound of an engine broke the quiet. "Kelly's here with Doc," Durer said briskly. He had picked the knife up carefully with a plastic bag: a big lock-blade with the Corps' turreted castle on the handle. "I'd like to keep this kind of quiet." He stared bleakly a the knife. "This is all we need right now."

"What are you going to do, Carl?" Sandy's voice shook. "Just let it go? Pretend it didn't happen?"

"Hell no, woman." Durer flushed. "I'm going to ram this down Voltaire's throat 'till he pukes, and he's going to do a DNA test on every damn man on that base. But I'm doin' it in private. Word'll get around soon enough," he said grimly.

"Stupid to throw the murder weapon away like that," Dan said. "'Specially when it has your name on it, sort of."

"Yeah, I thought of that," Durer said heavily. "I haven't convicted yet."

Yeah, whatever Durer's private feelings were, he was a fair and honest man. Kelly had driven up with the doctor, and Dan watched Durer surreptitiously pocket the bagged knife. He needed to talk to Carter. Kelly had the biggest mouth in town. Knife or no knife, folks were going to draw their own conclusions once word of this got around. He might have to try the back way onto the base. It was a big risk, with tensions as high as they were. Getting shot wouldn't help anything.

"Can you drop me back at the market?" he asked.

"Sure." Durer nodded, giving Dan a sideways glance. "Someone's got to tell the Wilmers." He cleared his throat.

He had done this kind of things too many times already. Dan wondered suddenly whom they would tell first, when he got shot. Sandy?

"I'll do it, Dan." Sandy touched his arm, her face calm and in control again. "I know Anne real well. Dan? What I said before . . ."

"I know." He touched her lips to silence her, kissed her gently on the forehead. "Thank you," he murmured. "For doing this."

He and Durer didn't talk much during the ride back to the market. From Durer's expression, he was as pessimistic as Dan about the future situation. Someone outside was trying to set Army against the locals; Dan was more sure of it than ever. And they were doing a damn good job. The only question was who. If he had that answer, Carter would listen to him. He'd have to listen. "You haven't heard any news of that Bill guy?" he asked as Durer turned down the main street. "You know — the red headed trader I was asking about?"

"Yeah, I know who you mean. No, no one's seen him that I know of." Durer pulled over against the curb. "Looks like someone borrowed your truck." He nodded.

It was just pulling up. Dan walked over. Nita sat in the passenger seat and a stranger drove. She'd been crying.

"What's up, Nita?" He eyed the stranger, who had shut off the engine, but sat still behind the wheel. "Are you all right?"

"I sold all the beans. I had to go . . . check on something." She slid down from the cab, not meeting his eyes.

Something was very wrong.

She looked up quickly, as if he'd spoken his worries out loud. "Can I tell you later?" she asked, her voice unsteady.

"Sure," he said gently. "Or not at all." The blond driver had come around to their side of the truck. He was leaning on a stick, had some kind of joint disease from the look of his crooked hands.

He remembered a boy with hands like those. Dan felt a cold breath on the back of his neck. A kid, out in the Dry. A kid who had had . . . magic in his crippled hands. He had been twelve, which would make him thirty-two now. Dan met the stranger's eyes, his flesh contracting into goose bumps. "Jeremy?" It was as if something had waked the past today, drawn it out of the dry soil like smoke rising from a buried fire. "Your name isn't Jeremy, is it?"

"Hello, Dan." An insect popped into the air between them, glowing like pale fire in the sunlight.

He'd called it a firefly, all those years ago. He'd asked Dan if that was what a real firefly looked like. "My God." Dan stared at it. "I heard someone was doing a magic show in town, but people said it was some kind of light show."

"I always wondered how you made out. I wondered if I'd ever run into you again." Jeremy didn't hold out his hand, just stood there.

Dan became aware of Nita, still and silent, watching them intently. "I thought after . . . that they might have killed you." He said it awkwardly. It was hard to meet those cool blue eyes. "I almost went back for you," he said. "Made you come along. But I didn't. I just . . . kept on running. I'm sorry."

"Don't be." Jeremy shrugged. "They didn't kill me. You didn't run out on me. *I* decided to stay, remember?" He reached into the bed of a pickup and retrieved a battered pack.

"Do you need a place to stay? I've got room." Awkward words. From the expression on Jeremy's face, he heard that awkwardness.

"I'm fine. Thanks." He slung his pack over his shoulder. "Take care of yourself, Nita."

"Did he ever understand? Dan asked softly. "Your dad?"

Jeremy stared out into the riverbed without answering. For an instant, Dan caught a flash of green from the corner of his eye, an afterimage of grass and gray water, like one of Jesse's paintings.

"No." Jeremy shrugged, finally. "I scared him. Listen." He frowned, threw Nita a quick glance, then turned back to Dan. "Not everyone thinks that what I do is wonderful. Don't tell people it isn't a light show, okay? She'll tell you." He touched Nita's arm, and his face softened suddenly. "Take it easy."

"I will." She took his hand.

Bemused, drowned and surrounded by ghosts and the past, Dan watched Jeremy limp down the street and disappear around the corner. "Where did you meet Jeremy?" he asked absently.

"Right here in The Dalles." Nita was looking at him, her forehead creased in thought. "I didn't realize you knew him."

"It was a long time ago." Dan shook himself, wanting to brush the nagging past away as if it were a cloud of springtime gnats. "You look beat," he said. "Which is how I feel. Let's go home."

"Sounds good," Nita said, and sighed.

The town looked ugly in the level beams of the setting sun, dry and dusty. Empty. A scrap of paper skidded down the middle of the street, pushed along by the wind. Dust eddied in a doorway. But the town wasn't empty. It was full of invisible murmurs. I don't want to hear them, Nita thought. She leaned back against the seat as the truck climbed up to the rim of the Gorge, missing the dry folds of the coast mountains with a terrible intensity. Their tent had smelled like honey. David had laughed when she tickled him awake in the dawn coolness. He had put his arms around her, kissed her face and neck, made love with her on the rumpled blankets. His love had the feel of beesong, soft and gentle.

She had traded the tent for the food she had needed for the trip. The bees were dying. Nita stared down at the angled line of the dam as they drove up along the wall of the Gorge. The gray concrete wall looked forbidding, like a fortress built on the stony dryness of the riverbed, closed and unfriendly. Nita held her restless daughter tightly in her arms as the truck bumped along the narrow road. Dan was quiet, full of his own shadows, small darknesses flecked with razored bits of pain and guilt. He had hurt Jeremy, or thought he had. And Jeremy thought so, too. He had been angry — closed up and resentful.

I don't want to know this, Nita thought sullenly. I can't change anything, Jeremy. What do you want from me?

Something. The memory of his needing nagged at her, making her angry.

When they reached the house, Nita busied herself with Rachel, nursing her, cleaning her with the oil that she'd bought at the market. For once Rachel was all too willing to fall asleep. Nita pinned a diaper on her daughter and tucked her into the bed. Rachel's eyes were blue, like David's eyes. Pain moved inside her, squeezing a lump up into her throat.

Whose bones lay under that rock? David's? Do I *want* them to be his? she asked herself. A tear spilled over to slide down Nita's cheek. She sighed and wiped her face as she felt Dan's quiet approach. He held the blue pack in his hands, the flap folded over to show the crooked letters. He didn't say anything, just looked at her.

Nita nodded, then turned back to the riverbed. "Someone found it," she whispered. "Near some bones."

"I'm sorry." Dan's sadness fell around her like the twilight shadows. He came to stand beside her, and as he looked down at the rocky falls of Celilo far below, his sadness deepened. "The past is walking tonight." He tried a laugh, but it came out crooked. He was staring down at the dry falls as they vanished into darkness.

"Who died down there?" Nita asked softly.

"My sister, Amy." Dan looked at her sideways, a little startled. "It's that obvious?"

Nita shrugged.

"She raised me. I guess she just got tired out eventually. We weren't doing too well. She jumped." He frowned down at the shadowed falls. "You know, I asked Jeremy once to make her face for me, so I could see it. And . . . he did." He let his breath out in a rush. "It wasn't just a picture, it was Amy, like he'd brought her back to life."

The dry falls had vanished into shadow, and it was getting cold. Nita shivered and Dan put his arm around her. For a long time they looked down into the riverbed. The sky had deepened to a royal blue and the first stars winked like dry eyes, low on the horizon. Nita leaned closer against Dan's warmth. His arm tightened around her shoulder and Nita felt the warm stir of his desire.

She closed her eyes. If she tilted her head, he would lean down and kiss her. Once their lips touched, there would be no going back. They would go into his room and make love on the narrow bed, beneath the paintings of Jeremy's river. When she woke in the darkness tonight, she would feel his warmth beside her, smell his sweat and his skin, hear the sound of his breathing.

She would be safe.

Nita took a small step away from him. He gave her a wry smile, lifted his arm from her shoulders gently. Silently, without touching, they went back into the dark house.

"You need to be careful." Dan switched on the solar lantern and hung it over the table. "We had a rape-murder last night. Out near Sandy's place."

Nita listened in growing horror as he told her about Candy Wilmer and her death. "Maybe it wasn't one of the soldiers," she said hesitantly. "Maybe someone just wanted it to look that way."

"That occurred to Durer and me." Dan set the pot of leftover beans on the table, his expression grim. "But a lot of people aren't going to look beyond that knife. The only hope we have is to find out who's behind the sabotage. It's not someone local, or we'd know who was in on it by now. I can see someone busting the Pipe for revenge, but what about the rest of this stuff? Someone wants to start a war between the Corps and The Dalles. Why? Dan leaned his elbows on the tabletop, staring moodily at the bean pot. "Carter asked me that question and I can't answer him. Who wins? No one. There's only so much water and there's only so much land under hoses. Carter's right. The equation only comes out one way, no matter what." He sighed and spooned cold beans onto his plate. "I'm losing my touch. People want to listen to the Ransoms, not to me."

"It's my father," Nita said harshly. "That's what keeps you here. Why don't you let it go?"

"Sam's part of it." Dan put his fork down. "Maybe you're right. Maybe it's time I quit."

He was thinking defeat, not release. He was thinking death. Something tickled the back of her mind. It had something to do with what Dan had just said, but she couldn't put her finger on it. She spooned beans onto her plate, not really hungry, but not wanting to face the darkness of her bedroom. At least Rachel was there.

"I'm going to bed." Dan stretched, his fatigue filling the room like a haze of dust. "Are you sure you're all right?"

"Yes." She met his eyes. Smiled for him. "Thanks."

He disappeared into his bedroom. Nita sighed, feeling her own weariness. She scrubbed her plate clean in the pan of sand that stood on the counter. It was getting dirty; she'd need to get a fresh panful tomorrow. Renny's unexpected visit this morning had made her forget. Renny! The trucker's name jogged her memory. Frowning, Nita hesitated, wondering if it was really important. Right now, tonight, she didn't want to knock on Dan's door.

With a shrug, she grabbed the lantern, walked resolutely across the floor, and tapped lightly on the warped panels of Dan's door.

"Come in." He was sitting in bed, the sheets across his lap, eyebrows arched with his wondering. The yellow light made his tanned shoulders gleam like polished wood, edged his wiry muscles with shadow.

"Renny told me something odd." Nita licked dry lips, didn't look at his erection prodding the sheet. "She said they were putting new land under hoses down in the Valley. To grow more bushes."

"What?" Dan sat up straighter. "Carter told me that the reduction was intended to keep the Valley's share constant, that there would be crop losses down there if they cut the flow at all."

He wasn't thinking about sex anymore.

"If Renny's right, someone is handing out a line of bullshit. You don't get a federal permit for new fields if water's tight. I wonder who's shitting who," he said softly.

"It's not Carter." Nita bit her lip as Dan looked at her.

"I think he was telling me the truth — or what he thought was the truth," Dan said slowly. "Remember I said that no one stood to win?" He frowned, his face lined with shadow. "This changes things. I'm not so sure that's true anymore. Somebody may be pulling strings to get new fields in." His frown deepened. "If so, it has to be someone who's big enough to pull those strings. If Carter isn't behind it, he needs to know what's going on. He should have the sources to check it out. If he believes me. I guess this is where I throw the dice and find out how my luck is running."

"I'm coming, too."

"No way." Dan shook his head, gave her a crooked grin. "I can add two and two and come up with four. Do you think Carter is going to listen if you're standing at my side? I'm sorry if I messed something up between you."

"You didn't." Nita flushed and looked away.

"He'll listen if I can give him something concrete. He doesn't want a war here any more than I do."

"They won't let any civilians on base, so you're going to sneak in, aren't you?"

Dan smiled at her. "The worst he can do is jail me for trespass."

Her father had trapped this man, on that dusty afternoon when the men had come. The blood that had stained her had hardened into a chain around Dan Greely's throat. "That's not the worst that can happen to you," Nita said bitterly. "You can get yourself shot."

"I said the same thing to your father once."

"And he didn't listen either. Well, he should be proud of you." Nita turned on her heel and fled to the sanctuary of Rachel's dreams.

CHAPTER SIXTEEN

It was late when Carter looked up. He felt a mild sense of shock at the flood-lit darkness beyond his office window. It had been late afternoon when he had finally made it back to his deskful of flow reports. He stretched, wincing at the crackle of vertebrae in his neck. It had been a relief to bury himself in solid, comprehensible numbers. He understood turbulence and flow dynamics. The numbers always meant the same thing.

Private First Class Carolyn Allison had been shot today while out on patrol. Someone had hidden in the rocks along the riverbed, had shot her in the chest with a 30.06. An old hunting rifle, probably. Possibly the same rifle that had killed Delgado's brother. Carter stared at this reflection on the window glass. Stranger's face — flat and unfamiliar, the mouth set in hard lines, the eyes unreadable. He had spent part of the afternoon in the infirmary. Carolyn Allison would live, but it had been close.

My fault? How much? The face in the window stared back at him, eyes accusing. If he had come down hard on the Shunt demonstration, would it be better now? Or worse? Carter shook his head. A flood of transfer requests cluttered his desk. He had denied them all — although he couldn't blame people for wanting to bail out. Hastings had told him he couldn't expect any new people for at least another week, and maybe not even then. Sick calls were escalating. The accident rate had soared. Tired people made mistakes, and the doubled patrols he'd had to put out were wearing them all ragged. Morale sucked. And now Durer was on his case, claiming that a Corps member had committed a rape and murder in The Dalles. He'd undoubtedly broadcast his damned verdict to everyone in town — which had probably resulted in the shooting. Carter had ordered an armed fast-reaction team to be kept on five-minute alert status. Things were that bad.

A knock on the door made him jump. "Come in." He turned away from the window.

Delgado marched in and saluted, his posture stiff and straight. "I have exceeded my authority, sir, but I've come up with something that I have to show you."

"How exactly did you exceed your authority, Major?" Carter reined in his temper with an effort. Since the beating incident and his subsequent discipline of the major, relations had been strained, to say the least. Damn Hastings, anyway. "You're walking a thin line with me," he said coldly.

"I understand, sir." Delgado stared at a spot on the wall above Carter's head. "I had one of my men keep an eye on Greely."

"The Dalles is off limits. By my direct order."

"Yes, sire, but I sent him out before you gave the order, sir. He was discreet." Delgado pulled a tiny digital camera from his pocket. "Permission to upload this to your computer, sir?"

Carter jerked his head and Delgado plugged the camera into his CPU. The screen flickered as the camera uploaded and suddenly a photo blinked to life on the screen.

Two men stood together in front of the government store, apparently deep in conversation. Dan Greely and the red haired agitator, or someone who looked a hell of a lot like him. Greely had said that he didn't know the man's name, that he'd only seen him around. "Who took this?" Carter asked heavily.

"Sergeant Roth, sir, from Support. He's good with a camera."

"I want to talk to him. Right now."

"Right away, sir." Delgado gave him a brisk salute and departed.

Carter stared at the screen. He had liked Dan Greely, and he had resisted the evidence that was all around him — dismissed it as too convenient, as circumstantial. He swallowed, tasting bile in the back of his throat.

By the time he finished interviewing Roth it was very late. Carter printed up a copy of the photo and pocketed it, locking his office on the way out. His footsteps echoed in the empty corridor. There would be coffee in the mess. He should go get a sandwich, he told himself, but he wasn't hungry. A private was coming in as he reached the main doors.

"Sir?" She saluted. "I just escorted Chief of Police Durer off the base. I called your office, but you'd left."

"Oh, yeah." Carter ran a hand across his face, realizing just how tired he was. "He stuck around this long?" That meant he hadn't found anything very useful. Carter swallowed his anger and looked more closely at the woman. "You kicked that local off me at the Shunt," he said, recognizing her. "Wasson, right?"

"Yessir." She grinned. "I was glad to be of service, sir."

"Did Durer find anything?" Carter asked as they walked to the doors.

"He copied all the gate logs." Her face was carefully neutral. "And he took prints from tires down at the motor pool. I don't think he was satisfied, sir."

"He thinks we're covering up for someone, never mind that we've given him full cooperation." Carter's lips tightened. "He wants to pin this on the Corps so bad he can taste it. Damn local."

"Sir."

Carter looked at Wasson. Her face had gone tight, closed. "Something wrong, Private?"

She shook her head, eyes averted.

"Hold it a minute." He put out a hand as she started to open the door. "I'd like to know. It's not an order, Wasson. I'm asking."

She looked at him, looked away, obviously angry. She had something to say, but he was a colonel. "I . . . grew up in Hood River, sir." Twin spots of color glowed on her cheeks and she stared stiffly at the wall. "It's hard for us, sir. We're locals. Our families are 'hicks.'" She gave him a hard, bright look from the corner of her eye.

Expecting a reprimand? Carter sighed. "I haven't given much thought to that, and I should have," he said wearily. "Tell me about it, Private."

"We're . . . caught in the middle," she said tightly. "We're *Corps*. They were our friends, the ones who got killed, one of us. I knew Sonny and Tom real well. Sonny and I were . . . close." Her lips twitched. "My family used to grow pears in Hood River, but the trees were old and they died off when I was young. Mom's still there, living with my brother. I don't know how they're going to make out with this water cut. I mean —" She stared at the doors in front of her, struggling for words. "I know we don't make the rules, but I feel like the goddamn enemy sometimes. Excuse me, sir."

What he should tell her, of course, was that she was Corps, first and foremost. But she knew that, or she wouldn't be hurting. Carter sighed. "It's tough, isn't it? You catch shit from your buddies for siding with the locals and you feel like a traitor to your family at the same time. You're damned either way." There weren't too many locals on base, but there were some. He'd better find out who, first thing in the morning. He should have found out at the beginning.

"I was stationed in Chicago when the big riot started," he said. "We got sent out to break down the barricades afterward and help pick up the bodies. I . . . recognized one. We used to play ball together, after school."

Domino had been one of the few people in Johnny's crowd who had accepted Carter. How the hell had he ended up on the lakeshore, ragged and dirty and dead? "I felt like shit."

"If you'd had to shoot at him, would you have done it?"

Carter met Wasson's eyes, seeing the fear in them. "Chicago won't happen here," he said flatly.

"Yes, sir. Thank you, sir." She snapped him a brisk salute.

Carter watched her march down the corridor. That salute was the first one he'd seen in days that had really been meant. He pushed through the doors, leaning against their weight and the heaviness in his chest. He sure hoped he could keep that promise he'd just made.

Outside, he shivered in the night chill. The wind was picking up. Grit rasped on concrete and Carter blinked, his eyes tearing as they filled with dust. His goggles were on his desk but he was too tired to go back for them. All he wanted to do was fall onto his bed and sleep. Even a shower could wait. He cut through the alley, seeing nothing. Who had grabbed him and why? In the glow of the porch light, Carter fumbled with the lock, swung the door open . . . and froze. Dan Greely was sitting on his sofa.

"We need to talk," Greely said.

"You're right. We do." Carter stepped inside and closed the door very softly behind him. "I have something to show you." He walked past Greely, into his bedroom, his anger a cold weight in his gut. He opened the drawer of his nightstand and took out the Beretta. Greely was still on the sofa. He went very still as Carter reentered the room.

"I'm not armed, not even with a knife." He fixed his eyes on the gun. "What's gotten into you, Carter?"

"Keep your hands on your knees. Where I can see them." He lifted the phone, called Security.

"Carter, will you wait for one minute?" Greely said urgently. "What the hell is going on here? I snuck in because what I have to say is important. If you really give a damn about what's happening on the riverbed, listen to me, for God's sake."

"Did you ever find that agitator?"

"No." Greely shrugged. "He split as far as I can find out. I never did catch up to him."

The cold anger was spreading through his body. The man had a damned golden tongue.

"You need to hear this." Greely spoke rapidly. "Someone is getting permits to irrigate new acreage down in the Willamette Valley."

"Bullshit," Carter snapped. "They're already irrigating to capacity down there. That's why we have to absorb the flow cut."

"That's what you told us." Greely's eyes were intent on Carter's face. "Do you know this for sure?"

"General Hastings gave me the numbers himself."

"How good are his sources?"

"You have proof?"

"No." Greely looked troubled. "I was hoping that you could check this out. That's why I came here — to ask you to do that. I think maybe we're all being set up."

"You talk very slick," Carter said. He edged sideways to the computer desk, slipped the CD into its tray. The screen lit with the photo, the agitator's red hair flaming in the bright sun. "After I talked to you at City Hall, my car broke down. And a little welcoming committee was waiting for it to happen. And my phone was gone." He watched Greely's eyes fix on the screen. "Someone fixed the engine very neatly. And we found a wrench down in the engine compartment. It had the initials DG on it." He stared at Greely. "If Judge Lindstrom and Durer weren't in your pocket, you'd be in jail right now."

"They're not in my pocket but they're fair men. Who took that?" He jerked his head at the screen.

"One of ours. I talked to him."

"He's lying to you. That's a fake." Greely's shoulders slumped. "I wondered who swiped my tools. It's a frame, Carter. A good one."

"It's uploaded right out of the camera. And don't tell me about any three days for trespassing. This time, we hold you for the US Marshal. We're charging you with tresspass, tampering with government property, and water-flow obstruction. And kidnap."

"I don't think you can make any of that stick. Except the trespass."

"Maybe not, but it will be at least two weeks before the marshal even gets around to collecting you. I can't spare anyone to transport you, and he's down in Medford right now. If you are innocent, you'll have a great alibi for anything that happens."

"You're making a mistake." Greely's eyes were bleak. "Sandy Corbett and I have been working our asses off to keep a lid on things. You need our help a lot more than you realize."

"If that turns out to be true, I'll apologize."

"It'll be too damn late to apologize by then."

Security knocked on the door and Carter let the MPs in. Greely stood quietly as they cuffed him, his face expressionless. He looked over his shoulder as the MPs ushered him out of the room. "You're wrong," he said. "About a lot of things."

Carter waited until the door latched behind them, then he went to put the Beretta away. He had never thumbed off the safety. "Hell," he said and slammed the drawer closed.

And what if Greely had been telling the truth? About the new Valley fields?

He was lying. Feeding Carter a new line of bull.

But if he wasn't lying . . . the Corps was cutting water that didn't need to be cut. Carter remembered Private Wasson's face as she talked about her family in Hood River.

Pacific Biosystems? They were the prime suspect of course. Carter shrugged as he stripped off his coverall. It would be easy enough to check. They couldn't keep that kind of thing secret; the permit application for any new irrigation line had to go on record, and the records were accessible. Just to be sure, just for Wasson's sake, he'd check.

He threw his dirty coverall into the corner, feeling less sure of himself than he had on his first day here.

CHAPTER SEVENTEEN

The wind picked up during the night. It blew down the Gorge in fierce gusts, shaking the old house, tugging at the dried-out shingles, sifting dust and grit between the cracks in the walls. Awake in the darkness, Nita listened to the wind, listened for the sound of Dan's truck. Rachel whimpered and struggled in her sleep and Nita held her close.

"It's me, isn't it?" Nita touched her daughter's face. "I'm giving you bad dreams, worrying about Dan." Her daughter's dark hair felt as fine as milkweed down beneath her fingers. Her fault, her DNA. The windows rattled, closed against the blowing dust. Nita slipped out of bed and tiptoed across the room to peer through the glass. The sky was dark and starless, and Nita shivered in her thin shirt. Maybe Carter would listen. Maybe he would believe Dan.

Carter didn't trust anyone. Not really. He wasn't going to believe Dan.

The wind rose to a booming crescendo just before dawn, but by the time the sun was well up, it had dropped to fitful gusts. Nita fed Rachel, wanting to start for town right now. It wasn't to be. Outside, the dust storm had bowed the plants to the ground. If she didn't do something about it, Dan would lose his crop. She had been hired to take care of the beans. Chafing at the delay, Nita spread Rachel's blanket in the shade of the box that housed the water meter and set her daughter down. Rachel grabbed for her toes, drooling and grinning. "You *are* teething, aren't you?" Nita peered into her daughter's mouth, then tickled her round belly until Rachel laughed.

Draping her sunscarf over her head, she stared down the bean rows, propping up the wilting stems, shaking dust from wind-shredded leaves. The powdery dust stuck to her skin as the morning crawled by, turned muddy by her sweat. Nita wiped her face, back aching, unwilling to take a break. Only a few more rows. The water would come on at dusk and soak the field. Maybe it would help.

Finished, at last. She scooped up Rachel, started for the porch. The figure limping up the track to the house caught her by surprise. Jeremy. In spite of her worries, she smiled as the landscape shimmered into a thousand shades of green. "Did you walk all the way from town?" she asked as they met at the porch. "Would you like a drink?"

"Yes, and yes, thank you. People used to say 'hello, how are you?' a generation ago." He grinned at her. "Now, we say 'hello, would you like a drink?' I guess thirst is more important than your health and well being now."

"I never thought of it that way. Sit," she said because his knees hurt him. "I'll bring it out here." The pain had a worn feeling to it, like a piece of stone that had been polished by wind and water until the sharp edges had worn away. They had hurt him all his life, she guessed.

She carried two mugs out onto the porch, handed him one. "Is there anything I can do? For the pain?"

"You feel it, too?" He looked down at the lumpy bulge of his kneecaps. "That must be rough sometimes."

"Yes." Nita drank half of her water, her eyes on the dry gash of the riverbed below. "My father used to sit on this porch. I wonder if he could remember it — water in the riverbed. Maybe that's why he worked so hard to save this town. Or maybe it was because he was like me," she said softly. "Maybe it trapped him — all those needs and hopes and fears around him. Maybe he couldn't say no, Jeremy. She's going to blame me." Nita poked a finger into Rachel's palm, swallowed hard as Rachel clutched it. "I did this to her."

"Only if you hide it." Jeremy's face was still, without sympathy. "Only if you deny what you are."

"How can I deny it?" Nita blinked as the ground around the house went green with short, tough-looking grass. She reached, passed her fingers through a thin stalk of white flowers. "It still surprises me." And she smiled because she couldn't help it. "Are you doing it on purpose?"

"I can't really control the visions. They just happen." Jeremy crossed his arms on his raised knees, moody suddenly. "I came up here to . . . apologize to Dan. For yesterday. I was . . . rude."

"He felt guilty." Nita studied his face. "That he left you behind."

"Did he?" Jeremy looked surprised. "I wasn't angry about that. What he told me, back then, was that my makings were wonderful. I stayed behind because I believed him. But he was wrong." Jeremy shrugged. "They're nothing. They're dangerous." He touched his chest, remembered pain clouding the air between them. "I needed someone to blame for that. I never really expected to see him again."

The hurting inside him was worse than his knees. Nita reached for Jeremy's hand and his fingers tightened around hers.

"The past matters, Jeremy."

"No, it doesn't." He stared down into the riverbed. "It just makes the dust seem worse, it makes people crazy. So, is Dan here?"

"No." Nita lifted her head, her worry coming back in a rush. "He went down to the base last night, and he didn't come back. I was just about to go down there." She picked up Rachel, went to get her sling, and twisted it over her shoulder.

"The base is closed to civilians."

"Maybe Carter will talk to me. I hope so."

"Carter Voltaire? I've met him," Jeremy said thoughtfully. "I like him. I get the feeling that he's caught in the middle of this water war and it scares him shitless."

"He doesn't trust Dan." Nita tucked Rachel into the sling. "He thinks Dan is behind the sabotage and stuff and he isn't."

"So go tell him that. Tell him how you know."

"He won't believe me." She looked away.

"Won't he?" Jeremy followed her into the house as she filled a water jug at the tap. "I think he will. Is that what you're afraid of?"

"Cut it out." Nita scooped Rachel out of the sling as she started to fuss. "What do you want from me, Jeremy?"

"I want you to use your talent." Jeremy lifted Rachel out of her arms. "Would you fill mine, too?" He held out a plastic two-liter. "I think I can get us onto the base."

She turned on the tap hard, not caring that she splashed water all over the counter, about to tell him that she didn't want his help. But the sound of an engine interrupted her. It wasn't Dan, she knew the sound of his truck, but she ran outside anyway, wanting to believe that someone else had given him a ride home for some reason. The car was just pulling up beside the porch, a new all-electric, covered in dust. Nita halted at the top step as the driver got out. It was Carter's friend.

"Hello." He smiled at her, but he wasn't pleased to see her. "Is Dan Greely around?"

"No, he's not," Nita said quickly. "He's in town. Could you give us a ride, on your way back?"

"I'm sorry." His expression of polite regreat covered a stab of irritation that made Nita wince. "I'm going straight back to Bonneville. I'm on a tight schedule." He glanced pointedly at his watch.

"Which means you have to drive right into The Dalles to pick up Eighty-four." Jeremy had come out onto the porch behind Nita. "Out here folks don't say no when someone asks for a ride. Walking in the sun is grim."

Nita watched the friend — Johnny, she remembered his name — notice Jeremy's hands. His revulsion showed briefly on his face, clearly enough for Jeremy to see it. "Maybe I'll just wait around for Dan for awhile." His smile was wearing thin. "I'll pick you up on the way down, if I pass you."

"If we've got to walk, we'd better get moving." Jeremy shoved his hands into his pockets.

Nina hesitated. This man wanted them to leave. Why? What did Dan have that was worth stealing? Nothing this man couldn't buy with the money he probably had in his pockets, from the look of his clothes. "I'm not going to town." She sat down on the top step, ignoring Jeremy's surprise. "I told Dan I'd wait for him." She lifted Rachel from her sling and sat her on her lap.

"Oh, forget it, I'll give you a ride." The man's smile was more in keeping with his sour mood, now. "No point in sticking around here for hours."

He knows, Nita thought, and felt a sudden chill. He knew that Dan wasn't coming back. A fist closed tight in her chest, making it hard to breathe.

"I think I'm lost." Jeremy gave her a narrow look. "Are we getting a ride or staying here?"

"Let's go." Nita stood quickly. "We appreciate the lift." She gave this Johnny a very sweet smile.

He didn't speak to them as they climbed into the car. Cool air whispered from the vents, making Rachel chuckle with delight. He didn't say one word as he eased the car down the rutted road into The Dalles. He was pissed that they'd been at Dan's house — what had he been after? Was he doing something for Carter? She almost asked him, but something made her hold her tongue. He pulled over at the interstate ramp and stopped the car with a jerk. "I hope this is okay."

And to hell with you if it isn't? "It's fine," Nita said as they got out of air-conditioned car. What did Carter owe this man? The car peeled away with a scatter of gravel and she jumped as Jeremy put his hand on her arm.

"Want to tell me what was going on?"

"I don't know." She frowned at him. "He doesn't know Dan, and he wanted to get into the house. He was mad that we were there."

"Maybe one of us should have stayed," Jeremy said thoughtfully. "Is he connected to the Pipeline mess?"

"He's Carter's friend," Nita said reluctantly. Full of nagging dread, she and Jeremy walked to the base gate.

The guard scowled at them, but Jeremy wasn't worried. He smiled at her and gave her a thumbs up. The dread thickened in her belly, growing heavier as the minutes ticked by. Carter finally appeared, walking fast. She didn't need to see his face to feel his frown as he spotted her.

"Jeremy?" He glanced at Nita, avoiding her eyes. "Don't ask me to let Greely go. I assume that's why you're here."

"You arrested him?" Until that moment she hadn't realized how much she had feared that he was dead, like her father. "He's here?"

"Yes." His face tightened. "With cause. I'm sorry."

He was hurting inside. He hadn't listened to Dan, didn't want to listen to her. In a moment, he would turn around and walk back through that glittering metal gate. "Carter, you need to hear me," she said. "Because you care about what's happening here."

"Call it payment," Jeremy said to Carter.

Carter frowned, looked at Jeremy and away. "I can spare you a few minutes. That's all." He sighed, not wanting to be here. "It's not going to change anything," he said. "It's beyond me, now."

"We'll take what we can get," Jeremy said cheerfully. And gave Nita a look.

She walked through the ugly gate. The unformed guard saluted Carter and his eyes slid to Nita. He leered at her behind Carter's back and his lust raked her. She lifted her chin. A moment later a strangled squawk made her look back. The guard was slapping frantically at his back, neck craned to stare over his shoulder. Nita sneaked a look at Jeremy.

He walked serenely next to her. His face was calm, but she felt his amusement. She touched his arm lightly, smiling in spite of her apprehension, and kept her hand on his arm as they walked down the dusty street between the sterile blocks of buildings. Carter wasn't taking them to his apartment. She looked up at the looming cliff-face of the dam, hoped they wouldn't go any closer. The air was full of anger, fear, and tension. It pressed around her, smothering as a heavy blanket, making Rachel start to cry. The dam leaned over them, seemingly ready to fall. Carter turned aside and held open the door to a long, low building.

It was cool inside, as cool as the car had been. The sweat on Nita's skin chilled instantly, and Rachel cooed. They were walking down a pastel-walled hallway lined with doors. Two uniformed men passed them, their bland faces masking hostility. Nita nearly stumbled into Carter as he stopped to open a door.

He stepped aside quickly, not wanting to touch her, and ushered them into a cramped office. "Dan Greely trespassed on Corps property last night." Carter closed the door with a small bang. "He's safely locked up, waiting for the U.S. Marshal. I can't let him go and that's the bottom line. Is there anything else?"

Rachel began to cry again, fretful and shrill. Without a word, Jeremy stepped forward and lifted Rachel from Nita's arms. "We'll wait for you in the hall," he said, and walked out.

Nita felt a flash of panic as the door closed behind them, cutting off the sound of Rachel's fretting. "Dan came here to tell you something important," Nita faltered.

"He didn't have anything important to say to me."

He hurt. "Damn it, Carter." Nita groped for anger, seized it like a lifeline. "Didn't you even listen to him? About the new fields in the Valley?"

"It's not happening." Carter lifted his shoulders in a shrug. "I'm busy, Nita."

"It *is* happening." Words, words, she needed words. Nita took a deep breath. "Renny Warren — a trucker — told me about them, and I told Dan. He thought it was important — important enough to risk getting arrested or shot to tell you. Doesn't that matter to you? Or are you in on this? Is that it?" She felt a sudden chill. "Your friend Johnny gave us a ride this afternoon. He was snooping around Dan's house. Are you both in on it? Are you getting some kind of cut for giving water to the Valley?"

"No," Carter said. "I'm not. And neither is Johnny."

His anger stung, but it filled her with relief. He wasn't in on it. "Okay, I apologize. But Renny Warren was telling the truth. Dan said you had to cut the Gorge because the Valley crops would die — but that's not true, is it?"

"It is true. I can't help but think you're saying this so I'll let Greely go. Johnny's in San Francisco, by the way." Carter turned his back on her and leaned over his desk. "I have a lot of reports to catch up on."

"He's not in San Francisco. He was at the market yesterday, too." Nita walked around his desk and leaned on it so that he had to look her in the face. "You still think I've made some kind of choice between you and Dan," she said bitterly. "The choice was never between you. I didn't walk away from you. I ran away because I cared too damn much and I didn't know if David was alive or dead back then. I couldn't love you when I didn't know . . ." Her voice broke and she looked away, fighting tears.

"Nita." Carter crossed his arms tightly. "This Renny was lying. As for Greely, I have proof that he was involved with the people who dumped me in the Dry. He also sabotaged my car last time I was in town. I'm sorry, Nita. But the proof is real. He did it."

"What kind of proof can you have?" Nita clenched her fists. "He didn't do it."

"I have photos and an eyewitness."

Now was the time to tell him. "They're wrong. Fakes," she gasped, failing, failing. "I'll bring you proof," she said, despising herself in that instant. "I'll bring you proof that those fields are real. If I do that, will you let Dan go?"

"If you can get me solid proof . . . it will make a difference." Carter looked at her and looked away, doubting himself, doubting her. "I can't promise any more than that. Dan might be safer here, Nita."

"I'm not just worried about Dan." Her voice caught. "I'm worried about you, too."

He stood up suddenly, and she stepped into his arms. Their kiss was a hard and bruising sharing this time, full of anger, doubt, love, and pain . . . hers and his, all mixed up ant twisted together. She thrust herself suddenly away from him, tasting blood on her lip, trembling. He made no move to touch her again, but stood stiff and still beside his desk.

Someone tapped lightly on the door and they both jumped.

"Come in," Carter said shortly.

Nita remembered the uniformed man who pushed the door open. He was the one who had found Carter that night up on the Gorge rim. His familiar, ugly darkness filled the office like a sour smell.

"What is it, Major?" Carter sat down stiffly behind his desk, frowning.

"We got a report from the team at the Shunt." The man turned deliberately to stare at Nita.

"Say it," Carter snapped.

The major hesitated just long enough to make his point. "Corporal Roscoe reported in, sir. He and his team spotted some suspicious activity in the hills above the riverbed. A hick fired a couple of shots at them and took off. The corporal is asking for permission to pursue, sir."

"They can't leave the Shunt unguarded."

"By the time another team gets out there, the bastards'll have vanished." The cold eyes flicked to Nita and away. "I could have another detail at the Shunt inside of a half hour, sir. The hicks'll never know there's no one there." Hot eagerness flared like lust in the man. "We could catch 'em."

"No." Carter stood. "Tell the corporal to go after them, but one man stays at the Shunt. Get the alert team out there pronto, and put a squad on alert in case there's trouble. Armed, Major."

The officer snapped a brisk, pleased salute and strode out of the office. Nita started after him, her skin dotted with goosebumps. He was so full of hatred. Was it her imagination, or had some of it been directed toward Carter?

"You have to go." Carter was staring at the map on the wall. "If . . . you turn up anything concrete, come to the lower gate. The guard there will contact me."

He wanted her to leave. "Who was that man?"

"Major Delgado. Why?"

"He . . . doesn't like locals."

"His brother was one of the people who got killed last spring." Carter wouldn't meet her eyes. "You have to leave now."

"Carter." She paused at the door. "Who betrayed you?" His lips tightened but he still wouldn't look at her. "I'll bring you proof," she said, and fled.

CHAPTER EIGHTEEN

Carter half rose as Nita left, then sank down into his seat again. Nothing more to say between them. Nothing. He stared at the riverbed map on the wall, not really seeing it.

Who betrayed you? What had made her say that? He leaned his face in his hands, remembering the single spot of blood on the bathroom rug. She had always been so neat, Mom, so careful not to make a mess. Why this memory? Why now? He shook his head to banish the image. Could you call suicide a betrayal? He let his breath out in an angry rush.

His phone beeped. Swearing softly under his breath, Carter flipped it open.

"Hey, Carter." Johnny's voice came cheerfully over the line. It wasn't a video connection, just voice. "I'm tearing through town," he said. "Got time for a quick lunch?"

He *was* here. "I thought you were down in San Francisco," Carter said cautiously.

"I had some official business with the general. Carter . . ." He hesitated. "I need to talk to you."

"Can you come here? I can't get away."

"Damn. I'm on a tight schedule." Johnny sounded harried. "This is important. Remember what we were talking about over lunch? Paul's little theory?"

"Yes." Carter frowned. "About a Corps link to Pacific BioSystems."

"I can't say more on a cell — but it seems to be in your backyard."

Delgado? Hastings? "Who?"

"Like I just said . . ." Johnny cleared his throat. "Listen, we don't have concrete proof yet, but we're working on it." His tone was guarded. "Watch your back, okay? I'll let you know as soon as something breaks. It's big, Carter. Keep that in mind, okay?"

He meant Hastings. "Thanks," Carter said. "Oh, were you up at Dan Greely's house this morning?"

"Yeah." Silence hummed in his ear. "Who told you?"

"Nita." So she had been telling the truth about that. "She said you gave her a ride."

"So that was Nita?" Johnny was trying to sound casual. "She was . . . up at the Greely place. Is she . . . living there?"

"Yes, she's living there," Carter growled. "It's a free country."

"Hey, I'm sorry." Johnny laughed awkwardly. "I don't know anything."

"Forget it. So what were you doing up there?"

"I thought I'd meet this local agitator face to face. It's . . . part of what I was telling you about. I needed to check out a few loose ends."

"Check out some things? What the hell are you doing, Johnny?" Carter swallowed sudden anger. "Playing amateur detective? People are getting shot around here, damn it."

"What do you think it means to be a regional director for Water Policy?" Johnny's tone was cold. "We're supposed to be out here, in our districts. This isn't supposed to be a desk job, Colonel Voltaire. This is my responsibility more than yours, remember?"

"I'm sorry." Carter flushed. He had thought of Johnny as sitting at a computer screen reviewing other people's reports. "I apologize. But let me deal with Greely. He's locked up right here, as a matter of fact."

"He is? Well, I guess I can stop looking for him, then." The harried town was back in his voice. "I'm outa here. Watch yourself, remember?"

"I always watch myself. Thanks, Johnny." He put the phone down slowly.

Hastings? He was big enough to make it worth Pacific Bio's time, and he had access to every patrol schedule. Through Delgado? Maybe his dislike of Carter hadn't been due to his unexpected promotion. Maybe Hatings had been worried that Carter was a plant, sent to spy. Had he been worried enough to shoot him full of drugs and ask? Whoever had grabbed him from the base had learned the schedules and routes to a T. Or had been wearing a uniform.

Greely could be the local connection. That fit, too, no matter what Nita wanted to believe. Cold inside, Carter touched numbers on his phone. This connection was a video link. His neutral smile felt stiff as a clay mask on his face.

The general scowled from Carter's screen. "Colonel? Anything wrong?"

"I don't know, sir." Carter frowned, watching Hastings' expression. "I have some news that I thought you should hear. A trucker claims that new fields are going in down in the Willamette Valley. "

"They're not." Hastings frowned. "The farms are hurting for enough water to keep the crops up off the ground as it is. You know how truckers talk. Is that all?"

"I didn't believe it either," Carter said quickly. "Not at first. But the woman involved says she can give me proof. If she's right, sir, then there's a cover-up going on. A big one, and we're being had. I think it's worth looking into, sir."

"Proof changes things." Hastings grunted. "What kind of proof and who is it?"

He seemed genuinely surprised, Carter thought. An act? "A woman named Warren, sir. She . . . didn't have the proof with her."

"Renny Warren?" Hastings waved a dismissive hand. "She owns the land Greely works and she's one of the biggest black market operators in the Northwest. Renny Warren is slick enough to keep her ass out of jail, but I wouldn't call her trustworthy. Not by a long shot."

"I see." Carter frowned. Yet another link to Greely.

"I guess I can't blame you for being taken in." Hastings reached for something out of range of the video pickup. "You didn't know the connection. Did she tell you what she had?"

"No, sir. She's supposed to bring it to me," Carter said briskly. "I'll call you when I get it."

"If it checks out, call me. Don't bother me otherwise." He scowled, his expression faintly contemptuous. "I don't need to waste my time on a wild-goose chase. I didn't think you had the time to waste either. I'm glad you have everything under control out there."

Carter clenched his teeth. "With the general's indulgence, I am respectfully requesting permission to pursue this matter." It would be damned easy to believe that Hastings was pulling the strings behind all this. "I think it matters, sir."

"Do what you want." Hastings made a chopping gesture with one hand. "Just don't let any of those damn locals hole that Pipe. You got it."

"Yes, sir." Carter broke the connection. So Nita's source of information had a direct connection to Greely. Carter leaned his chin on his hands and stared at the blank screen. All threads in this tangled web led smack to Dan Greely. Either he was the center of all this . . . or Nita was telling the truth and he had been well and solidly framed.

By whom? Hastings? Carter shoved his chair back and stood. Maybe he was just a bastard. It occurred to him as he brought up the day's flow reports on his screen that he wouldn't shed many tears if Hastings ended up in a court-martial.

CHAPTER NINETEEN

Nita walked down the hall from Carter's office, her shoulders drooping. Jeremy was sitting on the floor near the main door, with Rachel asleep on his shoulder. "I don't need your gift to know that we locals aren't very popular here." He got to his feet, careful not to disturb Rachel.

His unspoken question hummed in the air. "I didn't tell him," she snapped. "He wouldn't have believed me anyway. So let's drop it, okay?"

"I didn't say anything," Jeremy said mildly.

Nita pressed her lips together, took Rachel from him, and tucked her into her sling. He *wouldn't* have believed her. It wouldn't have made any difference.

Jeremy was disappointed in her. Nita stalked toward the gate, furious; at Jeremy, at Carter, at herself for being afraid. She almost welcomed the hostility of the uniformed men and women around them. The guard took their passes, his eyes cold, and waved them through.

"Now what?" Jeremy struggled to keep up with her fast pace. "What next?"

"He wants proof that Dan's not involved." She didn't slow down, didn't wait for him. "I have to prove that the new fields exist. I have to go talk to Renny Warren."

"The trucker? I've heard of her." He was wary. "She'll be at the plaza. If she's in town."

"She won't help me," Nita said bitterly. Jeremy's knees were hurting him and she finally slowed down, teeth on edge from his pain. "She doesn't like Dan."

"You can persuade her."

"What do you want from me?" She swung to face him. "Why don't you just lay off?"

Rachel woke up with a jerk and began to cry, kicking her feet and squirming in the sling. "No," she yelled. "Not you, too. No, do you hear me, I can't stand it." She turned and ran. The stony ground jarred her feet and sweat stung her eyes, muddy with dust, salty as tears. Rachel screamed and struggled in the sling. Sobbing for breath, Nita finally staggered into the shade of the culvert. "I'm sorry, honey." She scooped her shrieking daughter into her arms. "I'm so sorry . . . I love you." She buried her face against her daughter's rigid body. "I do. Rachel, honey, stop crying. It's all right." Only it wasn't all right, and it would never be all right, not as long as she lived.

A green dragonfly popped into the air above Rachel's angry face.

"Go away," Nita whispered.

"No." Jeremy leaned against the wall beside her, sad. "I remember when our milk goat had a crippled kid. From the water or the dust, my dad said. That kind of thing happens a lot out in the Dry. Deformities and . . . strangeness. "

Slowly Rachel's angry wails subsided into hiccoughing sobs. She reached for the dragonfly, batting at it irritably at first, then grabbing for it with a tentative smile.

"I don't want to believe that it's the Dry that causes people like you or me to be born," Jeremy said softly. "I don't want us to be a bunch of dust-induced mutations. What if we're the first sign of change? What if the whole human race is . . . adapting somehow? So that we can live with what's happening, live through it? Instead of killing ourselves and the land trying to fight it?"

"What does it matter, *why*?" Nita said bitterly. "What difference does it make?"

Jeremy sighed and laid a gentle hand on her shoulder. "Dad said that crippled goat kid wasn't worth the water it would drink. It would never get around well — never be of any real use. So he took it out to the garden. He cut its throat with the big knife from the kitchen. He held it over a hill of beans, so that its blood watered the plants. I want us to be hope, Nita. Not mistakes."

Nita looked sideways at the thick, gentle fingers on her shoulder. His father had thought about the knife when he was born. Jeremy knew it and that knowing echoed in his words. Nita closed her eyes, shivering. "I love Rachel," she whispered. "No matter what she is."

"Do you?" Jeremy turned her gently around to face him. "If you don't accept yourself, you'll never really be able to accept Rachel."

"That's not true!"

"Isn't it? Ask yourself, Nita, and listen to the answer." He sighed. "Are you going to go see Renny Warren now?"

"Am I going to manipulate her into helping Dan, do you mean?"

"Yes."

"Fine. Let's go find her." Nita straightened. "Right now." She pulled her sunscarf from her pack and draped it over her shoulder to shade her daughter's face.

Rachel yawned and Nita held her close, sweat soaking through her shirt like blood. The sun was still high overhead. Shadows were no more than slivers of darkness at the base of rocks, and the whitewashed walls of the Plaza Inn glared white in the harsh light as Nita approached. The faded red roof of the building had a scabby look. Fallen tiles littered the cracked asphalt beneath the eaves, and four semi rigs with triple and quadruple trailers baked in the asphalt lot.

"They look so shiny," Nita murmured. "As if they've just been polished."

"They probably have been." Jeremy eyed the glittering chrome and black of the nearest truck. "Truckers wash their rigs. It's a symbol. You're doing pretty badly if you can't afford the water to keep your rig clean."

Nita looked at her distorted reflection in the gleaming door of the cab beside her. Washed with water. She remembered the precious minutes spent in Carter's shower and wrestled with outrage. How did they wash these monsters? Coiled hoses hung on the side of the building. There was a tap on the wall, too, safely caged away behind locked, steel-mesh. Did they uncoil the hoses and spray gallons and gallons of water across the trucks, then let it evaporate in the sun? Nita tried to guess how much it would take to wash a single truck. Enough to wash diapers for Rachel for a month? Enough to wash them every time, instead of putting them out in the sun to dry until the smell got too bad? A puddle had collected beneath one of the hoses inside the enclosure. Nita's toes twitched with the desire to walk through it, to feel the tickle of sun-warm water splashing across her dusty skin.

"That's awful," she breathed. "How can they do that?"

"I wouldn't talk like that in front of Renny." Jeremy smiled faintly. "Truckers have their own values. They can be a little . . . touchy."

Jeremy was thirsty. Nita could feel it, but the wasted water and the spotless trucks didn't bother him. Nita frowned, shifting Rachel into a more comfortable position on her hip. Sometimes it seemed as if Jeremy had no real allegiances. He could be friends with Dan and Carter and the truckers with their wasted water. Maybe because he really belonged to his green past? Not this dusty present?

"This way." Jeremy took her hand, his smile warming his pale eyes. "Only the cops use the front door." He pulled open a gray metal door with no markings. Cool air rushed out, chilly enough to make Nita gasp. "The rigs have good air-conditioning," he said. "The truckers like it cool." They walked into a dimly lit, windowless hallway. Doors opened in the dirty pastel walls every few feet. Metal or plastic numbers had been pried off the panels, leaving ghostly images behind. The grimy magenta carpet underfoot smelled of dust and dirty clothes.

"You know a lot about truckers." Nita looked apprehensively down the hallway.

"I keep moving. Someone always figures out the projector scam sooner or later, so I don't stay long in any one place." Jeremy shrugged as he led her down the hallway. "I ride with truckers a lot. Some of them pair up, but you cut your profit that way, so they mostly drive solo. They're bored and lonely, so they'll trade miles for a little entertainment. They like my makings. I don't have much trouble getting around."

"Truckers waste water."

"They drive through the Dry because it takes too much fuel to go around it. Big convoys are pretty safe, but you can't always hook up with one. Hijackers get some. You break down, you're prey for the salvagers."

"Okay." Nita let her breath out. "I'll stop bitching. Maybe Renny'll let me sit on the hood of her truck next time she washes it."

"Don't even joke about it."

A door opened suddenly and a man stuck his bearded head out into the hallway. "You lookin' for someone?" he asked casually.

It wasn't a casual question. "Renny." Nita blurted the name out. "Renny Warren. She said she was staying here."

"Did she?" The man's deepset eyes moved slowly from Nita to Jeremy and back again. "You friends of hers?"

"Nita is." Jeremy nodded at her. "You're Wasser, aren't you? You gave me a ride from 'Frisco up to Portland a few months back."

The man's face went still for a moment; then his thick lips smiled in the carefully trimmed nest of his reddish beard. "I remember you," he said. "They guy with the butterflies. How ya takin' it?"

"As it comes." Jeremy shrugged. "You?"

"Same." The man jerked his head toward the far end of the hall. "Renny's on this floor. Second from the end. Take it easy." His maned head disappeared and the door closed softly.

"I think he had a gun. In his hand, where we couldn't see it." Nita eyed the closed door.

"Probably. Truckers don't kid around. You don't wander through here unless you're invited. Come on."

Second door from the end. Nita took a deep breath and tapped softly. Renny hadn't scared her at the house. Down here, in this dim, dirty corridor, her pulse fluttered.

"Yeah?" The gemstones winked in Renny's ear as she peered through the partly opened door. "Change your mind about digging dirt, babe? And who's this?" Her eyes roved over Jeremy, dismissed him.

"Jeremy Barlow, a friend of mine." Nita made no move to touch the door. "Can I talk to you, Renny? It's important."

"Why not? I'm awake and I got nothing better to do." Renny opened the door wide with a single, tight swing.

Nita walked past the muzzle of the small automatic in Renny's hand. For some reason it wasn't as frightening as the gun in the hand of the bearded trucker. Renny would make sure it was a killing shot, Nita guessed, but she wouldn't pull the trigger unless she figured she needed to. She looked around the room surprised. She had expected more grime, but the room was light and clean. A luxurious bed took up most of the space with a shiny, silky looking covering. An expensive flat screen hung above a polished wooden table flanked by chairs upholstered in rich, crimson fabric. After the corridor, the luxury took Nita's breath away.

"So, why the visit?"

Nita sat down in the chair Renny pointed to, trying to gather her thoughts. Jeremy had seated himself on the far corner of the bed, obviously staying out of the way. "I wanted to know more about the new fields down in the Valley," she said. "The ones you mentioned at the house."

"Why?" Renny was suddenly wary.

Nita frowned, thinking fast as she bounced a chuckling Rachel in her lap. "The Corps cut the water flow in the Gorge. They said they had to do it to keep Valley crops from dying." She looked at the trucker from beneath her lashes. Renny was leaning against a tall dresser, arms crossed, frowning a little. She wasn't angry or even very curious. The yellow light from the ceiling fixture struck sparks from the chains around her neck and a trace of sleepy lust hung in the air. "I think someone's running a scam," Nita ventured.

"So? Danny got you playing politics after all?" Renny gave her a whip-flick glance. "Danny likes power games."

Now what? "Dan's out of the picture." Nita used a tone of mild regret. "He got himself arrested."

"Did he?" Hot emotion flashed and faded behind Renny's benign look of surprise. "So why the interest in the irrigation water?" She raised one eyebrow.

This time it was a serious question. "Leverage comes in handy sometimes." Nita smiled at the wiry trucker. "I thought I might try a career in local politics. My father was a name here, once, and the time seems about right."

"While Danny's in jail, you mean? You're a sharp little bitch, aren't you?" Renny's laugh filled the room, too large for the small woman. "So good-hearted Danny took an operator under his wing, did he?" She grinned at Nita. "By the time he gets his ass out of jail, you'll have his perch on top of this shit pile all sewed up?"

Approval. Renny understood this type of move. Nita gave her the small, sleek smile she expected. "I need to know who's getting a cut from those new fields," she said softly.

"Now that would be worth something, wouldn't it?" Renny chuckled. "You'll own someone's ass, honey. Myself, I can't see why you want to bother with this dumpy town, but that's your business." Renny crossed her ankles and leaned back on her elbows, sure of herself, sure of Nita, now. "What's my cut?"

Nothing for free. Not from this woman. Nita made a show of considering, wondering what she would value.

"How about Danny?" Renny said softly.

Nita shrugged, listening hard to the resonances behind the trucker's words. Careful . . . "Sure." She made her voice casual, put *casual* into the slant of her shoulders and the curve of her spine. "Tell me how and when." She felt Jeremy's twitch of reaction. You wanted me to play this game, she thought sullenly. You shut up.

Renny was watching her, debating, trying to decide if Nita was acting or not. Rachel started to fuss. She wasn't really hungry, but Nita lifted her shirt, the fabric sliding up over the curve of her milk-heavy breast, felt the heat of Renny's stare as Rachel groped lazily for her dark nipple.

"Hell." Renny smiled. "Danny'll dig his own grave. He's been working on it for years. No, I don't think I'll let you off the hook that easily."

Nita's skin prickled and she stifled a desire to bolt out of the room.

"We'll make it an IOU and we'll talk about it later."

"That's too vague." Wrong thing to say, but it popped out before she could stop herself.

"Take it or leave it." Renny straightened. "I don't bargain."

Game over. "All right." Nita drew a shaky breath. "An IOU. After I get something I can use. Concrete proof."

"Not an issue, girl." Renny reached over to grab Nita's hand, her eyes traveling slowly down her body, full of creamy anticipation. "What do you need? Names? Title transfers? All the sneaky little back-door connections?"

"Everything." Nita let her breath out in a rush. "In hardcopy."

"I think that's going to cost you a little extra." Renny's eyes flickered and she made a flicking motion with her fingers, as if brushing away invisible flies. "I know a lady in Portland who makes her living on the net. She can dig up everything you need. No one keeps Lydia out."

"Great." Nita stood, settling Rachel on her hip. "When can you get it for me?"

"*We'll* leave right now." The wiry trucker grinned at her. "I've got half a load for the city. That's enough to pay expenses. Why wait?"

We? "How do I get back here?" Nita fished in her pack for Rachel's beads, trying to hide her unease.

"Babe, you can hop a ride anywhere you want. Even with the kid." Renny sounded dryly amused. "You looked in a mirror lately? But I might pick up an eastbound load, you never know." Her grin widened. "And if I don't, I'll find someone who owes me a favor. A little gift from me. Keep it in mind." She eyed Rachel dubiously. "Those boobs mean you got to bring the kid, right? She's not going to scream the whole way, is she?"

Nita shook her head, looked at Jeremy. "Would you stay up at the house for me? If the beans don't get watered on time, they'll wilt. The automatic valve's broken and you have to do it on manual."

"Sure." Jeremy nodded. "I've worked fields before."

"You got a half hour." Renny opened the door. "I've got to pick up my stuff and warm up my rig."

Jeremy walked past her, out into the grimy hall. Nita followed him outside and around to the front entrance of the inn, the one the cops used. She squatted on the cracked concrete walk, in the narrow strip of shade, cradled Rachel on her lap and leaned her forehead against her daughter's small heat.

Jeremy put a hand on her shoulder, his sympathy falling on her like dust.

"It was that or Dan. She hates him." She didn't lift her head. "What if I say no?"

"It wouldn't be a good idea," Jeremy said reluctantly. "Truckers back each other up and they have long memories."

"Thanks a lot." A big engine rumbled a bass note in the parking lot and Nita caught a whiff of ethanol on the hot breeze. She swallowed a hard knot of apprehension, gathered Rachel into her arms and stood. "I hope this satisfies Carter," she said bitterly.

"I'll meet you at the house when you get back." He touched her lightly. "Good luck."

As Renny swung the door open, Nita straightened her shoulders, tucked Rachel into her sling, and clambered up into the high cab.

Renny sat in a padded seat — the only seat. Embroidered cushions, a tiny kitchen unit, shelves, and cupboards turned the rest of the cab into a plush — if cramped — living space. Even a flatscreen hung on the side wall, and a little GPS screen glowed on the dash. Nita looked apprehensively at the gleaming bank of gauges and displays that surrounded the screen as she settled herself gingerly on the carpeted floor beside Renny's seat.

"Relax, babe." Renny ran a blunt-nailed finger down Nita's arm, her eyes glinting with amusement. "You scared of me or the truck? I don't collect 'till I deliver your dirt, so you're safe 'till then."

Needling again. Nita lifted her chin and managed a smile. "I've never been in a truck cab before. It's . . . amazing."

She didn't have to pretend awe. She could feel the power vibrating through the cab but it was quiet inside, so cool that her skin had gone tight and bumpy. She brushed her palm across the thick crimson carpet. The dashboard was paneled in what looked like real wood. Nita touched the satiny finish, tracking the rich grain. Silver winked at her from knobs and the rims of the digital display. Blue green numbers and letters winked indecipherable codes at her.

"You've got your mouth hanging open like a native, babe."

"I can't help it."

Renny tossed her head. "Take a good look — she's a sweet rig. I won't waste power specs on you, but she's one of the best on the road. Custom design, state of the art engine. If the kid gets sleepy, you can put her on the futon back there. Don't let her piss on it."

"I've got diapers on her . . ." Nita gasped as the truck suddenly swerved. She fell against the door, grabbing for Rachel.

"What the hell?" Renny snarled. The truck swerved again. "What's that hotshot trying to do? If he scrapes my fender I'll run him into the damn riverbed."

Clutching the door, Nita peered through the windshield. A battered van was crowding the truck, forcing Renny to steer close to the rough shoulder of the highway. Here, the ground dropped off abruptly into the riverbed. If the truck went over, Nita thought in terror, it would roll.

"Duck," Renny yelled and hunched down behind the wheel.

Bits of glass stung Nita's face and she heard a sound like a distant backfire as she crouched over Rachel.

"The bastard's shooting at us." Bent low, Renny clutched the wheel.

The truck shuddered and lurched. Renny cursed in a continuous monotone, her voice barely audible over the roar of wind and engine noise. More glass stung Nita's neck and she gasped at a white explosion of shock. I'm hit, she thought, and then; it's Renny. Rachel started to scream as the truck swerved again. Nita caught a flicker of cold, focused hatred, lost it. That wasn't Renny. She recognized that hatred. The cab shuddered and metal crunched. Renny gave a wordless cry as another impact shook the truck.

Triumph, not pain. It was over, whatever was going on. They weren't going to roll down into the riverbed. Nita raised her head cautiously. Vibrations shook the cab, but they were still moving, still on the highway. Renny clutched the wheel with both hands, her face set and white, eyes squinted against the dust in the air. More holes pocked the window in Renny's door, and blood soaked her left sleeve.

"I ran the bastards off the road," Renny said between clenched teeth. "Good thing they were so low. Door's bulletproof and you can't hit much anyway, shooting up. A 'jacker would've sprayed the windshield and we'd have gone over for sure."

"Stop," Nita said. "You're bleeding."

"I sort of noticed, babe." Renny bared her teeth. "But I don't think they went off fast enough to do serious damage. We'll stop down the road, where we've got better high ground."

Her arm was beginning to hurt with a hot, grinding pain. Nita clenched her teeth. Rachel was still screaming. Nita soothed her as best she could, and used her sunscarf to block the holes in the windshield so that Renny didn't get too much dust in her face. Renny didn't stop until they reached the Mosier detour. Once off the interstate, she pulled over onto the shoulder of the two-lane road, struggling one-handed with the wheel. The truck finally jolted to a halt and Renny leaned back against the seat, her face white.

"I want the medical kit from that top storage cupboard," she said. "There's a gun under the seat. Get that first."

Nita put the crying Rachel onto the futon and found a squat rifle in a concealed holster beside Renny's seat. She handed it to Renny, then took down the green plastic box of medical supplies.

"You handle the gun if I pass out. It's full auto." Renny opened one eye. "Nine millimeter hollow point, not much kick but it'll stop someone. Point it and pull the trigger. Don't swing it around — aim steady and you'll probably hit something. Safety's there."

"Let's hope they don't show." Nita put the gun on the floor and opened the box.

Renny carried a lot of medical supplies. Nita fumbled through bandages and surgical instruments, vials of antibiotics, pain-killers and stimulants. This was all black-market stuff, worth a small fortune. This was where the antibiotics on Dan's shelf had come from. She looked down the road, but saw no sign of the van. She reached for Renny's injured arm.

"I'll take care of it." Renny slapped her hand away. "Give me those scissors."

"Shut up and sit still." Nita clenched her teeth against Renny's pain. "I have two hands." She began to cut away Renny's blood-soaked sleeve. "What pills do you need to take?"

"You're a gutsy little bitch. You'd better do a damn good job." Renny swallowed a groan as Nita swabbed blood from the wound with an antiseptic pad. "I'll need the white tablets for infection and two of the orange capsules for pain," she mumbled through tight lips. "They're loaded with meth, so I won't nod off. Custom mix."

"The bullet went through," Nita said over Rachel's cries. "It's bleeding pretty badly." She dug her fingers into Renny's armpit to compress the main artery. David had taught her a lot, out in the hills. Nita pressed a fresh gauze pad against the ugly exit wound, relieved as the bleeding slowed.

The orange capsules worked fast to dull Renny's pain. Rachel finally stopped screaming and fell into instant, exhausted sleep. Feeling shaky herself, Nita finished cleaning the wound and bandaged Renny's arm. Blood had run down Nita's arm to her elbows, had dripped onto her worn jeans. She taped the bandage in place, wiped her hands, and began to put the supplies away. Renny looked better, not so pale.

"Nice job." Renny managed a faint grin. "I was right. You wouldn't make a half bad trucker." She pushed her door open and slid awkwardly to the ground. "Look at my rig." She glared at the crumpled skin of the truck's gleaming fender. "I'd like to get my hands on the bastards. Do you know who they were?" Her good hand locked on Nita's wrist.

"I think so." Now that it was over, Nita's hands wanted to tremble. "It was a Major Delgado in the van. From the base. It's because of the fields. He doesn't want me to get that proof. I'm sorry, Renny."

"You gave me his name," Renny said flatly. "We're even. Don't worry. You'll get your proof, babe. You just make damn sure you twist someone good with it. Delgado's days are now numbered." She touched the bandage on her arm, flexed her fingers, and winced. "Let's go," she said as she swung herself into the cab. "I want to get to Portland before those caps wear off. There's some fiber tape in that cupboard. You can patch the windshield while we drive. Leave the gun where you can reach it."

CHAPTER TWENTY

Carter left his office and went down to Operations, needing to be there in person. He had taken a risk, leaving the Shunt valves with a single guard, even for half an hour. The safe thing would have been to deny Corporal Roscoe's request, to have had him wait until the relief detail showed up. But by then, the sniper would have vanished. He wanted a wedge into who was behind this, and the sniper would give him that wedge.

Carter paused outside the big double doors. He needed that wedge and he needed it damn badly. He couldn't afford to believe anybody here, not Nita, not Greely, maybe not Hastings. His cell buzzed.

"Delgado, here." The major's voice sounded harsh in his ear. "We've got a situation. The relief team was ambushed, just west of the Shunt. Roscoe called in for support. We've got casualties, sir."

The war had finally started. Carter felt cold. "I want that squad rolling now," he said harshly. "Major?"

"Sir?"

"No local people on this mission. Pass it on to the unit's CO."

"Yes, sir," Delgado said briskly. "We're rolling."

"You stay," Carter snapped. "I'm taking it."

"Sir?"

Carter hung up on him. No way Delgado handled this. He ducked into Operations, where Major Bybee gave him the all-clear. No problem with the flow — not yet. He left Operations almost at a run and burst out into the baking afternoon heat. The squad was riding two of the battalion's new AAVs — armored and baled to take any dry terrain. The captain in charge saluted and Carter returned it as he scanned the troops. His eyes narrowed and he veered around to the rear of the nearest truck. "Private Wasson?"

"Sir." The private's sandy head jerked up as she snapped him a salute.

"You're off this assignment. Get out."

"Sir?" Her face flushed. "You can't to that. Captain Westerly . . ."

"You heard me," Carter snapped. He'd deal with Westerly later. "Move it, Private."

Face sullen, she climbed down. The first vehicle was already pulling out and the grunts on this one were looking carefully elsewhere. Wasson yanked her rifle out to the truck bed and stalked away, her shoulders rigid.

"Sir?" Westerly saluted, her face tight.

"Later." Carter cut her off. "Let's go, Captain." She hadn't expected him to come along, and looked for one instant as if she was going to protest. Her salute was razor sharp, but her eyes were almost as sullen as Wasson's. Carter swung himself up into a seat without returning it, angry at Westerly, angry at himself. He'd handled that badly, but hell, there hadn't been time to handle it any other way.

The grunts behind him were silent. Because he was there. "This is a hell of a situation," Carter said. "We're supposed to be running water, not shooting people." The AAV lurched forward and he grabbed for a handhold.

"I'm tired of just takin' it." The low voice was just audible.

Carter felt the sudden stillness all around him. "You think I'm pretty soft on the hicks, don't you?" Carter looked back, picked out the dark-haired kid who'd spoken. A private — Carter read his name, Andy Stakowski. "They can shoot us a hell of a lot easier than we can shoot them. You think about that, Private." The kid looked angry. He was, what — nineteen? Twenty? "If that Pipe leaks we have to go out and fix it. That makes us sitting ducks. If a war starts, we'll lose it. But we'll take out the bastards who are shooting at us. In spades."

"You said it," someone said, farther back in the truck.

Carter watched the walls of the Gorge slide past. They were all scared. We're not combat troops, he thought bitterly. People joined the Corps to design lifts, fix pipe, drive a dozer, or watchdog flow turbulence. The vehicle rocked as it hit a stretch of bad pavement, throwing him back against someone's shins. "Sorry." Carter glanced over his shoulder to find himself looking into the young private's face.

"It's a rough ride, sir." He hesitated, blushing red. "I'm sorry, sir. About what I said, sir."

"It's okay," Carter said. "We've got people down out there. Let's get to them." The kid's eyes were bright with excitement or fear or maybe both. He was ready to be a hero. It's not like the videos, kid. Carter stared out at the passing landscape, remembering the stink of blood and bowel and dust after the Chicago riot. The bodies they'd picked up had bloated and split open in the heat.

The rattle of automatic weapons echoed back and forth between the walls of the Gorge, coming from everywhere and nowhere. The AAV was slowing and Carter's stomach clenched. "Keep your heads down," he yelled as he leaped from the back of the still-rolling truck. "Scatter and get under cover. If they're up on the rim, they've got us."

He landed lightly as the rest of the grunts piled out. The men and women hit the ground running, scrambling for whatever cover they could find. Roscoe was waving from a jumbled pile of rocks near the bottom of the riverbed.

"They're in the bunker," the corporal yelled. Another short burst of weapons fire rattled down the Gorge. "They're not using hunting rifles, sir. Not this time."

Doing *what* in the bunker? "We've got to get in close enough to lob gas. Carter crouched beside Westerly. "Send one team around to the north, another along the Deschutes side of the bunker. If they can come up on it from behind, they can get in pretty close under cover. We'll keep the bastards busy here."

"Yes, sir." Westerly scuttled away, crouched low.

It might already be too late. It wouldn't take much to wreck the automatic valves. Carter snatched his cell from his belt, using the secure channel.

"Operations. Yes sir, Colonel?"

"Any trouble?"

"Negative, sir. It's running fine."

"We've got intruders in the Shunt bunker. Put an override on all manual controls. Lock 'em down tight." Worst case scenarios unrolled in his head. "Get ready to shut down the flow fast. Call me if anything at all shows upon the boards." He snapped the phone closed and scrambled down the slope toward Roscoe's rock. A Corps 4x4 lay on its side at the bottom of the bed; Carter thought he could see a body behind the wheel. Corporal Roscoe, a light-skinned black man with a long, bony face, reached for Carter as he got close and pulled him down behind the shelter of the dusty boulder.

"I sure am glad to see you all." His Louisiana accent softened his words. "The relief team walked right into an ambush. They were waiting for us."

Carter looked past him. Another Corps body lay in the sun — a dark-haired woman.

"The hicks had it all set up, sir." Roscoe's eyelids flickered. "Lopez and I were up on the rim, sir. We couldn't do anything. Lopez got it when we tried for the truck. They were already in the bunker, sir. Amesworth was in there." His shoulders jerked.

Carter put a hand on the Corporal's arm, then slithered around the side of the boulder to peer up at the bunker. Its concrete walls gleamed white in the glare. If one of the teams he'd sent out could get gas in there, they'd have them. He'd have salvaged something from this mess, and he'd damn well wring some names out of them. Carter looked back up the bank. His people had spread out over the rocky slope of the riverbed. Sporadic bursts of gunfire rattled down the Gorge — all Corps fire. They were keeping the bastards busy, as ordered. Carter's jaw tightened as two new vehicles pulled up along the highway. Media. Who the hell had called them? He reached for his cell again. "Any trouble?" he asked Operations.

"Negative," Bybee told him. "Thumbs up. We've locked out the manual controls."

Carter frowned as he replaced the phone. "I haven't heard any more shots from the bunker. I wonder if they sneaked back into the Deschutes bed. They'd be out of sight from this angle. I don't like it." Carter felt a growing uneasiness. "They had plenty of time to screw up the valves before we got here. What are they up to?"

"Colonel?" Roscoe cleared his throat. "They knew every move we were making out there. I think someone set us up, sir. Someone from the base."

And had called in the media to come watch the action.

An explosion cut off their words, roaring through the Gorge like a vast roll of thunder. A fist of concussion slammed Carter flat. Rocks and dirt showered down, some chunks big enough to hurt. Ears ringing, blinded by dust, Carter wondered why the thunder of the blast didn't stop. It went on and on and its low, hissing rumble shook the ground. Dazed, blinking, he lifted his head, caught a glimpse of brown motion, as if the entire riverbed had lifted and was sliding toward them. With a flash of horror he realized what he was seeing.

Water.

"Up to the road!" He staggered to his feet. "Move it, move it!" he yelled hoarsely.

Captain Roscoe was already scrambling up the slope. Carter started after him and nearly tripped over a limp body. It was the kid, the private. Face bloody, he groaned as Carter hauled him to his feet. He slung the kid's arm across his shoulder and staggered as the first rush of water hit him. Debris rode a crest of dirty foam, tugging at him with incredible force. Why the hell didn't they shut down the flow? The flood washed higher, shoving the barely conscious private against him, tearing at them both.

He went down on one knee under the weight of the boy's body and the water seized them both, cold and deep now. Something slammed into his side and pain blazed through him. He couldn't stand up, felt his footing going, his feet sliding as the water torqued them both. His arm had gone numb. Then the water pulled him off his feet and he stifled a cry as water closed over his head. Stand up, he told himself. It couldn't be that deep. But the kid's body twisted in his grip, dragging him down. His shoulder scraped sand . . . riverbed? Which way was up? They were rolling, tumbling. He slammed against rock and a new spear of pain blasted the air from his lungs. His mouth filled with water and his lungs spasmed as he struggled not to cough and breathe water.

Let go, his brain screamed at him. Let go and you can make it. But his fingers had turned to stone, locked into the fabric of the kid's coverall. He had to breathe *now*. One more kick. His legs felt like lead, but his toe caught a rock and shoved him a few inches forward.

A hand closed on his collar and fingers dug into his armpit. Carter's head broke water. He sucked in a blessed, agonized breath, choked on water, and gagged. Sunlight dazzled him, turned the world to a blinding kaleidoscope of silver light. Someone was yelling. The hands locked under his armpits dragged him higher, out of the cold clutch of the water and onto the welcome heat of the rocks. Carter took another breath and cried out as pain knifed through him.

"Keep working," someone said loud and close by. "Got a pulse yet?"

I'm alive, Carter wanted to say, but it hurt just to breathe. He coughed and the world went gray and fuzzy. He coughed again and groaned, sucking the searing, wonderful air.

A face moved into view, blocked out the glare of light. "You're the biggest fish I ever caught." Johnny gave him a faint grin. "The only one, for that matter. Not bad for a beginner." Water dripped from his hair, ran down his face.

"What the hell?" Carter whispered.

"I showed up with the cavalry. Or the media, as the case may be. Not too many people can drown in a dry riverbed. You sure tried hard. They got the flow shut down, by the way." Johnny's face looked pale in spite of his flip tone. "It was something, seeing water in the riverbed. Scared the shit out of me, if you want to know."

"Thanks." Carter forced the word out through the pain that banded his chest.

"Any time." Johnny raised his head and his face went grave.

Carter heard the murmurs. The kid. They had been talking about his pulse. He tried to look, but when he moved, pain filled his vision with wavering black spots.

"Take it easy." Johnny put a restraining hand on his shoulder. "They're going to bring a stretcher down for you in a minute."

"Did he make it?" Carter didn't need Johnny's headshake. He had heard the answer in the hushed voices. Damn, damn, dam. He closed his eyes. He had held on to him. He hadn't let go. It should have counted. He should have lived.

It seemed to take a small eternity for a medical team to arrive from the base and struggle down the bank with their equipment. Shaded from the sun by a makeshift awning rigged from a shirt, Carter watched the mud dry in the riverbed. The saboteurs had vanished, had probably set the charges and slipped up the Deschutes bed. The blast had shattered the multiple pipes where they entered the Shunt complex. The emergency system should have shut down the upstream flow as soon as the pressure dropped, but it hadn't. Something was wrong about that, but pain fogged Carter's brain and he couldn't think straight.

"How're you doing, Colonel?" One of the paramedics bent over Carter, settling a plastic-framed stretcher down beside him. "We're going to move you in a minute, okay?" He wrapped a blood pressure cuff around Carter's upper arm, pumped it tight, frowned at the dial for a minute, then jerked a nod at his buddy. "All right, let's go. Just relax and let us do all the work here." He and his partner slid arms beneath Carter's neck, back, hips, legs. "One, two . . ."

"Three."

They slid him sideways onto the hot plastic padding of the stretcher. Carter had been prepared for pain, but something moved inside of him, and bone grated on bone. Sickness welled up in his belly. I'm going to throw up, he thought, and passed out.

CHAPTER TWENTY-ONE

Where exactly are we going?" Nita asked Renny. Bonneville was behind them. Up ahead the interstate curved away from the riverbed, veering west toward Portland.

"Lydia works for Pacific BioSystems — the big vat company." Renny concentrated on the road. "It's north of the city, out where the Willamette bed hits the Columbia."

"Oh." Nita shifted Rachel on her lap, dangling the beads for her daughter's clutch. Rachel batted at them, her face screwing up again, still cranky.

Because of Renny. She hurt. Nita stared out the window. In places, the riverbed ran narrow and deep and steep cliffs leaned over the road, like curtains of stone. What did Jeremy see when he walked along this highway? Nita turned away from the window, cuddling her daughter. We sacrifice the unfit to the Dry, Nita thought; beans and beats to biomass bushes that can live on salt water, goat kids to thirsty plants, a crippled child to abandonment. What was my father sacrificed to? she wondered bitterly. Water? Water is our god. No, she thought. Drought is our god and we offer it water. And blood.

She thought about the Robinson boy Seth had told her about, shivering at the memory of his molten hatred. She shivered as Rachel's hand closed over the beads, and she stroked her daughter's cheek lightly. Jeremy wanted them to mean something. Not mutants or demons. Not crippled goat kids.

"This is our turn-off." Renny worked the wheel awkwardly, eased the rig off the wide asphalt lanes and onto a curving exit ramp.

A lot of cars crowded the road — more cars than Nita had ever seen at one time. They made her nervous as they whispered by. People must be rich in the city. She had never even been to Eugene, much less Portland. She hunched her shoulders, oppressed by the people. It was like a huge crowd murmuring, murmuring, all around her. The truck had exited onto a wide city street. Buildings, concrete, brick, or flaking metal, crowded the road. Green grass grew on some of the roofs. Nita stared at it, wide-eyed. Why? Next door, weathered machines crouched on an asphalt lot. Nita recognized a front loader and tractors. Others were larger, their functions less comprehensible.

"This was an industrial district, years ago." Renny raised her voice to be heard over the engine noise admitted by the broken window. "A couple of good mechanics still operate here, but the city bulldozed a lot of it for the camp."

The road curved sharply around a mound of rubble. The rubble had been shaped into a wall of gray, crumbled concrete, twisted metal, and debris. Orange electrified wire, strung on white plastic poles, topped it. Beyond the fence lay the camp. Originally it had been laid out as neat rows of barracks, spaced by wide streets. Now haphazard shacks, cobbled together from plastic, cardboard, and scraps of rusty siding, crowded the spaces between the buildings. Dark knots of humanity huddled in strips of shade, or the doorways for the shacks. A flock of naked children chased each other through the dust near the fence.

The government guaranteed water, housing, and basic medical care, if you needed it. You lived here if you had to take them up on it. Nita looked away. Despair drifted from the camp like the stench from a pit toilet. This was why Dan had driven down to the base to talk to Carter, Nita thought suddenly. People he knew — Sandy Corbett or Bob in the government store — might end up here. The camp had been here when her father was alive. Nita hoped suddenly and fervently that her restless, angry brother Ignacio wasn't in there.

That would have hurt her father more than anything else.

The rubble-and-wire fence ended and Renny shifted gears. Nita was grateful when the dark echoes of the camp's occupants faded.

"This is the place." Renny braked, turned down a wide, new-looking street. "I'll park us behind the loading dock tonight, run on into town with the rest of my load tomorrow."

Nita looked out the window at an enormous building. "The roof looks like a tent," she said. It rose above stained concrete walls in jet-black peaks and billows, shining in the sun.

"It's made out of photo-cloth." Renny slowed as they approached a wide, chain-link fence. "This used to be an old racetrack — horses or dogs, I forget which. Pacific Bio put one of those new roofs on it. It converts sun to battery power." She pulled a plastic card from an inside pocket and handed it to a uniformed security guard.

He ran it through a slot in the tiny gatehouse behind him, then handed it back. "Run into some trouble?" He eyed the truck's battered fender.

"Nothing I couldn't handle."

"Dock R." The gate began to rattle laboriously open. "Around to the right."

Renny put the rig into gear and the truck crept forward with a growl. "I usually make this stop." She looked at Nita from the corners of her eyes. "I've got some good customers here. Very inside folk."

Customers for what? Renny was waiting to see if she'd ask. Baiting her again? Nita leaned against the door, tired of the game, tired of Renny's pain.

"I get them some good deals on antibiotics. I've got a sound connection in Chi. I used to have a couple, but the other guy got his in the riot." She clucked her tongue. "Lost a lot of good contacts in that nasty little war."

Would it happen in The Dalles? Carter was afraid it would. They were circling the huge building, passing loading dock after loading dock, concrete ledges that jutted out in front of wall-mounted valves and racked lengths of corrugated plastic pipe.

"This is where they unload the tankers," Renny said conversationally. "They digest the chopped-up biomass at local plants — use some pretty fancy bacteria to do it. Then they haul the digested sludge — syrup, they call it — to the plant here. Add a few chemicals and some cloned tissue and bingo, you can grow a ton or so of cherry or wheat cells."

"Do you carry the syrup?" Nita asked.

"Not me, babe." Renny's lip curled. "That's for the tanker jocks. That stuff stinks and it's sugars, mostly; hell to get off the metalwork." She and Nita clenched their teeth as she used both hands to back the truck up to a wide platform. Rachel fussed.

"Everybody out." Renny killed the engine, leaned her head back against the seat. "End of the line."

Her face looked gray. Fresh blood has soaked through the bandage on her arm.

"Can someone here look at that?" Nita gathered up Rachel.

"You did a good enough job." Renny's eyes snapped open. "I'll get unloaded and then we'll find Lydia." She shoved her door open and hopped out.

Nita wasn't fooled, but she stood silently below the concrete dock as a coveralled kid hurried up. He took the e-pad Renny handed him, thumb printed it, and scurried away.

"I deliver custom office supplies," she said dryly.

Which were really antibiotics. Nita watched Renny open a hand-sized panel on the side of the trailer to key in a long string of digits and letters on a keypad.

"Some of the hotshots use palm locks. Techie toys." She sneered. "All a 'jacker needs is your palm. It doesn't have to be attached to you. Numbers they have to dig out of you, and sometimes it buys you a way out."

She sounded so matter-of-fact.

The kid reappeared, followed by a rectangular platform on wheels. It had a rail along one side and its wheels squeaked as it trundled along the dock after him. The hair on the back of Nita's neck prickled. The kid wasn't touching the thing. It was following him like a dog, creaking along at his heels.

"Magic." The kid noticed her expression and leered at her. "I trained him myself. Stop, Max. Sit." The platform obediently halted. Slowly the bed sank between its wheels until it rested on the dock.

"Stop trying to impress the natives and get the boxes, punk." Renny scowled up at him. "Those cargo trucks are voice activated with a three-chip brain," she said to Nita. "The kid wears a transmitter and it follows him. Pacific Bio likes gadgets. You've got to stop gawking, babe."

Nita grimaced at Renny's mix of irritation and amusement. "So I'm a native," she said. "Whatever that means."

"Means you're no trucker and you don't know the city from squat. Give me that." She snatched the e-pad the sulky kid was holding out and thumb printed it. "Take good care of that merchandise." She showed her teeth briefly and tossed a folded leaf of scrip in his direction.

"Yessir." The kid grinned, caught the script deftly, and tucked it into a pocket. "I'll take real good care of it." He turned on his heel and whistled two notes to the wheeled truck.

It lifted itself obediently and trundled after him, four small cartons stacked neatly on its bed. Renny slammed the trailer doors. "Let's find Lydia," she said. "Then I want to sleep for a while. Damn that bastard." She touched a raw scrape in the truck's gleaming paint. "I hope he went through the windshield."

Nita shifted Rachel onto her hip and didn't offer her arm to the trucker. Renny would bite her head off, no matter that she was feeling shaky. An echo of the woman's cold nausea tightened Nita's stomach as she followed Renny up the flight of concrete stairs that led to the loading dock itself.

"We'll take the back way." Renny fished the plastic card out of her pocket and swiped it through a reader beside a green metal door with no handle.

A bell chimed and the door slid sideways into the wall. Humid air puffed into their faces and Nita wrinkled her nose at the thick, almost fetid smell. A maze of gleaming pipes and round tanks surrounded them, and a low, throbbing hum tickled Nita's ears, making her feel as if her bones were vibrating inside her flesh. Rachel squirmed on her hip, chuckling.

"Like it, child?" Nita touched her daughter's nose, smiled at her wide grin.

"You coming?"

Nita hurried after Renny, ducking beneath overhanging pipes. Some of them were no thicker than her finger. Others were as big as tree trunks. "What are these for?" she asked as she caught up with the trucker.

"The big ones carry the raw syrup. The little ones carry all kinds of stuff. Trace elements, chemicals, antibiotics." Renny shrugged. "Ask Lydia. She's the one who plays with all this shit."

"They were skirting the main floor of the vast building now. Sunshine filtered through wide strips of translucent plastic in the black fabric roof, filling the space with soft light. Huge tanks stood in rows; round, silver, domed with clear plastic. Nita caught a whiff of citrus on the heavy air as she climbed a metal stairway after Renny. From up here she could look down into the nearest tank. Thick yellow sludge filled the tank, scummed with an oily layer of clear liquid. Like fat on a pot of meat soup, Nita thought. She wondered what it was, feeling slightly revolted. She'd eat beans any day, thank you.

Renny waited for her on the narrow walkway that ringed the factory, radiating fatigue, pain, and irritable impatience. Without a word, she pushed open one of the doors that lined the walkway. It opened into a small office. The color struck Nita first; every square inch of wall space was covered with pictures of flowers, some old, some bright and new, holos and what looked like the pages from old magazines. Rachel cooed with delight. The rainbow of colors overwhelmed Nita. She recognized a few of them from the dusty hills above the valley — yarrow, desert parsley, and fleabane. David had told her the names of the plants as they hunted bees together. Real flowers even grew beneath a small, shaded light tube. Petals like the wings of a butterfly unfolded above crystal dishes of pale golden jelly.

"Well, well. And when did you wander in?" A small woman stood up from her seat in front of a large, flat-screen. "Renny, you should have told me you were coming. My God, what happened to you this time? Hijackers?" She walked into Renny's embrace, careful of the trucker's bandaged arm.

She looked as if she was maybe in her thirties, with a thick mane of carefully cut short hair so blonde that it looked white. Her skin was paler than any skin Nita had ever seen, and her eyes were a vivid lavender as she turned to smile at Nita. "Hi," she said. "I'm Lydia."

Nita took her hand, surprised at the strength in the petite woman's long fingers. "I'm Nita." She felt awkward and grimy and out of place.

"Nita needs some answers, so I brought her to you. I think I'm going to go crawl into your bed and sleep," Renny said. "I'm feeling a little frayed."

"You look like hell." Concern flickered in Lydia's eyes, and she kept her arm around the trucker's waist. "You all right? You going to tell me what happened?"

"Yes, I'll live, and later. I'm just ready for some rest."

"So go rest," Lydia snapped. "I haven't changed my door code. Refrigerator's full and there's good scotch in the top cupboard. Nita can tell me what she wants."

Renny laughed suddenly, disengaged herself from Lydia's arm with surprising gentleness. "Yes, ma'am." She gave Nita a lopsided smile. "She'll get you everything you need, babe." The door closed behind her.

"Damn that woman." Lydia let her breath out sharply. "I don't suppose you're her lover, are you?" She raised a pale eyebrow at Nita.

"No. I'm . . . not." Nita felt her face heating. Jealousy? No, that wasn't what she was feeling.

"Too bad. She's such a bloody loner." Lydia lifted her shoulders in a jerky shrug. "So. What is it that Renny thinks I can do for you?"

"Renny said you were good at finding . . . information."

"Yes, I am. Spill it." Lydia perched herself on the edge of her terminal console, one foot flicking in the air like a cat's tail.

Worrying about Renny. "I need proof that someone is putting in new fields in the Valley. I need to know who's doing it. Renny thought you could find out for me." She held her breath.

"Is that all?" Lydia hopped down and dropped into her chair. "Honey, that should be no problem. It's in the public domain — field permits. Didn't you know that?" Her long fingers danced across her keyboard and one quadrant of her big flat-sceen flickered.

Rachel was kicking, fussing a little. She wanted to get down. Nita shrugged her pack off her shoulder, took the quilt out, and spread it on the floor. Rachel wanted the flower pictures. Her frustration flared like heat lightning as she rocked onto her hands and knees. One hand moved, then a knee. With a frustrated screech, she flopped onto her face, but she was closer to the bright wall.

"Kid, you just crawled." Nita laughed softly. "All you need is practice now."

Rachel rocked to her knees again, made it two crawling steps closer to a picture of a yellow trumpet-shaped blossom. Her chin banged the bare floor this time and she started to cry, angry more than hurt.

"It's all right, all right." Nita picked her up. Her daughter's body felt tense, rigid with her effort. Hers was a hot, pure emotion, simple and direct. *I want!* Nita held Rachel close to the wall, smiling at her gurgling pleasure. Did any flowers grow in the camp they had passed? "You won't grow up there," she whispered to her daughter. "I promise."

"This is turning out to be more fun than I expected." Lydia spoke up. "Someone has gone to a lot of trouble to misfile permit applications in some very creative ways."

Lydia was pleased. Nita leaned over her shoulder, but the jumble of letters and numbers on the screen meant nothing to her.

"Apparently a new company is behind the applications. The interesting thing is that this particular company — AgriCo — is owned by a dummy corporation. The majority stockholders are keeping a low profile."

"Does that mean you can't get the information?"

"You've got to be kidding." Lydia sniffed. "What it means is that I have to sneak into some very tight stock exchange files and find out who really holds the reins here." She hummed to herself. "Whoever did the hiding was good," she said after awhile. "I bet it was Rico. It's his style . . . although if it is Rico, he's getting just a wee bit careless in his old age." A second quadrant of the big screen flickered.

"What do you do here?" Nita asked, fascinated.

"Record keeping, inventory, formula integrations, payroll. Drudge work." Lydia grimaced. "But Pacific Bio has bucks for tech, so I have state of the art hardware and software and they don't bother me when I upgrade. Can't ask for more than that. Aha!" Her fingers pounced and the screen flashed a column of numbers and letters. "It was Rico. Someday I'll tell him about the hole he always leaves in his security jobs. Maybe. Your permits are burning now. I'll have the CD for you in a moment and the hardcopy's in the laser tray," she said absently. "They're all to AgriCo but in a minute . . ." She hissed softly, tapped more keys. "In a minute you'll have the rest of what you need to link AgriCo to your mystery shareholders. There are only two real ones. The others are ghosts." She lifted her hands from the keyboard and spun her wheeled stool around. "It's all yours, honey. Got anything else I can play with? That was fun."

"I don't think so." White sheets were sliding silently out into the tray, a squat plastic box, settling delicately into a wire tray. Nita lifted the top sheet.

"Your mystery duo went to a lot of trouble to hide. Smart of them to hire Rico, but they should have hired me." Lydia smiled, full of satisfaction. "It wasn't nearly as much of a challenge as I'd hoped. Rico must have been having a bad day."

"I'm not sure I understand this." Nita looked at the sheets. Some of them seemed to be copies of legal documents; others were lists of dates and dollar amounts.

"It's all there — records of stock transfers to the dummies, sub-corporations, the whole messy electronic trail. Those are your men." She pointed. "The names on line one. I'm a little surprised. I know Pacific Bio's been trying to lever the general's ass for years, but I thought he was cold steel legal."

Nita stared at the paper, her skin flushing hot and cold. William Hastings. That was the first name. Carter's boss — which put him squarely in the middle. But it was the second name that shook her.

Dan Greely.

"You're wrong," Nita said, and flinched with the hot flash of Lydia's reaction. "I didn't mean it like that. Renny said you were the best."

"I am, at that. Nice that she noticed." Lydia's anger eased. "I'm not wrong, honey, I'm sorry. What happened to Renny's arm, by the way? If I know her, she won't tell me."

"Someone shot at us. Because we were coming here to get this." Nita shook the papers gently. "Lydia . . . I know that Dan Greely isn't involved with this." She looked at the woman's strange eyes. "Is there any way that this might have been faked? To fool someone like you?"

"Honey, I trust my information a hell of a lot more than I trust your intuition." Lydia crossed her arms, her eyes hooded. "I'm sorry your friend is twisted, but it happens. People lie all the time. Yes, someone could have gone to a whole lot of trouble to fake this, but I doubt it."

She was worried about Renny and offended, too. "You're the best," Nita said desperately. "Maybe whoever did it wanted to make sure that they could fool even the best. Will you see if there's anything else?"

Lydia shook her head. "I would have spotted something."

"Someone's going to laugh if you're wrong."

"Let them." Lydia raised one eyebrow. "If they're able to fool me they're entitled to laugh." She stood. "I'm going to go check on Renny."

"She's asleep." Nita stepped in front of her. "I know she is. The same way I know Dan Greely isn't in on it." She sucked in a breath, feeling as if there wasn't enough air in the room. "I can read minds. Sort of. That's how I know Renny is asleep. And Dan didn't do this. The information is a trick." She ran out words, lightheaded.

Lydia was staring at her, eyes thoughtful, her surprise will hidden behind the calm mask of her face. "So how do you *sort of* read minds?"

"I . . . hear emotions. Not words or anything . . . not thoughts. But I know when someone's . . . lying."

"You could be lying." Lydia laughed suddenly. "But I rather think you'd do a better job of being convincing if you were. I don't think I'll ask you to prove it." Lydia tilted her head, considering. "Some truths I don't think I want to know. Or the lies either."

She was thinking of Renny. And she believed her. Nita felt dizzy with reaction. She had considered, doubted, and made her decision. Just like that. Nita swallowed the lump in her throat. "Will you do it? Find out what's going on here?"

"Yeah, I'll go look again." Lydia frowned at her flowered wall. "I wish you *were* her lover," she said quietly. "That's about what it would take, to live with Renny. A mind reader. She needs . . . to care about someone enough to be careful. One of these days she's not going to come back."

Love? Yes. And anticipation of that day.

"She cares about you," Nita blurted.

"I know." Lydia's eyebrows rose above her strange eyes. "She does, but I'm no empath. She pisses me off when she won't tell me stuff, and I let it show, and she snarls at me, and we fight. I hate trucking and Renny goes nuts cooped up here." She laughed. "But other than that we love each other."

"I'm sorry."

"Me, too. Sometimes." Lydia shrugged and went to stand in front of her lights. "This is a cymbidium." She picked up the buttery flower. "One of the techs cloned it for me. The original plant came from old-time Hawaii. This one is a ladyslipper, from a swamp that dried up decades ago. The cells come from the international germ plasm bank in northern China."

Lydia's flowers grew from frozen bits of the past. She would understand Jeremy. Nita watched Lydia replace the delicate blooms beneath the light. Renny didn't talk about the past. She only looked ahead, at the road in front of her. Nita touched Lydia's arm lightly. "Do you have a med kit or something?" she asked. "Renny just woke up and her arm was bleeding when she went to lie down. Her kit is locked in the truck."

"I'll get you what you need. If you can get Renny to let you do anything about it, you're ahead of me." Lydia sighed. "She's so damn macho."

They clattered down the stairs, past the vat of yellow sludge. "What is that?" Nita grimaced.

"Corn cells. They're engineered to produce large amounts of oil. The pressed cells go into the new fake meat."

"I see." She'd definitely stick with beans.

Lydia took Nita to the company infirmary. The bright, clean room, crammed with a cupboards and equipment was empty. "Where is everyone?" Nita asked.

"It's all automated. You've got a few maintenance people and Security. This is from when we had more workers." Lydia collected a roll of gauze, tape, and sterile pads from various drawers. "What antibiotic is she on?"

"I don't know the name. White tablets?"

"Like this?" Lydia opened a bottle, tipped two tablets into her palm.

"I think so."

"You're probably right. It's one of the new ones that still work. It's what she brings in with her 'office supplies.' Too bad I can't have the doc look at her, but company policy is very very tight on that score."

"Won't you get in trouble for taking this stuff?" Nita looked up at the dark eye on a video camera. She'd noticed them in every corner. "Won't they see?"

"Relax." Lydia followed her gaze. "These are all digital pickups. I ran a handy little pre-edited segment before we came down here. We've got four and a half more minutes before Security sees anything but an empty plant." She ushered Nita into the corridor. "I'll check this situation again for you. I thought Rico was a little careless. Maybe he was careless on purpose." She smiled a little sadly, her lavender gaze on Nita's face. "I don't envy you, honey. I don't envy you at all. Go talk Renny into taking care of herself, will you? I'll go see if Rico was being cute."

CHAPTER TWENTY-TWO

Y ou have screwed up in every possible way in this command." Hands
clasped behind his back, General Hastings paced across Carter's small
bedroom. "You had no business letting Roscoe leave the Shunt, and your
negligence cost us the lives of six soldiers." He spun around, his finger
stabbing at Carter, face as hard as carved stone. "I will personally see that
you get busted for this, mister."

"Sir." Carter forced the word through tight lips. Whether or not Hastings
had anything to do with this, he was right. He remembered the feel of the
private's coverall as the flood slammed them down the riverbed. He had
clutched it in his dreams, coming out of surgery, had waked with bloody
nailmarks on his palms. "Sir?" He pushed himself higher on the pillows,
sucking in a breath as his broken ribs stabbed him. "I had a reason for what
I did. With all due respect, sir . . ."

"Cut the formal crap, Voltaire."

"All right, I will." Hell, he was screwed anyway. "We need to find out
who's behind this." Or do you want to, General? "It's an outside setup, sir.
I'm sure of it. And they have someone on the base." He struggled higher in
bed, fighting the buzz of the doctor's painkillers, watching Hasting's face.
"Someone is trying to start a shooting war between the Corps and the
locals and yes, the locals are playing right into it, but they're not behind it. If
we could have caught those snipers yesterday, we'd have found our connection. Sir." He clenched his teeth as the room wavered in front of his
eyes. "I made a bad judgment call yesterday, but we were set up. They
know where and when we'd show up, right down to the last detail, sir. I'm
trying to stop this war from happening."

"Are you?" Hasting's tone was icy. "I think everyone realizes that
someone is tipping off the terrorists about patrol schedules. And that ambush yesterday."

"Yes, sir." Carter drew a shallow, careful breath. "I suspect it's Major
Delgado, sir."

"The major has been reporting directly to me." Hastings's eyes pinned Carter. "On my orders. He's been here as long as I have, and I trust *him*. I have my own theories about who is the leak around here. I've been keeping a close watch on your local connections. You and Greely are in on this together, Voltaire. It's pretty damned obvious."

Carter stared at Hastings, stunned. If anything, this confirmed his suspicions about the general. Johnny had been right. "I've dealt with the local leaders," he said tightly. "But I've never betrayed the Corps. Sir." Unlike you, you bastard, he thought.

"We're going to look into that." Hastings's expression didn't change. "Do I make myself clear, Colonel?"

"Yes, sir," Carter said between his teeth.

"What action I decide to take will depend on my investigation here. Meanwhile, the situation calls for drastic measures, and I'm going to take them." His gray eyes glittered. "These local troublemakers got away with it last time they acted up. Water Policy was soft and it wouldn't endorse emergency measures, but it's not so soft this time around. This time I put these terrorists in their place. After this we'll get a whole lot more cooperation around here."

Revenge, Carter thought. For his son. "What are you going to do?"

"I'm going to shut this stretch of riverbed dry, from the Klamath Shunt to the Willamette Shunt. Not one drop of water beyond the federal minimum goes through the meters. "

Which meant cutting it to the Personal Maintenance Allowance, the minimum share of water guaranteed to each citizen served by a federal water system. That wouldn't give people around here enough water to keep kitchen crops alive, or do anything except survive. "You can't do that." Carter couldn't stop himself. "General, that's going to start the war for sure."

"It already started. I've been granted full emergency powers by Water Policy. They're scared that a big water loss will short Mexico and give Canada a reason to kick over the traces. Ask your buddy." His lip curled. "I've been authorized to take whatever measures are needed to keep the southern share up to maximum. It comes right out of the share here — every drop. The break should be repaired by tomorrow, but the Willamette and Sacramento systems have lost over twenty-four hours of flow. If we divert everything over the calculated minimum down the shunts, we can minimize crop losses in the valleys and keep Mexico's share constant. It'll teach these terrorists a lesson they won't forget for a long time."

"Sir?" Carter swallowed. "Only a handful of people are involved in the sabotage. A lot of innocent farmers are going to lose their crops and their land."

"They could have turned these terrorists in. They know who they are." The general's eyes had gone hard. "No innocent people live along this riverbed. I've asked for Rangers as backup, and my request has been granted. They're unloading now."

Rangers. Stunned, Carter sank back onto his pillow. Rangers were the elite and they hated this kind of call. Rangers had been brought in to back up the 82nd Airborne in Chicago. That had been when things got out of hand, although that particular fact had never made it into the media.

"Voltaire?" Hastings paused in the doorway. "Tell me what you know about Greely's escape."

"What?" Carter stared. "What escape? What are you talking about?"

"Someone sprung him while the Shunt was going down. Two men in uniforms. The guard saw that much before they hit him."

"I don't know, sir." His head was full of buzzing.

"I finally heard how you ended up here." Hastings's gave him a contemptuous look. "Seems this senator did a little string pulling for a particular posting. As a favor for a friend. Targass is tight with Water Policy." His lips twitched as if he wanted to spit. "Your buddy might be Water Policy but he can't save your ass."

Carter stared after him, barely registering the slam of the door. Someone had pulled strings to get him posted here. Through Senator Targass. The name rang a bell but the where and when wouldn't come.

Nine Corps deaths this year, including Private Stakowski who had barely turned twenty. If Hastings shut down the local water, fields along the riverbed would dry up and blow away. How long would it take? Two days? A week?

"Sir?" A hesitant voice roused him. "Colonel Voltaire, sir?"

"In here."

"I'm sorry, sir. I knocked." Private Wasson appeared in the doorway to his bedroom, half hidden by the doorframe. "I'll pull cleanup for a month if my sergeant hears about this." She glanced nervously over her shoulder. "But I heard you got hurt bad, sir."

"I'll live." Carter pushed himself painfully up onto the pillows again. "Thanks, Private." She was waiting to ask him something. Not that he could do much. "What's up?" he asked wearily.

"Sir, is it true that we're going to shut the water down along the riverbed?"

Rumors got around way too fast in this place. He wondered if he'd heard that Hastings was out to bust him yet. "Yes. It's true."

"*Sir.*"

The anguish and anger in that single tight syllable finally penetrated.

Carter narrowed his eyes, seeing finally what she was trying to hide. "Private, come into the room. All the way in."

She marched stiffly to the foot of his bed and stood at attention. The bruises on her face were dark and new. Her mouth was swollen and Carter saw a raw, ugly scrape on her arm blow the sleeve of her coverall.

"I was ready to go, yesterday," she said in a low, taut voice. "I got permission from Captain Westerly, and I was as ready to shoot as any of the others. Maybe my family does live along the riverbed, but I'm Corps, sir."

The rumor about Roscoe getting set up surely had gone around by now, too. Carter sighed, rubbed his face. "You made a tough decision and I took it away from you. I didn't do it very well, either. I apologize, Private. I hope they look worse than you do."

"Thank you, sir. One of them does." She lifted her chin. "This would have happened sooner or later anyway, sir."

"I'm sorry about your family," he said. "I'm sorry about all the people who are going to pay for this when it isn't their debt. I did my best to keep the promise I made to you."

The private was silent for a moment, her eyes fixed on the wall above Carter's head. "Sir? Is it true that the guy we've been holding has escaped? The head honcho from The Dalles?"

"It's true."

"You weren't . . . moving him, sir? Like down to Bonneville?"

Carter shook his head, his eyes on her face. "He wasn't going anywhere until the U.S. Marshal showed up to claim him. Why?"

"I saw something, while everyone was . . . at the Shunt." Wasson scowled at the floor. "An officer and an NCO were taking this man out to a car — graying hair, kind of tall, wearing jeans and he was kind of wobbly. I stopped to see if they needed any help. The guy was in cuffs, and the lieutenant said he was a prisoner, that they were moving him down to Bonneville, sir. I'm pretty sure it was the guy from town, the one who's always in front of things."

"Would you recognize the others again?" Carter sat forward gingerly.

"I . . . *did* recognize the corporal. He's down at Bonneville. I was there before I got transferred up here." Wasson looked at him finally. "He's from Hood River."

Back to Hastings again. A cold anger was forming in his belly. "Thanks." He held out his hand to her. "You're Corps, first. I won't forget it."

She gripped his hand hard, released it abruptly. "If someone from the Corps is behind this, I'll find out."

The smoldering heat in her eyes worried him. "We'll do it my way," he told her urgently. "I'll pull a personnel record for you, and you see if you can recognize this corporal's name. Don't discuss this with anyone, is that understood?"

"Yes, sir. I'll keep my mouth shut and my ears open."

"I'll call your CO and get you assigned to HQ platoon as my aide. We'll go over the records together."

"Yes, sir. Wasson saluted smartly, her eyes glittering. "I'll recognize that guy's name." She spun on her heel and marched out of the room, nearly colliding with Johnny as he came through the front door.

"What was that all about?" Johnny pulled off dust goggles and tossed them onto the chest of drawers. "Man, it's windy out there today. You look a lot better than the last time I saw you. They were wheeling you into surgery, as I recall."

"What are you doing here?" Carter grimaced as he leaned forward. "How did you mange to show up in time to pull me out of the water?" He managed a grin for Johnny. "Talk about timing."

"I tagged along with the media." He sat down on the foot of Carter's bed. "I've got an inside source on the payroll, and she tipped me off. I guess someone called them and told them about the fireworks. You didn't see the newscasts, huh? It's all over the net."

"Yeah, so I hear." Carter clenched a fist. "The country thinks we're in a war and in a day or two, we will be."

"Hey, the public's pissed at the locals, not at you guys." Johnny shrugged. "You're heroes. Keeping the water flowing, all that stuff. Another food shortage is hitting the east coast hard. You'll get applause for anything you do, believe me."

"It's not the publicity angle. It's what's going to happen here that worries me."

"That's the locals' problem." Johnny shrugged. "They started this mess. They get to deal with the results, not you."

"You don't get it." Carter groaned and slumped back onto his pillows as pain gripped him.

"Hey, are you okay?" Johnny leaned forward, worried. "They wouldn't let *me* on the base, yesterday. Hastings has this place nailed shut. I had to go through Washington to get past the old fart."

"No wonder he was snarling about Water Policy today." Carter breathed shallowly, waiting for the spasm to pass. "I broke four ribs, one nicked a lung. I've got a rubber drain in for a couple of days, but everything should grow back together. Johnny, I'm essentially under arrest," he said bitterly. "Hastings accused me of setting this up."

Johnny leaned back, arms crossed, face thoughtful. "Can't say I'm surprised."

"You did mean him. On the phone."

"I couldn't say so. Not on an unsecure cell. We have absolutely no concrete proof." Johnny shook his head, his expression sober. "I think I almost got you killed."

"My own stupidity almost got me killed." Carter closed his eyes as the fanged python squeezing his ribs finally relaxed. "I wish I'd known sooner, though."

"I just found out. My buddy Paul in DC has been snooping around for me, digging whatever dirt he can on the general. I thought you might need it."

Paul. The name clicked. Paul Targass. "You did it." He stared at Johnny. "You had Targass get me posted out here. *Goddamnit,* Johnny."

"Hey." Johnny recoiled. "Take it easy. Yes, I did that," he said harshly. "Why not? You're a good officer and I needed you out here. Pacific Bio's already on my back, I couldn't trust Hastings. If I mess up here, the rest of the Committee will be after me like sharks. I'm not . . . very popular." He met Carter's eyes. "I had a chance to get you stationed out here and I took it. I needed you to watch my back. So I'm a selfish prick, okay?" He looked away. "Buy you know that."

"I wish you hadn't done it." Carter sighed. That was Johnny. Do it first and apologize later. Or never. "Well, I'm here, and I think you're right about Hastings. I'm almost sure Delgado is in on it, too. That flood happened because of a fried board. The flow should have shut down in seconds, but it was three minutes before Operations ran the override and shut the valves. That emergency system is checked weekly. The last recorded inspection was only two days before the break."

"You think Delgado sabotaged it?"

"I think Andy Stakowski and five others died because of it," Carter said. "Someone gets to pay for that."

Tomorrow a truck would carry the six caskets to the dry plot of ground that was the base's cemetery. A flag would cover each casket. They would flutter in the dusty wind as a firing party fired three volleys. The chaplain would read a moving service, a bugler would play 'Taps,' the flags would be folded and presented to the next of kin. The river had covered that piece of ground once. Jeremy would see water if he looked at the graves. That's what those men and women had died to protect, Carter thought bitterly. Not freedom, not democracy. Just water.

Life.

"Wasson — the private you met on your way out — might hand us the key. She recognized the corporal who sprung Greely. He's from Bonneville, but she can't remember his name. I'm going to pull a personnel record for her."

"That might give us the link we need to Hastings." Johnny was nodding. "Good for Private Wasson."

"Yeah." Carter swung his legs over the side of the bed, hissing between his teeth. "Hand me the phone, will you? I've got to call Personnel."

"While you're doing that, I'm going to try searching Greely's place. If he's in with Hastings on this . . . and it sure seems likely . . . something will be there. Something that will point to Hastings."

"It's too dangerous," Carter said.

"He wouldn't dare go back there." Johnny's eyes were glittering with the old, school-days, go-for-it fire.

He was going to do it. "Get your car. I'm coming, too."

"You can't go running around in your condition." Johnny frowned. "I'll call you when I get there."

"You'll get yourself shot, is what'll happen, Johnny." Carter gave him a weak grin. "Not without me. I want that proof more than you do." He stood, wavering a little, one hand on the wall for support. "Park right in front of the door. I don't know if they've got orders to stop me at the gate or not."

"Lie down on the floor and I'll toss some stuff over you."

Well, what difference did it make if he went AWOL? Carter limped over to his closet as Johnny left and rooted out a jacket and folded bedspread to add to the camouflage. That cold anger curdled in his gut. Whoever was behind this . . . Hastings? . . . owed for a lot of lives right now. Carter opened his dresser drawer, took out the Beretta, and made sure it was loaded.

CHAPTER TWENTY-THREE

Crouched on the floor of Johnny's car, Carter held his breath as Johnny braked at the gate to surrender his pass.

"You better watch yourself out there." The guard's voice sounded as if she were in the back seat with Carter. "Something big is going on. The whole town's on its way out to the Shunt. I hope you're heading west — you're not going to get anywhere going east."

Another demonstration? Sweat stung Carter's eyes. Hastings had his Rangers out there. He closed his eyes, urging Johnny silently to step on it, get them the hell out of here. The car lurched forward, gathering speed.

"It's clear." Johnny glanced in the rearview as Carter threw off the stifling camouflage.

"Did you hear that? About the Shunt?" Carter eased himself onto the seat, tried to brace himself against the cars motion. It hurt. "If anyone does anything, this is going to blow up."

"I heard." Johnny shook his head. "You can't do squat there. You need proof that Hastings's doing this." He braked at the truck plaza, then swung left onto the state highway. "I'll bet you a hundred bucks we find it at Greely's."

He was right. Carter drew a cautious breath. Nita might turn up with something . . . or she might not. She wasn't willing to see Greely as anything but a hero.

The afternoon sun streaked the Gorge wall with stark black shadows, giving the rocky bones of the earth an austere beauty. Those rocks would still be here tomorrow, whether a hundred people died or none at all. They wouldn't care, one way or the other. The events of this day, of this past month, were nothing more than a flicker of light and darkness to the planet, he thought. A millisecond in the planet's lifetime. They topped the rim of the Gorge and Carter clung to the door, breathing in quick, shallow gasps as the car bounced across the rocky track that led to Greely's house. He pressed his arm to his side, felt wetness at the surgery site. The doc was not going to be happy with him.

He needed some kind of solid proof. Something.

Greely's beans were already wilting. Johnny pulled up in front of the weathered little house and Carter climbed stiffly out. Last time he had pulled up here things had looked so hopeful. Slowly, painfully, he climbed the warped steps while Johnny checked around the buildings. The main room looked as barren as he remembered it; table, chairs, woodstove, and sink. One bedroom door stood open. Greely's, he remembered, and spied the bright paintings on the walls. Nita had walked through the other door, flushed with sleep. He tensed as the handle turned.

"Jeremy?" Carter blinked. "What are you doing here?"

"I *was* watering Dan's beans for Nita. Only there's no more water." Jeremy yawned and gave Carter a quizzical look. "What's up?"

"Have you seen Greely?"

"I thought you had him locked up?" Jeremy's eyes narrowed.

"Who's this?" Johnny burst through the door. "He was here before."

"Carter, what's going on?" Jeremy ignored Johnny. "You look bad."

"He got a rib through his lung when the Pipe blew." Johnny walked past him, began opening kitchen cupboards. "Wow. Whatever else this guy's into, he's got good black-market connections." He waved a brown pill bottle. "*I* can't even get this stuff."

"You want to butt out?" Jeremy limped over and slammed the cupboard door. "What's this all about, anyhow?"

"I need to search the house," Carter said wearily. "Right now."

"He's on your side, Carter."

"How do you know?" Carter clenched his fists. "How the hell do you *know*, Jeremy? You give me a solid reason, and we'll both believe it."

"Nita told me."

The quiet words hit him like a blow. "She's . . . biased."

"I don't think so." Jeremy's tone was mild. "Relax, Carter. I'm not going to take you on. If you want to search, do it. I don't think Dan would mind. Where is he, if you don't have him?" He was frowning now. "He didn't come back up here."

"He escaped." Or he had been taken and then he was likely dead. Bad way to prove your innocence. Carter turned his back on Jeremy and yanked a drawer open, sorting quickly through a handful of kitchen utensils. Johnny was going through the cupboards, looking into pots, lifting stacked plates. Jeremy sat down on the corner of the table, watching them rummage. Carter left the main room to Johnny and went into Greely's bedroom. Watercolors lined the walls. They had been painted on sheets of rough paper, and Carter wondered if Greely had done them. They all showed water in the river. Carter stared at a picture of gray-green water cascading over gray rocks. It looked . . . real. Like Jeremy's visions. A flat photo stood on the small table beside the bed. Carter picked it up. A gray-haired woman with a strong face looked out at him, smiling quizzically, a little warily. Carter put the picture down carefully, wondering who she was.

Greely's drawers yielded clothes, odds and ends, and a sheaf of hardcopy that turned out to be old bills, receipts, and meter records. Carter peeked behind the watercolors, but nothing had been hidden there, either. Hand on Nita's door, he hesitated, afraid, angry at that twinge of fear. He shoved the door open. Her room smelled faintly of honey and piss — her daughter's contribution, no doubt. The bed was neatly made and her pack stood against the wall. She had put her clothes into the top drawer of the dresser. She didn't have much — an extra pair of jeans, a couple of pairs of underwear, and two shirts. Carter turned the soft folds of cloth over, catching a faint whiff of her scent. Had she ever owned more than this? He slammed the drawer and checked the next one down.

It was there, under the pile of stiff, dry diapers, tucked beneath the yellowed newspaper that lined the drawer. Stock certificates. Pacific BioSystems stock, made out to Dan Greely. And a handwritten note, stuck between two of the certificates. *Here's the next installment. We've got a new CO coming in and I've got to talk to you about strategy. Same place, tomorrow night.*

It wasn't signed, but Carter recognized the handwriting. Hastings put those jagged tails on his Y's.

Very carefully, he folded the certificates and tucked them into his pocket. Very carefully, he straightened the pile of diapers. She didn't know, he told himself. But it didn't really matter if she did or not. Dan Greely and Hastings had put strings on him and made him dance. Carter touched the butt of the Beretta lightly, feeling the paper crackle in his pocket. It might be enough to send Greely to prison for life and put Hastings in front of a court-martial. And it might not. Hastings was a general. Politics would come into it.

"Carter?" Johnny stood in the doorway, his expression eager. "You find something?"

"No." Carter shrugged. "Maybe you ought to look. I'm getting fuzzy."

"Sure." Johnny stepped past him and yanked a drawer open. "Go sit down. You look pale."

He felt pale. Carter limped through the house, not looking at Jeremy, his ribs searing him with every step. He thought he could make it, but Johnny caught up with him as he collapsed into the driver's seat.

"What the hell are you up to?" Johnny put a hand on the door. "Carter?"

Carter hit the electric locks, rolled the windows up.

"Hey!"

"This isn't your fight." The engine roared and Johnny leaped backward as he gunned it in reverse, spinning a rooster tail of dirt as he backed the car around in a tight arc. Icy sweat stuck his shirt to his skin. He could drive one-handed. He could manage that much. He floored it and peeled out of the yard, the rear end fishtailing, Johnny's shouting left behind in an instant. Breath whistling through his teeth, he roared up the drive, the car rocking and bouncing, driving lances of pain through his chest.

Johnny didn't get to die for Carter's mistakes. At least he'd have that. If he got to the Shunt in time, maybe the war wouldn't happen.

CHAPTER TWENTY-FOUR

The countryside looked different from the cab of a truck. Kneeling on Renny's plush carpet, Nita watched the riverbed unreel beyond the highway. Your perspective changed up here; you saw the dust and rock and the pump stations from a different angle. Nita stroked the cab's carpet — not really carpet but acoustic skin, Renny had told her, reinforced by an electronic noise-cancellation system. With the windows intact, you could barely hear the purr of the engine. The quiet and the cool dustless air made the wind-scoured land look even less real.

"We're so . . . removed in here," Nita said out loud.

"How so, babe?" Renny tossed her a quick glance, then turned her attention back to the highway.

"They aren't real. The rocks, the riverbed." Nita squirmed. Renny's arm was hurting her again, but she wouldn't take any more of the orange painkillers. "I wish I could take a turn and give you a break," she said.

"I've been worse off. Quit clucking at me like a mother hen." Renny smiled faintly. "You're right. It's not real, all that dust out there. I don't particularly want it to be real, either. I don't want to look any farther than the road in front of me. Give me a nice room in a plaza somewhere, a good dinner, and a sharp deal. That's real enough."

"You don't look behind you," Nita said. "Lydia keeps it all around her, doesn't she? The past?" Preserved in the succulent leaves of long-dead plants.

"You say some strange things, babe."

Past and present. A dusty barrier divided one from the other. Only Jeremy really straddled it. Nita sighed, urging the truck to move faster, watching the rocky scar of the riverbed drift past.

"That stuff Lydia dug up is worrying you, isn't it?" Renny said.

Yes, someone planted those names, Lydia had told her. *Sorry, I don't have the real names yet. Rico's getting better in his old age after all.*

It's going to take me a little while to pick out the threads for you. But don't worry. I'll find 'em.

"Yes, I guess it is."

"She'll get you what you're after. No one hides anything forever from Lydia."

"It . . . might not be in time." Nita pressed her lips together. A terrible sense of urgency nagged at her. "Something is happening," she said. "I know it."

"You fed me a line back there, didn't you, babe?" Renny shot Nita a look. "You're no operator. You're in this as deep as Danny."

"I didn't mean to be." Nita looked at the trucker, trying to read the barbed tangle of her emotions. "It was strange, coming here. People are nice to me because I'm Sam Montoya's daughter."

"So you're Sam's kid, huh? Small world. Maybe not." Renny chuckled. "Yeah, Sam was another one like Danny. Kind of a hero around here, too. That why you came back?"

"No." Nita twisted to look into the rear of the cab, but Rachel was still asleep on the futon, sucking on her fist. "He was no hero to me. I think I hated him. Because he let those men kill him. He left me to get all Mama's blame for it." The blood that spattered her had never washed off.

"You don't hate him any more?"

"I don't know." Nita frowned. "I think I understand why he did what he did. He knew those men would come for him. Sooner or later. But he didn't want us — the whole town — to die, too. I hope — when he saw them — it still mattered to him."

Renny grunted. "I never gave a damn about Jesse. We scratched to live, and she would've done a lot better without a kid. I was an accident. If she'd had the guts, she would have left me out in the Dry when I was born. I chained her to that hose farm and we both knew it."

Nita shivered at her hurt. And anger. "And then Dan came along."

"Yeah, then Danny came along. He's my age, did you know that? Almost exactly. I was twenty-three when he moved in with her. I heard about it from a friend of mine. I'd been working the east-west routes then, driving as an apprentice for an old witch who could make a rig fly, setting up with a partner of my own." She gave a dry laugh. "I didn't get back here much, didn't want to. I guess Danny had something to offer Jesse that I didn't. What happened the day they came for your dad?"

"He stopped to hide me, so they wouldn't kill me, too." Nita let her breath out slowly. "They probably would've killed him even if he had run. You could see for miles around our place and they had rifles."

"How old were you, babe?"

"Five. I think. About that."

"It's a damn dusty world we grow up in," Renny said. She shook her head and concentrated on wrestling the truck off onto the Mosier detour.

Nita looked at the folded hills where Julio Moreno had buried the bones he had found. Such an easy place to die among the rocks and stumps of the long dead orchards. The truck growled a low note as it climbed up over the crest where Jeremy had showed her spring. "This land is full of our ghosts," she said. "It's crowded with ghosts."

"Ghosts, huh?" Renny shifted on her padded seat as she eased the truck back onto the freeway again. "Jesse talked about ghosts, but I never tried very hard to see 'em. Could be that's what Dan did for her. Shared her ghosts with her."

The bitter thorn of Renny's hunt had softened just a little bit. Nita reached out, met Renny's hand halfway. For a silent moment their hands clasped; then Renny winced and let go to use both hands on the wheel.

"Come down to the plaza before I take off again." She gave Nita a crooked grin. "I'll teach you to drive this baby. Then you can take over next time I get shot."

"I will," Nita said.

They passed the abandoned car dealerships and stripped, empty shopping centers that fringed the west end of The Dalles. "We'll drop the rig at the plaza and pick up one of their loaner cars." Renny eased the truck down the exit ramp. "I don't drive this baby on that goat track to the farm."

"I'm going to the base." Nita drew a slow breath. She had no proof to offer Carter yet, nothing that would save Dan. Except for herself. What she was. "I can walk from here," she said as they turned onto the plaza access road.

Dust eddied across the asphalt lot. A single rig baked in the sun. "It's too empty." Renny scowled. "Stay put a minute. I'll find out what's up."

The dust sifted into the truck as soon as Renny cracked the sealed door. She cursed and slammed it behind her, ducking her head against the hot wind as she ran across the parking lot to the door. Something was wrong. Nita played with Rachel as she waited, trying to ignore the clench of unease in her gut. Rachel fussed and slapped at the dangled beads. No puddle lay beneath the caged hoses today. A dust devil twisted at the corner of the building, and Nita hugged her cranky daughter. Renny was coming back and Nita winced as she yanked the door open.

"Bad news." Renny scowled at the distant wall of the dam. Curtained by blowing dust, it bulked like a cliff wall across the riverbed. "Somebody blew the Pipe while we were on our jaunt. A lot of uniforms got killed."

Carter? Nita sucked in her breath, afraid to ask, afraid to say his name out loud. "Do they know who?" she managed.

"No names, babe. A bunch of them got offed in an ambush and a couple more drowned when the Pipe went. Drowned, can you believe it?" Renny's laugh carried no trace of humor. "Josie says it's war around here. Water's cut off and they aren't going to turn it back on. Uniforms blew away a truck last night. Turned out to be a family with a kid. The locals are crazy mad, on their way down to the Shunt to kill uniforms and turn the water back on. Josie's on her way out of here right now." Renny gave Nita a sharp look. "She's right, babe. How 'bout if I give you that driving lesson in Boise?"

Nita shook her head, full of fear. "Will you give me that ride up to the farmhouse?" she faltered. "Before you leave?" Jeremy would know what was going on.

"You're as thick-headed as Danny," Renny growled. "But I figured that out already." She pulled a key from her pocket. "I got us a loaner. We'll have to go through town and cut over to the house by the back way. The Army shut down the highway between here and the Deschutes bed. Even the rigs have to wait for an escort before they can go through. Josie said everyone is pissed as hell. I don't know any more than that."

And Carter? Had he died in that ambush? His name kept sneaking into Nita's head as the battered little loaner car chugged its way along the winding road that followed the rim of the Gorge. An ambush. Carter would have been in charge. There. Rachel squirmed and Nita bounced her, trying to distract her, trying to distract herself from her own fears.

Beyond the windows, rows of irrigated beans or beets swung past. The plants were wilting, yellowing in the sun. The landscape still looked unreal, but this sense of unreality had the dull gloss of a nightmare. They had been gone only twenty-four hours. The Dalles was dying.

Renny turned the car onto the narrow track that led to the farmhouse and braked to a halt. "Listen to me, babe. You got nothing to bargain with, right? People are about to start shooting." She studied Nita's face for a moment, then started the car moving again. "I've already offered Boise, so I won't say it again. But you be careful, babe. Hear?"

"I hear you," Nita said as the car pulled up behind the sagging gray house. "I'll be careful, Renny." She climbed out, Rachel clutched awkwardly in her arms. "Take care of yourself."

"Hell, I'm not running off quite yet." Renny looked grim. "I'll stick around to see what's going down. If it's bad enough, I might want to cross the bridge and haul up to Goldendale and ninety-seven. That gets me back to the riverbed, and I can give this dog and pony show a miss." She got out and slammed the door.

Renny was worried. About her? "Thanks," Nita said softly. Out in the fields, the beans lay dying. What if Jeremy wasn't here? What if no one was here? What had happened to Carter?

Jeremy and Johnny Seldon were on the porch, sitting in the shade. "Nita!" Jeremy's relief hummed in the air. "I didn't hear the car for the wind noise. Hello, Renny. Want some water?"

"What's going on?" Nita's voice threatened to break. "Is . . . Carter all right? Was he at the Pipe?"

"He was just here a few minutes ago, Nita." Jeremy limped to the steps and put a hand on her arm. "He got hurt, but he'll be all right." For all his comforting tone, no comfort lay beneath his words.

"What's wrong?" she whispered.

"He ran off and stranded me here." Johnny peered around the corner. "I could use a ride."

He was angry. Nita turned her back on him. "I don't understand," she said, hugging Rachel to her. "I don't understand, Jeremy."

"I don't think I do, either." Jeremy put an arm around her. "Come on inside, put Rachel down, and have a drink of water. I'll get you a glass, Renny." He urged Nita gently into the dim interior of the house. "I think he found something." He looked at her sideways. "They were searching the house, looking for proof that Dan's involved with the sabotage. All of a sudden he bolted out of here. He acted . . . pretty upset."

"He found what we were after." Johnny had followed them inside, pulled out a chair, and dropped into it. "He found proof that Greely's connected with Hastings. Where the hell did he go with it?" He banged a clenched fist down on the table. "Goddamn idiot."

"There's no proof." Nita stared at him. "Not here."

"There had to be. A letter." Johnny gave her a cold stare. "Something."

He was so easy to read. "You know he found something," she breathed. "You put it here." Her eyes widened. "That's why you came up here the other day. To hide it. And you just came back after you dropped us off in town. I knew you didn't really want to see Dan, but I couldn't figure out what you wanted. You meant to put it here and get Carter to find it."

"You got a problem, lady?" Johnny crossed his arms, gave her a crooked smirk. "You been watching too many mystery vids."

"You're lying," she said matter of factly. "You planted something to link Dan to Hastings. We found other stuff. You probably planted that, too. The shares with Hastings' and Dan's names on them. It'll tie them together and tie them to Pacific BioSytems. So everyone will think they've been making money from those fields Renny talked about."

Rachel was squirming in her arms, protesting that Nita was holding her too tightly. They were all staring at her. Renny perplexed, Jeremy listening carefully. And Johnny — behind his cold, untroubled face — was afraid.

"You're behind it," she whispered. "You hired Rico to fix the records and make it just obvious enough to find. You've done it all, haven't you? The sabotage — the shooting. How could you do this to Carter?" Her voice trembled and broke. "My God, he *loves* you."

Johnny lunged up at her, then gasped as the heel of Jeremy's hand caught him hard in the chest, jolting him back into his chair.

"Sit still," Jeremy said mildly. "I think that's about enough." This time, they all looked at the small automatic that had appeared in his hand. He didn't look very clumsy, holding the gun.

Johnny clutched the tabletop with both hands, breathing through his mouth. "She's making it up." He didn't take his eyes from the gun. "She's Greely's lover, sticking up for him. I want to see one single shred of proof."

"I have it. I'm not showing it to *you*." A lie, but he wouldn't know. "He's at the Shunt." She turned to Jeremy, pleading now. "Josie at the plaza said everyone is going there. To turn the water back on. That's where he went." And he wouldn't care if he died, trying to stop it. "I have to go there, Jeremy. Now."

"Nita are you sure?" He frowned at Johnny. "The Shunt is probably the most dangerous place in the country right now. If he's there, he's with the Army and you'll get yourself killed if you go near them. They're shooting at us, Nita. To kill."

Jeremy wasn't going to go. "Renny?" Nita faced her. "I need the car."

"You're worse than Danny, babe. At least he has some sense." The wiry trucker snorted, her eyes fixed on Jeremy's gun. "You got a tank up your sleeve? Heavy hardware? What the hell is the *point*?"

"I don't know." Nita met her eyes.

"Oh, shit." Renny's scowl moved from Jeremy's face to Johnny's and finally back to Nita. "You and Danny. Load up, babe. You don't know these goat tracks for squat and I do. No point in your getting shot any sooner than you have to."

"Thanks, Renny," Nita said softly. "I owe you again."

"You sure do. It goes on the account. Let's go." Renny turned her back on Jeremy's gun to push through the door and out into the glare of hot sun.

"I'm coming." Jeremy limped after them. "I guess I'm in on this, too."

Renny already had the engine running by the time they reached the car.

"What about me?" Johnny followed them, wary, scared, and furious. "How the hell do I get out of here?"

"Walk," Jeremy suggested as he climbed into the backseat. "Better take a water jug." He stared at Johnny. "West might be a good idea."

Renny growled something under her breath, put the car into gear. She hadn't been kidding when she had talked about goat tracks. The car bounced like a ball on the rutted trails that led back from the rim of the Gorge and down into the Deschutes bed. No one said anything. Only Jeremy looked serene, but he wasn't. The rough track scored Renny's arm with white agony, but when Nita offered to drive she nearly bit her head off. They didn't pass a single car — the countryside might as well have been deserted.

The deep scar of the Deschutes bed opened out in front of them as they topped the rise. The narrow track dove straight down toward the bottom of the riverbed. Trucks and cars clogged the flat ground along the old bank, blocking the road that led down to the Columbia bed itself. Renny eased the car down the slope, rear wheels slithering in the loose gravel. "Busy place down here," she said dryly. She pulled the car over behind a battered blue pickup and turned off the ignition. It was quiet. A bird chirped somewhere, an incongruous sound that set Nita's teeth on edge. The tension in the air made her want to scream.

"Everybody out," Renny said. "You all do what you want, but I don't plan to die for any natives."

She was speaking to Nita. Jeremy climbed out silently, tense but calm. Nita scooped up Rachel and followed him. She heard no gunfire, no screams, no shouts, but the air felt ready to explode. A pump station gleamed in the sunshine in the distance.

Rachel whimpered and Nita held her daughter tightly, acutely aware of her daughter's warmth. "Renny?" She walked around to the driver's side. Held out Rachel.

Renny's eyes narrowed and Nita braced herself.

With a muttered curse, Renny shoved the door open. "Until you get back." She took Rachel from Nita's arms. "I'm no mother, babe. You come get her damn soon."

"I will," Nita whispered. She walked away as Renny slammed the car door. I am never going to see my daughter again, she thought.

What goes around, goes around again. And again. She closed her mouth against a laugh that would turn into a shriek.

"Bad?" Jeremy touched her arm, his eyes dark with worry.

"Yes." She was trembling. "It's never . . . been this strong before."

"You've never been in the middle of a riot before." Jeremy took her arm. "Are you sure you can handle this?"

"I don't know." Nita drew a shuddering breath and managed to stop shaking. "Carter's here. He doesn't know about Johnny. He thinks Hastings is behind this. And Dan."

"Carter said Dan escaped." Jeremy shaded his eyes. "I'm not sure that's what happened, but he's not in jail anymore."

Which meant what? Johnny had set this up. He had taken Carter to find that damning evidence so . . . what would happen? She didn't know, couldn't make thoughts come together in her aching head. She held Jeremy's hand very tightly as they threaded their way between the parked vehicles, grateful for this presence. He was no longer scared, was simply . . . calm.

He didn't care if he died or not, wasn't afraid any more. She focused on that calm, used it to fight the storm of fear/hate/anger that grew steadily stronger. She stumbled. People ahead. Lots of people. They filled the Deschutes bed like a dark, undulating plain. She shuddered. More cars. Trucks. They were so angry.

"I was up on the rim when the Pipe blew," Jeremy said softly. "I saw the water come down the bed in a wave. It wasn't a river, it was a flood. It was the scariest thing I've ever seen. Can you find Carter in all this?"

This was a flood, too, a dark, destructive torrent. "I don't . . . know," she gasped.

She could hear the mob's voices now, a low, growling murmur that had been cut off by a trick of acoustics and a bulge of the riverbed wall. A rough barricade made up of vehicles and junk blocked the interstate. Most of the people milled behind it. A lot of them had guns. She was panting, suffocating, as if the anger and desperation burned up the oxygen in the air.

"Nita!" Sandy Corbett separated herself from the crowd, haggard and dusty. "What are you doing here? Do you know where Dan is? We heard he'd been arrested."

"Dan's disappeared." Nita swallowed, her throat dry as dust. "Sandy, what's happening?"

"What does it look like?" Sandy said bitterly. "Everyone has their back to the wall. Not one of us is going to have a crop left by tomorrow night. If the Army won't turn the water back on, we will. Ransom's bunch started it. We scraped together enough money to hire a Portland law firm to get an injunction to turn the water back on, but it's already too late for some of the crops. I don't know." Sandy spat into the dust, her face gaunt with anger and exhaustion. "This time I'm about ready to listen to Ransom. What have we got left to lose?"

"Sandy, you have to stop it. John Seldon from Water Policy is behind all this. I've got proof. He set this up to happen, I don't know why."

"Seldon? Water Policy?" Sandy looked away from Nita, shoulders drooping. "I can't make this stop, honey. Dan couldn't make this stop. It's too late."

"It's not too late, don't you understand . . . Carter'll die because he can't see another Chicago happen and that's why he came down here . . . once this happens it's all over, The Dalles is dead forever, it's what he *wants*, Sandy, this Johnny, we have to stop it."

"Nita, stop it!" Jeremy grabbed her by the shoulders, gave her a single hard shake. "Calm down. You're reacting to the crowd. Come on, Nita."

Yes, reacting. Nita clutched Jeremy, gasping for breath, realized Sandy was staring at her, thinking *crazy*. "All right." She sucked in a breath, shivering violently. "I'm all right." Barely. Her nails had left bloody marks on Jeremy's forearms. "It's so loud, I don't think I can pick out Carter," she said in a small voice.

"He'll be back behind the barricade anyway." Jeremy scowled at the Shunt bunker. "He's a lot safer there than here. I think we need to get out of here in one piece so you can deliver your proof to him."

Which she didn't have. Nita shook her head. He wasn't down here to be safe.

Someone was yelling at the mob over a loudspeaker. An officer. Any second now the shooting would start. Whatever the uniform had said, it was the wrong thing. A howl of rage shook her.

"*You've had your chance*," Ransom was bellowing over an electronic megaphone, his voice echoing down the riverbed. "*It's our turn now. Let's turn the water back on!*"

A shot cracked out. Another. The mob moved, surging forward, voices rising in shouts, screams. Automatic weapons fire rattled and the crowd-roar was punctuated with screams. Bodies crushed in behind them and Jeremy yanked her into a stumbling run.

Everything that had mattered to her father, everything that had mattered to Dan would be gone, swept down the riverbed in this ugly feud . . . "Jeremy, wait." She dug in her heels, clinging to him, dragging him into an eddy of clear space behind a parked truck. "You saw it — the flood. Make it. Make it again, but big. Really big. Fill the riverbed with it. Like the whole river's flooding."

"I can't." He jerked to a halt. "I can't control the visions. Just the little stuff. And what good would it do."

"Yes, you can. You made spring for me on the crest. You did it, it didn't just happen. Do it!"

"It won't help," he gritted.

"If you admit you can do it, then you have to use it for something." She stared into his pale, angry eyes. "You'll have to be responsible instead of just running from it."

He slapped her across the face.

Stunned by the blow and the white hot slash of his rage, Nita sprawled face down in the dust. He wouldn't do it. Nothing would stop it now. Her father had finally lost. Dan had lost. Gunfire, screams, and shouts pierced her Terror clawed at her, growing louder in her mind, swallowing the rage. Nita lifted her head . . . and screamed.

A wall of water towered over her. It filled the upstream riverbed with foamy madness, stretching from wall to rocky Gorge wall. Bigger than the dam, a wall of darkness, it curled over them ready to crash down on them, smash them, drown them. Nita struggled with panic...even as she told herself it was only Jeremy, that it was only a making.

People were seeing it. Not everyone saw it at first, but those first, sensitive ones panicked, dropped their weapons and ran. As if their fear had soaked through the mob mind, allowing everyone to see it, too, more and more people froze, threw aside whatever they were holding until the entire mob charged for the riverbank in blind panic.

It's only Jeremy. The knowledge began to erode as the mob surged past them and the dark wave of their terror beat at her. The nightmare wave curled higher, closer, in nightmare slow motion, streaked with dirty foam. Nita struggled for sanity. In a few moments that water would sweep over the bunker, thunder down on her head, smash her, choke her, drown her.

It's only Jeremy. It's only Jeremy. A burly man in a Corps uniform stumbled by, his eyes white-ringed and wild. *It's only Jeremy.* Nita fought the wash of emotion that threatened to send her stumbling and scrambling up the bank. She clung to the truck that sheltered them. Slowly . . . slowly . . . the crest of terror weakened as people fled. Car engines growled and the riverbed emptied. Nita sobbed once as the world began to reshape itself. Jeremy's wave still curled in the riverbed, closer, but moving very slowly.

Horns blared and the roar of engines began to diminish. The few men and women who still milled in the riverbed looked dazed and bewildered. Jeremy knelt in the dust, his fists clenched, eyes fixed on his hovering flood.

"Jeremy?" He didn't react as Nita knelt beside him. In a spurt of fear, she shook him. He resisted for an instant, his muscles rigid, then sighed and slumped.

The wave crest vanished, leaving the sunbaked riverbed nearly empty.

"You did it. Everyone's running." Nita put her arms around him, trembling with the aftermath of the terror. "You stopped it, Jeremy."

"I did . . . didn't I?" He was trembling, too. He got unsteadily to his feet, leaning heavily on her, as if the terrible vision had sucked all the strength out of him.

"This way." Nita put her arm around him, guiding him toward an outcrop of rock. "I'm going to try for the bunker. I think . . . the general will be there and Carter is going to find him. The wave won't scare him. He'll know it had to be you." Now that the worst of the mob mind had thinned she could think again. "I have to tell him about Johnny."

"I'm still in this. I'm all right." Jeremy pushed hair out of his face. "Can you listen for people, Nita? I don't want to meet some freaked out uniform with a gun."

"I can do that." Individual emotions should stand out sharply against the dull background of the retreating mob. "We're okay. I think the soldiers mostly ran, too." She clutched his hand and they began to pick their way along the riverbed.

So little sign of the flood and its effect remained. The baked clay of the bed didn't hold footprints. Someone had dropped a battered hunting rifle and it lay wedged between two rocks. They worked their way around one of the long lava ridges that cut the riverbed here. A body lay in the dust on the far side — a boy. Nita recoiled. He lay on his back, head twisted at a sickening angle, his wide-open eyes staring at the sky. He looked about fifteen.

Jeremy groaned.

"He would have been shot by a uniform," Nita said fiercely. "Or he would have ended up in a camp. And how many more?" She grabbed Jeremy's arm, suddenly aware of a familiar touch against the murk of the distant confusion. "Carter," she breathed. Alive. Not dead.

"Wait." Jeremy yanked her to a halt. "Slow, Nita, or we'll both get shot. We're pretty close to the bunker."

Not slow, no. The feel of him terrified her. It was full of death. She tore free of Jeremy's restraining hand and broke into a run.

CHAPTER TWENTY-FIVE

Reason finally penetrated Carter's cold rage as he sped away from Dan's house on the Gorge rim. He was wearing a Corps uniform, which meant he wasn't likely to make it back to the base alive, never mind to the Shunt. And he had to make it to the Shunt. Hastings would be there — with his Rangers.

Carter braked, fighting the car one-handed onto the rough shoulder of the main road. Pain from his ribs was making him dizzy, but he fished in the backseat and found a shirt. It was a white dress shirt with a food stain on the front — part of Johnny's dirty laundry. He slid his arms into the too-large sleeves. It would do. With his coverall rolled down around his waist, he looked more local than uniform — as long as he stayed in the car.

He put the car into gear and headed down the hill, toward the highway bridge that crossed the riverbed. The few locals he passed barely glanced at him. The town might as well have been a ghost town. Everybody must be down at the Shunt. He would have to come up on the Shunt from the Washington side of the Gorge. That was going to slow him down a lot, but Hastings would have thrown roadblocks across 84, and he wasn't sure what orders concerning himself might have been issued. Probably none, since he wasn't officially under arrest, but he wasn't taking any chances. Purpose had contracted to a cold lump in his gut.

Killing Hastings wouldn't bring anyone back to life and probably wouldn't save The Dalles, but it would balance the scales just a little. He crossed the bridge and turned eastward on the Washington highway. Hastings would have thrown barricades across this road, too. He braked, stripped off the shirt and pulled his coverall up over his shoulders again. The Corps insignia gleamed on the collar. He had sworn an oath of office when he had been commissioned. The words came back to him suddenly and clearly, as if he had just spoken them only this afternoon. *I do solemnly swear that I will support and defend the Constitution of the United States . . .* And the Corps, by its very existence, had shredded the Constitution. Water counted a lot more than individual rights any more. . . . *against all enemies, foreign and domestic* . . . Hastings was the enemy here. And Dan Greely. He drove fast, carrying death inside him like an unhatched egg or a bomb set to go off. A guided missile. Nothing more.

The Shunt bunker came into view, across the riverbed on the Oregon side. A dark mass of humanity seethed at the mouth of the Deschutes bed. Carter shivered, seeing Lakeshore in those dark figures. A wooden barricade barred the access road that led down to the bunker from this side. Two guards lifted rifles, sighting on the windshield as a third man waved him to a halt. Carter stared impassively at the muzzles of their guns, waiting for them to recognize him.

"I'm sorry, sir." A corporal leaned in at the window. "The general said no one was to come through here."

"He didn't mean me," Carter snapped.

"I'd better check, sir . . ."

Carter stepped on the accelerator, and because Hastings hadn't named him specifically, and he was, after all, a colonel, the corporal nervously waved him through. The Shunt was right ahead. Carter drove down into the riverbed and parked the car, his skin tightening. No one was working on the Pipe. They were all behind the parked trucks, crouching low, rifles locked and loaded. Rangers and regular Corps.

He was too damn late.

As Carter flung the door open, gunshots cracked. The rear window of the car disintegrated in a glittering shower and he dove for the ground, realizing that he was in plain sight, well within the range of rifle fire from across the riverbed. Locals were running down into the riverbed, taking cover behind the lava ridges that scored the bed along here, firing. One of the running figures fell. Another. Carter spotted Hastings near the bunker. Crouching low, he started running, zigzagging from rock to rock.

Someone screamed hoarsely. It was a cry of fear, not pain. Carter glanced up, then tripped and fell, pain from his ribs blasting the breath from his lungs. Water! The dark wall curled over their heads, streaked with foam, ready to break. Carter heard more screams, heard his own voice yelling in fear. *Run*, his brain screamed at him, but his chest spasmed, pain doubling him over. In a moment the raging water would seize him again, tumble him down the riverbed, suck him down in its cold, terrible grip.

Jeremy. The tiny, sane thought blossomed in his head. *It's Jeremy.*

Panting, he lifted his head. Yes, the wave was too slow — not like the ugly brown flood from the Pipe. It wasn't real. Soldiers ran past him. A wide-eyed corporal dropped his rifle and it bounced, the barrel barely missing Carter's face. Blind with terror, people stumbled, fell, were pulled to their feet by friends and ran on. "It's all right," Carter shouted. "It's an illusion."

Nobody listened. Well, it looked damn real. Even knowing it had to be Jeremy, he still wanted to run.

For a seeming eternity it threatened and then . . . it vanished. Carter found himself staring at baked clay and dusty rocks, his heart still pounding. "Damn," he whispered. He drew a shallow, cautious breath and looked around.

The riverbed looked as if the wave had actually hit. The mob had scattered, and cars and trucks were pulling out on the Oregon side. The barricade was nearly deserted. Dust blew away on the dry wind, and a few sprawled bodies lay in the sun. Drowned by an imaginary flood? Carter wondered numbly. Killed by real bullets. For the moment, it was over. What had Jeremy *done*?

Maybe now he had time to stop it. Touching the folded shares in his breast pocket, Carter staggered to his feet and touched the cold weight of the Beretta. Hastings would still be at the bunker. He wouldn't have run far. Carter limped toward the bunker, black spots swarming at the edges of his vision. Blood soaked the side of his coverall. He wasn't going to be able to stay on his feet much longer. Long enough, maybe. The Shunt appeared deserted although a small detachment of Rangers was already scrambling back toward it. No Hastings.

"Carter? Carter, wait!"

Nita's voice? Carter turned, relief that she was all right leaping like flame in his chest, turning sick as he remembered where he'd found the stock certificates. And then she was running toward him, her black hair loose from its braid, whipping in the wind, her arms reaching for him. And his arm went around her, never mind where he'd found the certificates, because one of those bodies might have been her. He groaned as she pressed against him and staggered.

"You're hurt," she said. "You were there, weren't you? When they blew the Pipe?"

"Yes, I was there." He touched her face lightly, pierced with loss. "Get down. A lot of people still have guns out here." He pulled her down behind a rock, searching the bed for any sign of Hastings. "Get out of here, Nita. Now. Head for the Oregon side, keep low, and get away from the riverbed. Please?"

"You're wrong." She grabbed his hand. "Carter — whatever you found in Dan's house it was planted there for you to find. It was meant to look like Dan and General Hastings are behind this, backed by Pacific BioSystems. They're not. It's a set up." She clung to his hand as he tried to pull away. "That's why I came here. To tell you."

"I'm sorry, Nita." Maybe she saw her father in Dan Greely.

"I'm not just wishing." She clung to his arm as he started for the bunker. "Carter, I know who did it. He admitted it. He gave himself away. It's Johnny Seldon. It was so easy for him to use you. I'm so sorry."

"Johnny?" Her accusation stopped him. "Nita, get out of here *now*. You're going to get killed."

"He wanted you to find it . . . he took you up there to find it. That's why he came up there the other day. To plant it. He went back after he gave Jeremy and I a ride into town."

"How do you know this?" He twisted savagely out of her grasp. Because Johnny had been up there. "Tell me how come you're so sure." A shot boomed out and he ducked, pulling her flat. "Stay down. I'm going to have to get you out of here somehow."

"Dan." She bolted to her feet and ran, upright, a perfect target for anyone in the riverbed.

Carter swore, and scrambled after her as best he could. She vanished down into the old channel. At least it was out of sight of much of the riverbed. He slid down after her, calling her crazy and an idiot, afraid for her. He rounded a spire of water-worn lava and halted in his tracks.

Hastings sprawled face-down in the dust between the ridges of lava. His face was turned toward Carter and his eyes stared sightlessly at the rocks. Dark blood stained the dust beneath him.

Greely leaned against the rocks less than ten feet from Hastings's body, a large-caliber revolver in his hand. Carter looked at him, felt no surprise.

Nita stood squarely between them.

He watched her, watched Greely, his gun in his hand. Greely didn't even seem to notice them. He stared at the gun in his hand with a confused expression on his face, let it drop into the dust. It landed with the dull sound of metal on stone.

"Don't," Nita said softly.

"You are some bastard," Carter said softly.

"No." Greely's voice was slow and thick. "I didn't . . ."

Nita stepped back against Greely, shielding him with her body, her face full of pain.

Carter edged sideways, purpose beating in his head. The scales were almost balanced. Almost. He might be able to yank her out of the way before Greely could reach for the gun. He just stood there. Looking at it.

"Stop." Nita said. "You hear me, first." Her cold, icy tone made him glance at her. "Johnny is behind this. With Major Delgado, I think. At least he shot at Renny and I when we left for Portland."

"I've heard you on the subject of Dan Greely," he snapped. Delgado. Yeah, he was for sure part of this. "Prove that Johnny is behind this."

"Johnny told me he hadn't planted the things at the house and he was lying. He recognized Rico, the name of the hacker who planted the fake information to tie the general and Dan to Pacific Biosystems. He told me he wasn't behind the sabotage and he was lying."

"He wasn't lying, Nita."

"Nobody can lie to me, Carter." She faced him, fists clenched at her sides, her head up, meeting his stare. "I hear what you're feeling inside . . . what everyone feels. Do you understand? When you lie, I can always feel it. You can't hide a lie from me. Not ever."

He shook his head.

"Right now, you're doubting. You think it maybe was Johnny." She said each word flatly, without inflection. "You're thinking that he could have done all this. And you're afraid that it's true. What the hell do you owe this man? You're nothing to him."

She flinched as he jerked, fear bright on her face.

"Did you think I was going to shoot you?" He looked down at the Beretta, lowered it.

She was right. About his doubts.

And the debt.

She shouldn't be able to be that right. Nobody knew.

Tears gleamed on her face. "Dan didn't shoot this man," she said. "He isn't behind this. If you wait, I can give you the proof. You have to wait, Carter."

His hands were shaking. Pacific Biosystems. That was the tie in. Johnny had said something about them, had jumped on Carter when he had followed up on it. If she was telling the truth. About reading minds.

Half an hour ago, a man had filled the dry riverbed with an imaginary flood.

Carter shoved the Beretta back into its holster and lifted his head to look Dan Greely in the face. "How did you get here?"

"Someone . . . grabbed me. Out of . . . your jail." He spoke with an effort and seemed barely able to stay on his feet.

"Maybe it's a frame. I don't know."

Nita gave a small, choked cry, her face turning up to the rocks above them, her body stiffening.

"You fool." Delgado rose from behind tumbled boulders. "You dumb asshole. Why didn't you just shoot him? Then everything would fit, and we'd be home free."

He'd been there all the time. Carter stared up at him, keeping his hands away from the gun and still. Delgado's eyes were on Nita, black holes in his dust-grimed face. "You hick bitch, you messed it all up. You want proof?"

"Nita, down!" Jeremy's voice, hoarse and urgent.

Carter caught a glimpse of movement, blond hair from the corner of his eye. Delgado swung the barrel his way, then jerked it back toward Nita, Dan lunged for her, stumbling and clumsy, too slow. Carter yanked the Beretta from its holster, heart pounding. Delgado saw him and the rifle barrel swung back in Carter's direction, moving too fast.

"No," Nita screamed, leaping straight up the bank at him.

They were all moving now and the rifle barrel jerked and wavered. Carter brought the Beretta up just as Delgado fired. The short burst of ugly sound crashed from rock to rock, and the Beretta bucked in Carter's hand. The slug caught Delgado in the chest, spun him sideways. He skidded down the slope in an avalanche of stones and dirt.

Behind him, Nita cried a hoarse note of anguish.

Carter turned slowly, not wanting to see. It wasn't Nita. It was Jeremy. He lay sprawled on his back and she crouched beside him, her face twisted. Bright blood soaked the bottom of his shirt. A lot of blood. Dan went awkwardly to his knees beside her. He fumbled his shirt off, wadded it into a pad. Cold inside, Carter touched Jeremy's throat. He had a pulse; thready and uneven but there.

"He's dying," Nita said.

Her eyes scared the hell out of him. She *felt* this. His last doubt vanished.

"Try to stop the bleeding," he snapped at Dan. He had his cell out, was calling for paramedics, pronto. Snapped orders into the phone.

"Hurry," Dan said.

Carter started for the bunker and the trucks, his ribs screaming. He was shaking by the time he reached it, clammy with icy sweat. Back up med teams were arriving from the base and he met one on their way to answer his call, sent them scrambling down to Jeremy.

He wanted to follow them. Not yet. He had to find the Rangers' CO, pronto. Sort out the confusion, assess injuries, Shunt security, and the needs of the moment. Troops were reassembling, shaken, eyes flicking up the riverbed as if another flood could appear at any moment. Rumors were flying. Ghost flood. He heard that twice before he found the Rangers and their CO. Good enough, he thought. He sent people down for Hastings and Delgado, got a medic to give him painkillers and enough amphetamine to keep him on his feet.

The stretcher team hurried past with Jeremy, IV bag swinging. "How is he?" Carter asked, got a head-shake in reply. Alive, still. He could hope.

Carter saw no sign of Nita or Greely. They had vanished. He issued strict orders against retaliation against locals in any form, saying a silent prayer it would keep them safe.

He sent out details to search for any injured people who might still be in the riverbed. Soldiers and locals both, and don't miss any locals, he told them. It was time to start healing this breach, but it was going to be a damned tough breach to heal. The bodies were coming in. Six locals, so far. Two Corps people, not including Delgado and Hastings. For the moment, he was letting them remain victims of the riot, so that made four. Slowly he sorted through the mess as the day waned into dusk.

The painkillers didn't help much, and even cranked to the eyebrows with amphetamines he finally had to stop. Or he was going to end up on a stretcher, too. He leaned against the side of a truck, his coverall stiff with blood seeping from the surgery site. The doc was going to scream at him, he thought fuzzily. The sun was going down and shadows streaked the dry riverbed. He could see a stretch of the east bank from here. Once a park must have occupied that space. The dusty ground was divided into little rectangles by the remains of asphalt paths and parking strips. People had probably parked their RVs or pitched tents there in the old days. Now dust drifted over the curbs, and only stumps remained of the trees that must have shaded the campground.

Suddenly he wanted to see Jeremy's version of that campground, wanted to see grass, leaves. Maybe the ghosts of kids playing, swimming in the river? Carter wondered if those kids had lived to see the river go dusty and dry as they sunk the Pipe. Only so much water existed and a lot of people needed it. If Jeremy died, he'd never know what that damn park had looked like.

Now he had to think about Johnny. Carter closed his eyes, remembering the day he'd come home from school. He'd called her name, even though she was often out of it, doing the pills she got from Doctor Warrington, after she'd finished with his big house. He knew why Warrington had paid Carter's tuition to the pricey school. Everyone knew. And he heard her cry some nights, when she came back late. He wondered why she had cut her wrists instead of using some of the many many pills she had.

He had called 911. Because that's what you did. And then . . . Warrington had walked in. He had looked at her and turned to leave. Just like that.

Carter didn't remember much after that — just blurry images of Warrington on the floor, and paramedics, and cops. They cuffed him and hauled him off to jail. The images were like someone else's old photos, found in a drawer. He had been just too old for juvenile court. And the charge had been murder. Johnny's dad had paid for the lawyer and the expensive experts who had testified that Mr. Warrington had died of an aneurysm that would have happened anyway, and not because Carter had hit him. They pointed out to the jury the shame that Carter had lived with, and brought in teachers from the expensive school to testify to the bullying they hadn't much bothered to stop at the time.

He ended up with an assault conviction and a suspended sentence.

Because of Johnny.

Carter wiped his face, feeling sweat and mud beneath his fingers. Time to finish up fast, before the drugs wore off. Time enough, later, for Nita's proof. And Johnny. He turned away from the dusty park with its ghosts of playing children. The riot was over but it wasn't an ending. Even if they got the water back on tonight, some people were going to lose their crops. When would the next flow cut come down? The struggle along this river-bed would never end. Not until the rains came back. Carter took another painkiller and had an NCO drive him back to the base.

He stopped in at Operations to make sure that the flow meters in The Dalles were being reset. By morning, they'd be back to the original settings. Maybe that would be soon enough, he thought. For at least some of the farmers. He leaned against the door of Operations, staring up at the dry glitter of the stars. He hoped Nita and Dan had made it back to the farm okay. This wasn't the time to send soldiers through The Dalles to check. With an effort, he straightened, and headed for the infirmary.

CHAPTER TWENTY-SIX

Hospitals smelled alike, he thought. Military or civilian. Carter tried to decipher the odor as he waited for the doctor. Disinfectant, urine, and fear? He looked up as the doctor stormed into the sterile little waiting room. She wore blood spotted-surgical greens and her mouth pressed into a straight line as she faced him. "What the hell are you doing? You had surgery less than forty-eight hours ago. The only reason I didn't keep you in here then was that you said you'd stay in bed. Do you know how very lucky you are not to have bled to death today? I'm admitting you right now."

"Not yet." Carter raised a hand. "Believe me, if I've lived this long, I can last another couple of hours. Then I'll go to bed. I promise."

"I'll remind you of that when the stretcher detail brings in your body." Her shoulders slumped and fatigue etched lines around her mouth. "You wanted to know about your civilian. He was the worst that came in, but he's stable. In Recovery, so you can't see him." She sighed. "I did the best I could, Colonel, but the bullet passed close to his spine, and he sustained some damage that's going to need stem cells to fix." She stared past him at the pastel-green wall. "Any chance he has good health insurance?"

"What kind of damage are you talking about?"

"Too soon to tell." The tired eyes got more tired. "Maybe paralysis from the hips down if there's no intervention. Maybe only partial loss of use. Can you give me some ID and any kind of history on this guy?"

"His legal name is Jeremy Barlow and he was born in the Dry with the joint deformities he has now. That's all I know." Carter sat down hard on a chair.

"Colonel . . ." The doctor hesitated. "What do you know about this . . . ghost flood? Everybody's talking about it."

"He did it." Carter raised his head, met her dark eyes. "The guy you just patched up. It was . . . an illusion. He saved a lot of lives with it, doctor. Pretty damn bitter reward, if you ask me." His lips twisted. "Don't be surprised by what you see as he comes out of anesthesia. Better warn the nurses."

"Illusion . . ." She shook her head, doubtful. "You can put in a request for emergency medical assistance for him," she said slowly. "I'll do the paperwork tonight."

"Do that."

"I will, but don't get your hopes up." She looked away. "Usually it takes two to four weeks for approval, even if you mark it urgent. You have to apply stem cells within thirty-six hours of injury. Or it's ineffective."

"Do it anyway," he grated. At least it was something to hope for.

The doctor insisted on checking his blood pressure and temperature and changing the bandage on the surgery site. She reamed him thoroughly about his condition, but decided he wasn't dying. He didn't really pay attention. He refused any more pills — he'd had more than enough and exhaustion had walled him in with a gray fog so that even the pain from his abused ribs didn't come through very strongly. He told the doctor to call him if there was any change in Jeremy's condition and left.

Outside, he stopped, leaned against the building and pulled out his cell. Johnny answered on the first ring, his voice bright and worried. "What is going on up there? The media's full of all kinds of crazy rumors. Officers shot, a flood in the riverbed that wasn't a flood. Jeeze, I'm glad to hear from you. Where the hell did you go after you took off like that?"

"You knew where I went." Carter closed his eyes. "You know where I am right now. You put a chip into me, didn't you?."

"What . . . are you talking about? Carter?" Johnny's voice was bright and concerned. "Are you okay? Where are you?"

"I'll see you in my apartment. Leave right now, Johnny. They'll let you through the main gate. Don't make me wait." He hung up.

His cell rang again immediately and he shut it off. Slowly he made his way across the base. The last dose of amphetamine was wearing off, leaving trembling exhaustion in its wake. Carter pushed his door open, fumbled for the switch and flicked on the light.

Dan Greely was sitting on his sofa.

"You do this a lot, don't you?" Carter closed the door and leaned against it. "Why don't you try the gate?"

"Not tonight." Dan's eyes narrowed. "You look like hell."

"So the doctor told me. You don't look so good yourself." Carter made it to a chair and leaned his head back against the upholstery. "Where's Nita?"

"At the truck plaza with Renny. Worrying about Jeremy," Dan said. "Worrying about you. How is Jeremy?"

"In Recovery." He decided not to mention the doctor's prognosis. "I'll call the government store when I know something. Tell me what happened." Carter sat up with an effort, realizing that he had stopped doubting Dan. "I'm too beat to be judgmental, so I'll listen."

"The red headed agitator and someone else showed up at my jail cell in uniform," Dan said slowly. "The idea was to make it look as if I'd shot Hastings. I think Delgado was supposed to shoot me afterward. They shot me full of something when they grabbed me and everything is kind of blurry. I think I was in a basement somewhere. We missed Jeremy's show, I guess. I think we were driving down into the riverbed when it happened. I remember someone yelling and the car we were in slammed into something. Nita says he scared everyone right out of the riverbed."

"He sure did." Carter rubbed his aching eyes. "He stopped a war."

"I . . . don't really understand what he does," Dan said hesitantly. "But it's really something." He shook his head. "I don't know how Delgado got Hastings down there, but next thing I knew I heard a shot. Someone shoved a gun into my hand. I guess it was Delgado. I still wasn't too clear. And that's about the time you showed up." He shrugged. "You know the rest."

"I forgot about that gun." Carter's eyes snapped open. "It had to have killed Hastings. And it has your prints on it."

"Not a problem." Dan looked at him sideways. "I made it disappear for good."

"You don't take chances, do you?"

"Sometimes I do." Dan leaned back against the sofa, closed his eyes. "Think we can start over, Carter?"

"I think we have to." Carter sighed. "I've got to trust you. I can't do this by myself. I'm a uniform. I'm sorry . . . that I got taken in by that frame."

Dan grimaced. "It was a damn tight frame."

Yeah, it was. Carter leaned his face in his hands. "We'll have water restored to the local lines by morning. I've got a crew working all night on it. I'm going to do some horse trading and I think we can make up the difference without cutting The Dalles much. I'll have the final numbers by tomorrow night, I hope." If he could stay out of the doctor's clutches. "For the interim, I have the power to set the flow. But we may have to cut after all."

"We're both going to have our work cut out for us." Dan gave him a crooked smile. "But you boosted my stock by arresting me. That shut up the people who claimed I was in bed with you."

"We'll do our best, I guess." Carter noticed the fresh bruises on Dan's face and the red weals on his wrists where he'd been cuffed or tied. "You need a ride back?"

"Not really safe for you folks right now. I'll stay at the plaza tonight. Nita's really worried about you." Dan levered himself to his feet. "She cares a lot about you, Carter. Just so you know. I didn't . . . know what she could do." His eyes flickered.

"I didn't either," Carter said. It bothered Dan. You could see it in his face. It would be scary. To think that someone knew what was going on inside your head. How did *he* feel? He scowled and forced himself to his feet. He didn't know. Not tonight.

He'd have to answer that question.

"I'll get you an escort to the gate." He pulled out his phone, surprised at how much it weighed. "Dan? How the hell do you get in here?"

Dan gave him a crooked s mile. "There's a low spot on the riverbed side of the fence, out behind the kitchen compost bins. This kid was stationed here about two years ago. He was a Corps electrician, and he was Sandy's nephew. He diddled the fence a little, just enough so that you can slide under without getting zapped or setting off the alarm. Sandy and I know about it. Nobody else."

"Thanks," Carter said. "Use the gate after this, okay?"

Dan lifted a hand in a half salute as the escort knocked on the door. Carter felt a small flash of relief as he recognized Private Wasson. "Make sure this man gets out the gate safely," he told her, then held up a hand. "Private, were you out at the Shunt today?"

"Yes, sir. We got sent in as backup, sir." Her eyebrows rose. "What happened?" Awe colored her tone. "Do you know what it was? Some kind of hologram or something?"

"Something," Carter told her. He glanced at his watch as Dan followed her toward the main gate. He'd give Johnny a half hour to show.

He knocked less than five minutes later.

"You must have been breaking speed records." Carter stood aside as Johnny breezed into the room.

"You weren't making any sense at all. Are you sure you shouldn't be in the infirmary right now?" Johnny peered at Carter. "You look like you're going to pass out."

"Not quite yet."

"What happened at the Shunt? Fill me in, will you? And where's the stuff you found at Greely's house?" Johnny sat down on the sofa Dan had just vacated. "What was it?"

"How did you know I found anything at Greely's?" Carter leaned against the door.

"Uh . . . that guy. He said you had something in your hand when you left." Johnny shrugged. "Why else go tearing off like a crazy man?"

"I didn't have anything in my hands when I left." Carter crossed his arms. "Tell me about Pacific BioSystems, Johnny."

"What about 'em?" Johnny's eyelids flickered. "We've got inside information that they've cut a deal with Hastings, we just don't have any proof yet." He sighed. "That's what I was hoping we'd find at Greely's. No luck, huh?"

"I want to know what you were trying to do." The words came out leaden. "Why frame Hastings and Dan Greely? Why ruin the farmers along the riverbed? What does it gain you?"

"What are you talking about?" Anger flashed across Johnny's face, turned into sudden comprehension. "That Latina chick of yours." He snapped his fingers. "What's her name? She's been giving you an earful, hasn't she? Carter, I know how you feel about her." He shrugged, his face full of sympathy. "I think you're going to have to face the fact that she's Greely's lover. I saw it for myself. She'll say anything to clear that guy."

"Heard from Delgado this evening?" Carter watched Johnny's face go still.

"Who's . . ."

"You planted the information that ties Greely and Hastings to PacificBio systems, Johnny. A better hacker than the one you hired found the real deal." He sure as hell hoped Nita was right about that. "So proof exists, Johnny. You hear me? Proof." He paced across the room, turned back to stare at Johnny. "Hastings is dead. So is Delgado, so he can't testify against you. But you can't slip out of this clean." He drew a shallow, painful breath, remembering those cell bars, so long ago, the slippery feel of blood on his fingers. "I won't cover for you," he said unsteadily.

"I didn't kill anybody." Johnny looked away from him, his face twitching. "You got to look out for yourself, Carter. The world won't look out for you. You'd do better to save your friends, let the rest go."

"Delgado said something like that."

"He was crazy. He wasn't supposed to kill that girl."

"Just Hastings and Greely?" Carter's blood chilled. "What about Private Wasson, Johnny, the one who could identify the corporal who helped kidnap Greely?"

"Why couldn't you just leave it *alone*?" Johnny lurched to his feet. "You wouldn't have gotten hurt. I had it all set up. You were going to come out of this like a hero."

Like a hero. He stared at Johnny, realizing he had wanted him to deny it, wanted him to come up with a good reason why Nita was wrong, why it wasn't him. He had been as ready to believe him as he had been ready to believe in Dan's guilt. "Why, Johnny?" he asked numbly. "Why did you do this? You've got it all."

"Yeah, I have it all," Johnny whispered. "Do you know how fast I could lose it? After Amber and I split, I went a little crazy for awhile. You were so busy with your Army games and I . . . was on my own." He stared down at Carter, haggard in the yellow light of the overhead fixture. "This little whore I'd been seeing tried to shake me down. Yes, she was underage, but it was no rape, that's for sure. She solicited *me*. I didn't mean to kill her. It . . . was an accident. And then . . . Morissy showed up two days later. With pictures. They could do a DNA match, of course. The cops. If she tipped them off. She'd set the girl on me, planning to lever me with the sex charge. And I handed her my ass on a platter." His face had gone white.

"Morissy thought she owned me, Carter. No one owns me. No one. This was the way out. Do you know what would have happened once it came out that Pacific BioSystems had bribed a Corps general to give them extra water, that they had caused a local water war? The media would crucify them with joy, and we'd have an excuse to really bring them to heel. Someone needs to yank them into line, and if they leaned on me then, I could claim it was a frame. Revenge for exposing them. Carter? His lips trembled. The girl . . . it really was an accident."

"Did you give Wasson's name to Delgado?" Carter asked softly.

"Yes." Johnny wouldn't meet his eyes. "She could ID the guy he was working with in Bonneville."

"What did you think Delgado was going to do? And meanwhile, The Dalles ends up another Chicago."

"I told you, you wouldn't have gotten hurt." Johnny made a chopping gesture with his hand. "I made sure of that. Hastings and Greely would have taken the heat and you would have been a hero for finding out about it. I'd never let you get stuck in the middle. Your ass has been covered the whole time. Everything would have worked out fine," he said bitterly. "They should be growing bushes along the Columbia anyway."

"I fried out in the Dry. Did you have your hired help dump me out there just to turn me against the locals? Ten people died down in the riverbed today. Ten! Delgado almost shot me. Did I mention that?"

"We knew where you were, " Johnny said sullenly. "You were right about a chip. That's what the grab was for. Delgado wouldn't have shot you. He was supposed to . . ."

"Shoot Greely? And any other witnesses? My God, I don't believe you're saying this stuff." Carter buried his face in his hands. "Does it matter so much? A seat on Water Policy?"

"Yes, it matters."

The hissing intensity of Johnny's voice brought Carter's head up, raised the hairs on the back of his neck.

"My father's one of the top economists in the world. He's an *icon*, and I'm just Trevor Seldon's son. Not John Seldon. All my life I've been Trevor Seldon's son." Johnny's eyes glittered. "But now I'm Water Policy. *I* control his water. He drinks because I let him. He's never had this much power, Carter. He never will."

Carter looked away, hearing Nita's voice in his head. *You mean nothing to him.*

"I didn't shoot anyone," Johnny said hoarsely. "No one can connect those deaths to me. I didn't murder that girl. What do you want from me?"

"I should turn it all over to the media." He stared at the flowered paper on the wall. It would exonerate The Corps and Hastings. It would exonerate Carter. "If you resign from Water Policy . . . I won't," he said softly. "Because once . . . you were my friend."

"I can't just *resign*. Listen, wait a minute!" Johnny bounced to his feet, his voice high and tight. "I think we can cut a deal. You brought a civilian into the infirmary, yeah, I still have my sources, Carter — is this a friend of yours?" Johnny's eyes were desperate. "I heard he's in very bad shape. I'll pay for whatever it takes to put him back together — if you'll dump anything incriminating — just forget we ever had this conversation. I'll keep my hands off the Corps and your command. Do we have a deal?"

His hand on the knob to open the door and usher Johnny out, Carter hesitated. What had Hastings said — that there were no innocent people along the riverbed? He'd been wrong. There was at least one innocent person in all this: Jeremy. He had never taken sides in this war, and he had saved an awful lot of people.

Carter closed his eyes briefly. Johnny would always come first. Not the numbers, not the thirsty men and women who lived or died by Water Policy's decisions: it was Johnny Seldon, first and foremost. "No," he whispered. What had Jeremy said about the Dry? – that sometimes you had to make ugly choices. "I want to hear on the news tomorrow that you've resigned."

Johnny marched past him and into the night, his face set like a stone.

Nita would know. She would know that he had done this to Jeremy. He closed the door behind Johnny and locked it.

CHAPTER TWENTY-SEVEN

The hospital corridor oppressed Nita. It was white and sterile, filled with echoes of pain and sickness. Everybody hurried and seemed to be very busy. She tiptoed down it, her skin tight with gooseflesh even though it wasn't particularly cool, half expecting someone to stop her and demand to know what she was doing here. She had been surprised at Renny's ready agreement to drive her all the way here to Portland, to the big city hospital where Jeremy had been transferred. The receptionist downstairs had told her his room number, but the numbers didn't want to behave rationally up here. Nita closed he eyes briefly, her head buzzing with the fog of discomfort that filled this place.

A chunky young woman in green pants and a loose green shirt passed on her way down the corridor. "Are you lost?" she asked with a smile.

"I'm looking for Jeremy Barlow. In four twenty-one," Nita said. The woman's pleasant feel eased some of her tension. "I think I *am* lost."

"Not really. He's down here." The woman nodded down an intersecting corridor. "I'll take you." She fell in beside Nita, her curiosity like the smell of flowers in the air. "He has quite a talent, Jeremy. Everybody in the entire psych department here has been down talking with him and testing what he can do. We moved him into a room where he could look out at the Willamette bed. Has he showed you the city he sees? It was so *beautiful.*" Her eyes had gone dreamy. "Pictures just don't do it, do they? You know, when I see it, really *see* it, I can believe it'll be like that again, some day."

Nita halted in the middle of the corridor. "He shows you?"

"Sure." The woman raised a quizzical eyebrow at her reaction, but decide to let it pass. "The more I do it, the better I can see it. I just caught a few glimpses at first, but some people see everything the first time. Cara, one of the surgical nurses is really good at it. Doctor Lazarus, the head of Psych, had a name for what he does, but I can't remember it now."

"That's wonderful." Nita felt dazed. He was doing this? Here? Where he couldn't escape?

"This is the place." The woman lifted a hand, smiling. "I'm Amelia Cary, by the way. A lowly intern. Say hi to Jeremy for me, will you? I'm supposed to be elsewhere five minutes ago."

"I will," Nita said, and pushed the oversize door open as the woman hurried away.

Jeremy was asleep. His face looked pale and fragile on the white pillow, haloed by his fair hair. Tubes trailed across the bed, IVs and a catheter, dripping fluid into his veins, carrying away the excess, as if Jeremy himself had become nothing more than some kind of living filter removing a few nutrients from the slow, steady trickle of liquid. It frightened her. She shivered suddenly, wanting to shake him, wake him up so that she could be sure he was still Jeremy.

As if he had felt her anxiety, Jeremy's eyelids fluttered. "Hi." He turned his head on the pillow to look at her, and his smile was his own. "When did you get here?"

"A little while ago. Renny drove me down." She reached for his hand, closing her fingers tightly around his. "Jeremy, it's my fault. I should have heard Delgado. If I'd listened, I would have known he was there. But Carter was going to kill Dan, and I just didn't listen . . ."

"Hey, stop." He squeezed her hand. "It's not your fault. Any of us could have ended up dead. It's kind of a medium-sized miracle that we didn't. And I'm not going to die, so relax." He squeezed her hand again, then grimaced and fingered the tubing taped to the back of his other hand. "It itches," he said. "I guess I'll be on this thing until they're all done with the treatments. But they don't have to do any more surgery. That's what Dr. Carey told me this morning. Although she said some of the doctors were talking about working on my hands. And my knees." He stretched his knotted fingers. "If they decide to, they'll do it for free. I guess they're seeing more cases of this and they want to see if they can fix it."

He wasn't sad. Or scared. "Jeremy?" Nita framed the question she wanted to ask, but the words wouldn't come. *Spinal damage*, Dan had told her. *He might never be able to walk again.*

"Dr. Imenez was in this morning." Jeremy smiled now, reaching up to touch her cheek. "He's the one who's been doing the fancy stuff — something with stem cells. He stuck me with a needle this morning. Up and down my legs. I couldn't feel anything when he did it before, but this time . . . I did. Not all the sticks, but some of them. He was pleased, Nita." He pushed her braid back over her shoulder. "I guess it looks good."

"Jeremy, I'm so glad." She held his hands, smiling with the bright glow of his hope. He wouldn't have to spend the rest of his life in a bed in Dan's house. Surely. "I met Dr. Carey. She said hi. And she told me you're show-ing people your visions."

"No kidding." He smiled, a little more tentatively this time. "I guess I really stirred things up. A whole bunch of doctors are trying to figure out how I do what I do. It scares me some . . . you can feel that, right? But it's okay. They're running all kinds of tests while I'm making stuff. They don't have a clue. But the nurses all sneak in here to look at the river. I still don't know why everybody saw that flood in the riverbed like they did."

"It had to be because of all the people," Nita said. "I *knew* it was you, and it still panicked me. I think it was like a few people saw it, and their reaction sort of set off others around him. Does that make sense?"

"No, but it happened anyway." Jeremy closed his eyes. "You were right, you know? About my not wanting to face what I could do. The vi-sions, I mean. My dad could see them. I showed him what the land had been like once, and . . . I think something broke inside of him. I think he died sooner . . . because of that."

"You don't know that."

"You could have told me, right?" He kissed the back of her hand, lightly. "Too bad you weren't there. Or maybe I'm right. We'll never know. And I am . . . facing it. The visions. Trying to figure out what they're good for."

"Dr. Cary said they gave her hope," Nita said softly. His face looked thin, shadowed with recent pain. "She said they made her believe the world could be like that again one day."

Jeremy's smile warmed her. "It's still going to scare some people, make some people crazy. But I guess there's a price for everything, right?"

"Yes." Nita felt the smile tremble on her lips, made it stronger.

"What's wrong?" Jeremy's fingers tightened around hers. "Carter?"

"So who reads minds now?" She laughed, but it caught in her throat.

"I don't need to try very hard. He was here earlier this week." Jeremy wouldn't let go of her hand. "I asked him about you. He said he hadn't seen you."

He was sad for her. "He's been pretty busy and...I don't feel comfort-able walking up to that gate. Even though the base isn't closed anymore. I got the proof he needed from Renny's hacker friend. Dan gave it to Carter. Johnny resigned from Water Policy. I heard it on the news. I've been busy." She made her voice light. "Dan, Sandy, and I have all been busy trying to smooth things out between The Dalles and the Corps. It's not easy." *We.* "You know, I'm doing what I told Dan I'd never do — what my father did."

"You're doing what you need to do." Jeremy smiled.

"I think so." And it still surprised her at times.

"You want to know something weird?" Jeremy stared up at the ceiling. "Johnny Seldon paid for my treatment."

"Him?" Her eyes widened. "Why?"

"I don't know." Jeremy touched his sheeted abdomen lightly. "He came to see me the first day I was here. He's a strange man. I kind of wished you were here." He fell silent for a moment, frowning. "He made me promise not to tell Carter. Then he said it made things even. Then he left. I'll take it," Jeremy said lightly. "I don't care where it comes from."

He had been terrified he would end up paralyzed. She could hear echoes of that terror even now. "It's all right now." Nita brushed a wisp of hair back from his face. His yes were so blue — the color of the sky above the riverbed on a windless day. David's eyes had been almost that color. "I've got to go," she said. "Renny's got Rachel at the car."

"Renny?" He laughed. "She sure doesn't seem like the motherly type to me."

"She says Rachel's not bad for a kid. She told me she'd take her on as an apprentice as soon as she can reach the pedals on the truck."

"She could do worse."

Through the window, she could see the river. Green grass fringed the sparkling sweep of the river full of water, glowing in the sun. Trees bloomed along white sidewalks, their bare branches clouded with pink blossoms. "It was so beautiful." She leaned forward to kiss him on the lips. "I'll be back when I can."

"Nita?" Jeremy's eyes were full of sympathy. "When I finally get out of here, I plan to head back to the Tygh Valley. To see if that kid they stoned might still be alive somewhere. He's like us, Nita. There are others like us. I've heard about 'em. I think I'm going to start looking for them. If you want to come along, I'd like the company."

If Carter is afraid of you, he meant. Dan was. Just a little. "I might take you up on it." Nita smiled for him. "I'll let you know." She left the room before he could see her tears.

"You took your time." Renny sat in the strip of shade cast by her battered loaner. Rachel stood between her knees, wobbly and delighted. "The kid's ready to start running," Renny said. "She gets ticked off when it doesn't happen. I like her attitude." She laughed and handed the drooling Rachel up to Nita. "Let's go, babe. Feed her in the car if you've got to. I'm due to hit the road."

"Can we make one stop?" Nita asked her as she climbed into the car's baking interior. "Just for a couple of minutes?"

"Where and why?"

"Mosier." Nita looked away from the comprehension in Renny's eyes.

"Sure, babe," she said, and a trace of sadness lurked beneath her words.

It was one of those rare, windless days in the riverbed. Nita left Renny at the car with the sleeping Rachel and walked up the steep little street, past the sagging white house where Julio Moreno sold his secondhand clothes and furniture. He was out on his cluttered porch and he raised his good hand in a gesture that was almost a salute. Nita nodded and smiled, but didn't stop.

Dust puffed up from beneath her feet to hang in the still air. The heat stifled Nita, baking her flesh on her bones. The single tree in the tiny cemetery cast a thin shade across the dust. The newer stones were just pieces of lava or river rock; names and dates had been scrawled across them in black, or blue, or silver paint. Leaf shadows dappled the grave where Julio had buried the bones. Nita knelt in the dust beside the stone. She hadn't been able to find any flowers this late in the year, but she laid the small bunch of greenery that she had gathered on the grave: desert parsley and wheatgrass, a sprig of yarrow. At least the leaves were green and alive, even if they were already wilting. The stone was rectangular, reddish brown, smooth enough to have been shaped by hand instead of by nature. Nita touched the surface with her forefinger, feeling the tiny grains of sand beneath her fingertip. A few feet away another rough stone marked a grave. Luis Hansen read the fading blue letters. There were no dates on the stone, just the name.

Child? Nita wondered. Old man? She sighed and pulled the nail from her pocket. *D.* She scratched the letter into the surface, wavery white lines as crooked as the embroidered letters on the pack. *A.* David, I loved you. I still love you. *V I D.* You gave me space to grow up. You kept me safe. *A S.* I don't think I need anyone to keep me safe any more. *C H E R.* She put the nail back into her pocket and laid the bunch of greens on the stone. "If you're here, know I love you. If you walked away . . . I hope you find happiness."

"David Ascher," Renny said from behind her. "You made up your mind, huh?"

"Yes, I have." Nita stood up and took Rachel from the trucker's arms. An ending and a beginning. She would ask Dan where her father was buried. Julio had disappeared from his porch and the little town looked deserted as people waited out the afternoon heat. Water was running in the soaker hoses again — for now. When it got cooler, men, women, and children would go out to work the fields until it got too dark to see, shaping their lives to fit the harsh rhythms of sun and water. This is what matters, Nita thought. We can look at Jeremy's green visions and hope for that future, but right now, this is what has to matter.

"Thanks for the ride," Nita said.

"I had nothing better to do." Renny slid into the front seat, reaching for Rachel who yawned and blinked. "You know, when we made our little bargain, I thought you were sleeping with Danny. I could tell you weren't real thrilled with the idea of crawling into my bed and I figured I could wing two birds with one stone."

"I still owe you," Nita said. "You took Rachel in the riverbed, too."

"She'll make a good trucker, that kid. I was serious about taking her on." Renny handed Rachel to Nita and pulled her door closed. "We're even, babe. You make me think about things." She reached inside her denim shirt and pulled out a brown envelope. "This is for you."

Nita opened the envelope, removed the folded sheets. It was a hardcopy of a land title, in her name. "Your farm?"

"Jesse's farm, not mine." Renny pulled onto the hold highway. "It was never mine. You can give it to Dan if you want. Or you can keep it and cut your own deals." She shrugged, looking sideways at Nita. "Lydia told me a weird thing. She said you can hear what people think. Is there anything in that, babe?"

"I hear a little bit," Nita said softly.

"Too bad you didn't come along earlier." Renny turned her attention back to the road, but not before Nita caught the glint of tears in her eyes. They were climbing up over the crest now, the engine growling with protest. Up ahead the promontory where Jeremy had called up a long-ago spring jutted out over the riverbed. Different, she thought. That's all we are.

"Could you let me off here?" she asked suddenly.

"I can't wait, and it's a long walk to town. You sure, babe?"

"I've got my water bottle. I'll walk back when it gets cooler."

Renny pulled the car into the crumbling circular drive. People might have come here just to look down on the riverbed — no, the river — in the old days. Nita looked at the dry rocky gash, remembering shimmering water and the soft tints of green life that Jeremy had showed her. Yes, it would have been worth coming up here just to look.

"See you next trip," Renny said. "Take care of yourself."

Regretful? "I will." Nita leaned down for Rachel. "You take care of yourself, too. Can you let Lydia help?"

"We tried that once. Hell, who knows." She gave Nita a crooked grin. "We might give it another shot sometime." She pulled the door closed.

The engine roared and the car leaped forward, down to The Dalles where Renny would pick up her rig and head eastward: toward Boise, the next plaza, and the next deal. Always looking at the road ahead, never back. Holding carefully to Rachel, Nita climbed the tangled ruin of old fence and walked out onto the promontory. No pool lay here today, just dust and stones and a view of the riverbed. For a moment, Nita regretted her decision to com here. Veins of rock marched across the far side of the Gorge, streaked brown and gray, carrying her eye farther and farther east, to where the walls of the Gorge and the rocky bed of the river blurred into opalescent haze. Nita spread Rachel's quilt in the strip of shade cast by a crumbling stone wall and sat with her back against the relative cool of the stone.

"This is our world." Nita propped her daughter against her raised knees as the sun crawled slowly across the dry dome of the sky. "There's beauty in it, if you look for it. We'd better look for it, because that's all we're going to get."

Rachel cooed and drooled, reaching for Nita's hair.

The sun was dipping toward the horizon and she was drowsing in the heat when the sound of a car cut through the quiet. Nita looked over her shoulder as the engine throbbed and died. A Corps pickup had parked by the ruined fence. She knew who it was before he had even opened the door — she would probably have recognized him in the middle of Portland.

Carter stepped gingerly across the rusty wire and walked toward her, a little hesitant. "I went looking for you . . . to offer you a ride to see Jeremy. Renny said you went today, that she left you here."

"He's getting some feeling back in his legs, Carter."

"Really?" His relief flooded the air. "That's great. They weren't offering a lot of hope." He sat down beside her on the quilt, close enough that their bodies touched, arm against arm, leg against leg. "I . . . need to tell you." He kept his eyes on the riverbed. "Johnny offered to pay for stem cell treatments for Jeremy. If I'd lose that proof. Nita . . . I couldn't do it. It . . . would have hurt too many people to let him off."

She touched his arm, awed by the echo of what that choice had cost him.

"I'm sorry. That I haven't come by." He kept his gaze on the riverbed, frowning, shy inside, unsure. "I ended up in the infirmary for a couple of days." He grimaced. "I . . . vanished the evidence that the hacker gave

Mary Rosenblum

me. I don't know who actually did the shooting around here, or killed Candy Wilmer. Probably the people who were working for Delgado. If Durer catches them, they might implicate Johnny, but so far they seem to have disappeared." Carter drew a slow breath. "I'm going to let it go at that. Dan's pissed at me for not giving Johnny to the media, and he has reason to be, but he's going along with it. I . . . owed a debt to Johnny."

"I know." She leaned against him. "Johnny paid for Jeremy's treatment. That's why he's getting better."

"What?"

"He told Jeremy it was a gift from him. And that you're even. You are, Carter. You repaid that debt a long time ago and he knew it."

"Do you *know* that?" His voice quivered, just a hair.

"I know that." She looked down at her daughter and stroked a wisp of dark hair back from her face, hurting with his hurt.

"I'm going to stay on here," he said slowly. "With the Corps or without it. People need to stand in the middle around here. They need to stick their necks out — like Dan." He looked at her at last. "I . . . didn't come looking for you right away," he said. "It wasn't just that the doctor stuck me in the infirmary. It was . . . because I had to know how I felt about you . . . about what you are."

Nita waited, her heart pounding suddenly, wanting to cover her ears or get up and run.

"I'm always going to feel a little guilty for letting Johnny off, and you're going to know that. And a lot of other things. And sometimes it's going to drive me nuts. And sometimes . . . it's going to be wonderful." He drew a slow breath, his eyes as dark as the rocks beneath the dust. "I'm not afraid of what you are, Nita. Was that what happened with David? Was he afraid?"

"Yes." And he *wasn't* afraid. Nita took his face between her palms and kissed him, and he put his arms around her, pulling her against him. The kiss went on a long time.

Rachel's delighted crowing finally broke them apart. "Child, you are going to get educated young," Nita said breathlessly.

"It's going to be tough around here." Carter put his arm around her. "A lot of people have already gotten foreclosure notices from the Federal Credit Bureau. It's going to take some time to untangle those illegal permits and get the new fields off-line. Even pulling some water from the Great Lakes, we still may have to make some cuts to keep Mexico's share secure."

"No good answers, huh?" Nita looked into his eyes. "Maybe all we can do is choose the best of bad choices. Sending Johnny to jail wouldn't have saved those people in the riverbed."

"I guess not. Dan said the same thing. He's not too pissed." Carter shrugged, but an edge of bitterness in him had eased. "I guess we'll do the best we can." He pulled her lightly against him and kissed her again.

Nita closed her eyes, breathing his scent, tasting him, remembering, anticipating.

Rachel fussed.

"She's hungry." Nita sighed. "See what happens when you get involved with nursing women?"

"I see," Carter said soberly, and then he laughed.

It was a happy sound: she couldn't remember ever hearing him laugh like that. He stretched out on the quilt in lengthening afternoon shadows and Nita pillowed her head on his shoulder, careful of his injured ribs. Tucked between them, Rachel nursed contentedly.

Rite of Passage
by Alexei Panshin
trade paper: $16.99
ISBN: 0-9789078-2-5

Summer of the Apocalypse
by James Van Pelt
trade paper: $17.99
ISBN: 0-9746573-8-7

Human Visions: The Talebones Interviews
by Ken Rand
trade paper: $17.99
ISBN: 0-9746573-9-5

Last Flight of the Goddess
Ken Scholes
limited hardcover: $25
ISBN: 0-9789078-0-9

Rocket Science
by Jay Lake
trade paper: $17.99
ISBN: 0-9746573-6-0

**The 10% Solution:
Self-editing for the Modern Writer**
by Ken Rand
paperback: $9.99
ISBN: 0-9668184-0-7

The Last of the O-Forms
by James Van Pelt
trade paper: $17.99
ISBN: 0-9746573-5-2

Dreams of the Desert Wind
by Kurt R.A. Giambastiani
trade paper: $17.99
ISBN: 0-9746573-3-6

Green Grow the Rushes-Oh
by Jay Lake
specialty chapbook: $6.99
ISBN: 0-9746573-2-8

ABOUT THE AUTHOR

Mary Rosenblum first published in *Asimov's Magazine* in 1990 with "For A Price," one of her Clarion West stories. (She attended that boot camp for writers in 1988.) Since that first publication, she has published more than 60 short stories in SF, mystery, and mainstream fiction, as well as eight novels. Her SF stories have been published in *Asimov's*, *The Magazine of Fantasy and Science Fiction*, *SciFiction*, and *Analog*, among others. She won the Compton Crook award for Best First Novel, The Asimov's Readers Award, and has been a Hugo Award finalist. She has been on the short list for a lot of awards but she doesn't keep track. She publishes in mystery as Mary Freeman, and also teaches writing.

When she is not writing, she practices a sustainable lifestyle on her country acreage, growing all her fruits and vegetables and keeping sheep. She also trains dogs in tracking, herding, and obedience work. You can find out more about her at: **www.maryrosenblum.com**

CPSIA information can be obtained
at www.ICGtesting.com
Printed in the USA
FSHW012003190821
84192FS